THE EXTREMIST

Nadia Dalbuono has spent the last eighteen years
working as a documentary director and consultant for
Channel 4, ITV, Discovery, and *National Geographic*
in various countries. *The Extremist* is the fourth book
in the Leone Scamarcio series, following *The Few*, *The
American* (longlisted for the 2016 CWA Steel Dagger),
and *The Hit*. She divides her time between the UK and
northern Italy.

the extremist

NADIA DALBUONO

SCRIBE

Melbourne • London

Scribe Publications Pty Ltd
2 John St, Clerkenwell, London, WC1N 2ES, United Kingdom
18–20 Edward St, Brunswick, Victoria, Australia 3056

First published by Scribe 2018

Typeset in Dante MT 12.75/16.5pt by the publisher

Printed and bound in the UK by CPI Group (UK) Ltd, Croydon CR0 4YY

Scribe Publications is committed to the sustainable use of natural
resources and the use of paper products made responsibly from those
resources.

9781911344650 (UK paperback)
9781925322514 (Australian paperback)
9781925548716 (e-book)

CiP entries for this title are available from the National Library of
Australia and the British Library.

scribepublications.co.uk
scribepublications.com.au

In memory of
David Leon Hall
8 September 1934–29 May 2016

1

THE BOY ENTERS THE McDonald's. It is a relief to escape the cloying heat and its undercurrents of summer drains and tourist sweat. He wipes his forehead with the back of his hand, shrugs the bag off his shoulder, and looks around. He counts fifteen people queuing at the tills, most of them teenagers — clutching backpacks and squinting at iPhones. To his left, nearly all the tables are full — more students and a cluster of Japanese tourists. He takes in a few young families, kids no more than four or five. Panic is stirring in his gut, turning it liquid. He tastes acid on his tongue and wants to retch. He swallows, tries to take a breath.

To his right, the place is a little emptier — only four of the tables are occupied. His eyes settle on a group of schoolgirls in uniform, their checked skirts too short, their laughter too loud. Behind the girls is a dishevelled old man, probably a vagrant. He's tearing the wrapper from a meagre burger, his eyes darting furtively as if he's afraid someone will swipe it.

The boy feels sweat running down the back of his neck; he notices a tremor in his leg. He turns and sees his three companions standing in the doorway. Just the sight of them makes his heart hammer. He swallows again: his throat dry, his tongue bulky. He wishes he'd taken something like they'd suggested.

He waves them forward, his arm a little shaky. Dafiq frowns. The boy doesn't understand why. When the others are level with him, he closes his eyes and tries to slow his racing thoughts. He counts to five, then gives them the sign. The air shifts, and he knows they're reaching for their guns now. He nods, and the AKs emerge quietly from beneath their coats.

The firing starts before even he expects it. His ears are humming, and the sweat is now slick between his shoulderblades. He coughs — the air is already dense with cordite. People are running, screaming, falling. Food is tumbling, being trampled into the floor tiles, where it mixes with blood. Someone slips on a patch of mayonnaise and rams their hip into a rubbish bin. A baby cries, a woman sobs. The boy closes his eyes and raises his weapon.

'Allahu Akbar,' he whispers as he pulls the trigger.

'Who wants to show me what they're drawing?' asks the young teacher.

A little boy thrusts up an arm. 'Me! Me!'

'OK, Simo.' She walks over and picks up the piece of paper in front of him.

'Is it an elephant?'

'A dinosaur ...' He looks disappointed, but bites his lip, takes back the paper, and carries on drawing.

'Excellent. Who's next ...?'

There's a commotion at the back of the room. Four men are running through the door, screaming something in a language the teacher doesn't recognise. They're dressed in black, and their faces are obscured by balaclavas. But even though she can't follow what they're saying, she knows immediately who they are.

'Gather close. Don't worry, it's just a game!' she shouts, pulling the toddlers to her, trying not to succumb to her terror. Rita, the classroom assistant, has run over, and she, too, is grabbing as many children as she can, shakily trying to wedge herself between them and the men.

The leader of the group is just a couple of metres away, and the teacher notices that he has young unlined eyes beneath his balaclava. She looks for a suicide vest, but can't see one — just rifles: at least three or four strung across his chest and back. He's now so close that she can smell the nicotine on his breath and the fear beneath it. His hand is on his gun; his fingers are hovering above the trigger. She looks up into his haunted eyes and reads uncertainty. There might be hope, she thinks. They might still have a chance.

2

I THINK WHEN YOU reach the end you'll agree that this is just a small story about nothing out of the ordinary. It's the tale of a boy from the suburbs who always did what was expected — smiled when required, excelled at school, hung out with the good girls. It's the story of a boy who came to realise that it doesn't matter if you've lived in a place five years or fifty, if your IQ is 40 or 140 — because in the end, if your face doesn't fit, you're out. You'll remain on the fringes and will never be allowed in from the cold.

Scamarcio had never seen the squad room so full and so quiet. It seemed like every detective he had ever worked with was huddled around the wide-screen TV, deep in thought. Some had their hands in their pockets; others had them bunched at their mouths. A few stood with their arms barred across their chests, their feet set wide, as if braced for whatever horror was yet to come. It wasn't clear whether the intense silence was due to shock or because no-one dared speak for fear of missing a development.

'News is reaching us here of a third incident at a coffee bar near the Colosseum. It is believed hostages are inside. As yet, numbers remain unclear,' said the news anchor.

'Jesus Christ,' someone hissed, shattering the silence and causing the atmosphere in the room to shift.

'It's the usual method: they make sure the emergency services are tied up in one place, then they launch attacks elsewhere. It'll be a bloodbath.'

'That's right, think positive,' muttered Sartori, a detective from Rimini.

Scamarcio heard scraping and turned to see Chief Garramone trying to clamber up onto a desk. It was a strange sight. The chief was carrying a few excess kilos and he wasn't manoeuvring his bulk with particular skill. He had one leg on a chair and the other almost on the table, but Scamarcio couldn't see how he was going to free the other leg while maintaining his balance. He realised that he'd never seen the chief stand on a desk for anything. Then again, these were extraordinary times.

Garramone eventually decided to use both his hands, and managed to find a semi-dignified position from which to hoist himself up. When he was finally standing, he adjusted the waistband on his trousers and smoothed down his brush of hair. Scamarcio thought he looked quite nervous — another first.

Garramone coughed, then said, 'Listen up.' Heads turned, and a few people shuffled nearer.

'I've just spoken to Chief Mancino. We're going to be working on background. Once these guys are ID'd — and he tells me it's imminent — they want us running down family, friends, neighbours. Who are these men? How did they get here? And, most importantly, what do they want?'

'Isn't it obvious?' someone shouted.

'Isn't all that Intel's turf?' came another voice.

'Intel are up to their eyes, as are the anti-terror squad. They need our help,' said Garramone calmly.

The sound of a loud explosion from the TV made them all turn. The cameras had switched back to the McDonald's, where an intense white glow was illuminating the restaurant from the inside. Scamarcio could just make out the silhouettes of people beyond the windows: some crouched, some flat. He watched as one keeled over and slumped slowly to the floor, like a ragdoll. All at once, the glow transformed into a series of bright-white flashes. Scamarcio counted five of them.

'That sounds like firing coming from inside the restaurant,' said the news anchor. 'We will need to wait for confirmation, but from what we're seeing it definitely looks and sounds like gunfire. Monica, can you hear me? Was that gunfire?'

But no reply came. The firing had ceased, and an eerie silence was descending on the street. The waiting news crews said nothing; the emergency services were still. It was as if they'd all fallen under a hex. Smoke was moving across the TV screen, and Scamarcio could no longer make out the forms beyond the glass.

'They're shooting hostages,' said Garramone quietly. 'They have no interest in negotiation.'

'Why aren't we moving in?' asked Sartori, full of outrage.

'The SWATs are waiting for the go-ahead from the negotiator. That's the playbook, but it's bullshit. The negotiator probably thinks he still has work to do, but these bastards couldn't give a fuck about a deal. They just want their sixty virgins or whatever the hell it is.' Garramone shook his head, disbelieving.

A young female voice came over the TV, hushed and breathless. 'We were told to step back, there. I can confirm that *was* gunfire. The terrorists appear to be following through on their earlier threat.'

'Where the fuck is everyone?' shouted Scamarcio at no-one in particular. 'Where the fuck are *we*?'

'Depends how many hostages they've got,' said a voice from across the room. 'They need those numbers before they start deploying.'

'They're holding units back. It's the procedure,' echoed Garramone. 'There could be another attack.'

'If they start killing those little kids ...' said Sartori. 'Christ.

That school is just a few streets from me. Those poor children, they can't ...'

'They'll claim it's no different to what happens in Palestine or Syria every day ...'

'It's just so fucking warped ...'

Someone's mobile rang, and Scamarcio turned to see Garramone answering. After a few moments, the chief's face folded in shock. For an instant, Scamarcio wondered if he'd just learned that he had a relative caught up in the carnage. But inexplicably he was now looking straight at Scamarcio as if this call somehow concerned him personally. He felt his chest grow warm, his stomach tighten. *Jesus, did Fiammetta step out for a coffee and stumble into that? But it's only 7.30, and she never really gets up before 11.00 ...*

'Yes, he's here,' Garramone was saying, still staring at Scamarcio, his forehead lined with confusion. 'At the coffee bar? ... But what the hell could they possibly want with *him?*'

3

SCAMARCIO SAT BESIDE THE police driver and watched as Via Nazionale flashed by. There was an unusual emptiness to the streets, as if the whole of Rome had scurried home to watch the news or was too scared to venture out. But as the car neared the Colosseum, small clusters of people started to appear. They seemed to be a mixture of tourists and locals, and many of them kept glancing nervously over their shoulders as if they feared they were about to be ambushed in plain sight.

After they'd driven on for another half a minute, Scamarcio realised he was now looking at a thick crowd held back behind a police cordon. They were all focused on an inconspicuous coffee bar set in a row of shops running along the street. Scores of emergency-response vehicles were blocking the roadway, light bars flashing, back doors open. His stomach lurched.

The police driver pulled up at the kerb just beyond the cordon, and a tall, fair-haired man in plainclothes hurried over, wielding a walkie-talkie. The stranger opened Scamarcio's door, and he stepped out gingerly, his legs weak. The smells of baked tarmac, summer cologne, and diesel were heavy on the air.

'Detective Scamarcio?'

Scamarcio nodded and shook the man's hand. He had a firm, confident grip.

'Thanks for coming at such short notice.'

Scamarcio swallowed, his mouth dry. 'I don't understand ...'

'Follow me. I'll bring you up to speed.'

He turned and headed towards a large white van parked twenty metres up the pavement, to the right of the coffee bar. It was impossible to see what was going on inside the bar; the windows had now been obscured by large monochrome flags bearing the characters of the Shahada. Scamarcio could see a few spots of red on the steps leading to the front door, and wondered if he was looking at blood.

The stranger knocked on the back of the van, and the door opened immediately. He stood back to allow Scamarcio to enter. Scamarcio climbed a couple of steps and was momentarily blinded by a wall of lights. A bank of CCTV screens and what looked like switchboard consoles covered one side of the darkened vehicle. Seated in front of the screens were about seven people — all of them wearing headphones. He spotted the police negotiators immediately: they were sitting next to each other, and while one of them was talking into his mike, the other was taking notes. Scamarcio heard the lead negotiator say, 'He'll be here. You have my word, Ifran.'

'I don't want your bullshit word.' It was a heavily accented voice, and sounded slightly distorted as it came through the speakers.

A young man with a worried expression tapped the lead negotiator on the shoulder and said something in his ear. The negotiator turned and nodded at Scamarcio, then swung back around. 'I'm going to sign off now, Ifran. I'll be back on when the detective arrives. Here's Andrea.' His colleague adjusted the position of his microphone and resumed the conversation in low, neutral tones. Scamarcio tuned him out and focused his attention on the first guy.

He had pushed back his headset into his thick mane of long, grey hair, and had removed his bright-red-framed glasses to rub his eyes with wide, nicotine-stained hands. The stranger who had accompanied Scamarcio coughed, then said, 'Let's fill in the detective on why he's here.'

The negotiator rolled forward in his chair and replaced his glasses. As he pushed up the sleeves of his shirt, Scamarcio was surprised to see a faded tattoo of a rose on his right forearm.

The man pulled out a thin pack of Marlboros from his top pocket and extracted a cigarette, tapping it invitingly against the side of the box. Scamarcio hoped he'd offer him one, but he didn't.

Scamarcio glanced away for a second and took in the other men, and the one woman, in the van. They were all looking at him. Among them, he recognised Leopardi, the deputy head of police. He wondered who the others were, but it didn't seem that he was going to be offered an introduction.

'So here's the thing, Detective,' said the negotiator, after he'd taken a quick drag. 'One of the terrorists inside the café, Ifran, is asking for you personally. You're the only one he's prepared to deal with.'

'But I've never met him,' said Scamarcio. 'I've never even *heard* of him.' He realised he sounded way too defensive.

'But he's heard of you.'

'How can that be?'

'You ever met a guy called Vincenzo Guerra?'

Scamarcio's mind drew a momentary blank, then returned a hit. 'What?'

'Vincenzo Guerra — former terrorist with the NAR. Now residing in Opera prison ...'

Scamarcio nodded slowly. 'I interviewed him in connection with a case last year. He provided some background.'

'What case was that?' asked the fair-haired stranger who had met him at the kerb.

Scamarcio didn't really want to explain, but he knew he had no choice, especially with Leopardi present.

'An American man was found hanging from the Ponte Sant'Angelo last autumn. Turned out he worked for US Intel and had been active in Italy during the Years of Lead. An academic I spoke to advised me to talk to Guerra. I did.'

'Was he helpful?' asked the stranger.

'In a manner of speaking ...' Scamarcio eyed the deputy chief, but his expression was unreadable. 'So what's Guerra got to do with all this? He's behind bars.'

'All I know,' said the negotiator, 'is that he gave Ifran your name. That's what he told us anyway.'

'How does Ifran know Guerra?'

'They were in Opera at the same time.'

'Ifran was in prison?'

'Hit and run,' said the blond-haired guy.

'So he's known to the authorities?'

'Yes, but not as a terrorist.'

Scamarcio took a breath and gestured in the direction of the bar. 'How many people has he got in there?'

'Fifteen, we think,' said the negotiator.

'All still alive?'

'Yeah, and we're working hard to keep it that way. We can't have a repeat of McDonald's.'

'People were killed?'

'We have serious injuries — no deaths as yet.' The negotiator paused, then spoke quietly. 'We need you to go and talk to Ifran — find out what he wants.'

Scamarcio was shaking his head; it was almost an involuntary reflex. 'But he could be wearing a suicide vest, they could have the place rigged, it could be a set-up — hell, it could be anything.'

'He tells us he's not wearing a vest,' said the negotiator.

'Oh, well that's fine then,' muttered Scamarcio.

'There are a lot of lives at stake,' said the fair-haired stranger.

'I don't need you to tell me that. Who the fuck are you,

anyway?'

'Fabrizio Masi — I work for AISE.' The guy pulled out his ID.

Scamarcio studied the guy, then the Intel ID. There was something plastic about him, both in the flesh and in the picture.

'I don't get it. Aren't the police running this?'

'It's a joint effort,' said Leopardi, from the back of the van.

The second negotiator pushed back his headphones and swung around. 'We need to get a move on. He's nervous.'

'He's not the only one,' said Scamarcio.

Masi laid an unwelcome hand on his arm. 'We'll have you covered. Just get in there and find out what the fuck he wants, and then get back out. Don't promise him anything. Just tell him you'll pass on his request.'

'You got a Kevlar?'

'He doesn't want you wearing one.'

'*What?*'

No-one said a word.

'What if he doesn't let me back out?'

'We think he will.'

'And how did you reach that conclusion?'

Masi took him by the elbow and angled him towards the door. 'Come on, Detective. The clock is ticking.'

Scamarcio was led past the clusters of elite sniper units and waiting ambulance crews, stretchers ready on the pavement. He felt a hundred eyes tracking him. He could just tell them all 'no'; it was a free country. But, as Masi had said, there were lives at stake. If he walked away now, could he ever look at himself in the mirror? What would people say? He'd forever be Leone Scamarcio, son of a mafioso *and* a coward.

'Here we are,' said Masi, as if they'd just arrived at a picnic. 'Good to go?'

Scamarcio nodded, but couldn't manage to speak. Masi barked something into his walkie-talkie.

'Detective Scamarcio is entering the building. We repeat, Detective Scamarcio is entering the building,' came a voice from a loudhailer.

Scamarcio felt the snipers beside him tense, and then he noticed the mass of TV cameras for the first time, blinking in the sun like a thousand reptile eyes sizing up a kill. 'Shit,' he said, not caring who might hear. He hadn't had time to call Fiammetta and tell her what was happening. She was going to find out from the news. *Shit, shit, and triple shit.*

He exhaled and took in the scene ahead: the black banners, the opaque glass, the shadowy figures moving beyond the small strips of window that were still visible. A hand nudged him forward, and he started the long walk to the bar, his legs suddenly light and unpredictable, as if they were no longer connected to his mind. He trained his eyes on the door, decorated with the ubiquitous stickers for MasterCard and the metro network. It could have been any door on any bar, but who knew what hell lay beyond.

Sweat was running down his forearms now, dripping into his palms. His new Aspesi shirt, a recent present from Fiammetta, was already pasted to his back, its collar wet. He noticed a strange prickling between his shoulder blades, as if his nervous system was getting ready to trip. He was halfway to the door now, and his heart was hammering so violently he feared he was about to go into cardiac arrest. He hoped Fiammetta would not have to watch *that* play out on national TV.

He took a long breath. Just a few more steps and he'd be inside. Were there any injured? Surely Masi would have said so, but perhaps they didn't know. He spun through his training in his head and checked off the First Aid basics. He reminded himself to stay calm, maintain control: give an impression of command.

He reached for the fat brass handle and noticed the finger smudges. People had popped in for coffee and had been dragged into a nightmare. He pushed the handle and held his breath.

Suddenly, someone grabbed his wrist and yanked him into blackness. It was too dark to make out the figure before him, but the smell was easy to decipher. The stench of fear was everywhere: a sweetish mix of sweat, excrement, urine, and something primal that Scamarcio had never quite been able to pin down.

'Get away from the window.' The voice was young, male, and fragile. He sounded scared and out of his depth. Scamarcio knew this wasn't necessarily an advantage.

'Over here,' barked the boy.

Scamarcio followed him to the back of the bar, where a dim light was pooling. For the first time, he noticed the silent line of people slumped on the floor, their clothes a rumpled mess and their hair askew. He counted four men guarding them. They were wielding AK-47s and had a string of other rifles, large and small, slung across their backs. *Why so many?* he wondered, before realising: *They figure there'll be no time to reload.*

The light was coming from an open doorway, and, as they drew nearer, Scamarcio started to make out the features of the man ahead. He was indeed young, no more than twenty-five, and the lost look in his wide eyes confirmed Scamarcio's initial assessment: he didn't feel in control.

'Ifran?' Scamarcio asked.

The boy gave a barely perceptible nod. 'Wait,' he snapped at Scamarcio, gesturing to his fellow gunmen, guarding the hostages.

Several seconds passed while the men spoke to each other in an Arabic language Scamarcio didn't understand. Then Ifran said, 'Follow me.'

He led Scamarcio past the pool of light, and they made

their way down a steep staircase, before entering a storeroom. Scamarcio took in rickety shelves full of filter coffee, paper towels, and bottled water. A bare bulb hung from the ceiling.

'Over here,' said the boy, walking towards the far wall. 'Get right away from the door.'

He came to a stop and leaned his right shoulder against the wall while he patted his jacket pocket. After a second or two, he produced a pack of MS cigarettes and began to light up. Under the stark light, Scamarcio noticed his pockmarked skin and dense, dark brows. His hair was shaved short in a military crop.

Ifran offered him a cigarette, and Scamarcio gratefully accepted. While the boy lit up for him, Scamarcio looked for any signs of a suicide vest. There was no bulk beneath his T-shirt, no unexplained shapes.

'So,' said Scamarcio, after he'd taken a few puffs and thanked the God he still didn't believe in that this boy was a smoker, 'all I know is that Vincenzo Guerra gave you my name.'

Ifran frowned. 'In Opera.' His accent was coming through strongly.

Scamarcio took another pull on the cigarette and tried to steady his nerves. He remembered that he'd never liked MSs — there was a grittiness to them, a sharp aftertaste. 'I'm just a detective in the Flying Squad. I don't see where I fit in.'

Ifran rubbed beneath his nose and stared. His gaze was hard and uncompromising. He seemed less afraid now. 'Vincenzo told me you understood the way it all turned — that if I ever found myself in trouble on the outside, you were someone I could ask for help.'

Scamarcio wanted to yell '*What the fuck!*' but instead said calmly, 'Right now, you're in a lot of trouble, but I don't see how I can get you out of it.'

'I don't think you quite understand the nature of the trouble I'm in.'

'It's obvious ...'

'You need to look beyond the obvious.'

Jesus, thought Scamarcio. *Are we going to talk in riddles all morning, while the hostages above us soil themselves in fear?*

'Tell me,' he said, trying to keep his voice even.

'When you look at me, what do you see?' said the boy softly, his eyes narrowing through the smoke.

Scamarcio started to weigh up a response, then just tossed it to the wind — there wasn't time. 'I see a young guy who has taken fifteen people hostage, and who has much of Rome's police force outside, armed to the hilt. I see a young guy in deep shit.' He swallowed; it made no sense to rile him. The boy might be out of his depth, but he was wielding an AK and he was on edge.

'What else do you see?'

'Excuse me?'

'What else?'

Scamarcio took a breath. 'I see someone who seems scared.'

Ifran rolled his eyes. 'No. Do you see an Italian or a foreigner?'

Sure, he had an accent, but his Italian was flawless. Scamarcio knew this was *the* toxic question. 'Did you grow up here? In Rome?' he tried, knowing it was a cop-out.

'You didn't answer me.'

Scamarcio took a hurried drag; there just wasn't enough time to think. 'I see a mixture of both, I guess. You wouldn't speak Italian like you do if you hadn't lived here for a long time.'

'A mixture of both,' Ifran repeated. 'A mixture of both is a confusing thing to be.'

Scamarcio blinked. He was struggling.

'I think you understand, Detective.'

'What?'

'You're also a mixture of both.'

'Am I?'

'You are the son of a mafioso *and* a top policeman. You have

16

come from one world, but are attempting to make a life in another. This is no easy feat.'

Scamarcio said nothing.

'The question is whether one *can* trade one world for another, or whether, despite all our efforts, it's impossible. If you are born into a certain environment, perhaps you're forever condemned to inhabit it?'

Scamarcio breathed out slowly, his mouth a small 'o'.

'Why aren't you answering?'

'Because I don't know — I'm still working it out. I still have a foot in my old world, as much as I wish I didn't.'

'Ah,' said Ifran, triumphant. 'That's why I knew we could talk. We're in the same boat, you and I.'

Scamarcio took a moment to absorb this. He wasn't so sure.

'I guess you're thinking I've been radicalised.'

The question took Scamarcio by surprise. 'I really hadn't got that far ...'

'If a Muslim army started bombing Rome from the air, wiping out homes, hospitals, supplies, killing women and children, if this same army then went around Europe, fomenting coups in some places, pushing regime change in others, bringing poverty and destitution, suffering and starvation, wouldn't you want to strike back? Wouldn't you want to fight?'

'Of course.'

'If you did, would people say you'd been radicalised?'

Scamarcio said nothing.

'There's no such thing as radicalisation. It's a bullshit term. There's anger, that's all. Anger at the suffering brought on our people.' He said the last part under his breath, almost as if he was embarrassed.

'"Your" people?'

'My family is from Libya, but I speak for the whole of the Middle East.'

'When did you leave?'

'Fifteen years ago, when I was eight. My parents were ahead of the curve.'

'But you still feel part of all that?'

'Of course. Italy has never let me in.'

'Have you tried?'

'Do you mean to insult me?' he asked, but he didn't seem that angry.

'So all this is about getting back at the West?'

The boy stubbed out his cigarette and went to light up another. 'That would be the simple analysis.'

'Give me the complicated one.'

Ifran took a few drags and closed his eyes for a moment. 'I was in Opera 'cos I ran someone over and killed them. I didn't stop to check they were OK.'

'Yes, I was told.'

The boy rubbed a hand up and down the back of his neck, as if the muscles there were bothering him. 'I was sorry for what I did. It was a moment of madness — the not-stopping. I hadn't seen the guy come out from the other side. It was a sunny day and I'd been blinded for a moment, and when I spotted him, it was already too late.' He brought a hand up to his eyes and closed them at the memory.

'Right,' said Scamarcio quietly.

'Before that day, I'd been active — politically. I'd been a member of a protest group; we organised marches in Rome against the Israeli occupation.' He stopped and sucked on his cigarette. Scamarcio noticed that it was nearly down to the filter already. 'Guerra was like a mentor to me. We understood one another. He warned me about what might happen — what might happen when I got out of Opera.'

'Happen how?'

'When I was released last year I wasn't working, just

organising a few demos. I met these two guys. They'd been to Syria; they'd seen it all. We got to talking …'

Scamarcio stayed quite still.

'Over time, they persuaded me that something more serious needed to be done than a few marches. Slowly we started planning, organising — getting our ideas together.'

Scamarcio took a long final drag on his cigarette and stubbed it out beneath his shoe. He wanted to ask for another, but didn't want to interrupt the boy.

'Then, about three months ago, something changed. One of the guys left his phone in my living room while he took a slash. It rang, and I answered it.'

Scamarcio pushed a hand across his mouth. It was cool in the storeroom, but he felt a new trickle of sweat start its way down his spine.

'The accent on the other end of the phone was surprising. He said, and I remember the words exactly, "Hey, Maalik. How's the weather?" I don't know why, but I decided not to tell him I wasn't Maalik. I say, "Not bad," or something like that. He says, "Glad to hear it. You ready?" I say, "Yes." He says, "July twelfth." Then he hangs up.'

July twelfth. That's today's date, Scamarcio realised. 'What was the significance of that call, do you think?'

'I didn't understand the significance until Maalik told us we'd be going into action on July twelfth.'

Scamarcio struggled to prioritise. 'This Maalik, where is he now?'

'At the McDonald's.'

'He's one of the terrorists?'

Ifran nodded.

'And the voice — you say it was a surprising accent?'

The boy just nodded again.

'What was surprising about it?'

'It was from a place I wouldn't have expected.'

'European?'

'American.'

'If you believe the hype, the US is full of home-growns. An accent means nothing.'

'Well, then I got to digging.'

'And?'

'And that's what I want from you. I need you to finish where I left off.'

'I don't follow.'

'I've got proof that this guy wasn't who he said he was — that he was working for the wrong side.'

'The wrong side?'

The boy smoked the rest of his second cigarette right down to the stub, then tossed it to the floor and ground it out hard with his foot. The gesture made Scamarcio nervous.

'Don't pretend you don't understand, Detective. Like Guerra said, you know the way it all turns.'

'But why would an American be involved?'

'That's the million-dollar question — well, billion-dollar probably.'

'What?'

'You'll see.'

'So what do you want me to do? Take all this to the negotiators?' Even as he asked the question, Scamarcio knew that it might not be the quickest route to the truth.

'No.'

'What, then?'

'I need you to travel thirty kilometres outside of Rome to a villa by the sea. Then, I want you to walk to the bottom of the garden. Right down the end, beneath the hanging branches of the peach tree, you'll find a box buried in the earth. Open it and bring me the contents.'

'What the fuck?'

'I want you to do all of this without telling the authorities. You can't relay one single detail of your conversation with me.'

'You've got to be joking.'

'Do I look like I'm joking?' The boy chose this moment to ram the rifle butt hard into Scamarcio's chest. The blow shocked him, and he forgot to breathe for a moment.

'If you don't do what I ask, thousands will perish.' The boy's wide eyes seemed assured now, full of new self-belief.

'But you're not holding ...'

'None of you understand what you're dealing with here,' said the boy calmly. 'This siege hasn't even *begun*. If you *don't* do this for me, you'll see rivers of blood by nightfall.'

He thrust a scrap of paper into Scamarcio's hand. 'You've got until 9.00 a.m. tomorrow. Then I need you back here with a news crew from CNN. I want the handover of the contents of the box broadcast to the world in real time. And remember: not a word to anyone. You're on your own.'

4

'WE WILL THRIVE IN Italy,' I remember mum saying. 'Rome is the place where democracy began. It's the home of freedom and fairness.'

When I think about those words, I want to laugh, then cry. You can't throw a small child into the water and expect it to swim. Worse, you can't then beat that child for sinking.

Scamarcio stepped back out into the sunshine, a million camera shutters clicking as he made his way towards Agent Masi, who was waiting for him at the head of the cordon.

'Let's get you away from this madness,' Masi said crisply. To Scamarcio, it seemed as if the madness had yet to begin.

He figured they'd head back to the van and the negotiators, but instead Masi led him to a waiting Mercedes. He held open the back door. For a second, Scamarcio thought about protesting — perhaps doing a runner — but the world's media was watching, so he climbed in, compliant, already sensing that he was about to be led a dance. As he sank back against the cool leather, momentarily grateful for the respite, he noticed Colonel Andrea Scalisi, head of AISE, in the front passenger seat. Scamarcio no longer felt able to relax.

There'd been no time to decide how much to say, but just the sight of Scalisi stilled his tongue. His encounters with him on the American case had led Scamarcio to believe that he was the go-to guy for dirty men with nasty secrets, and he reminded himself that whatever Scalisi said, he'd need to think long and hard before revealing the truth about his conversation with Ifran.

'Why aren't the police here to meet me?' Scamarcio asked. 'Surely this is a matter for them and the negotiators.'

'That depends on what our little friend had to say,' said Scalisi, scratching at the corner of his narrow mouth.

'Not much, as it happens,' said Scamarcio, looking out at the hordes of media trying to steal an image of him as the Mercedes sped away.

'Detective, you'll understand that AISE can't be perceived to be playing catch-up. We need anything you can give us on these men so we can start pinning down identities and drawing up backgrounds. There could be others. And if so, we need to find them fast.'

Scamarcio thought of what Ifran had said: *None of you understand what you're dealing with.* Wouldn't it be a serious dereliction of duty *not* to share this? Shouldn't he let Scalisi know that there probably *were* others — that they could be looking at mass casualties? But the boy's warning was still ringing in his ears. And then there was the core problem: he simply didn't trust Scalisi.

'How can you hope *not* to be seen to be playing catch-up? There are three groups of terrorists holding hostages in three different locations, children among them. The public is asking how you *didn't know* — why didn't you have these guys in your sights?'

'Who's saying we didn't …?'

'But …'

'But nothing. We fucked up. We took our eyes off the ball, and now we need to get back in the game. Talk, Scamarcio — I'm running out of patience. Mancino and I go back a long way, and I know he's still watching you.'

Scamarcio had formed the impression that Chief of Police Mancino detested the colonel, but he let the comment hang. He was too thrown by Scalisi's uncharacteristic display of humility.

'The boy didn't tell me his full name. He's young. I'd say no more than early twenties.'

'We know his name,' muttered Scalisi, frustrated.

'He mentioned Vincenzo Guerra several times — said he was his mentor.'

'Cut the crap. Tell me something useful.'

'He's not wearing a suicide vest; I don't think the others are, either.'

Scalisi just grunted.

'He seemed to want reassurance.'

'Reassurance?'

'That when it all goes to the wall, he'll be OK.'

'He's a fucking terrorist, for Christ's sake.'

'I'm just telling you what he said. I got the impression he'd been forced into this — that he wasn't too happy to be there. I dunno, maybe you could lean on him for info. He didn't offer that, but ...'

'What about the other men with him?'

'There were four.'

Scalisi shook his head quickly, like he didn't want to waste time on trifling details. 'How did they respond to you being there?'

'My guy seemed to be the boss. They didn't say much.'

Scalisi frowned as if he wasn't happy to hear this.

'So what did you tell him?'

'Well, the negotiators said not to promise him anything, so I didn't.'

'Good.'

'So, what now?'

'You're coming with us to HQ. I need you where I can see

you. I don't like any of this. I don't like you, and I don't like Vincenzo Guerra, and I don't like the two of you being in the middle of this shitstorm.'

'What the fuck? You don't have the right to detain me. It's a free country.'

'Not at the moment, it isn't.'

Masi left him alone with a cup of decent coffee in a small room two doors down from Scalisi's office. Scamarcio had wanted to call Garramone and Fiammetta, but Masi had seized his cell phone. Scamarcio worried about being out of contact. Things with Fiammetta were good: solid. Finally he'd found someone who was interesting and challenging, as well as being unafraid of who he was. He couldn't allow today's events to compromise that.

He thought about summoning his lawyer to remind Scalisi and his goons of his basic human rights, but he knew there wasn't time. He needed out of there quickly; he needed to find a way to read the scrap of paper in his pocket and locate an exit. Given that he was sitting in the headquarters of the country's foreign intelligence service, pulling out the note now and reading it seemed like a bad idea. *The hidden cameras watching me are probably sending a feed back to Scalisi's computer in real time, the sick freak*, thought Scamarcio.

It occurred to him that all this might be used as a way to get back at him after his clash with Scalisi and his powerful friends on the American case. He spent a long moment thinking about those friends, and then wondered about the strange call Ifran claimed to have answered. Scamarcio reflected on why AISE had collected him from outside the bar. Strictly speaking, this was an internal security matter. AISE were the external agency dealing in foreign intelligence. It was almost as if Scalisi had been wheeled in because he'd dealt with Scamarcio in the past — because he was familiar with the troublesome detective.

'Masi!' Scamarcio shouted. He waited, but there was no response. 'Hey, Masi!' Scamarcio waved at a corner of the wall, certain that he was looking into a concealed camera.

Within seconds, Masi was back in the room.

'I need to use the bathroom.'

Masi seemed wrong-footed.

'Or don't I have the right to do *that* anymore?'

Masi rolled his eyes. 'No need for drama. It's left down the hallway, just before the swing doors. Don't be long. Chief Scalisi and some others are coming in for a debrief — they want the spit-and-cough.' He threw Scamarcio a concerned look, then left. It seemed that no-one had time for chitchat today.

Scamarcio waited a minute, and then got up and walked down the corridor, the sound of numerous TV sets, all tuned to the same channel, following him as he went. He half-heartedly tried the swing doors, but, as expected, they required a swipe card to exit. He located the bathroom and quickly chose a cubicle, impressed by the cleanliness of the place. Flying Squad HQ might take note. He sat down and pulled the scrap of paper from his pocket, hunching over so that his hands were obscured from above. Before he opened the note, he looked up at the ceiling. He couldn't spot any cameras, but knew this didn't mean much.

He unfolded the paper. On it were five words scrawled in blue biro: *Villa Morena, Via Roma, Ostia.*

He pushed the note back in his pocket, rose from the toilet, pulled the chain, and exited the stall. He noticed that there was just one window in the wall to his right, but it was very high and very narrow. There would be no way to reach it from the ground. He wondered about the wisdom of putting a window all the way up there — what was the point?

While he was standing there, staring, there was a noise,

and he turned to see a small Asian man wheeling in a cart of bathroom supplies. The cart was deep and high, and had a kind of short curtain in blue check running around the sides. Scamarcio looked at the man, then at the cart again, and knew that this might be his one opportunity. He patted his trouser pocket for his wallet. Fortunately, Masi hadn't taken it when he confiscated his phone. He flipped through the notes and counted two hundred and twenty euros in cash. He'd been to the ATM on his way into work that morning — he seemed to be burning through money lately, but that was what happened when your life was full. He pulled out two fifty-euro notes and showed them to the cleaner, expecting to be frogmarched back to Masi for even trying.

'This is yours if you get me out of the building,' Scamarcio said, trying to sound more confident than he felt. There was no way this stern-faced guy was going to cooperate — no doubt he'd been trained for this very eventuality. But the man surprised him by nodding calmly, as if this wasn't the first time he'd acceded to such a request. Scamarcio handed over the cash, and the man pocketed it quickly. Scamarcio studied the cart. He figured that, bunched up, he could perhaps get inside, but that the guy would need to drape a towel or something over the top to hide him. 'You'll have to cover my legs. The curtain won't be enough,' he said.

Wordlessly, the man started removing the supplies and stacking them against the wall as if it was all part of the service. Scamarcio helped him. When the space under the cart was empty, Scamarcio scrambled inside, worried that Scalisi or Masi would storm in at any moment. There was even less room than Scamarcio had imagined, and his back was already hurting from the awkward angle.

He saw some kind of striped material descend, then, within seconds, the cart was in motion. Scamarcio felt himself being wheeled down the long corridor, and then heard a button being pressed and the singsong bleep of a swipe card being accepted by the reader. The trolley lurched forward, and there was a suck of rubber as doors sealed shut behind them.

After a brief pause and another bleep, he felt the ground below him drop — they were in an elevator. Then he heard the suction sound of the doors opening again, and they started moving more rapidly, the wheels click-clicking beneath him. The trolley suddenly swung right, and they rolled up some kind of ramp and came to an abrupt stop. Scamarcio's back scraped painfully against the top of the cart. A hand reached under the curtain and grabbed him, and soon he was scrambling to his feet.

They were in a janitor's room. He took in shelves lined with cleaning fluids, and a row of brooms and long dusters hanging from the wall. The cleaner was pointing to the right. Scamarcio followed his gaze and saw another window, this one standing open. The layout was the same as in the bathroom.

'You need to get up there,' said the guy, in a thick accent. 'Is only way. You lower down now — fall won't kill you.'

The guy pointed to a small ladder resting against the wall. It didn't look anywhere near high enough to reach the window. 'Use that.'

Scamarcio took the ladder and pushed it into place, while the cleaner stood watch at the doorway. Even at the top of the ladder, Scamarcio was still about a metre beneath the opening. He was glad he'd decided to return to the gym — a few months back he wouldn't have had the strength to lift himself. He reached out above his head for the window ledge, took a breath, and then heaved himself up and through in one movement. There was no space to swing around, so he just let himself fall, catching only the quickest of glimpses as the concrete rushed towards him. He landed hard, and for a moment he lay quite still, his legs bent, fearing that he'd broken something. He felt no pain, but wondered if that was necessarily a good thing.

He rose and looked around. He was at the back of the building. Several white-and-yellow recycling bins lined the wall, along with some disused gas canisters. He scanned the area and spotted a small alleyway running to the right of the building, away from the main drag. This was good, he figured. It wouldn't make sense to use the major roads, which were covered by CCTV. He hadn't yet decided exactly *what* he was going to do, but the one thing he was sure of was that he wanted to get away from Scalisi as fast as possible — he wanted to exercise his human rights.

As he made his way down the alley, he thought of all the hostages who were injured at the McDonald's, of the people who lay huddled in the bar, and of the children at the nursery. What were his options? Should he go back to Garramone and seek advice? Or should he take Ifran's words at face-value and do what had been asked? Could he really live with deaths on his conscience? Even if he was just dealing with hypotheticals, could he just sit idly by? He didn't want to heed it, didn't even want to acknowledge it, but his instincts were telling him to listen to the boy — that if there was any real chance of helping these hostages, he would need to work with Ifran somehow.

Scamarcio pulled out the scrap of paper and read it again. The question was, how was he going to get to Ostia without a car and without being spotted? He turned left into an alley, which ran behind a large Fascist-era building that looked like another government institution. There was a man standing beside a Vespa some twenty metres ahead. His helmet was in his hands; he was fiddling with the strap, getting ready to leave. Without even thinking, Scamarcio shouted, 'Hey, you!'

The man turned, helmet aloft.

Scamarcio ran towards him, pulling out his badge, but making sure that his thumb obscured his name. The man stowed the helmet under his arm and leaned in to study the ID.

'I've got an emergency. I need to borrow your bike.'

'No way.' He was a big guy, heavy-set, and Scamarcio wasn't too sure of his chances in a fight.

'I promise that it will be returned in full working order, and that you'll be paid for the trouble.'

'Do I look like I was born yesterday?'

Scamarcio decided that he didn't, so, on impulse, he kneed him in the groin. He watched, almost shocked, as the guy dropped what he was holding, toppled to the ground, and writhed around, his hands clawing at his crotch. Scamarcio grabbed the helmet and keys from where they'd fallen by his feet.

He jumped on the bike, shouting 'Sorry!' as he sped away. He glanced over his shoulder, but the man was still prone and didn't seem to hear.

Scamarcio knew that he was in the northwest of the city, and that to reach Ostia he'd need to travel south. The centre was probably in lockdown, and there might be blockades in place on the ring roads, so he decided to take the smaller streets and just hope that there would be enough road signs to direct him. The west of the city was not an area he knew well, so he was winging it. At least the helmet would prevent him from being picked up by CCTV for a while.

His mind stuck on Fiammetta again. There was no doubt she'd have seen him on TV by now, and would be going crazy. He thought back to their conversation before he'd left for the day. She'd seemed preoccupied, and when he'd asked her what was wrong, she'd just smiled and said she had a surprise, but that she'd tell him what it was at dinner. There was something about that smile that had bothered him; it had seemed half-hearted, strained. Now, he wasn't even sure if he'd make it home, and there was no way of letting her know. Aside from the immediate issue of having no phone, there was a second problem: he knew that once Scalisi realised he'd done a runner, he'd place a tap on his landline and, most probably, Fiammetta's mobile. Any communication would be impossible. Scamarcio sighed and tried not to let the worry distract him. Fiammetta was tough — she'd find a way to handle all this.

He returned his focus to the muddled streets. Here in the west of the city, it was almost as if life was attempting to carry on as normal. He saw pensioners wheeling shopping trolleys, mothers pushing small children in carriers, elegant society ladies towing coiffured pooches. But the illusion was soon shattered when, through the windows of bars and cafés, he noticed small crowds huddled around televisions, heads all turned in the same direction. He passed a petrol station forecourt that was full of motorists, all their radios tuned to the same station.

After a few minutes, Scamarcio spotted the first sign for Ostia and merged to join the dual carriageway. He wondered about the villa. Would there be anyone home? If so, how the hell was he going to dig up their garden? And what the fuck did he think he was doing anyway?

He soon realised that he hadn't dressed for a forty-minute ride at maximum speed. Even though it was a hot day, by the time he left the dual carriageway and entered the outskirts of Ostia, there was a chill on his skin. The sea breezes didn't help. He stopped at the side of the road to take stock and let the sun warm his back.

Ahead of him, he noticed a sign with a tourist map embedded in plastic. He left the bike and ran his finger down the index. Via Roma was just below where someone had stuck a piece of used bubblegum. He was surprised to see that it ran directly opposite the seafront. He knew that street — there were some art deco masterpieces across from the beach, and he wondered if Villa Morena would be one of them. *Why did the boy choose such an exposed spot?* he wondered. He hoped the place was set back behind a high wall. Anything else would make his task too difficult.

He got back on the bike and made his way towards the seafront, navigating against the crisp swatch of blue ahead. Ostia could never be described as beautiful: the soulless modern apartment blocks lining the approach to the beach looked as if they'd been plucked straight from a Milan suburb; the fascist functionality of the place robbed it of all charm.

Scamarcio swung the Vespa onto Via Roma and made his way along the seafront, looking for a point where the bland apartment blocks gave way to more elegant villas. After a minute, he spotted the first — an ornate pink affair with pastel green shutters and dense bougainvillea. He checked the plaque for the house number, and after just thirty seconds found himself outside Villa Morena.

The high stone walls didn't allow much of a view of the residence beyond, and he hoped the back garden would be equally protected. He dismounted and, out of habit, checked the street. The question was whether to walk right up and ring the bell or whether to try a subtler approach. A lot of these villas lay empty in the winter, but, given it was now the middle of summer, the chances of someone being home were high. He needed to come up with a legitimate reason for being here. He'd have to talk to the owner and convince them to let him in — it was the only way to gain access without a drama unfolding.

He pressed the keypad and waited. After a few moments, a female voice came over the intercom.

'Who is it?'

'I was hoping to speak to the owner.'

'He's not here. He lives abroad.'

Great, thought Scamarcio. 'Are you the tenants?'

'Yes. And you are?'

'Would you mind if I came in for a moment and explained? It's kind of a long story.'

There was a small sigh down the line, but within seconds the high oak doors groaned open to reveal a wide gravel driveway. Scamarcio saw a small but immaculate lawn off to the right, with a round granite fountain at its centre. He approached the front door, a buzzing in his ears. The house was vast and reminded him of a wedding cake with its creamy façade and light-pink shutters.

A tall blonde woman was standing in the doorway; she didn't look too happy to see him. But as he drew nearer, he thought he saw her expression soften. He put her in her mid-forties, and found himself hoping that her marriage was tired, and that he might be able to use this somehow. In the next instant, he remembered his situation and prayed that she hadn't been watching the news. He thought he saw something cross her features that suggested he seemed familiar to her, but that she didn't quite know why. Fine — as long as it stayed that way.

'I'm so sorry to disturb you,' said Scamarcio, extending a hand up to where she stood on the front steps.

The woman tucked a loose strand of hair behind her ear and accepted the handshake. Her sparkly blue eyes narrowed. 'How can I help you?'

'Have you rented this place long?'

She eyed him with suspicion. 'This is our first summer. You still haven't told me who you are.'

'Oh yes, sorry. The thing is, I used to stay here as a child.'

She frowned. 'Oh, really?'

'This is going to sound like a strange request,' he raised both palms, 'so please forgive me if it seems out of order, but the thing is, I just lost my brother in a motorbike accident — a few days ago. When we stayed here as kids, we buried a box in the garden by a tree — it was a box with sketches and little essays on this and that — and I'm in the process of writing the eulogy, and I'd really like to retrieve it. I want to be able to include some of his memories from our time here when I write the tribute.'

Scamarcio looked down at the ground and took a breath. He

actually felt the hollowness of real grief for a moment. He didn't have a brother, so God knew what was going on. Maybe it was all the flotsam of the past bubbling up to the surface once more. Or maybe he was just worried about Fiammetta.

He felt a hand on his arm and looked up. The woman had descended from the top step and was standing directly in front of him.

'I'm so sorry,' she said, her eyes wide with compassion. 'I know what that's like. There's no pain like grief.'

Scamarcio just nodded.

'You buried it by a tree, you say?'

'Yes. There's a peach tree in the back garden. We hid it there.'

She nodded, but he could tell that something was troubling her.

'I'd *so* like to help you, but I don't feel like I can give you permission. It would be up to the owner, you see ...'

'Is he contactable?'

'He's very ill — he's living in Tunisia, I believe. His son is handling the rentals for him.'

'Could we contact him?' This was the last thing Scamarcio wanted, but he knew he had to show willing.

The woman looked at her watch. 'He's in Chicago. It will be late there now.'

Scamarcio sighed softly and made to turn away. 'Please don't worry — I knew it was a long shot.'

'Can you give me your name?'

Scamarcio thought quickly. 'Riccio. Piero Riccio.'

'Mr Riccio, could you come back tomorrow maybe? Once I've had a chance to phone them?'

He let his shoulders sag. 'I just drove down from Bologna today. I've got to be back north tomorrow for work. I'd have called ahead, but I didn't know the number.'

The woman fell silent for a moment, and he could see she was wrestling with it.

'Listen,' she said, more decisively now. 'Do you remember exactly where by the tree you buried it?'

'It was just below the hanging branches — well, they were hanging back then — with the house behind us.'

'So you wouldn't need to dig a large hole?'

'I don't think so.'

She nodded. 'OK, go ahead. If this helps you with your grief, I'd very much like to make it possible.'

'Thank you, that's so kind of you.'

She smiled conspiratorially. 'I don't get the feeling the son comes here often, so hopefully the grass will have grown back by his next visit.'

'I can always pay for a gardener to neaten things up.'

She waved the thought away. 'Don't worry.'

She led him around the outside of the house and through a small, ivy-covered archway that led to the back. Scamarcio had been about to marvel at the beauty of the garden and its pristine English lawn, but reminded himself that he was supposed to have been here before. 'It's still beautiful,' he said.

'Isn't it? It was the garden that convinced us. I know there's the sea right opposite, but this is a real oasis of calm. You know how crowded the beaches can get in the summer. You're packed in like sardines.'

'As a kid it was fun, but I don't think I could face all that now.'

'We're just here for our children. When they've grown out of it, we'll be going somewhere else. I much prefer Liguria.'

He smiled. They were approaching the peach tree, and he realised he had nothing to dig with.

'I'm really sorry — could I ask you for a spade? I think I was half expecting not to get this far, so I didn't bring anything with me.'

'Well, lugging a spade with you all the way from Bologna wouldn't have been much fun. Give me a sec.'

She jogged back towards the house, and he took the chance to look around the garden. *What is Ifran's connection to this place?* he wondered. *Has he even been here?*

The woman was soon back, and he took the spade and thanked her. He removed his jacket and folded it over a metal garden chair. He hoped she wouldn't stay and watch him dig, so he tried to convey some discomfort, in the hope she'd think he was grieving and leave him to it.

As if on cue, she said, 'Oh, do forgive me. You probably want to be alone. Can I offer you something to drink?'

'You're very kind. A glass of water would be great.'

'Sure. Come up to the house when you've finished.'

He thanked her again and set to work. The earth was hard, and he didn't feel like he would be able to make much progress; he seemed to be doing no more than chipping away at it, and like this it would take forever. But, as he dug, he found that beneath the surface the soil was softer. He worked on for a few minutes, but didn't make contact with anything solid. He decided to widen the area slightly around the spot where he had first begun. The spade was reaching further now, and he soon realised that he had already made a deep gouge. He glanced back at the house, worried about the woman's reaction — the hole was starting to look big.

Ten minutes later he wondered yet again if Ifran's story was just an elaborate hoax. He checked the house again, anxious that the woman would be growing restless. But he couldn't see her watching. He returned his attention to the soil, and after a couple more minutes, the blade made a tinny *clang* as it came up against something hard. Whatever it was was blocking the movement of the spade. He felt a small surge of excitement as he started to probe around the edges to get some sense of the shape of the thing. It seemed square and small, although he wasn't yet sure how far it extended down into the earth. Keeping the object on the right, he pushed down with the spade, until he found earth once more. He levered the blade underneath and brought the object up to the surface.

As he pulled it out, he realised that it was a box — oblong, rusted, and covered with grey-green mould. He scraped away the soil to reveal an old biscuit tin, a green-and-black illustration of an aristocratic woman in a wide hat and long frilly dress on the front. It might have been an antique from the late nineteenth century. The lid had rusted along the seal, and it took him quite a bit of effort to prise it off. When he'd finally managed it, he looked inside and saw what looked like a DVD in a plastic cover. It was the only item in the box.

He replaced the lid, refilled the hole as best he could, and headed up the garden. He did not have his laptop with him, and had no idea how he was going to play whatever was on the disc. He realised that his shirt was damp and quickly put on his jacket.

As he neared the house, he noticed the woman waving at him, her face partially obscured by a shaft of sunlight hitting the window. As the sunlight shifted, he saw that she was motioning him to the right. He weaved around perfect flowerbeds of oleander and hibiscus, and wondered yet again about Ifran's links to this place. Had he stayed here? Worked here?

The woman was waiting for him in the doorway.

'Did you find what you were looking for?'

Scamarcio showed her the box. 'It's exactly as I remember it.'

'I'm so glad,' she said. 'Was everything still inside?'

He hoped she hadn't been able to see, but by his reckoning she would have been too far away. 'It seems like it. I'm not brave enough to go through it now. I'll wait until I'm home.'

'That's sensible.' She motioned him into the kitchen and passed him a glass of water from the counter. He saw that she'd gone to some trouble — added ice and lemon slices. 'If you prefer something else ...' she said nervously.

'No, water's great. Thank you.' He took a long drink. How should he phrase this? 'So, this is your first year staying here, you said?'

'Yes, the house was recommended to us by friends.'

'It's a good spot if you still need to get into the city.' This was stating the obvious, but he hoped it might lead him in the right direction.

'Oh yes, fortunately my husband doesn't need to go in every day.'

'Lucky him — is he one of those media types who can work from home?'

'Oh no,' she laughed. 'He's an accountant — for Rome city council.'

Scamarcio nodded. That was one potential link he could cross off the list.

'The owner of the property — his son's in America you say?'

He noticed her blue eyes narrow again slightly. 'Yes, he works there I believe. Our friends who were here before us said they never saw him. Then again, they were always out.'

'Well, if you've got the beach on your doorstep …'

She shook her head. 'You'd think so, but those two were workaholics. Frankly, we couldn't understand why they took the house if they were going to be in Rome all the time.' She looked strangely downcast, and he frowned, confused. She noticed and said, 'Unfortunately one of them died last year — it was a terrible shock. It made me think that we really shouldn't give our lives over to work. It's just not worth it when it could all be snatched away at any moment.'

'I'm sorry to hear that,' said Scamarcio. 'I can't think of any job that would make me a workaholic,' he lied. He downed the water and set the glass on the counter as if to leave.

'Oh,' she shook her head again. 'They're … they *were* both high up in government — intelligence, would you believe.

38

We'd known them for years, but they would never talk about it. Anyway, I shouldn't knock their work ethic — these are challenging times. My sister just called and said there's been some big terror attack in Rome.'

She reached for a TV remote. 'I was just about to switch on and find out what's happening when you came up from the garden. Mind if I take a look? My husband's at a conference in Frascati, so I'm not worried, but I *am* curious.'

'Listen, I won't take up any more of your time,' said Scamarcio quickly. 'Thank you so much for your kindness.'

'Not at all. I do hope the memorial goes well.'

He thought he detected a trace of disappointment — perhaps she'd expected more.

He thanked her again, and she escorted him to the front door. His heart was hammering as he crossed the gravel. He wondered how much time he had to get away before she called the police — or, better still, her friend in intelligence.

Once outside the gates, he retrieved the DVD from the biscuit tin and put it in the top pocket of his jacket. He discarded the empty tin behind a low bush, then jumped on the Vespa and headed north along the sea front, still thinking about these former tenants and their possible connection to the box. He needed somewhere he could stop to look at the DVD, but then remembered that this was a secondary issue — first, he required a means to play it. He'd have to find an electronics store, but asking a passer-by for directions was dangerous. Marginally less risky would be to approach a sunbather, who would be less likely to have seen the news.

He pulled up at the kerb, parked, and crossed the road to the balustrade that led down to the beachfront. A quick glance over the side revealed a relatively empty stretch with a few elderly sunworshippers scattered twenty metres away. He descended and looked left, then right. Next to the stairway was a small bar. He peered through the window, but couldn't spot a TV, unless it was on the far wall, out of view. Rather than traipse across the sand, he decided to risk it.

He approached the young guy on the till. 'Espresso, please.' He knew this was pushing his luck, but he needed a hit. After he'd knocked it back and paid, he said, 'You happen to know if there's a place round here that sells computers?'

The boy nodded and pointed behind Scamarcio's head. 'Go straight up the seafront, then take a right into Via Celli. It's on the left just after the lights. Say Mauro sent you.'

The guy behind the counter of the electronics place looked even younger than the boy at the beach bar. Scamarcio wondered if this was because he was getting old.

'You got a cheap laptop that plays DVDs?'

'No-one watches DVDs anymore,' said the boy.

'I do.'

'You got a home computer?'

Scamarcio nodded, not understanding the relevance.

'You'd be better off streaming the DVD from there to your laptop or tablet.'

'I've not got time.'

The boy scratched sullenly behind his ear. Scamarcio noticed the acne scars beneath his deep tan, like craters in a desert road.

'I've got a sneaky little piece of software called Handbrake. It converts DVDs so you can watch them on your iPad. It takes a while though, and uses a fair bit of storage.'

'Listen,' said Scamarcio, trying not to lose it. 'I came here to buy a cheap laptop on which I can play a DVD. Do you have such a thing, or do they no longer exist?' As well as feeling old, he now sounded it.

The boy shrugged. 'Well, if that's the way you want to go, but it would be a dereliction of duty on my part not to advise you that you're making a big mistake.' He looked genuinely concerned. Scamarcio wondered whether it seemed to the boy that he was from another era, another universe even.

'I've got an old HP 6530b out back. It's still in working order and it plays DVDs. It's yours for 100.'

There was a sly look in the lad's eyes, but Scamarcio didn't have time to haggle. 'Done.'

The boy disappeared through some fly strips, and Scamarcio heard him humming as he shifted boxes around. The low murmur of a radio was coming from somewhere out the back, but it seemed to be playing the usual banal summer hit the idiot nation had all got behind, rather than the news. After a few minutes, the boy returned, a laptop under his arm. He laid it on the counter and blew the dust off it. 'I'll throw in the power pack, too.'

Scamarcio wanted to say that you could hardly count the power pack as a bonus, but he let it go. 'Can you start it up?'

'You don't trust me?'

'I don't trust anyone.'

The boy rolled his eyes. 'You'll need to reset the password — it's "tits" at the moment.'

'Nice.'

'I think so.'

Scamarcio shook his head and waited.

When the home screen had appeared, the boy swung the laptop around to show him. 'All hunky dory. It's still got Microsoft Office, and the license is in date. You want to give me the DVD so we can check the drive?'

'No,' said Scamarcio quickly. 'I'll take my chances.'

The boy frowned. 'I thought that was the whole point.' Then as an afterthought, 'I hope you're not up to anything dodgy 'cos

41

I don't want it coming back to bite me. We've got the pigs at our door enough as it is.'

If only he knew, thought Scamarcio as he handed over the cash. 'You got a bag? Something that I can put over my shoulder — I'm on a bike.'

The boy eyed him strangely, and then disappeared through the fly-strips again. After a few moments, he reappeared with a plastic shopping bag, one of the durable ones that were meant to last. 'On the house. It won't go over your shoulder, but you could hang it from the bars till you get home. Perhaps I could interest you in a backpack — I've got the new Microsoft ones just in?' He gestured to the shelves to his left.

'No,' snapped Scamarcio, grabbing the bag and hurrying out.

Once he was outside, he realised that he'd wanted to ask the boy something, but had forgotten what it was. The comment about the pigs had thrown him. He finished attaching the bag to the bars and was about to start the ignition when he felt a hard grip on his shoulder. He turned to see the lad standing there, weirdly wild-eyed and covered in sweat. 'It *is* you. I *knew* it. You're the guy on TV everyone's looking for. What the fuck?' He glanced around in a panic. 'It's the terrorist guy everyone's after! Look, it's him!' he shouted to an oblivious elderly couple who were crossing the road, the old man hunched over his cane. 'Call the police! Call the *police*!'

Scamarcio pushed the boy out of the way and pumped the gas. He heard him fall hard to the ground, but didn't care.

5

'MOST PEOPLE GO THEIR *whole lives without making any kind of difference,' Kadeem used to say. 'They're just parasites, consuming resources and polluting the planet.'*

'We're no better.'

'No. We'll be among the very few who actually do something.'

'Thousands go on marches, wave banners. It never changes anything.'

'Ifran — I'm not talking about marches, I'm not talking about banners. I'm sick of fucking banners. We need to do something — something meaningful. We need to teach them a lesson that they'll never forget — for all the shit, all the suffering.'

I don't remember what I said at that point, but I do remember that I felt afraid. But at exactly the same moment I felt afraid, I also felt excited. It was the same excitement I used to feel as a kid when I freewheeled down the hill with my eyes closed, not knowing whether a car would be coming round the bend.

Scamarcio took the coast road south, wondering about his chances of finding a place where he could watch the DVD unnoticed. He'd toyed with the idea of heading back inland, but the problem with that option was that the police might now be monitoring the main roads leading into Rome. He'd probably need to keep well clear of the city until it was time to hand over the DVD. He had a vague memory of some kind of national park south-east of Ostia with a lot of woodland where he'd once taken a girl for a weekend hike. If he could find it, it might be a place to sit things out until he understood what he was dealing with.

He reached the outskirts of Ostia, then drove on for a few kilometres, worried that he may have already missed the turn-off for the reserve. As he passed through one small village after another, he was struck again by the emptiness of the streets. The same scene was playing out time and again: in a bar on the right, he saw a cluster of customers huddled around the wide-screen TV as if Roma were hammering Juventus. In the next bar along, it was the same story. The entire country, it seemed, had ground to a halt. The more time went by, he realised, the greater his chance of being recognised. He wondered whether he should turn his thinking on its head: whether it made more sense to head back early. But his instincts kept drawing him to the woods; something was telling him to stay well away from Rome.

He left the village and its dusty streets, and continued along the coast, figuring that he should spot the park soon enough. As he indicated to overtake an Apecar, his attention was drawn to a chink of light blinking from inside the laptop bag. He gave a start — *that* was what he'd meant to ask the boy. They hadn't checked the battery power. He could have kicked himself; it might yet prove a serious mistake.

Up ahead on the left, he spotted a trio of parked coaches, and as he drew closer, he noticed a wide gravel area with a large black-and-white sign announcing the nature reserve of Castelporziano. Walking into this public place was not without its risks. He slowed and pulled into the motorbike parking area, where he dismounted and removed his helmet. He lowered his head and strode towards the gates. A few metres beyond them, he spied a souvenir kiosk selling baseball caps, postcards, and all the usual tat. He walked over and pulled out his wallet.

The cap was a rip-off at fifteen euros, but right now it seemed like a necessity. He chose a blue one with the Italian flag on it; it might prove useful should his patriotism be called into question. Unfortunately, he'd left his sunglasses in the squad room, but he couldn't spot any for sale here. Wordlessly, he handed over his cash to the bored girl behind the counter, then he turned and quickly walked away, ripping out the label as he went.

Up ahead were a few picnic tables and several tourists enjoying their morning coffee and brioche. He made for a spot well back from the path, pulled out the laptop, and checked his watch. It was 11.45 already. He had to fight the temptation to look around and check whether he was being observed, knowing it would only make him conspicuous.

The ancient computer seemed to take an age to boot up, and when the home screen finally appeared, his heart sank. The battery was almost dead — there was less than five per cent remaining. He wondered how long the DVD was, and how much time he would need to make sense of it. He could just watch it now to check, but he didn't know what the disc contained, and he couldn't risk the images drawing attention.

He rose from the table and made his way back to the souvenir kiosk. The girl was now nibbling on a manicured nail as she flicked through a celebrity magazine. Scamarcio spotted a series of paparazzi shots of Alessia Marcuzzi on a beach in Formentera with her new husband.

'Excuse me,' he coughed.

'Yes?' The girl huffed as she set down the magazine. He noticed the bee-stung lips and huge brown eyes, which had escaped him the first time around.

'I was wondering if I could ask a favour? I've got a work emergency and need somewhere to plug in my laptop.' He realised that on its own it sounded lame. 'My boss is making my life a misery. If I gave you twenty euros would you charge it for me?' He hoped he looked sufficiently desperate. He certainly felt it.

She hesitated for a moment, then said, 'We really shouldn't …'

'I'm begging you. My job's on the line. I'll throw in a beer.'

She smiled, and he noticed her strong cheekbones.

'Well, maybe this time I can make an exception.' She pointed under his arm. 'You got the cable?'

He nodded and handed it all over.

'Where will you be? So I can tell you when it's ready.'

'It's OK,' he said quickly. 'I'll just come back in half an hour.'

As he was about to leave, she said, 'You must think I'm an idiot.'

He froze. He'd been crazy to even try this.

'Sorry?' He turned slowly, trying to keep his tone casual.

'You said you'd give me twenty euros.'

He remembered to breathe again. 'Oh, sorry — I forgot.'

She frowned, but it was quickly followed by a playful grin.

He handed over the cash. But as she went to take it, she seemed to think again, and said, 'No, you keep it. If you're about to lose your job, you'll be needing it.' There was something in her tone that suggested she didn't quite buy the sob story.

'Thank you,' he said, re-pocketing the money. 'I'll be back soon.'

'Don't forget to bring that beer.'

He smiled, feeling increasingly nervous about the amount of time he'd spent talking to this girl.

He didn't want to sit it out at the picnic tables, so he decided to head into the park a little way. He spent a few minutes at the entrance, studying the maps on the information board. They confirmed what he vaguely remembered: there were a couple of main roads running through the centre of the reserve. He would need to do his best to avoid them. At the centre of the park's woodland stood the Porziano Castle and its estate, and again he decided that it would be best to steer clear. He'd opt for some woodland not too far from where he'd left the Vespa, but not too close to the tourists.

A quick scan of the information box next to the map revealed a new problem: only pre-booked tour groups could enter. He looked around and spotted a guy in a small booth stamping tickets — Scamarcio knew he wouldn't be able to just wing it. His stomach began to growl, so he headed for the café beyond the picnic tables and bought two brioche and a cappuccino. He downed the coffee and stepped back outside to think while he ate. To the right of the map, there was now a party of around twenty tourists and their female guide, getting ready to enter the park. Scamarcio realised that this would have been a good tour to join had he not been waiting for the laptop. He headed towards them, wondering if he had time to grab the computer and tag on to their group.

'You've got ten minutes for a toilet and snack break, and then we'll be starting,' said the guide in English. There was some murmuring before a few of them broke away and headed towards the café.

Scamarcio swung around in the direction of the souvenir kiosk. It was already late in the morning, and there might not be another group where he could blend in so easily. The Japanese party standing off to his left wouldn't work. He'd retrieve the laptop now, and just chance it.

He hurried towards the kiosk, anxious and impatient, but when he was just ten metres away, he froze.

The girl was standing outside, talking to two Carabinieri and pointing in Scamarcio's direction. His chest tightened and his breathing became shallow. He turned. It took every ounce of self-control not to break into a run. He slowly walked away, expecting to feel a grip on his arm any second. When the tour group was just a few metres ahead, he stopped and pulled his cap down lower. He pretended to study a brochure he'd picked up in the café as he willed the minutes to pass. He just wanted to escape into the forest and disappear.

More tourists were beginning to hover around the guide now. He could hear footsteps behind him, but he didn't dare look. He just kept thumbing through the leaflet, the words swimming. After what seemed like an eternity, the guide said, 'OK, if everyone's ready, let's get going.'

The people in front moved forward, and Scamarcio kept in step close behind. The guide handed over the tickets, and they shuffled past the guy in the box. Scamarcio tensed, expecting him to shout out the error, but no sound came.

After they'd crossed a flat treeless area, and were approaching the woods, the guide began her spiel: 'This park covers fifty-nine square kilometres and stretches twelve kilometres inland. It is the most important coastal forest area in the country, and belongs to the President of the Republic.'

Scamarcio smiled grimly to himself at the irony of hiding from the secret services in the President's backyard.

'If you keep your eyes open, you might be lucky enough to spot wild boar, deer, hares, weasels, foxes, badgers, porcupines, and hedgehogs. The estate at the centre of the reserve is home to rare Maremma horses and cattle. We'll head over there shortly, but first I want to show you something.' She hunched down by the side of a lone tree. 'The trunks of these old and majestic oaks provide shelter to several species of woodpeckers, jays, and barn owls, as well as nocturnal and diurnal raptors such as buzzards. The reserve has been documented since the fifth century, when it was in the possession of the basilica of the Holy Cross in Jerusalem ...'

As she spoke, she hitched a backpack off her shoulder and laid it on the ground. Scamarcio saw that it was slightly open, the silver corner of something metallic glinting in the sun. He stepped closer so he could see better, and realised that he was looking at a laptop. He tuned out her commentary as he tried to think about how he might steal it. It seemed impossible — there were too many witnesses.

All at once, there was a commotion to his right. One of the tourists was shouting 'Deer!' and pointing at a cluster of dark smudges on the horizon. The group were all turning their heads in the same direction, and, as they did, Scamarcio made a split-second decision: he grabbed the rucksack and sprinted towards the forest. Behind him he heard camera shutters and cries, and he prayed to the God he still didn't quite believe in that the group's attention was staying locked on the wildlife.

He reached the shadows of the forest, his chest burning. He kept on running, branches and twigs cracking underfoot. After a while, the foliage started to thicken, bringing with it darkness and an unfamiliar musk. The air gradually grew cooler, the dank tang more intense. He had a stitch in his side, and he panted to a stop, laying the bag carefully on the ground. He thought he heard faint shouts in the distance, but wondered if this was just his imagination playing tricks.

He undid the zip on the backpack and felt the smooth metallic edges of the laptop. As he pulled it out, he saw that it was compact, but not miniature — still big enough to have an optical drive. He studied the side and exhaled when he saw a long slit and the DVD symbol.

He sat down, pulled out the disc from the top pocket of his jacket, and slipped it into the machine. The laptop had been left on stand-by, and the home screen loaded without a hitch. His luck, it seemed, was finally in.

He waited as the DVD whirred, his blood pounding. Whatever was on it might either confirm his actions as rank stupidity, or justify the risks. After a few seconds, a blurred image appeared, and he pressed play.

He saw a group of three men seated in free-standing plastic chairs on what looked like the edge of a football pitch or tennis court. There were a couple of tall sodium lamps and a white chalk outline on the patch of green behind them. From the low light and long shadows, it looked as though the video had been recorded in the early evening, just before dusk. The camera had framed the subjects from head to toe, and Scamarcio sensed that the cameraman was hiding out some distance away, because the figures sometimes became blurry, as if they were on the long end of a lens. The audio was good, and suggested some kind of microphone had been planted among the group.

Scamarcio studied the faces. Two of them were dark skinned, Middle Eastern in appearance — he thought they might have been the same men he'd seen at the café with Ifran, though it had been too dark to see anyone's face clearly. They both looked young, and were dressed in jeans, white trainers, and T-shirts. The third man was extremely blond, almost white-haired, with milky blue eyes and a handsome, tanned, angular face. He looked to be in his early forties, and although he was seated, Scamarcio could tell from his huge, long legs, which he'd stretched out in front of him, that he was big boned and very tall. He was wearing a navy-blue polo shirt, pale chinos, and smart brown boat shoes. To Scamarcio, the man did not look like a terrorist, but he told himself that that meant nothing.

'So, did you take them our list?' one of the young men was asking the giant.

The giant shifted in his chair and folded his wide hands. He looked ill at ease.

'I did ...'

Scamarcio immediately detected the American accent. Is *this the man who Ifran spoke to on the phone?* he wondered.

'And ...?'

'They're a little uncomfortable with what you're proposing, Barkat.'

'Uncomfortable?' the boy repeated, his voice thick with irony. Scamarcio noticed his long nose and large ears, and thought again that perhaps he'd seen him in the coffee bar that morning. 'You think *we're* fucking comfortable?'

The blond man scratched at his neck. 'No-one forced you into this.'

The young man shook his head, his thin mouth opening slightly. 'That's twisting it.'

'I don't think so.'

The darker skinned, slightly smaller guy frowned and turned away as if he didn't want to be there.

The boy called Barkat sighed and said, 'So, what's the problem? What are they so scared of?'

'It's what they call the chain of evidence — they need to remain in the shadows.'

The young man threw a hand out. 'Even I don't know who they are. They're just being paranoid.'

'Where I come from we have a phrase: plan for the worst, hope for the best.'

'So that's why you've been dragging your heels?'

'We can't do otherwise — it's due diligence.'

'So where does that leave us?'

'Things are going to take a little longer. And it won't be coming from me.'

'Who, then?'

'Some friends — with contacts down south.'

Scamarcio thought he read genuine astonishment in Barkat's eyes. After a few seconds, the boy said, 'You've got to be fucking kidding.'

The blond man shook his head. 'I haven't told you who these friends are. You're jumping to conclusions.'

The smaller guy seemed finally about to speak, but Barkat held up a hand to stop him.

'Whatever. When will we get it?'

The blond giant got up to leave, slowly unfolding himself like a massive spider. Scamarcio reckoned he stood at 6 foot 5, but without anyone else to compare him to, it was hard to be sure. The camera was trying to adjust to the new parameters, but the image was becoming shaky.

'I'll be in touch. Give me a few more days,' said the giant, smoothing down his chinos. With that he left the frame, and the camera made no attempt to follow him. Scamarcio caught the expression on Barkat's face — he looked worried.

The video ended. Scamarcio returned to the main menu of the DVD to see if there were any other clips listed. There was one.

He pressed play, and an image appeared of two young girls, a redhead and a blonde, playing ball in a garden somewhere. The lawn was lush, and there were neat flowerbeds behind them, full of roses and buddleias. He sped through the clip, but the image remained unchanged. The girls were still throwing the ball back and forth, laughing and singing in Italian. Then the screen went black. Scamarcio let the video play on, but although the tracker at the bottom had not reached the end, no more pictures appeared. He skipped to just before the end of the timeline, but found nothing more. It looked like this was the remnant of an old family movie, and that the disc had been reused to store the footage of the three men.

He played the first film again, looking for clues to where it had been shot, but he couldn't find any. There weren't any trees visible, which might have given him an idea of the surrounding landscape — coastal or inland, green north or drier south. He could hear the low hum of cicadas in the background, but that didn't tell him much. He searched for timecodes, but found nothing. What was the significance of the meeting between these men? Was there any significance? Was it even for real?

Yet again, he wondered if Ifran was playing him for a fool. But something about the film stirred his instincts. The blond guy seemed professional, and it was intriguing that he looked so different from the others. *Where is Ifran in all this?* he wondered. Had he been the secret cameraman?

Scamarcio sighed and played the clip for a third time, pausing on an image of the giant. He considered contacting his journalist friend, Blakemore, who had helped him on the American case. Then Scamarcio remembered he was without a phone. He thought about trying to connect to the internet, but knew that many a mafia fugitive had been located the same way. He took a long breath. Ifran had been right — he was on his own.

6

Scamarcio stowed the laptop in the backpack and rose to his feet. He checked his watch again. It was nearly 1.00 p.m. He needed to get back to Ifran and try to make sense of it all. He wished he could ignore the demand for a news crew. It would be better to discuss this in private — establish the facts before the boy broadcast his story to the world — but how was he going to negotiate that with so much at stake?

Scamarcio made towards the sunlight at the fringes of the wood — he wanted to head south, towards the coast, and find a route out of the park that was less public than the way he'd entered. The problem was that he had to get back to the Vespa. He moved quickly through the dappled light, the changing chatter of different birds marking his progress. After he'd walked for a couple of minutes, he stopped to take in the first breaths of ozone and coastal pine. They stirred within him a primal drive for survival, a need to resolve this fast.

He was nearly at the edge of the forest when the shrill ringtone of a mobile phone pierced the silence and rooted him to the spot. He was about to run, then realised that the sound was coming from inside the backpack.

'Fuck it,' he hissed. He'd been careless. He fumbled around, his hands shaking as he undid flaps, opened zips. After a long search, he finally located an old Samsung Galaxy inside a back pocket. He pulled it out and killed the call. He switched off the phone, then, not wanting to take any chances, he tore off the back and removed the SIM card and battery. He snapped the SIM in half and pocketed it, along with the battery.

He came out of the forest onto the side of the same road he'd taken from Ostia. By his calculation, the Vespa was now to his left, probably a good half-hour's walk away. He quickly realised he should abandon the bike and cut his losses. If the Carabinieri had been at the park because of him, then they may already have looked at CCTV, which would show him pulling up on the stolen bike. The very last thing he wanted was to have to find new wheels, but it was the safest option.

He began making his way along the side of the road, wondering how long he could keep this up before he was spotted by a passing police car, or an eagle-eyed member of the public. He'd hardly finished this thought when he saw what looked like a Carabinieri Alfa Romeo some thirty metres up ahead. He blinked, wondering if it was just his imagination filling in the gaps, but when he looked again an Alfa was indeed emerging from the heat haze, its telltale blue-and-red livery glinting in the sun. He swallowed, his mouth dry. There was nothing for it but to duck back into the forest.

He was only half way up the bank when the screech of tyres made him turn. A white BMW motorbike was skidding to a stop right behind him, churning up dust and pebbles, and turning the air black. He coughed as he tried to scramble up the bank and into the forest. He kept losing his footing, and was struggling to see for the dust. Then, in the next instant, strong arms were grabbing him, dragging him back down. He pushed back with his elbows, trying to fight them off, but in seconds he was being pulled to the ground, his breath catching on sand and grit.

Suddenly, the stranger released his grip and stepped back. Scamarcio realised that the figure towering above him was removing his helmet. For a few moments he couldn't make sense of it — couldn't take it in: the image in front of him was so unexpected, so out of place, he wondered if he might be hallucinating. Standing in the dirt, red-faced and sweating, was the journalist Roberto Rigamonti. Their paths had crossed on the American case, but Scamarcio hadn't seen him in over a year.

'Rigamonti ...What the *fuck*?'

'No time.' Rigamonti helped him up, then sprung open the seat of the bike. He pulled out a helmet and pushed it into Scamarcio's hands. 'Get on!'

Scamarcio wondered if he could trust him, but the Carabinieri's Alfa was now just a short distance away, and all other options seemed to be evaporating into the heat haze.

He scrambled on, the bike already starting to move, and they made a sharp U-turn, hurtling past the Carabinieri. Scamarcio worried that they'd drawn too much attention to themselves, and the Alfa would swing around and follow, but the Carabinieri, it seemed, were going to carry on their way. He took a long breath and tried to steady his wild pulse.

His relief lasted less than ten seconds. The air was suddenly shattered by the wail of sirens, and he swung around to see the squad car executing a sharp turn, its light bars flashing. Rigamonti pumped the gas, and the BMW roared, the world morphing into an angry mesh of noise and colour. They were weaving in and out of vans, Vespas, and oblivious Apecar drivers like slalom skiers, and the only thing Scamarcio could think was that they were about to die. Then all at once there was a shrieking sound of tearing rubber, followed by a blaring of horns, and he turned to see an unsuspecting truck lumbering across an intersection and into the path of the speeding Alfa. Both vehicles swerved and screeched to a halt, the front of the Alfa avoiding the side of the truck by inches. Scamarcio looked away, and finally remembered to breathe.

When the national park was far behind them, and the first

56

colours of Torvaianica were starting to dance on the horizon, Scamarcio heard Rigamonti's shaky voice coming through his helmet.

'Do you think they'll have read my plates?'

'They probably weren't close enough for long enough ... but never say never.'

'Fuck. I don't want to ditch my bike.'

'My instincts say we're good.'

'We won't stop here — too busy. I'm heading for Fossignano.'

Scamarcio had never been to Fossignano, so had no idea whether this was a wise decision or not. 'Right,' he said, his throat parched. 'I can't wait to hear how you just happened to be passing.'

'It's a good one,' said Rigamonti.

They travelled on in silence, the hotels and tourist bars gradually giving way to squat concrete buildings and drab housing, each territory marked out as a scorched stamp of grass. The side of the road was strewn with garbage, and Scamarcio wondered if Fossignano was one of the many places in the country where the town council was now bankrupt.

The bike began to slow, and Rigamonti turned past a rusting corrugated fence that looked as if it was about to collapse. They entered a car park, and ahead of them Scamarcio saw an unpainted concrete block boasting a bar and a gym in faded pink fluorescent letters. The place oozed neglect, and he hoped they wouldn't be hanging around. He took off his helmet, his hair slick with sweat. 'So, Rigamonti: what the fuck?'

'I could ask the same. Half the country's police are out looking for you.' The reporter wiped his face with one corner of his frayed Palestine scarf, then extracted a battered plastic bottle of mineral water from beneath the seat. He offered it to Scamarcio, but he waved it away. 'I'd have thought the police would have better things to do.'

'Everyone thinks you have the answers.'

'How convenient ...'

'So why did you scarper? What the hell were you thinking?' A smile played on Rigamonti's lips.

Scamarcio exhaled. 'It got messy. Then that dick Scalisi from AISE got involved, and it became a whole lot messier. I needed time to think — in peace.' He raised his chin. 'Anyway, you haven't answered me. What the fuck are you doing here?'

Rigamonti scratched above his nose. 'You're all over the TV. They're saying the terrorists may have blackmailed you into doing something sinister. I was listening to the police scanners, trying to work out if the cops had any idea where you were. Last sighting was Ostia, so I drove out and waited. After a while, someone called in a sighting near the south-western entrance to the national park. I decided to do laps in the hope I might get to you before the circus — fortune favours the bold, and all that.'

'You after a story?'

'Does the pope smoke hash?'

'Given that you didn't really get anywhere on the American case, what makes you think you'll be able to bring this one to the surface?'

'Fuck, I don't even know what the story is yet. But you should know that I'm not working for the big guys anymore — I decided to preserve my freedom.'

'They fire you?'

'Yup.'

Scamarcio remembered that he'd appreciated Rigamonti's no-nonsense approach the first time around. 'Well,' he sighed. 'I've got to hand it to you — you certainly go all out.' He extended a hand, and Rigamonti took it.

'Word on the grapevine is that you're seeing that showgirl ...'

Scamarcio frowned. 'Weird grapevine you have.'

Rigamonti shrugged. Scamarcio said nothing.

'So it's true?'

'Might be.'

'Actually it was in one of the celebrity mags.'

'What?'

'You were spotted outside a restaurant — La Pergola, I think.'

'I never go to La Pergola — it's way beyond my budget,' muttered Scamarcio.

'I heard your dad left you a tidy little legacy.'

'Are you going to try to help me find my way out of this shitstorm or not?'

Rigamonti took him by the elbow. 'There's a guy I know. He said we could use his place.'

'What guy?'

'Doesn't matter — you can trust him.'

'How can you be sure?'

'Oh for fuck's sake, Scamarcio, stop asking so many questions.'

Rigamonti took a left past the gym towards some overspilling rubbish bins. Behind the bins was a small alley, wedged between yew hedges. As they walked through it, Scamarcio was hit by the stench of rotting garbage and old urine. The cracked concrete path soon opened out onto the back lot of a row of unpainted houses, their bruised grey walls daubed with mucus-green graffiti. 'Immigrants out', seemed to be the overriding theme.

'Nice friends you have.'

'You should be grateful.'

Scamarcio felt a ripple of anxiety. 'It's not like I've got time to kill. I need to get back to Rome. The boy said if I don't meet his demands and return to the café by 9.00 a.m. tomorrow, the killing will start.'

Rigamonti stopped, but didn't turn. When he did eventually face him, his expression was grave. 'Scamarcio, we don't know each other well, but I've always regarded you as a realist. Have you considered that perhaps the authorities don't *want* you back?'

'You've just told me they're doing all they can to find me!'

'Right now, you're little more than a distraction, that's all. I don't know what that terrorist asked you to do, but isn't it possible that the authorities won't let you go through with it — that they'll do all they can to block it?' His speech had slowed, as if Scamarcio were simple.

'Of course I'd considered that.'

'So?'

'What?'

'So how the hell did you think you were going to get back to Rome undetected and give that terrorist whatever it is he wants?'

'I'll find a way.'

Rigamonti shook his head. 'Scamarcio, I don't think you quite appreciate the scale of the manhunt that's going down. Rome is practically on lockdown — you wouldn't make it halfway to the centre before they spotted you. There's no way in the world you could reach that boy.'

'Then we're fucked, because if I don't get back there, they're going to blow us all to shreds.'

'That's melodramatic …'

'You weren't *there*. Ifran told me this siege is much bigger than we realise. I think they've got other places wired, new guys ready to roll …'

'Intel are all over this …'

'No, they're *not*. And there may be more than one reason for that — it's not just incompetence.'

'What?' Rigamonti looked confused.

'Come on, let's find your friend.'

A bald man with several days' growth of beard, and tattoos along both forearms answered the door, and led them into his home.

What it lacked on the outside, it more than made up for on the inside. The place was well decorated, tasteful even: Scamarcio was surprised to see two huge cream sofas and some expensive looking oak furniture, carefully arranged.

'I'll leave you to it, then,' said their anonymous host. 'Roberto, you know where to reach me.' The man tapped the side of his nose, and Rigamonti looked nervous.

When the front door had slammed, Scamarcio asked, 'Who was that?'

'Better if you don't know, Scamarcio, better if you don't.' Rigamonti drew a pen and notebook from his jacket pocket.

'You don't waste time.'

'You just told me we don't have any.'

Scamarcio collapsed into the sofa. 'God, I'm tired.'

'So, what did he say, this boy?'

Scamarcio closed his eyes and started talking him through it: the call at the police station, the talk with Ifran, the drive with Scalisi, his escape, and the house in Ostia. The scratch of Rigamonti's pen against the paper was the only sound in the house. A couple of times the reporter was about to say something, then seemed to think better of it.

When Scamarcio came to the end, Rigamonti raised a languid eyebrow. 'This is *unusual*,' he murmured, almost non-committal. 'No-one will believe there's anything underhand going on, of course.'

'Why "of course"?'

'It's uncomfortable.'

'The internet is full of people asking uncomfortable questions.'

'I was thinking more about the print media.'

'Are you surprised?'

'That Ifran's suggesting some unorthodox involvement?'

Scamarcio nodded.

'A little, but not that much ...'

'Still chasing the next conspiracy?'

'I wouldn't be the first. So, this video?'

'I've watched it.'

'Any use?'

'I don't know.'

'Can I take a look?'

Scamarcio removed the laptop from the backpack and opened it. He handed the computer and DVD to Rigamonti.

When he had finished watching, the reporter said, 'Hmm. So the blond guy is the one Ifran believes he spoke to on the phone — the one who set the date as July twelfth?'

'I think so, but I have no way of knowing for sure.'

'Did Ifran film this?'

'That would be my guess. Interestingly, I found out that the villa where I dug up the box was formerly rented by a couple working for Intel.'

Rigamonti rubbed at his chin. After a moment, he said, 'You know, all this, it just seems too ... too neat really.'

Scamarcio didn't want to acknowledge it, but he knew what Rigamonti meant.

'If this blond guy is working for some foreign party — if some hidden entity *is* pulling his strings — I don't think they'd go about it like this. They'd use a subtler play. The guy they'd have inside the op would be one of *them* for starters.'

'One of them?'

'Middle Eastern, Arab. They'd never send in a white guy — it's too obvious.'

Scamarcio realised that this had been bothering him, too. 'Maybe whoever it is couldn't get *one of them*. Maybe they couldn't recruit them?'

Rigamonti pushed out his bottom lip and shrugged. 'Perhaps ...'

Scamarcio thought back to an article he'd read recently. 'Aren't there white jihadists? I remember reading about the Caucasus, the extremists over there ...'

'There aren't many left, and frankly, I doubt this guy's from there. There's the perfect American accent for starters.'

'So what is all this, then?'

'I dunno, Scamarcio. Right now, I have absolutely no bloody idea.'

'Well, we need to find out.'

'How did Ifran seem when he told you about the box?'

'Like he was for real — I can usually tell when my strings are being pulled.'

'That's significant. We mustn't lose sight of that. We need to find out more about Ifran. Who knows him? What's his real agenda?'

'That's exactly what the spooks will be doing. We're not going to be able to shake a stick at that stuff.'

'Not necessarily ...' Rigamonti looked like he was about to say more — but if he was, he thought better of it again.

'We don't even know where he's from.'

'That's where you're out of the loop. They've traced him to Torpignattara.'

Scamarcio was surprised at the fast work, but not the result. Recently, some commentators had been arguing that Torpignattara was Rome's equivalent of Brussels's Molenbeek. 'You know people there?' Scamarcio guessed.

'I did a story last year on whether Rome had its own banlieues, whether our suburbs harboured the same toxic resentments.'

'And what did you conclude?'

'After today, I can safely say I told you so.'

'So you're suggesting we head out there?'

'Yep.'

'But I risk getting picked up; the place will be swarming. I'll never get back.'

'Scamarcio.' Rigamonti's voice was rising now. 'You've got to let it go. You're not going to make it past the police in the centre!'

Scamarcio leapt to his feet. 'So we're just going to stand aside and let them kill thousands?'

'*Thousands*?'

Scamarcio nodded slowly, as if Rigamonti was too dumb to understand.

'You don't think he was playing you?'

'Like I said, my instincts say otherwise.' He tried to sound more confident than he felt. Fresh doubt was starting to creep in, but he didn't feel ready to share it.

Rigamonti pushed his glasses higher up his nose. Scamarcio noticed that they were the same unfashionable pair he'd been wearing last year, but now there was a small web of tape between the lens and the right-hand arm.

'What if we somehow buy ourselves enough time to check this thing out properly? We make contact with Ifran, tell him he might need to wait — that you're still working on it,' suggested Rigamonti.

'How the hell am I going to call him? The authorities are monitoring his line. They'll control all the calls coming in, and besides, I don't have his number.'

'Hmmm,' said Rigamonti helpfully.

Scamarcio walked to the narrow window and surveyed the miserable vista beyond. Two mud-brown birds were scrapping over a snail, pecking at each other as the shell came apart. A thought began to form: 'Actually there might be someone — Vincenzo Guerra. If I got him to call, got him to ask to be put through, they might allow it. He might be able to get a message to Ifran.'

'What's Guerra got to do with this?'

'They were together in Opera — he and the boy.'

'Why would the authorities allow a criminal like Guerra to

talk to Ifran? It wouldn't make for good headlines.'

'Yes, maybe that's too simple. What if we give Guerra a message to pass to the authorities that *they* can relay to the boy? There'd have to be some code which proved to Ifran that it was legitimate, and that the message really was coming from Guerra.'

Rigamonti sighed. 'How are you going to get to him? Can prisoners even take calls?'

Scamarcio pondered it for a moment, and then said, 'No. They can only phone out, once a message is received. The fucker is that I think they're only allowed to make calls in the morning. There's no morning left. We need to find a way to contact him, and he needs a way to call back immediately.'

'Can't you just go down the official police route? Tell them the truth and ask them to put you in touch with him?'

They both fell silent, knowing that wasn't going to work.

Scamarcio rubbed at his stubble. 'I could call my boss, but there's no guarantee he'd play ball. He'd be taking a huge risk.'

'What other options are there?'

Scamarcio struggled to think of any. He was about to give up, when an idea came to him. It wasn't an idea he particularly welcomed. 'There's a guy I know.'

'A guy ...' echoed Rigamonti, looking up from his notepad.

'He's from the wrong side of the tracks — a big player down in Calabria. He's bound to know people inside Opera: people who could get a message to Guerra, people who might have a phone.'

'Then let's call him!' Rigamonti's initial doubts seemed to have vanished.

'It's not that easy. I don't have his number — it's on a second mobile I keep at home.'

Rigamonti's eyes widened, and Scamarcio knew that the reporter was suddenly wondering whether the rumours about him were true — whether he was in tight with 'Ndrangheta after all.

Scamarcio's thoughts tumbled on. He realised that there was now a high chance that the police would search his apartment and find his secret phone stashed in the safe. He erased the call history after every use, and all the names had been changed, but he knew that wouldn't be enough. But Fiammetta was sharp; surely she'd find a way to make sure they didn't get to the important stuff.

'So you don't have any other ways to reach your Calabrian kingpin?'

Scamarcio turned from the window. 'There's a bar in Germaneto ...' He closed his eyes, still not sure whether he was doing the right thing. He tried to cast his mind back: when he'd gone to find Dante Greco for the first time, in Catanzaro, he'd left the car, walked up the street, and then the bar had been there on the right — shabby and peeling, battered chairs outside. He'd taken the steps, gone through the door. Had he even looked at the sign? He must have done ... but the name had been written somewhere else, too ... on the piece of notepaper that had been handed to him by Foti's messenger boy. Yes, that was it: *Bar Solari*.

'Bar Solari in Germaneto — his right-hand man, Mirco, can be found there,' said Scamarcio, triumphant.

'You want my phone?' asked Rigamonti, getting up to hand it over.

Scamarcio used the phone to run a quick web search for the number of the bar, not really expecting to find it, but the details were in the first hit. He rang and asked for Mirco. He thought he'd be fobbed off with 'wrong number', but the guy who answered said, 'Wait one sec — he's watching TV out back. They all are. It's a dead zone.'

Scamarcio swallowed and questioned the wisdom of what he was doing. But he still couldn't think of an alternative. It felt too risky to involve Garramone.

'Who's asking?' said Mirco gruffly, clearly put out to have been pulled away from the news.

Scamarcio's stomach tensed, and he felt fresh sweat breaking out between his shoulders.

'Mirco, it's Scamarcio. Leone Scamarcio.'

The line fell silent, and Scamarcio counted to five in his head. Eventually, Mirco whispered, 'Is this some kind of joke?'

'No joke, Mirco. It's me — the same guy who witnessed your boss, the boss of bosses, reading *Men Are from Mars, Women Are from Venus.*'

'Fuck,' hissed Mirco. 'You've got the whole fucking country out looking for you. Fuck, fuck, *fuck*, man. You are in *so* much shit.'

Mirco clearly hadn't spent much time improving his vocabulary since they'd last met.

'Yes, I'm aware of that. Can you put me through to Greco? I need a word.'

'Fuck,' repeated Mirco, under his breath. 'I don't believe this.'

'Will you put me through?'

'Wait — I need to ask him if he'll talk to you. He'll probably want to stay well clear.'

Great, thought Scamarcio. It seemed that there was a new hierarchy of criminal decency in place that he'd been hitherto unaware of. It might be OK for Greco to fraternise with Europe's most prolific drug and arms traffickers, but apparently it just wasn't form to talk to someone who might or might not be cooperating with terrorists. Scamarcio wanted to tell Mirco to go hang, but managed to hold his tongue.

After a long wait, Mirco was back, panting slightly. 'He'll talk to you. God knows why, but he will. Hang on.'

Scamarcio wondered if the Snake's curiosity had simply got the better of him.

The line clicked, then an unctuous voice said, 'Scamarcio, my word. You may be many things, but after today's little farce, I can safely say you're not a coward.'

'I'll take that as a compliment.'

'Please do. So, how can I help? I sense that whatever it is you want is tied up with the God-awful mess that seems to be unfolding all around you up in Rome.'

'Greco, I didn't have anything to do with those terrorists deciding to do what they did.'

'Ah, I don't care,' sighed Greco tiredly. 'Just explain what you want, and I'll tell you if I can do it. I have to say I'm intrigued.'

Scamarcio told him about the message he needed to get to Guerra inside Opera, trying to keep other details to a minimum. When he was done, Greco asked simply, 'What's in it for me?'

'You'd have helped save the lives of many, and I'd make that known. But that's as far as it goes. I can't swing prosecutions, I can't get the force off your back, I can't destroy evidence. Been there, done that, and I'm not going back. If those terms aren't acceptable, I understand.'

Scamarcio wondered if he'd just put his own personal advancement above the lives of others, but fuck it — he was not going to fall into the same trap with Greco as he'd done with Piocosta. He was moving on, and Fiammetta was a part of that — they'd talked long and hard. He was going to go as straight as he could, and she was going to stop whoring her soul around Rome's showbiz set — they'd reach their goals the *right* way. It might take a little longer, but they'd make it.

Scamarcio heard Greco suck the air in through his teeth, heard it whistle out again. Eventually he said, 'OK, Scamarcio. I'll do you this favour because I'm a good man. But don't insult my intelligence by trying to make me think you're going to pass me off as the hero. You'd never admit to a connection in a million years.'

Scamarcio stayed quite still. He wondered if Greco was recording the call.

'Neither would you admit to the fact we worked together on the Piocosta problem. That could cost you your career.' Greco paused. 'But perhaps not for the reasons you might think.'

The serpent was twisting and turning, slithering his way to a deal. Scamarcio felt acid in his gullet. 'And don't insult *my* intelligence by suggesting you're helping me out of kindness. I'm sure you'll name your price soon enough.'

Rigamonti looked up, alarmed, as if Scamarcio was pushing it.

But all Dante Greco said was, 'Yes, that's the beauty of our game — it's so fluid. Guerra will ring you in half an hour on the number you're calling from now.' With that he hung up — no *goodbye*, no *good luck*.

It was Greco's game, not his, was Scamarcio's first thought. His second was that it was unfortunate that the 'Ndrangheta's top boss now had Rigamonti's phone number. Scamarcio felt momentarily guilty, but really, what could he do? As always, it was a case of lesser evils.

Vincenzo Guerra called from Opera exactly thirty minutes later. Scamarcio marvelled at the precision of it — at the display of command and control Greco had executed for his benefit.

'Detective,' said Guerra, his tone grave.

'You know why I've contacted you?'

'I'm told it's about the drama being staged in the centre of Rome right now.'

'Staged' was an interesting choice of word, but Scamarcio didn't want to lose time pursuing it. 'I need you to get a message to Ifran. He wants me back there by 9.00 a.m. tomorrow, but if I'm to do what he asks, I may need more time. I could have trouble reaching him; the authorities may try to block me. I want Ifran to know that if there's any delay, it doesn't mean I've given up. He needs to know that I'll show.'

'He wants you back there, or what?'

Scamarcio preferred not to give him all the details. 'I'm sure you can guess. You played this game once.'

Guerra said nothing for a beat, then, 'How can I trust you?'

'I'm always interested in the truth, be it politically expedient or otherwise.'

Guerra grunted. 'Yes, that's what I figured. That's why I gave him your name.'

'You'll need to ring the negotiators — they probably won't put you through. You need to give them the message to pass on to Ifran. You'll have to use some kind of code, something that will show Ifran that the message genuinely came from you, that he can trust its authenticity.'

'How can we be sure the authorities won't screw it up?'

'Good question, but right now they're our only option. I can't call Ifran without them intercepting me first.'

'I think the boy's planning to do them some serious damage, but not in the way you might expect,' said Guerra, his voice almost a whisper.

'How do you mean?'

'It's complicated.'

'What do you know about him?'

'A little, but not a lot.'

Scamarcio didn't have time for the cat and mouse. 'Whose side is he on?'

'The same as you — the side of truth.'

That could mean anything, thought Scamarcio.

'What did he tell you today?' tried Guerra. 'What does he want?'

Scamarcio knew that it was too dangerous to give anything away. 'I can't go there, not now. The procedure you need to follow is this: Call Chief Garramone at Flying Squad HQ in Rome.' Scamarcio rattled off Garramone's direct line. 'Do *not* mention me. Tell him you need to get a message to Ifran via the negotiators, but don't tell him what that message is. He won't admit it, but basically he won't want to know — it's too messy for him. When he's put you through to the team dealing with the boy, give them the message with your personalised code — simple as that.'

'They'll be all over me after this.'

'I'd imagined they already were.'

'No, it's been surprisingly quiet.' His tone was thick with an irony Scamarcio didn't quite understand.

'So, you'll do this?'

'I'll do it.'

'Tell me about Ifran,' Scamarcio tried again.

'Nah, not on this phone. The Calabrians might think they have it all sewn up, but I don't trust anyone in here. If you want a proper chat, you'll have to make the trip to Milan.'

Scamarcio thanked him and cut the call.

'So, what now?' asked Rigamonti.

'We need to get moving, get things done as fast as we can in case the deadline still holds.'

'I'll need to contact my friends in Torpignattara.'

A vaguely familiar voice interrupted them from out in the corridor: 'Torpignattara? What the fuck are you doing going near that rat hole?'

Rigamonti quickly held a finger to his lips, and as he removed it, the owner of the house strolled back into the room.

'Come on, Roberto, I asked you a question,' said the tattooed guy.

Scamarcio hoped things weren't about to get nasty.

'It's just for a story,' said Rigamonti, hastily gathering his things.

'Do I look like I was born yesterday?' said the guy, but he didn't seem particularly angry. A bit put out, but not angry. 'There's been way too much peacemaking going on if you ask me. The pope kissing Muslims' feet, covering up statues ... Then,

71

if that's not bad enough, we have them moving in next door. It makes me spew.'

Scamarcio stayed quite still.

The tattooed guy jabbed a finger at Rigamonti. 'Everyone's forgetting what these fuckers have been telling us right from the start. Rome has been in their crosshairs since day one. Of the four metropolises of the ancient Roman Empire, how many are still standing? Just list them: Rome, Carthage, Alexandria, and Antioch — only the first still belongs to the West. Islam wiped out all the rest. One look at their shitty videos should have told us this day was coming — they've got the black flag of the caliphate waving over the Vatican, they've got the Colosseum in flames. Those bastards couldn't have sent us a clearer message if they'd scrawled it in blood on the Spanish Steps, but now everyone's running around like blind dogs in a meat market, like it's all some massive fucking surprise.'

'The Vatican certainly knew it was coming,' muttered Rigamonti.

'What?' asked his friend.

'Shifted all their gold to Switzerland, didn't they? Quite recently,' said Rigamonti to the floor.

Scamarcio broke in. 'Listen, I think we need to go.' He turned to Rigamonti's friend. 'Thank you for helping us — I appreciate it.'

The guy went to fist bump him, and Scamarcio spotted the letters 'S-K-I-N' tattooed across his forefingers. A quick glance at the guy's left hand confirmed his hunch — 'H-E-A-D' was tattooed on his other fist. *What charming company Rigamonti keeps.*

When they'd made their farewells and were heading back to the car park, Scamarcio said, 'What the fuck was that?'

'Met him for a story last year on white extremism. We're going full circle today — first him, and now my friends out in Torpignattara. I can safely say that we'll be getting the complete picture, the 360-degree view, as it were.'

'Doesn't it bother you, hanging out with blokes like that?'

'He's a means to an end — you'd know how that is.'

Scamarcio didn't like Rigamonti's tone, but he ignored it. Instead he said, 'All this talk of "extremism" — I mean, is it helpful? If you've lived through certain experiences, you'll have certain views. But does that mean you're an extremist?' He realised he was echoing Ifran.

'Yeah, the language is clumsy, and the narrative needs to change, you're right. But the media thinks we're all simpletons who can't deal with ambiguity. Or at least it suits them to think that. Anyway,' Rigamonti sighed and popped up the saddle on his bike, 'enough. I want to know what that lad is up to, then I want to put this exclusive to bed. After that, it's home, bath, and a nice glass of Ripasso.'

From where Scamarcio was standing, this seemed like a highly unlikely outcome.

7

IT'S FUNNY HOW THEY all felt the need to do drugs, get drunk, have sex in car parks. It was like they were looking for a way to escape the stability of their existence — the suffocation of success. For me it was different: if you've always been on the outside, and if your parents have always been on the outside, what is there left to rebel against? An outsider can never rebel. He's trapped in his own internal rebellion with no one there to notice it.

Scamarcio hadn't been to Torpignattara in a while. If anything, it had got worse in the years since his last visit. There seemed to be even less green in the parks, and the flaky, pale contagion of urban decay had spread, leaving more buildings boarded up and bereft. Conversely though, the pavements seemed fuller, the faces more diverse.

Less than a minute after entering the area, they spotted their first police car. Soon after, they saw a group of three patrol cars — Panthers — parked outside a smart-looking bar with silver letters and cream umbrellas that seemed to be trying too hard. Scamarcio noticed two uniforms talking to three dark-skinned men at a table outside.

Rigamonti swung the bike into a side street, and Scamarcio saw yet more squad cars and a couple of guys he made as plainclothes loitering by a bus stop, clearly waiting for orders. Up ahead were three uniforms strolling the street, armed to the hilt — it looked like a 'We're here, we have it under control', kind of patrol, with no real purpose. Rigamonti took a right and pulled to a stop in front of a run-down apartment block.

Scamarcio dismounted and almost stepped on a dead rat lying by a rubbish bin. The city was losing the war against the rat population. They used to say that there were three rats for every Roman, but he'd read recently that the ratio was now much higher. There was a level at which the rat population could no longer be contained, and they'd already exceeded that. Scamarcio thought of Scalisi — the rats were running amok in Rome.

Rigamonti rang the buzzer for the third floor, and a soft voice told them to come up. They were about to enter when Rigamonti tapped Scamarcio on the elbow and gestured subtly to his left. Two police cars had pulled up at the kerb some twenty metres ahead. A couple of uniforms were stepping out, followed by three plainclothes.

Scamarcio's instinct was to hurry inside, but he needed to check where the police were heading. After a moment's hesitation, the team tried the keypad of an apartment block two doors down from Scamarcio. Clearly no reply was forthcoming because, after a quick huddle with the plainclothes, they pressed the buttons again, then held an ID up to the glass. A guy soon appeared wielding a mop. After a brief back-and-forth, he led them around the side of the building, opening the wide metal gates to what Scamarcio presumed was the parking area.

'OK, I've seen enough,' he whispered.

When they were riding the elevator to the third floor, he asked, 'So, who is it we're going to see?'

Rigamonti rubbed beneath an eye. 'I met them for that story I told you about. They're two brothers who emigrated from Morocco ten years ago. I'm thinking they might be able to tell us something about your boy.'

When they knocked, a good-looking young man answered

the door. He was tall, with sharp cheekbones, almond-shaped eyes, and shoulder-length dark hair.

'Hamzi, how are you?' Rigamonti extended a hand. The young man took it, then eyed Scamarcio with a mixture of suspicion and concern.

'He's the guy from the news,' he said to Rigamonti, as if perhaps he wasn't aware.

'Yes, I was hoping we could have a quick word,' said the reporter.

Hamzi scanned the corridor, then ushered them inside. He stared at Scamarcio. 'This isn't going to cause any trouble for me, is it? I don't want hassle.'

'Where's Aakil?' Rigamonti asked.

'Out.'

Scamarcio took in a small lounge stuffed to capacity with dark wooden bookcases and chests of drawers. He guessed that the furniture had once stood in a bigger home. A couple of cheap fake-leather sofas occupied the centre of the room, elaborate antimacassars draped across the backs.

'There'll be no trouble,' said Rigamonti, probably too quickly. 'We won't be staying long.'

The young man gestured them to the sofa. 'So?' He took up a position on the settee opposite, but didn't look comfortable. He remained perched on the end, as if he needed to be ready to run at any moment.

'We're here about Ifran — I wondered if you knew him or knew of him?'

'You working for the police?'

'As usual, I'm just trying to get a story together.'

'But that guy's a policeman.' He pointed to Scamarcio as if he couldn't hear.

'Yep, but right now he's very much on the wrong side of the law.' Rigamonti sighed as if all this was an irrelevance. 'So, the boy — you know him?'

Hamzi barred his arms across his narrow chest. 'Not personally. But Twitter has kicked off — a couple of my mates know of him — a friend of a friend kind of thing.'

'And?'

'What's to tell? Looks like Ifran started hanging out with the wrong people — same old, same old ...'

'We're not sure it is.'

Hamzi shrugged. 'I couldn't judge. Like I say, we weren't acquainted.'

'What do they make of all this, your friends? Of Ifran's involvement?' Rigamonti asked.

'They say Ifran was into bling, liked to party — not your typical radical, if you know what I mean. People are surprised.'

Scamarcio made a mental note, then filed it away, unsure what to do with it. He didn't really want to know — there were already enough ambiguities, enough complications to consider.

'So he didn't seem particularly devout?' Rigamonti pushed.

'Not the way they tell it.'

'Was he popular?'

'I don't know — perhaps, if he liked to party. But I'm just guessing. I don't know him.' Scamarcio thought Hamzi was spelling this out a little bit too much.

'These friends of yours, do you think they'd talk to me?' asked Rigamonti.

Hamzi shrugged again. 'You could give it a go, but they don't know you. I can put in a good word, but I can't promise.'

'Let's try.'

Hamzi got up from the sofa and retrieved a mobile from the dresser. He punched the keypad and, after a few moments, began talking in a language Scamarcio didn't understand. The discussion seemed to grow quite heated, and Scamarcio thought he heard shouting on the other end, but then Hamzi fell silent and said 'OK,' before replacing the receiver.

'I think you're going to have to offer them something,' he said to Rigamonti.

'Cash?'

Hamzi nodded. 'They weren't keen. I told them you were straight, but that probably doesn't count for much. I didn't tell them about *him*,' he gestured to Scamarcio. 'If I were you, I wouldn't bring him — it will just freak them out.'

Rigamonti nodded. Scamarcio wondered where the hell he was supposed to hide out in Torpignattara with half the country's police patrolling the area.

'Thanks, Hamzi,' said Rigamonti, springing up from the sofa. 'I owe you one.'

'Yeah, well, if I ever need help, I'm hoping you can find me a good lawyer.'

'Done. Where are they, these friends?'

'A few streets down — Via della Rocca — it's near the park. Number forty-eight, fifth floor.'

They had finished shaking hands and were making to leave when Hamzi's door phone buzzed. He picked up the receiver, and Scamarcio watched the colour drain from his face. He pressed the button, smashed the phone back in its cradle, and pushed a shaky hand through his hair. 'It's the pigs. They're on their way up. Fuck, man, what have you *done?*'

'Nothing,' said Rigamonti, quite calm. 'They're just doing a routine house-to-house, that's all. Just say nothing, keep your head — all will be fine, I promise.'

With that, Rigamonti shoved Scamarcio out into the corridor. 'Let's take the stairs — they'll be in the lift.'

'Not if they're any good, they won't,' said Scamarcio. 'They'll take both to make sure no-one's doing a runner.'

'*So?*' said Rigamonti, the first hints of desperation in his voice.

'Follow me,' said Scamarcio, heading for the end of the corridor, quickly scanning the wall for the telltale panel. 'This building's old; we might have a chance.'

He soon found what he was looking for: a small silver handle marking the door to the rubbish chute. He pulled it open — the hole was just wide enough to climb inside.

'Are you crazy?' said Rigamonti, his eyes alive.

'Crazier to stand out here like a sitting duck ...'

'Oh, for fuck's sake.'

Scamarcio got into the chute and slid down to make room; luckily it wasn't so wide that they risked losing their grip. Scamarcio suddenly felt grateful for the fact that cohabiting had made him put on a few kilos. Fiammetta wasn't one for cooking, and they seemed to subsist on pizza, or oily take-outs from the Sardinian place down the road. The metal of the chute was warm beneath him, and the stink of old vegetables and rancid fats turned his stomach. He wondered how long they'd have to stay here. They might not be able to hear the police arrive; there might be no way of knowing when it was a good time to come out.

But, as if in answer to these doubts, he heard Hamzi's voice, much louder than natural, from further down the corridor. 'No,' he was saying. 'Let me go, you have no right!' He was shouting now. There were footfalls approaching, it was the sound of many pairs of boots, and Hamzi's cries were rising above them all, louder and louder. 'Under which law? You have no right! How can you do this?'

Scamarcio felt Rigamonti go quite still. Then he heard the sound of the elevator doors release and feet shuffling inside. Hamzi was still yelling. 'This is a fucking disgrace! It's unlawful! Get your hands off me, you racist bastards!'

When the groans of the cogs and pulleys of the lift had finally died away, Scamarcio tried to wet his lips and find some words. 'What the fuck?' he asked, already knowing the answer.

'They've gone and fucking arrested him, haven't they?' whispered Rigamonti.

'But it sounds like he's got nothing to do with it.'

'Either they're doing a sweep of the neighbourhood, or they know something we don't.'

'It's a sweep,' said Scamarcio, quite certain. 'They're desperate. It's bells and whistles — the normal rules no longer apply.'

'Let's go,' said Rigamonti, pushing his bulk against the door of the chute and pulling himself out. 'I want to get to Hamzi's friends before they do.'

Scamarcio scrambled out behind Rigamonti and stretched. His knees and back ached, and his neck was stiff. Yet again, he was reminded that he was fast approaching forty. 'They won't have the resources to arrest everyone.'

'Yeah, but Hamzi might be put under duress.'

'He wouldn't give them up, surely?'

'You said it yourself — it's emergency measures. What if the police go all Guantanamo?'

'I know the chief — he'd never countenance that.'

'Depends what pressure is being brought to bear.'

'No, I've seen him take the heat from AISE before, and he didn't bend.'

'Yeah, but this is different, Scamarcio. This time, the whole world's watching.'

'Chief Mancino's decent, he'll keep it clean. The last thing he'll want is all these non-suspects choking up the cells.'

'We'll see,' said Rigamonti, sceptical. He went to push the button for the elevator, but Scamarcio darted out a hand to stop him.

'We'll take the stairs. They might have forgotten something and be heading back up.'

'Like what, another suspect?' sighed the reporter.

8

WHEN THEY EXITED THE building, there was no sign of any police. Rigamonti had already entered the address of Hamzi's friends into the GPS on his iPhone. 'It's only a few minutes away. I'd walk, but given the circumstances, that doesn't seem wise.'

They clambered back on the motorbike, Scamarcio quickly flicking down the visor on his helmet. As they turned out of Hamzi's road, he spotted a platoon of Panthers parked alongside a disused market square. Then he noticed a type of black van with narrow windows that he knew was used by the SWAT unit of the anti-terror police. To the right of the van, standing on the pavement, were two dog handlers and their mutts. Scamarcio's impression changed: he sensed that the police knew exactly what they were looking for here. The elite snipers wouldn't have been sent in otherwise.

He scanned the area around the square. There were a few run-down apartment blocks and several shops. He couldn't tell where the units were headed, but it seemed clear that they were following a specific lead.

Rigamonti sped past the police vehicles, and Scamarcio's mind flashed on the possibility of a roadblock. But the way ahead was clear, and they moved freely into a wide street lined with semi-restored Art Nouveau buildings. Rigamonti took a swift left, and they pulled up outside what looked like a preschool. Paintings of trees and farmyard animals lined the glass windows.

'This has to be a mistake,' said the reporter.

Scamarcio looked around him and noticed a low building set back a few metres to the left of the school. It seemed like a work in progress, and had been partially painted brown along one wall. The building was squat, with just three floors. The ground floor windows were obscured by a crisscross of steel bars.

'Could it be that one?' he said, pointing it out to Rigamonti.

'Must be.'

They left the bike and traipsed across the threadbare patch of grass bordering the nursery.

Rigamonti scratched at the top of his head. 'I'm not sure how long we've got left until my name is mentioned,' said the reporter, sounding quite calm.

'You still think they'll make Hamzi sweat?'

'Sure.'

'My sense is that this is a major sweep, maybe the biggest they've ever staged. They're throwing all their resources at it, but it doesn't have much focus yet. It could be a while before they even start talking to Hamzi.'

'Hmm,' said Rigamonti, unconvinced. 'It looked like they knew exactly what they were doing up by that market square.'

'That's a separate issue, I think.'

'What do you mean?'

'Often in emergency situations like this, politics takes over, and money is spent doing the wrong things, just to give the impression that *something* is being done.'

'Sounds like wishful thinking.'

'Trust me. We still have some time.'

Rigamonti was about to ring the buzzer when he turned to Scamarcio. 'You heard what Hamzi said. Don't you think I should go it alone?'

Scamarcio ran a hand through the damp hair at the nape of his neck. 'Problem is, where the fuck do I go? The area is teeming. And I'd prefer not to loiter around inside this dump waiting for someone to spot me and call the cops.'

Rigamonti nodded as if he'd already reached the same conclusion: 'Right you are then, let's chance it.'

He rang the bell and explained loudly through the closed front door that Hamzi had sent them. Scamarcio heard a grunt before the latch clicked and the door swung open.

The young but morbidly obese guy standing on the threshold to his flat didn't seem particularly happy to see them. But when Rigamonti pulled out three hundred euros in cash, his mood seemed to lift slightly. Scamarcio distrusted him at first sight.

Once they were inside the filthy apartment, the reporter cut to it. 'Hamzi said you knew something about the boy Ifran, who's holed up at the café near the Colosseum, with all those hostages.'

There was a huge plasma TV playing Sky TG24 in the corner of the room, and the fat man glanced at it as Rigamonti spoke. Besides being dangerously overweight, the guy, who said his name was Aabad, was stunningly ugly, with bulbous eyes and a badly receding hairline. He turned from the TV and swigged nervously from a can of Coke before pushing the back of a swollen hand across his cavernous mouth.

'I don't know him, but my cousin Taaliq does. They used to hang out.'

'Used to?'

'Ifran suddenly disappeared, left the scene. He didn't want to party anymore.'

'Ifran liked to party?' tried Rigamonti.

Aabad shrugged and sniffed, then lowered his weight onto a decrepit looking sofa — foam was spilling from the cushions. 'They used to hit the clubs. He was quite a dancer. They were out three, four nights a week.'

Scamarcio couldn't square it. He couldn't fit Ifran into this picture, but then he reminded himself that he'd only spoken to him for a few minutes.

'Did they go to clubs round here?'

'Yeah, and in the centre, I think. Ifran had these ...' He hesitated as he tried to find the word *'particular* tastes.' Aabad pursed his huge lips in disgust.

'What do you mean, "particular"?' asked Scamarcio, not caring that he was drawing attention to himself.

Aabad looked strangely uncomfortable. He pinched his nose, then eased back into the sofa and scratched his oily brow. 'Well, let's just say that girls didn't really rock his boat,' he said nervously, almost as if he was talking about himself.

'He's gay?' asked Rigamonti.

The boy rubbed at the corner of an eye, apparently bored now. 'My cousin thought so, although he never saw anything specific.'

'When was all this — when were they hanging out?' asked Scamarcio.

'About six months ago. Then Ifran just disappeared.' Aabad clicked his fat fingers as though he'd been the one to make Ifran vanish.

'Six months ago?' echoed Scamarcio, his mind turning on something new, a thought he didn't have time to properly pursue.

'Yeah. He suddenly stopped returning my cousin's calls. Taaliq couldn't get hold of him.'

'And he never saw him again?'

'They passed on the street a few times, but Ifran just gave him the cold shoulder. Taaliq couldn't work it out; he didn't know what he'd done to offend him.'

'Your cousin, does he live around here?' asked Scamarcio.

'Yes, but he's away in Turin on business.'

'What business?' asked Rigamonti sharply.

Aabad nodded slowly and bit his bottom lip. 'No, that's not for you. I'm not going into it.'

'Fair enough,' said Rigamonti, looking away.

The fat guy tapped his chin a few times, seemingly thinking something through, then said, 'Do you want to see some pictures?'

Rigamonti swung his gaze back to Aabad. Scamarcio wondered if the guy was trading in filth — off-the-grid stuff.

'Pictures of my cousin and Ifran,' said Aabad impatiently, as if it narked him that they might jump to the wrong conclusion. He tapped the screen on his iPhone, then made to pass it across, but suddenly seemed to think better of it. 'That'll be another hundred.'

Rigamonti traded frustrated glances with Scamarcio. Scamarcio pulled out his wallet and extracted two fifty-euro notes, reluctantly handing them over. 'How come you have pictures?' he asked, feeling like he was being conned.

'I downloaded them from Facebook and Twitter when I heard you were interested.'

'How very helpful.'

'Supply and demand.'

Scamarcio stared at the gluttonous figure of Aabad, sprawled on the sofa like some rotting Jabba the Hutt, and decided that his agenda was most probably greed. It felt good not to have to deal with ambiguities for once.

'Just scroll to the right,' said Aabad, thumbing the fifty-euro notes and holding them up against a shaft of sunlight. Once he was satisfied, he pulled out a fat leather wallet and carefully slipped them inside.

Scamarcio studied the screen and saw a series of shots of Ifran smiling into the lens, another guy of similar age beside him. They seemed to be in a bar or nightclub, and both had bottles of beer in their hands, or elaborate cocktails of various shapes and sizes. They were dressed in tight T-shirts, their dense muscles visible beneath. In a couple of the pictures, Scamarcio spotted designer labels: Hugo Boss on one shirt, the Ralph Lauren polo player on the other. If anything, the two young men looked like poster boys for western materialism.

In the next shot, Aabad's cousin was gone, replaced by a good-looking dark-skinned girl in a shimmery halter-neck, her huge chest covered by a thick gold necklace. Scamarcio flicked to the next picture, then stopped. The girl was still on the boy's left, but on the right, grinning gormlessly, his eyes dark with drink, was the blond giant from the video. Scamarcio's heart began to race.

'You know this guy?' he asked Aabad, turning the phone to show him.

'The Chechen? Everyone knows the Chechen.'

'He's from Chechnya?'

'Yeah, but he's been here a few years now. He's not someone you'd want to mess with,' said Aabad scratching the side of his massive head.

'Why's that?'

'He's violent. I saw him beat a guy to a pulp once, just for looking at the woman he was screwing. And I know for a fact he wasn't even *interested* in that woman. He was just using her for sex.'

'He's got a reputation?'

'Everyone avoids him. My cousin hated him, but for some reason Ifran wanted to hang out with the Chechen. Who knows …?'

Scamarcio began to feel a prickling down his spine and inside his palms. It was the same feeling he'd had at preschool when he knew he'd made a mistake and was about to be found out. 'So they knew each other well, the Chechen and the boy?'

'Yeah, like I say, they hung out.'

'Even though he was violent?'

Aabad shrugged. 'I dunno. Maybe it didn't bother Ifran like it did the rest of us. There was always something a bit off about Ifran.'

'You said you didn't really know him.'

'I'm just telling you what I heard.' It sounded more first-person than that, but Scamarcio didn't push it.

'What was a Chechen doing living in Torpignattara?'

Aabad picked his nose and looked like he was about to inspect his finger, then seemed to remember he was in company. 'He wanted to work in Italy. Said that the war had destroyed everything back there.'

'He have a name, this Chechen?'

'Must have, but I don't know it — everyone just calls him the Chechen.'

'He'd come to Italy alone?'

'Yeah, I think so.'

'What did he do for work?'

'Is he dead or something?' asked Aabad, inclining his head, untrusting again.

'Why do you ask that?'

'You're talking about him in the past tense.'

It clicked for Scamarcio then. 'He's still here in Torpignattara?'

Aabad pushed out his bottom lip. For a moment, he looked like a huge mutant baby. 'Well, unless he's soared off above the rooftops like Superman, he's still in the laundrette where I saw him half an hour ago, watching his smalls go round.'

9

As THEY WERE HEADING for the door, Aabad flung out a huge flabby arm, barring their path.

'Do you think I was born yesterday?'

'Excuse me?' asked Rigamonti, looking like he might finally lose his cool.

Aabad jabbed a finger at Scamarcio. 'You think I don't recognise him?'

Neither man said a word. 'You think I'm not wondering what the fuck he's doing here, asking all these questions about Ifran?' Aabad angled his massive chest towards Scamarcio.

'Surely it must be obvious,' said Scamarcio, trying to resist the urge to look away.

'Obvious how?' Scamarcio saw a roll of fat shift beneath Aabad's huge tent of a T-shirt, and watched the wattle beneath his neck shake.

'Well, the whole world knows I met with the boy. I would have thought you'd have put two and two together and worked out he's blackmailing me.'

'Blackmailing you?'

'Yeah, and like you and your cousin's job, I'd prefer not to go into it. Suffice it to say that I need to know more about Ifran before I decide what to do next.'

'Why don't you just get your pig friends to help?'

'It's not that simple,' said Scamarcio. 'And they're not my friends.'

'Whatever,' said Aabad, adjusting the elasticated waistband on his grease-stained tracksuit bottoms. 'The pigs will be around here soon enough, asking questions about my cousin. Could be that I might have new, valuable information to share.'

Rigamonti shook his head, exasperated. 'Aabad, I have fifty euros left in my wallet. That's it.'

Aabad rubbed his spotty chin. 'Hmm. But I expect you have credit cards.'

Scamarcio thought quickly. Intel had an identity for Ifran; no doubt they knew where he lived. Right now, they'd be going through his phone records and his social media accounts, looking for contacts, people who knew him, maybe rooting out possible accomplices. It wouldn't be long before they hit on the cousin — indeed, they might have done so already.

'You spoken to your cousin this morning?' asked Scamarcio.

Aabad's chin wobbled as his mouth turned down. 'I tried to call him before you arrived, but it just rang out.'

Scamarcio took out his wallet and pulled out his MasterCard. He made no move to hand it across, but pointed a sharp finger at Aabad so that he was almost touching his shiny lump of a nose.

'*Don't* fucking call him and *don't* tell anyone we've been here. You manage that, and this card is yours for the next forty-eight hours before I cancel it. Wait an hour before using it.' He handed the card across.

Aabad looked at it, confused. 'What's the credit limit?'

'You don't need to worry about that.'

Aabad turned it over and examined the front. 'Yeah, I see it's a gold card. Life in the trough must pay well.'

Rigamonti was looking at Scamarcio as if he was out of his mind. Scamarcio understood what he was thinking, but by his assessment, Aabad was too stupid and too lazy to realise he was being played. Scamarcio knew that Scalisi would be monitoring the card, working out when to kill it. Sure, it would let him know that Scamarcio had been in Torpignattara, getting closer to the truth, but that was probably no bad thing. After the initial hit, the card would just cause confusion.

'Right then,' said Aabad, removing his arm and its undercarriage of flab from the doorframe. 'Fuck off. I've given you all I can.'

Aabad had told them the laundrette was at the end of his street on the left, next-door to a Japanese restaurant run by Chinese people. He'd claimed to have no idea where the Chechen actually lived.

They found the laundrette easily enough — hurrying inside after a couple of men who appeared to be conducting a drug deal in an overgrown scrap of park had sent hostile glances their way.

'We're looking for the Chechen,' said Rigamonti to a gaunt, weather-beaten blonde woman folding sheets behind the counter. Her eyes kept flitting to a small TV mounted on the wall. It was playing Sky TG24 like everywhere else. Scamarcio stole a breath and felt his palms grow damp — would she recognise him?

'You've just missed him,' said the woman, her eyes still on the screen. 'Fuck,' she said. 'Can you believe it? The world's gone mad.'

They both turned towards the TV, and as they did so, they heard a volley of shots ring out. Scamarcio stepped closer until he could read the tracker at the bottom of the screen. 'New gunfire heard at McDonald's on the Spanish Steps.'

'They're shooting hostages again,' he said, his voice low. 'What are they playing at?'

'They just want to scare us shitless,' said the woman. 'If you ask me, we need to ship those fuckers right back to where they came from. They're here to kill us, destroy our way of life. Just one look around this place should tell you that much. We're overrun.'

Scamarcio felt his spine grow warm. 'Has there been shooting at any of the other locations?' he asked. Given that the woman had shown no sign of recognising him, he decided to chance it.

'I only turned on the TV half an hour ago, so I couldn't say, but that's all they've been talking about since.' She finished folding the sheets, then bent low to grope around in a grubby blue laundry bag. She quickly pulled out a bunch of dazzlingly white T-shirts and deposited them on the counter.

'The Chechen — do you know where we might find him?' asked Rigamonti, his eyes darting nervously to the TV. Scamarcio followed his gaze and saw his own mugshot filling the screen. 'I'm going outside for a smoke,' he said quickly, heading for the door. He stepped out into the oppressive heat, which was now shimmering off the buildings, and turned away from the shopfront. He patted his jacket and pulled out his Marlboros — but the box was empty. He'd meant to restock, but had forgotten.

'Fuck it,' he sighed, defeated.

He looked back through the window and saw Rigamonti still chatting to the woman. After a long volley of back-and-forth, the reporter tossed back his head and laughed. But then the woman returned her attention to the TV, and Rigamonti swiftly held up a hand in farewell.

'Come on,' he said, grabbing Scamarcio by the elbow as he hurried into the road. 'She's going to come out looking for us any moment.'

They'd only made it half way down the street when they heard cries of 'Hey, you!'

They ran to the motorbike, Rigamonti firing up the engine before he was even properly in the saddle. They flew down the street, past the preschool outside Aabad's place, and swung a sharp right into a neighbouring street, which led to another road, dense with social housing. Children with Italian, Chinese, or South American features were playing on burnt scraps of grass outside.

'That harridan give you any idea about the Chechen?' Scamarcio asked.

'There's a bar where he likes to drink, but it's on that disused market square where all the cops are mustering. I doubt he's going to be around, and even if he was, how the hell do we get past all that?'

'She give you anything else?'

'There's a woman he's screwing — she lives back here — Via Rovetti. That's where we're headed. Well, I think it's where we're headed.'

Scamarcio hadn't seen any police cars for a while, but he wasn't sure whether to feel reassured. Beneath him, he felt the engine slow, and after a few seconds Rigamonti brought the bike to a stop outside a grey Fascist-era block. *The rationalist architecture coupled with the dead grass could crush the most hardened of souls*, thought Scamarcio.

Rigamonti dismounted and took a seat on a crumbling stone wall where some charming scribe had penned, *Your mother sucks dick Nino B*. The reporter ran a hand through his hair and leaned forward, his elbow on his knee, his head low. It seemed like a gesture of defeat.

Scamarcio followed him over. 'What is it?' he asked, not really wanting to know.

Rigamonti sniffed. 'I've got a bad feeling.'

'Tell me.'

'This Chechen, how does he survive?'

Scamarcio shook his head. 'I dunno.'

'I asked the woman in the laundrette if he had a job, where he worked. She said the Chechen doesn't work.'

'So?'

'No-one knows how he makes ends meet. He seems to have money, but he doesn't have a job. He says he's looking for a job, yet never finds one. But he likes designer gear and seems to have cash to burn in the bars. None of them can figure it out.'

'Has he ever explained it?'

'Not that she knows, and she sounds like she's at the heart of all local gossip.'

'What are you thinking?'

'I'm thinking that we've been looking at the photo the wrong way around.'

'How do you mean?'

'On the DVD, we saw a blond guy appearing to collaborate with the terrorists; he seems to be saying he'll help them procure something — my guess is they're talking about arms.'

'Mine, too,' said Scamarcio, glancing at his watch. There really wasn't time to be sitting on a wall going through minutiae.

'This guy has an accent — it's almost perfect American, but not quite. It suggests he's been educated in the US, but perhaps spent his early life elsewhere. We then find out this guy has told people he's come from Chechnya, we then find out he has no job …'

'Cut to it!' Scamarcio didn't like where this seemed to be heading, but they needed to get there fast.

'Scamarcio, don't you think it's likely that the Chechen is a plant — we all know how desperate the spooks are for human intelligence inside the suburbs. They want information on attacks that are being planned, who they should watch out for, newcomers to the area. My guess is that the Chechen — if he's even *from* Chechnya — is Intel's eyes and ears in Torpignattara. The fact he's white is no longer a problem. There are jihadists in Chechnya, so that's the disguise he's using.'

'No!' Scamarcio almost shouted it.

'Calm down,' said Rigamonti, raising both palms and taking a breath. 'Let's just try to paint the picture. You need to accept that Ifran's already lied. He told you he didn't know the blond guy, that when he heard the American accent on the phone it was a first, that it took him by surprise. But Aabad's photos clearly show that Ifran knew the Chechen, and probably knew him well.'

'Yeah, but we're not clear on the timeline — maybe he met him after the phone call, and then they became friends. Maybe it wasn't even the Chechen on the phone, and Ifran never made a connection between the two things.'

'No — I think he's known the Chechen for a long time. I also think there was no phone call.'

'What?'

'The boy wanted to get you to investigate the Chechen — he needed a story to get you hooked. The question now is, *why*? My guess is that he was trying to turn the tables on Intel. He knew the Chechen was a plant and he wanted to punish the intelligence services — make them sweat by suggesting that they were somehow involved. He's using you to launch a devastating first strike in a propaganda war.'

Scamarcio slumped down next to Rigamonti. His words made sense, it was a rational analysis, but the problem was that Scamarcio's gut wasn't listening. Both his instincts about the boy and his instincts about the film were telling him different. 'Why was the Chechen getting them arms, Rigamonti? That's straying so far behind enemy lines that it's almost entrapment. Hell, I reckon I'd have no problem finding a handful of magistrates who'd see it that way.'

'The game has got a lot dirtier, a lot more complicated, since 9/11. Yes, a few judges sometimes get their knickers in a twist, but Intel's not listening — they'll do whatever it takes.'

Scamarcio scratched at his jaw. 'Fuck it,' he whispered. He was about to suggest they make a move, when a thought struck him. 'OK, so if the Chechen's a plant, why are these attacks going ahead? Why didn't he warn the authorities? Why haven't they stopped them?'

At that, Rigamonti fell silent and studied the ground. 'There's been a breakdown in communications. Fuck-ups happen — maybe this is just one almighty fuck up.'

Scamarcio thought back to his conversation with Scalisi: *We fucked up. We took our eyes off the ball.* Scamarcio shook his head. No, it wasn't that simple. There was something bigger, something they were missing — he felt sure of it.

10

'COME IN OUT OF the heat,' he said. 'Do you want a coffee, a beer?' He seemed so confident, so in control, as if the prison and all its rules were meaningless, as if he could override them all.

'You've been through a tough time. These things can happen to the best of us, but justice is a brutal beast. It makes monsters of us all. We'd like to help, if we can. We think you deserve a fresh start.'

I took the seat that was being offered and looked around for a guard, but there was no-one. The visiting room was deserted — it was just me and the strange guy with the stoop.

It was the day my life began.

The woman the Chechen was screwing lived in a drab block around the corner from where they'd been sitting. There'd been no need to ring the bell because the downstairs entrance was ajar, the glass smashed. A couple of workers from the town council were trying to repair the damage, but the neighbourhood kids were making their lives a misery, pelting them with eggs and other liquidy missiles that looked a whole lot worse.

'Excuse me,' said Rigamonti, stepping over toolboxes and assorted rolls of tape. The council workers didn't spare him a glance. They were too busy wiping themselves down.

When they'd made it to the second floor, Rigamonti turned to Scamarcio: 'Her name's Nunzia by the way.'

'What if he's with her?'

'Then we can ask him to his face.'

'There'll be no time for that. He'll be straight on the phone, telling his Intel chums where to find us.'

'Ah, so you buy my theory now?'

'Partly — perhaps.'

Rigamonti knocked, and after a few moments, a woman in her mid-thirties with long, thick, curly hair and a generous bust opened the door. She wore heavy dark eye make-up and thick red lipstick. Scamarcio thought she was good-looking, but not beautiful. There was nothing delicate about her features — they were too solid, too permanent.

'We're looking for the Chechen,' said Rigamonti.

'He's not here,' she replied, trying to slam the door in their faces.

Scamarcio reached into his pocket and thrust his police ID through the gap. 'We need a word.'

Rigamonti raised his eyebrows, but Scamarcio sensed that this woman didn't recognise him; that she'd been too busy doing other things to watch the news. The gap inched wider. She adjusted the bra beneath her tight sleeveless top, then frowned. 'What the fuck is this?'

'It's the police, and if you don't let us in I'll send a bunch of blokes with a battering ram to do it for you,' said Scamarcio.

That seemed to swing it. She slowly opened the door, standing back against the wall to let them through. Scamarcio felt her eyes sizing him up as he passed and imagined that this must be how women felt when builders leered at them in the street.

'So,' he said once they were all inside, 'where can we find your boyfriend?'

She slumped into an armchair with a lurid pink plastic cover and reached for a box of fags on a side table. 'Which one?'

'The Chechen.'

'No idea, darling, we're not exclusive.' She sized him up once more, licking her lips, then smacking them together softly.

Scamarcio scratched behind an ear. 'Where does he live?'

'I couldn't tell you.'

'What, you don't know where your boyfriend lives?'

'The Chechen comes and goes. Literally.'

Scamarcio felt suddenly tired and took a seat on a shabby cane settee that looked like garden furniture. Rigamonti, he noticed, seemed occupied with something happening beyond the window.

'You known him long?'

'A few months,' she said, vaguely.

'How did you meet?'

'What do you care?'

'Come on, Nunzia, I haven't got all day.'

At the mention of her name, she smoothed down her hair, pulled it out from behind her shoulders, and rearranged it over her bust. Then she took a drink from a tumbler on a small table littered with battered cigarette packets and lottery scratch cards. The liquid inside the glass was clear, but Scamarcio sensed it probably wasn't water. Nunzia needed something to take the edge off her day, and she needed to start early.

'We met at a bar round here, he bought me drinks, I gave him a blow job.' She fixed Scamarcio with a hard stare.

'Has he told you much about himself?'

'He's not much of a talker.'

'He mention Chechnya at all?'

'He just says it was shit there, and that he needed to get out.'

'Did he say why he chose Italy?'

'Baby Jesus! Why is everyone so bloody interested in the Chechen all of a sudden?'

'What do you mean "everyone"?'

She held open a palm. 'Well, now you, then those arseholes this morning …'

'Which arseholes this morning?' Rigamonti turned sharply from the window.

'Blokes in dark suits — three of them — they were asking the same questions.'

'Did they say where they were from?'

'No.'

'Did they show you an ID?'

'No.'

'Why did you let them in, then?'

'They pointed a gun in my face. Seemed like the sensible thing to do.'

Nice, thought Scamarcio. If they were Intel, they'd tossed out the rulebook. He tried to focus. 'So, the Chechen didn't tell you much?'

'I just said that, didn't I? He claimed that he'd come here because everything was shit over there since the war — he saw this as his chance of finding a job ...'

'Has he found one?'

'No, but I don't think he's really trying.' She examined a chipped fingernail and turned her attention to Rigamonti, who was standing in the sunlight from the window.

'Why's that?' Scamarcio pressed.

'Well, he stays in bed till noon. Not much chance of finding a job if you can't be bothered to get up.'

He thought about that. He wondered what the Chechen was doing with his nights. But instead he asked, 'And you've been seeing him for a few months?'

'Yeah,' she said, frowning slightly. 'I didn't think he'd hang around, but he keeps coming back for more.' She picked at her teeth and tilted her head to the side, her eyes on Scamarcio all the while.

He stared at the woman before him and wondered quite *what* the Chechen was coming back for. Sure, she was good-looking, but she smelt of BO, and her hair was greasy at the roots. The handsome, well-muscled Chechen could do better. If he was indeed undercover, was it possible that there was something else bringing him here?

'What's your full name?'

'I'm not telling you.'

'Don't be ridiculous — I can get it from your ID card in an instant.'

'Why don't you, then?'

'Come on, Nunzia — you can save yourself a whole load of grief. I'll have you down the station on obstruction in seconds. Can you be bothered? I know I can't.'

She barred her arms across her huge bust. 'Basile,' she hissed, exasperated.

'Basile?' Scamarcio sat up straighter, more alert now.

'Yes,' she seethed, suddenly furious. 'But you can't lump us all in one basket. I have nothing to do with my brothers. It wasn't my fault we came from the same womb.'

Scamarcio exchanged glances with Rigamonti, who was looking confused.

'Your brothers run one of the most powerful clans in the area, Nunzia. How can you avoid them?'

He caught Rigamonti nodding slowly, the realisation dawning.

'Believe me, it ain't easy,' she sighed.

'You tell the Chechen about them?'

'Oh, he already knew, everyone does. With a name like Basile what can you do?'

'Quite,' said Scamarcio. Then: 'Did the Chechen ever talk to you about them?'

She scratched at an eyelid, and then below her nose. 'He might have done.'

'And what did he say?'

'You think I'm an idiot?'

'I will if you don't tell me. Give me a straight answer or you'll be in Rebibbia before nightfall.'

She scratched her neck and recrossed her legs. Scamarcio noticed a dappling of cellulite beneath her frayed denim shorts. 'He wanted me to fix up a meeting. He said he needed to talk to them about a business opportunity.'

'Did you?'

'Yes.'

'When was that?'

'A few weeks ago.'

Scamarcio could guess what that opportunity was. The Basiles were renowned arms dealers; it was said that only 'Ndrangheta had a higher turnover.

He got up from the sofa, motioning to Rigamonti to follow.

'Thank you, Nunzia, you've been most helpful. Where can I find your brothers?'

'Out by the industrial park — Via Zena,' she replied sullenly, pushing herself out of the chair, the damp plastic peeling away from the back of her thighs.

As he was heading towards the door, Scamarcio felt a hand on his back. He turned, and Nunzia was staring at him again, her face way too close. He could smell her breath — strawberry bubblegum with a bitter undercurrent, maybe vodka. The BO was overpowering. 'There's something you should know about the Chechen.'

Scamarcio was still trying to move towards the door, but for some reason, Rigamonti had come to a stop and was blocking his path.

All at once a voice from out in the corridor boomed, 'And what the fuck might that be?' The voice was male and abnormally deep. There was violence behind it and strength — immense strength.

Rigamonti turned to Scamarcio, quite pale. The Chechen

was standing before them, six feet six inches of pure muscle and sinew. But all Scamarcio really noticed at that moment was the Glock 43 levelled at Rigamonti's chest.

11

THE CHECHEN PUSHED THEM back inside the flat, saying, 'Not a word from either of you.'

Scamarcio picked up the strange American twang beneath the Italian. There was no hint of a Russian accent.

The Chechen gestured with his wide chin towards Nunzia Basile. 'You need to learn to keep your mouth shut.'

'They're the fucking pigs — what the hell was I supposed to do?'

He ignored her and thrust the gun into Rigamonti's chest, driving them back towards the rear of the flat. Scamarcio took in the Chechen's wide neck and the enormous biceps straining beneath his taut Jack Daniels T-shirt — just the sight of him made Scamarcio sweat.

'In there,' grunted the hulk.

Scamarcio felt his back come up against a door. It gave, and he almost lost his balance. They were standing in a narrow bedroom, an unmade double bed pushed up against the wall. Above the bed was a set of empty shelves, and on the small side-table lay a box of tissues, some KY jelly, and an open packet of condoms. There was a thin red curtain across the window, staining the sunlight. Scamarcio noticed a smell in the room he didn't much like.

'You're here until I say otherwise.' The Chechen pushed the Glock harder into Rigamonti's chest, and he toppled backwards onto the bed. The giant moved back out of the room, his eyes trained on them. He slammed the door shut, and they heard a key turning in the lock and then a series of loud bangs and thuds on the other side of the door as it trembled on its hinges. After a minute or so, the bangs were replaced by hammering. The Chechen was boarding them in.

'For fuck's sake!' Rigamonti exhaled and sank back against the bedhead, then seemed to think better of it and sat up quickly.

Scamarcio lifted the filthy curtain away from the glass. They were two floors up. They could jump, but they risked breaking a limb in the process.

'His accent bothers me,' said Scamarcio.

'That's all you're worried about?'

'There's no way that guy's from Chechnya.'

'Yeah, but he's got that Slavic look, that shape to the eyes, the cheekbones.'

Scamarcio shook his head. 'That means nothing.'

Rigamonti sighed and shook his head, angry now. 'It all comes back to the same thing. He's deep cover and he needs it to stay that way.'

'Deep cover for who? Our guys? Does that even make sense?'

Rigamonti had been about to reply when they heard shouts from the living room, then a loud slap followed by the sound of something hard, but at the same time soft, making contact with the wall. There was a quality to it that turned Scamarcio's stomach. 'Fuck, I think he's killed her,' he whispered.

Rigamonti paled. Scamarcio lifted the curtain once more and looked down at the kids pelting each other with water balloons. One of them was howling like a banshee, clutching his wrist, which was bent at a strange angle. Play was rough in Torpignattara.

One of the council workers was crossing the scorched grass towards a van on the pavement, his right hand wielding the toolbox. For a crazy moment, Scamarcio considered shouting down to him, asking for help, but he stopped himself. The guy's colleague was joining him at the pavement, and Scamarcio watched the two of them carefully deposit their equipment in the back before walking around to the cabin and opening the doors.

The first guy had been about to get in, but then he turned to the kids and raised his fist, slapping his bicep with the other hand — Italian for 'up yours'. The kids wasted no time in returning the gesture, and Scamarcio watched the smallest of them bite his own little hand meaning 'if I catch you, I'll kill you'. The guy from the council just shook his head in distaste and climbed into the driver's seat. As the van sped off, the children ran out into the road and hurled stones and bits of plaster, but from where Scamarcio was standing it didn't look like any of them had hit their target. At the sight of the van disappearing around the corner, he felt a sudden hollowness in his chest.

He turned to look at Rigamonti. He was hunched at the end of the bed, apparently deep in thought.

'What?' Scamarcio asked impatiently. He knew they were in trouble, but he wanted the positive spin. He didn't have the energy to keep geeing this guy up.

'We're fucked. Every which way we cut it, we're fucked.'

Scamarcio rubbed at the troublesome knot at the back of his neck and said, 'Come on, we'll sort this.'

Rigamonti was shaking his head. 'Yeah, and if we make it out of here, it won't be long before the spooks have our balls in a vice. We're probably better off letting the Chechen finish us.'

'Don't be ridiculous,' said Scamarcio, louder than he'd intended. But then he swung around as the sounds of shouting and screeching tyres rushed up from outside. He peered through the window and saw the kids hurling rocks at a couple of police Panthers that were shrieking to a stop at the kerb.

'It's the pigs, the stinking pigs,' the kids were chanting. 'Kill them! Kill the stinking pigs!'

'Shit it,' hissed Scamarcio.

Rigamonti joined him at the window. 'Jesus,' was all he offered.

They watched as the officers scrambled from the Panthers and ran up to the entrance, one of them wielding a steel battering ram. Then they heard glass smash, and Scamarcio thought briefly of the wasted council money. Why couldn't they have just tried the buzzers? The kids were now clustered on the steps in front of the door, clearly expecting to dart through the gap behind the police. It appeared that nobody was trying to stop them, because they soon disappeared, save for three of the younger ones — two boys and a girl, perhaps no older than seven — who were staring up at the apartment block open-mouthed, as if they hoped to track the police's progress through the mean slits of windows.

Suddenly, there was an explosion from somewhere out in the corridor, and Scamarcio heard, 'Hands up, you're under arrest! Drop your weapon or I'll shoot! Drop it now!'

A sharp volley of gunfire followed before someone shouted, 'There's a woman in the corner.'

There was silence for a moment, then Scamarcio heard a large weight being shifted. 'On your feet,' someone was yelling. 'On your feet, now!'

Scamarcio thought fast. This was the time to end it, to hammer on the door and declare themselves, but some unspoken force was drawing him back to the window. He pulled the curtain aside and opened the latch, releasing the window from its rotting frame.

'Hey, you,' he heard himself shout to the kids below.

The three tiny figures looked up, open-mouthed still.

'We need to jump — help us, and I'll give you fifty euros.'

The three little mouths seemed to open even wider.

'Quick! Find us something to land on.'

The kids looked about them, then the girl tugged one of the

boys by the arm, and they ran off. The seconds crawled, and Scamarcio was beginning to despair of ever seeing them again, but then they were back, dragging a filthy bundle of what looked like blankets behind them. One look told Scamarcio it wouldn't be enough.

Shouting was still coming from the living room. He thought he heard the ram against the bedroom door now, but wasn't sure. 'Rigamonti, time to go.'

The reporter looked startled, as if he hadn't heard any of the conversation at the window. 'What?'

'Come on! Now!'

Rigamonti hesitated, but then something clicked and he was behind Scamarcio, helping him scramble out. Scamarcio swung his legs through the gap, then sat perched on the ledge like a guy with suicide in mind. His heart started to race. He fixed his eyes on the useless pile of blankets, then let go, the air rushing past, the ground zooming towards him. He was light, then heavy, and then suddenly the burnt earth hit him with a thud. As he stumbled to his feet, dazed, the kids cheered, then held out their palms. But there was no time to find his wallet. 'Ask my friend,' he panted, sprinting for the bike.

But when he glanced behind him, there was no sign of Rigamonti. Scamarcio looked up at the window of the apartment and saw him staring down, motionless, a rabbit caught in headlights.

12

SCAMARCIO JUST KEPT LOOKING, willing him to jump. He knew he was wasting time, but he couldn't move. It was like watching the aftermath of a car crash and not being able to tear yourself away.

Then, there was a flash as the reporter tossed something from the window. The kids ran towards it, but Scamarcio got ahead of them and pushed them out the way — more violently than he'd intended. The keys to the bike were glinting in the grass. He grabbed them and ran. This time he didn't look back.

He reached the bike and had to stop and bend over. There was a stitch in his side that was becoming fierce. He felt like he might throw up. *What will happen to Rigamonti?* he asked himself. Where would they take him? But in the next instant, he wondered how quickly the authorities would find *him*. He tried to ignore the pain and scrambled onto the bike, his hand shaking as he fired up the ignition. The weight of the machine took him by surprise as he pulled away, and he almost lost control at the first corner.

'Fuck it,' he whispered as he flew past the battalions of police heading the other way, sirens blaring. But there was no-one there to hear him.

At first, Scamarcio thought that the best thing he could do was to head back to the centre and try to confront the boy. He needed to hear Ifran's explanation. Who was the Chechen, and what was his relationship with the Basiles? But then he reluctantly admitted to himself that Rigamonti was right — what were the chances that he would make it past the authorities?

He took a long breath as wrecked cars and broken houses flashed past. He did not want to hang around in Torpignattara, but it felt like the quickest route to the answers. Nunzia had told him where her brothers could be found, but Scamarcio asked himself exactly how he was expecting a meeting to go down. Did he really think he'd just waltz in there, and they'd tell him everything he needed to know? He tightened his grip and drove on, unsure of the direction in which he was heading. The police were thinning out, and the streets were growing full again. He continued on for a few more minutes, then stopped to ask someone the way to Via Zena. He'd get to the industrial park, and then work out how to play it — reckless perhaps, but there really wasn't time for anything more sophisticated.

It took him another five minutes to find the place. He drew to a stop opposite a series of dilapidated sheds where a heap of rusting bicycles had been abandoned. He stowed the backpack with the laptop in the top case of the BMW, and walked towards the compound. The metal gates were locked shut with a shiny padlock that looked new and unbreakable. He checked his watch. It was 4.30. God knew if Guerra's message had ever made it to Ifran.

Scamarcio skirted the long chain-link fence, but couldn't spot another way in. Beyond the fence were several low, grey buildings with sloping roofs — warehouses perhaps. A sudden chill crept through him; the whole feel of the place reminded him of a terrifying experience on a past case. He turned away and tried to focus. *What the hell am I doing here without back up?* As if to complete this tardy realisation, he felt a hard grip on his bicep and turned to see a weather-beaten oaf of a man looking as surprised as he was. 'What the fuck?'

Scamarcio stayed quite still.

'What are you doing here?' said the thug as if they were acquainted.

'Take me inside, and I'll tell you.'

The guy looked worried for a moment, then seemed to make up his mind, and pushed Scamarcio towards the fence. With his free arm, the mutt pulled out a bunch of keys and undid the shiny padlock. One of the metal gates groaned open.

'Hey, Nino,' he hollered as he pushed Scamarcio across the yard. 'You are *not* going to believe what I found sniffing around outside.'

But evidently Nino wasn't in, because no response came. The place was as silent as a morgue, save for the tap-tapping of something against a wall. Scamarcio turned and saw an old scrap of tarpaulin being battered by the breeze.

They passed a single-storey grey building and headed towards a small blue-and-white Portakabin behind it. The thug felt his pocket for the keys, then noticed a light inside the Portakabin and tried the door. It opened, and they entered a musty corridor, which smelt of old carpet and freshly brewed coffee. Scamarcio heard the murmur of the TV news. The sound became clearer as they moved towards a chink of light at the end of the hallway. 'One of the prime suspects in the Rome siege has escaped police custody. Police say he is armed and highly dangerous. The public is advised not to approach him under any circumstances.'

They're certainly upping the ante, thought Scamarcio. He was *not* armed and he was *not* dangerous — well, perhaps just slightly. But as they entered the room, Scamarcio saw the Chechen's huge face filling the screen. *He's a suspect? He's escaped?* Then he wondered if the authorities had *let* him escape. But if that was the case, why were they telling the media that they were looking for him?

Scamarcio turned and saw a well-built middle-aged man with

his legs up on the desk. His arms were folded behind his head as he watched the latest developments.

'Can you believe it?' he said to Scamarcio's jailer without looking at him. 'The Chechen went and got himself arrested, but then he managed to leg it.' There was a strong hint of sarcasm in his voice, as if he found all this highly improbable.

Scamarcio's jailer tightened his grip. 'Yeah, well, this day just gets stranger. Look what I found outside.'

The man at the desk finally tore his gaze from the screen, and even he seemed surprised this time. 'Jesus,' was all he said after he'd studied Scamarcio for a few moments.

'Sit,' barked the thug as he pushed Scamarcio into a chair opposite the desk. 'Don't move.'

He then fished around in a dented metal filing cabinet and quickly produced a pair of handcuffs, which he used to lock Scamarcio to the chair.

The man opposite leaned forward and rested his hairy forearms on the desk. Scamarcio noticed a gold Rolex and a steaming cup of coffee. It smelt good. 'You've got most of Rome's police out looking for you, *Detective*.' The sarcasm had returned.

Scamarcio sniffed and said nothing. He always found it was better to say nothing in these situations.

'So, what the fuck brings you to *my* door?'

Scamarcio stayed silent as he tried to craft a response that was direct, but would not offend. After a few moments, he said, 'That terrorist at the bar near the Colosseum has suggested that the powers that be may have been helping him. He's sent me to retrieve the evidence.'

At this the guy behind the desk threw back his head and guffawed. It was a thick deep laugh — the laugh of someone who'd grown up in the badlands and had developed the ability to spot a faker from a very early age. 'Fuck, what do you take me for?'

'It's no joke, that's what he said.'

The man stared at him, then said, 'Well, lad, he's playing you for a fool while Rome burns.'

He was too young to be calling Scamarcio 'lad'. 'Rome's not burning yet.'

The guy sighed and shook his head. 'Whatever. You're in serious trouble.' He looked at his goon. 'Would you say he's in trouble, Beppe?'

'That would be my assessment, Nino.'

Scamarcio thought that, beneath the bravado, the man called Nino looked slightly nervous.

'For a guy who's been selling arms to the intelligence services, for a guy who's going to be hauled in front of the magistrates quicker than you can say "maxi trial", you seem pretty calm,' Scamarcio tried.

'What?' Nino's eyes narrowed until they were black slits.

'Oh, I thought you'd already worked it out — you didn't seem surprised that the Chechen had managed to escape.'

'What the fuck are you talking about?' Nino pinched his nose and traded dark glances with the thug, Beppe.

Scamarcio could tell that they'd already discussed this; their street kid instincts had been warning them there was something off about the Chechen.

'You know what I'm talking about, let's not play games.'

'So, what do you want?' asked Nino, lunging forward across the desk. 'What the fuck has it got to do with you?'

'I want to know what he asked for, and when.'

'You think you can just walk in here ...'

Scamarcio had set his course and he intended to keep to it. From nowhere, he heard himself say, 'I have a friend, Dante Greco — you may have heard of him. Let's just say that if you don't give me what I need, Dante might make life difficult.'

Nino frowned and jolted his head back in surprise. 'I thought

112

you'd be threatening me with the cops.'

'They're probably all over you already — I wouldn't want to get in the way.'

'So, it's true what they say about you.'

'Nothing's ever black and white in this country. You of all people should know that, Nino.'

Nino just shook his head. Scamarcio watched his beady little eyes calculating his next move, and was reminded of Nunzia. He was sure that this was her brother, another Basile, but he didn't want to ask and let on that he'd met her — especially if she was now decomposing in the police morgue.

'Is Dante a friend from back home, then?'

Scamarcio nodded.

'You hear about what happened to Piero Piocosta?'

'Yeah,' said Scamarcio, wanting to get off that subject as quickly as possible.

Nino Basile eyed him with sullen curiosity, then said, 'So if I tell you, it won't make its way to the pigs.'

'You know as well as I that there's nothing they can do with hearsay. If I were you, I'd worry more about Greco.'

Basile pulled out a biro from a pot on his desk and began drumming the table. It was a strong, even rhythm. He let it run for a while, then stopped.

'Greco,' he repeated.

'Greco,' Scamarcio confirmed.

The drumming started up again, then stopped again. 'That Chechen — we don't know him well. He came to us a few months back wanting a truckload of shit: AKs, MP5s, grenades. He was a big spender.'

'How many?'

'About fifty of each.'

'And did you give him what he wanted?'

Basile nodded.

'And he's all paid up?'

'Oh yeah.'

'Euros?'

'Dollars.'

'How did you get the stuff?'

'What do you care?' The beady eyes widened, the pupils dilated. Scamarcio was reminded of a crocodile about to strike. 'Your Croat friends must be happy.'

Basile's expression gave nothing away.

'So you thought this guy was legit?'

Basile shrugged, but Scamarcio could tell there was something there — a doubt.

'Tell me.'

Basile scratched at his head. 'There was no problem with the money. He settled up.'

'So?'

'Well, I got the feeling he'd not done this kind of thing before.'

'Why?'

''Cos he paid before he'd even sampled the goods, before the handover. Who does that? It was like he couldn't get rid of the cash fast enough.'

Scamarcio had been about to ask them to remove the cuffs, to try to make a gentlemanly exit, re-summoning the phantom of Dante Greco, but there was a sudden commotion outside, and his gaze was pulled to the window. He heard panting, doors slamming, metal against metal, and the scuffle of heavy boots.

'Nino! Nino!' someone was half-shouting, half-wheezing. Scamarcio recognised the American accent immediately.

Basile looked alarmed, then sprang up from the desk. The Chechen was standing in the doorway, his white T-shirt transparent with sweat — it was as if he'd been running through the rain.

'Nino, help me. The pigs are after me.'

Basile just stood there, his mouth agape. The Chechen turned and in that moment saw Scamarcio handcuffed to the chair.

'You,' he said, his voice almost a whisper. Then he did something that none of them had expected. He bolted.

'Get these cuffs off,' Scamarcio yelled. The thug looked at his boss. Basile just nodded and grabbed something from his desk before darting out the door. As soon as he was free, Scamarcio followed Nino and his goon out into the yard. They were sprinting towards the entrance, and Scamarcio caught up with them at the gate. But the Chechen had been way too fast for all of them — he was already a faint blur half-way down the street. Scamarcio scrambled onto Rigamonti's bike, but the Chechen was just a dot at the end of the road now, and Scamarcio could barely make him out. He had no idea if he'd turned right, or left, or headed straight on.

'What the fuck was that?' panted Basile.

'God knows, but I'm going to find out,' said Scamarcio as he pulled away.

Basile and his mutt weren't even looking at him — their eyes were still trained on the end of the street.

Scamarcio reached the junction with the main road and stopped, scanning right, then left, then straight ahead, but there was no sign of the Chechen. He drove on, his eyes scouring the pavements, the side streets, the desiccated parks, but the giant was nowhere to be seen. When Scamarcio arrived at the next intersection, he stopped and checked the adjoining roads, but it soon became clear that the streets were empty.

It was as if he were chasing a phantom.

He continued driving back west towards the centre, expecting that it wouldn't be long before he encountered his first roadblock. Up ahead he noticed the traffic thickening and he pulled to a stop outside a boarded-up cinema. If there was a police checkpoint ahead, he wanted time to think first, to organise his thoughts, and try to clarify exactly what it was he was dealing with.

The reality was that he still had very little to go on. The only tangible evidence was the DVD, and that could be interpreted in any number of ways. He dismounted, put on his cap, and pulled out the laptop. Then he walked left down a side street. He'd find somewhere to watch the film one last time before he headed back to Ifran.

There was a small church a few metres up ahead, and he hurried inside, grateful for the cool, damp air. The church was almost empty, save for a group of young people occupying the front two rows on the right, who appeared to be waiting for someone. They were chatting quietly among themselves, and every so often glanced towards the door. Scamarcio took a seat in a pew at the very back and powered up the computer, turning the sound down low. He inserted the DVD and tried to concentrate. But, as the film played, nothing new struck him; there were no sudden nuances, no fresh clues as to the truth of the situation.

When the first film had finished, he replayed the second clip, with the incongruous footage of the two children in the garden kicking their ball back and forth, their laughter light and untroubled, their faces serene. There was nothing there. Or if there was, he just couldn't see it.

The screen eventually turned black, but he allowed the marker to complete its course along the timeline, realising that this was something he hadn't done the first time around. The next thirty seconds were empty, and he was about to shut it down when he realised that a sound was coming from the computer.

It took him a while to work it out, but he soon realised it was the voice of a young man, speaking deliberately low, the words hushed and barely decipherable. Scamarcio raised the volume, his pulse quickening.

'But we don't even know him,' the man was saying. It sounded like Ifran, but Scamarcio couldn't be sure.

'We know enough,' came the reply.

'We don't know where he comes from, we don't know what he does for a living. We don't even know if he's Muslim.'

'He fought in Dagestan with the IIPB, and then he was with the jihadists in the Caucasus Emirate — he's solid.'

'What's he doing in Rome, then? Why hasn't he left for Raqqa with the rest of them?'

'He lost his mother and sister in the second war. He wanted a new start, decided to come to Italy — to make a new life for himself.'

'Why's he hanging around with us, then?'

'He says that he feels he's not achieving anything — he wants to make a difference again.'

Scamarcio heard the first man suck in air. 'Barkat, I don't buy it. Where's he getting his cash? How does he survive?'

Barkat. The guy from the film.

'God — so many questions.'

'They're questions that need answers.'

Barkat said nothing.

'I've seen him eat pancetta. I've seen him legless ...'

'You eat pancetta. You drink Bacardi Breezers ...'

'I'm telling you, I don't trust this guy. He appears out of nowhere, wants to be our friend ...'

'That's why I checked him out, Ifran.' It *was* him.

'You what?'

'I know someone who knows someone in the Emirate — they confirmed they'd met him.'

117

'Met him when?'

'He'd been with them before he came here — he told them that he was leaving because he needed a break, wanted a change of scene. Same story he told me.'

Ifran fell silent.

'So, you see — he really is from Chechnya, he really was with the Emirate. OK, so he didn't go off to Syria with the rest of them, but remember that for a time that was frowned upon — it's a recent thing, this rush to join.'

'How did he get here?'

'Refugee.'

'OK,' said Ifran after a few moments' silence. 'But I still think we need to tread carefully. Don't give too much away — we need to keep testing him, making sure. It's too early to hand him everything on a plate.'

'Fine, if that's how you want to play it. But this guy's well connected — we need him more than he needs us.'

The marker reached the end of the timeline, and the audio died. Scamarcio quickly closed the laptop, as if there was something there he didn't want anyone to see. One question remained: how long had the Chechen been with the jihadists in the Caucasus before he came to Italy? Scamarcio wished *he* could have had the conversation with the contact from the Emirate — Barkat had not been thorough enough for his liking.

Scamarcio looked up at the ceiling and its peeling fresco of clouds and cherubs, sadistic smiles on their fat faces. He thought again about the Chechen's recent flight from the police. How could he establish the truth about this phantom? And where was he going to find it?

118

13

ACCORDING TO SCAMARCIO'S WATCH, it was now 5.30 p.m. He headed for the door of the church, wondering again whether Guerra's message had got through. If Scamarcio was to abide by Ifran's terms, he would need to find a news crew, and he would need to convince them to enter a hostage situation live. If he was even able to arrive at that point, which he doubted, the whole thing was going to take an age to set up: calls would need to be made, lawyers consulted, boards convened. The more he thought about it, the more impossible it seemed. It almost felt as if Ifran had set him up to fail.

Scamarcio hurried down the street, realising that he'd be returning without answers. He'd be trying to broadcast to the world something he didn't understand. It felt like a case of lesser evils, though — the risk of just walking away still felt too high.

He headed for the spot where he'd parked. He would use the motorbike to cover a few more kilometres to the centre, avoiding the more direct roads, which were covered by CCTV, and then he'd abandon it — he had no choice, the police would be looking for it now they had Rigamonti. But as he drew closer to where he'd left the BMW, the scene ahead told him his plan would need to change. Two uniforms were bent over the bike: one was taking photos with his phone while the other was knelt by the rear plates, apparently radioing the registration through to base. Scamarcio swung back the way he had come.

'One ... two ... three ...' he whispered, heading past the church, a bakery, a hardware store, then taking a left into a dusty street bordered by social housing, 'four ... five ... six ...' as he passed one neglected block after the other, 'seven ... eight ... nine ...' as a pet store, a pharmacy, and a barber's spun by. It was only once he'd made it to the end of the road that he allowed himself to run. He couldn't remember ever having run faster.

He was heading south now, away from Torpignattara, away from the centre again. He'd yet to spot a familiar landmark — anything that might anchor him and give him some sense of the area. The traffic was starting to thin, and he thought he must be heading towards Ciampino and the airport, but he hadn't seen a road sign so couldn't be sure.

He walked on for another kilometre, and then came to a stop outside a bar. He had a searing thirst and knew he needed to see to it, but he couldn't walk in without being recognised — all the customers had their eyes glued to the news. He rooted around in the backpack, hoping to find something of use. Besides the laptop there was nothing save a few coins amounting to the spectacular sum of five euros. He checked his wallet: he had just two notes left — a five and a ten.

He scanned the street. Opposite him was a series of shops, Chinese lettering across the windows of one. It looked like the kind of place that might sell junk for a few euros. He crossed the street, his head bent low. Once inside the shop, he quickly found a pair of sunglasses, but it took a while longer to settle on a pair that wouldn't draw attention. He fumbled in his wallet for the five euros, bowing his head as he handed over the coins, and then stepped back outside, heading for the bar. He made straight for the drinks fridge and pulled out a large frosty bottle.

He'd paid, pocketed the change, and was almost out of the

door when someone yelled, 'Turn the sound up, Marco, it's that showgirl di Bondi! What the hell has she got to do with anything?'

Scamarcio froze. He turned back slowly, measuring his movements, trying to make himself invisible.

'The showgirl Fiammetta di Bondi has been escorted by police from her home near Via Boncompagni,' said the newsreader. 'It is believed the authorities want to question her in connection with the whereabouts of her boyfriend, Detective Leone Scamarcio.'

Fiammetta looked stressed and dishevelled as two officers led her out of Scamarcio's apartment building. One shoulder of her white T-shirt had dropped down to reveal her bra strap. Her long blonde hair had fallen loose from its clip and was hanging in untidy bunches around her un-made-up face. Scamarcio wanted to run up and adjust the T-shirt, then deck the two goons manhandling her for subjecting her to such indignity.

He suddenly realised that she was shouting something, was shouting the same thing over and over. There was a touch of the madwoman about it, and his stomach started to knot. He tried to make out what she was saying, but couldn't — the words were running into each other. He drew nearer to the bar, not caring now if anyone spotted him. 'What's she saying?' a guy asked helpfully. The barman turned the sound up again.

After a few seconds, Scamarcio finally made it out. 'Oak tree,' she was repeating, like a savant in the throws of some painful delusion.

Scamarcio turned towards the door. 'Has she lost her marbles?' asked a voice behind him as he hurried out, wondering the exact same thing. Fiammetta was in some ways fragile, at times eccentric. Could it be that the pressure of all this was killing her? He felt a sharp stab of guilt; how he wished he could call her.

But as he hurried away, his shirt wet with sweat, realisation slowly dawned: Fiammetta hadn't gone crazy at all — in fact she was nothing short of a genius.

14

AWARE HE WAS STILL heading south, Scamarcio turned right at the first opportunity, aiming to reach the Tiber where it snaked its way through the lower reaches of the city. After he'd walked for ten minutes, he spotted the Parco della Caffarella, and knew it would be around three quarters of an hour before he hit Trastevere. His mind was racing. The huge oak tree on the left bank just below the hustle of Trastevere was a key location in his history with Fiammetta. It was beneath its branches that she'd told him recently that she loved him; something she'd claimed she'd never said to anyone. He'd decided to wait until another time to explain his feelings because he didn't want to sound trite, but he regretted that now.

What is waiting for me under that oak? he wondered. He felt a disturbing mix of anxiety and exhilaration.

As he crossed the Via Ostiense and made his way towards Trastevere, the anxiety grew. Would the police and Intel find a way to put pressure on Fiammetta? Get her to explain those words? But perhaps it didn't matter. Despite her apparent fragility, there was a strength to Fiammetta — a deeper solidity. She'd stay cool under fire.

A few police cars sped by. He wondered if there would be much of a presence in Trastevere. It was a touristy area — the authorities might consider it a risk. Yet he guessed that they were overwhelmed, what with the operation in Torpignattara and the siege at different locations around the centre, there wouldn't be many officers left to spare.

At the first sight of the Tiber, molten and stagnant under the sun, his heart flipped — again the same toxic blend of nerves and anticipation. He spotted some stone steps leading to the riverbank and quickly made his way down, figuring that he'd be less visible on the towpath.

He headed north, his thoughts churning; he passed a familiar bar and realised that the oak tree couldn't be more than ten minutes away now. He knew he'd be able to recognise it immediately thanks to its enormous, gnarled trunk where hundreds of Romans had scored their names. He wondered quite what he'd find in its shade; whether he'd be looking at something, or someone.

After he'd walked for about five minutes, the ancient oak came into view, its limbs dipping low as if testing the water for a swim. Beneath its branches stood a small, heavy-set man. As he drew closer, Scamarcio realised he was a stranger. Despite Scamarcio's sunglasses, however, the stranger seemed to recognise him.

'Leone,' he whispered. He held out a wide palm, and Scamarcio took it tentatively.

'I'm Pasquale. Dante sent me.'

'Dante Greco?'

'Who else?' said the man, running a quick hand through his brush cut. Scamarcio didn't much like his face — he read a capacity for cruelty in the man's small rodent eyes. Why had Fiammetta told him to come here? It didn't make any sense now.

'I guess you're wondering what's going on.'

'Yes,' said Scamarcio, quietly.

'You have a contact, a Professor Letta, whom you met on another case ...'

Scamarcio said nothing.

'Letta has been moving heaven and earth to find you. Word

got back to us that he was looking — we were asked to help track you down.'

'That's crazy.'

'It's been a crazy kind of day.'

'Where does Fiammetta fit in?'

'Dante makes it his business to stay abreast. We asked her to help.'

'And she suggested this place?'

'Yes.'

'What does Letta want?'

Pasquale pulled out a scrap of paper from his pocket and handed it over.

Scamarcio unfolded it quickly. All the note said was, 'Meet Mr Di Mare at the Basilica di Santa Maria.'

'That's it?'

'That's it.'

'There's no time on the message.'

'The man is waiting for you — he's been waiting a while, I think.'

Something wasn't adding up. 'Why is Greco helping me?' Scamarcio asked.

The man frowned and raised his palms. 'I can't speak for Dante. Maybe he just wanted to do you a favour?'

Scamarcio sniffed. He sensed that Greco didn't do favours for anyone.

He thanked Pasquale and walked on, heading north towards the basilica. After a few minutes, he had to leave the shelter of the towpath and enter the tangled web of side streets that led to the church. All the while, he was painfully aware that he was nearing the biggest police presence Rome had ever seen. What was Letta playing at, and who the hell was Mr Di Mare?

As Scamarcio emerged from the side streets and approached the basilica, he noticed a few tourists milling around the arches, posing for photos in the lengthening shadows. Scamarcio was surprised that they weren't all holed up in their hotels, sitting it out. He took the steps and entered the church, the cool musk of old stone hitting him immediately.

There were a few more tourists inside. To his right were a couple of blonde women lighting electric candles on a stand. To his left was a Japanese tour group clustered around a mosaic of the Virgin, the guide explaining something with exaggerated hand gestures.

Scamarcio scanned the central aisles: it didn't take him long to find him. Halfway down the rows of pews, quite alone, sat a man in a long black raincoat. As Scamarcio drew closer, he saw that the stranger was clutching a brown A4 envelope, and that his hands were trembling. Scamarcio passed him, and then turned. Sensing he was being observed, the man looked up. 'You made it,' he said, his voice low with surprise.

Scamarcio just nodded.

'Sit down.'

He did as instructed, taking a seat at the end of the parallel pew across the aisle. He studied the man he'd come to meet. Di Mare had close-cropped grey hair, intelligent brown-green eyes, and an angular, tanned face. The sinews on his neck looked taut, and Scamarcio guessed he still worked out. He'd have put him in his early sixties.

'Letta sent you?' Scamarcio asked.

'Not exactly.'

'I don't follow.'

'The professor and I share a contact. This contact told Letta about me, and Letta believed that, given today's events, you and I should talk.'

Scamarcio glanced at the envelope in the man's lap.

'I'm in trouble,' said Scamarcio. As comments went, it was inane, but somehow he felt the need to voice his fears, share them.

'Maybe I can help.'

'How?'

'I used to work for AISE. I retired a few months ago.'

'So, you know Colonel Scalisi?'

The man nodded, but his expression gave nothing away. 'I could have put in a few more years, but I wanted out.'

Scamarcio's interest spiked. 'Why?'

'We were running a project that I believed had gone sour. We should have called it a day and moved on. But we didn't.'

'How do you mean, "sour"?'

'We had an asset, well-placed. We'd spent a considerable amount of time and money on him. He was a serious investment.'

'And?'

'It was the old Frankenstein scenario: we'd created something important, but then it got out of hand — we lost control. The problem was that not all of my colleagues saw it that way. Or at least, they didn't *want* to. It was too painful — they'd invested too much to admit defeat.'

'You talking about Scalisi?'

'Among others.'

'So you walked away?'

'Call it a cop-out, but I preferred not to be there when the shit hit the fan.'

Scamarcio read guilt in his eyes.

'Is that what's happening today?'

'Yes.'

Scamarcio took a few moments to absorb it. So Intel *had* been behind the Chechen, just as Rigamonti had suspected. But now they no longer had a grip on him. *What made him turn?* he wondered. Or had the Chechen been playing them all from the start? Scamarcio remembered the question that had been needling him from the audio file.

'The Chechen — he'd been with the jihadists in the Caucasus? Surely that must have meant you couldn't *ever* really trust him?' Then the beginnings of a new idea struck him, and he looked up at the ceiling as he allowed it to take shape. 'Or was the Caucasus just a cover story?'

When he looked back, he was surprised to see Di Mare's brow lined with confusion. His mouth was slightly agape, and his cheeks were flushed. 'What Chechen?' he asked quietly.

'The Chechen in Torpignattara — the guy you've been running ...'

'No,' said Di Mare decisively. 'I was talking about *this* man.' He reached for the envelope and pulled out a series of surveillance shots, handing them quickly to Scamarcio. As he took them, Scamarcio felt his lungs tighten and his legs go weak. Standing next to Colonel Andrea Scalisi, smiling, was the boy from the café, the boy who had started all this: Ifran.

15

SCAMARCIO JUST KEPT STARING at the pictures, his mouth dry, his palms wet.

'I don't ...' He lost focus. 'I don't understand.'

'I'm not sure I do, either,' said Di Mare in a far away voice, as if his mind was struggling to make sense of this new turn. 'I've never known such a hornet's nest.' But then a new thought seemed to bother him, and he said softly, 'Of course, there was a Chechen ... some years back ... but he was being run from elsewhere. He was ...'

Just at that moment, without warning, Di Mare slumped forward and hit his head hard on the back of the pew in front. Scamarcio wondered if he'd suffered a stroke or a heart attack, but before he could lift him to check, he noticed a shiny trickle of red oozing from a hole at the back of his skull. Through the small hole he could see bone, and the grey slick of brain tissue.

Scamarcio sprang to his feet and scanned the back of the basilica, but he couldn't spot anyone hurrying out. The tourists were still going about their business, oblivious; the guides were still running through their spiel. He looked up at the balcony, but it was empty. The sniper, wherever they'd been, had vanished.

Di Mare was groaning softly. It sounded as if he was trying to say something. Scamarcio quickly bent down and brought his ear to the man's mouth.

'Ask Letta, he's ...' Then his voice drifted away as if it had been taken on the breeze.

'Fuck,' Scamarcio whispered. He tried to steady himself, find some calm. He knew he had to leave — before someone noticed. Keeping his head down, he made towards the altar, hoping to find a side exit. He didn't want to use the front steps with a gunman nearby. He hurried towards a chapel next to the altar, hoping that it might lead to the priests' changing area. He found a door partially ajar, and, as expected, it led to a small room.

Once inside, Scamarcio scanned the walls for a way out, but it was a sealed box — no windows, no doors. Then he noticed some narrow steps leading beneath the basilica. He took them, wondering whether it was a mistake, but still not wanting to return through the centre of the church.

He came down into a dank stone cellar, which he thought must border the crypt. He seemed to remember hearing that the head of one of the saints was buried down here, along with some remnants of the holy sponge. He cast around for an exit, not really expecting to find one. His gaze came to rest on a small door. He tried it several times, but it remained shut tight. He kept pushing, then pulling, but still it wouldn't budge. He'd just have to take his chances up in the church.

He sprinted back up the steps, through the antechamber, and out into the main body of the basilica. He slowed to a brisk walk as he made his way through the centre of the pews. There was a cluster of people around the dead man now. Scamarcio swung left and fixed his eyes on the main entrance, beseeching the Virgin Mary painted on the ceiling above to keep the police and whoever shot Di Mare at bay. He came out into the evening light, running past the fountain where a group of young people were laughing and chatting. There was no sign of any police or anyone else following him.

He finally panted to a stop, putting his head between his knees, and thought about what Di Mare had said. At no point had Scamarcio ever considered that Ifran might be involved with AISE.

All at once, he heard feet pounding, and turned to see two men in jeans and T-shirts running towards him. One was fumbling in his pocket, and Scamarcio knew he was reaching for a gun. Scamarcio took off down a small alleyway to his left that was thankfully full of tourists. People in the crowd turned and swore as he pushed his way through. He darted left into another street, where he spotted a courtyard just beyond the corner. He hurried towards the shadows of a series of ivy-covered archways, and came to a stop behind a group of tourists who were taking photos of a bust. He studied the alleyway. After less than a second, the two men tore past. Like cornered prey, Scamarcio waited for their return, his heart racing. But after several minutes had passed and they still hadn't reappeared, he stepped back into the light and tried to steady the rush of blood in his ears.

He had to find Professor Letta and tell him what had happened. But just getting to Letta was a problem. The university was near Termini, very much the city centre, so there were bound to be blocks and cordons in place all along the way. But Letta was the link to people with information, people who might be able to explain what the hell was going on. Scamarcio knew he had no option but to try to reach him.

16

'Do SIT DOWN, IFRAN, you're making me nervous. Take the weight off, have a drink.'

I didn't want to sit; I didn't want to drink. I just wanted to run away from the strange little hunchback: return to my cell, get some sleep. I already felt tainted, compromised, even though we'd yet to have a proper conversation. It no longer seemed like a fresh start. There was something about this man that made you feel dirty.

'How are you feeling about the trial?' he asked.

I remember that I was silent. I didn't want to talk. I didn't want to say a word without a lawyer present.

As Scamarcio had expected, the first roadblock appeared as he approached Via dei Serpenti. Via dei Serpenti led to the Colosseum. The police, it seemed, were trying to seal the street off, worried that the terrorists might also target the country's most famous tourist site. Scamarcio knew he was in the red zone now — Via Nazionale lay straight ahead, and Via del Quirinale to his left. The latter was home to the President's palace, so it was bound to be teeming with security. He'd been foolish to even try to make it this far. He turned back, knowing that he'd have to go the long way around, taking the roads running parallel with Corso d'Italia.

It took him more than forty minutes to reach the university, and only when he arrived did it occur to him that, given the hour and the day's events, it might be closed. There were very few people outside, and he began to think that his fears would be confirmed. But as he neared the front doors, he started to make out activity beyond the glass. He entered the wide lobby and approached one of the women at reception.

When he asked for Letta, she placed a brief call to his secretary. Letta was giving an evening lecture to some visiting students in the political sciences block — he was due to finish in ten minutes, so Scamarcio should hurry.

He realised that he hadn't been among such a concentration of people since Ostia. His nerves were jangling as he crossed the lawns where, in the mellowing light, students were sprawled reading books, or deep in conversation. He was still wearing his hat and sunglasses, and he kept his head low, only glancing up to check his progress.

He found the door to the lecture theatre easily enough. He entered, moving quickly along the side of the hall, worrying that people might turn and spot him hovering in the doorway. Letta was at the front, standing before a huge blackboard. Behind his head were the words, 'New Labour — necessary evolution or outright betrayal?'

The problem with trying to stay hidden, Scamarcio realised, was that Letta wouldn't spot him, either. He would have to sit it out until the end, and then grab the professor as he left.

He scanned the hall — it was packed, and most of the summer students seemed to be giving Letta their full attention.

'So why has the Left in this country never been able to evolve into something like New Labour? Why are our unions still strong? Our conclusion is simple — Blair was fortunate because Thatcher had already done his dirty work. She'd relieved him of the thorny problem of the unions.' Letta clapped his huge hands together. 'He was a lucky chap, this Tony Blair. But maybe a little less lucky now ...' Some students laughed.

Scamarcio tuned them out and tried to focus. Di Mare had suggested that AISE had been involved with Ifran, but had then somehow lost control of him. Where did the Chechen fit in? Had he played a part? The questions seemed to be mounting, and Scamarcio wondered whether he'd return to Ifran more confused than when he'd left — if he ever managed to find his way back.

Letta was winding up now, explaining that, given today's events, he was going to finish early so that they could all begin their journeys home. A few people started gathering their things, getting ready to leave. Scamarcio made his way slowly to the front, and as the students began to file past, he approached the desk. There was a pretty girl to Scamarcio's left, also waiting to talk to the professor. Scamarcio hoped Letta would spot him first.

'Shit,' Letta murmured as Scamarcio raised his sunglasses and finally caught his eye.

The girl tried to ask Letta something, but he batted the question away, muttering, 'I've got to run. Can you email me?' He grabbed his briefcase and took Scamarcio by the elbow, whisking him out into the corridor. 'What the hell do you think you're playing at?' he whispered.

'By coming here?'

'By getting involved in all this!'

'I'm doing what I have to.'

Letta fell silent as they crossed the lawns and headed for his staircase. Once they were inside his study, he locked the door, then lowered and closed the metal blinds on the window. Scamarcio removed his hat and sunglasses. It was now so dark that Letta had to switch on a desk lamp. He scrambled around among the detritus of open books, torn envelopes, and raggedy binders until he found a fat pouch of tobacco and some papers. He sat down and quickly began rolling one of his strange-looking cigarettes. Last time they'd met, Scamarcio had formed the impression they contained a little more than just tobacco.

As if to confirm it, Letta said, 'I'll keep it clean. I'd better have my wits about me.' He took a few quick drags, then fixed Scamarcio with a stare. 'What do they want, these terrorists? Have they got you over some kind of barrel?'

Scamarcio filled him in on Ifran's demands, the DVD, and the Chechen. When he was finished, Letta whistled softly. 'Dangerous.'

'It doesn't stop there.' Scamarcio told him about the conversation at the basilica and how it had been cut short. Letta closed his eyes and ran a slow hand across his lids. 'This is one hot mess,' was all he offered.

'As he was dying, Di Mare told me to come back to you.'

'That would make sense,' sighed Letta. 'He probably wanted me to put you in touch with Federico — the guy who told me to get you and Di Mare together. Di Mare was no doubt thinking that Federico might have something on your Chechen.' Letta paused for a moment. 'Shit. I can't believe they killed him.'

He reached for his desk phone and dialled, but the line seemed to be ringing out, because after ten seconds he replaced the receiver, his brow taut.

'If they shot Di Mare, isn't it likely that they're now onto your friend Federico?' Scamarcio asked, unease stirring.

'It's possible, but perhaps not likely. Federico keeps himself to himself — he lives in an isolated spot, some distance from Rome. It might just be that AISE were following Di Mare anyway — if he left under a cloud, they were no doubt keeping tabs.'

'You think AISE shot him?'

'Who else would it be?'

Scamarcio shrugged, realising he had no idea.

'These fucking Chechens — Intel bend over backwards to bed them, but then it's always tears in the morning.'

'What?'

'Federico and I have talked about it,' said Letta, dismissing the subject with a wave of the hand as if it were nothing. 'So that boy in the café was working for AISE, but he slipped the net? If that comes out, there'll be hell to pay.'

'But they won't let it come out.'

'They might not be able to stop it, Scamarcio.'

'But how many people know? Besides me — and now you?'

'You're thinking they won't let you talk?'

'I'm thinking they won't let me *live*.'

'Don't be silly, they can't kill you — it would look *off*. It's all out there now, you're on TV every two seconds — there's no way they could explain away your corpse.'

'They'll say I died in crossfire, a road accident, hung myself — couldn't cope with the guilt of letting all those people down. They'll think of something.'

Letta was shaking his head, but Scamarcio could tell that he wasn't one hundred per cent convinced now. 'Nah, don't worry. You just need to play it right. You want my advice? Go back there. Face the music. Sure, have a chat with Federico so you understand what you're dealing with, but after that, call it a day. I don't think you can win this one.'

Scamarcio frowned. 'I wouldn't have expected you to tell me to give up. Last time we met, you struck me as a bit of a crusader.'

Letta lifted his roll-up from the ashtray and took a long drag, blinking at Scamarcio through the fog. 'Yeah, but even I can see that you're badly outnumbered. You've got a life, a beautiful woman — or so I hear. Is it worth sacrificing all that to help a troubled boy settle some kind of score?'

'I'm not doing it to help him settle a score; I'm doing it to stop a bloodbath.'

'Do you really buy that? These terrorists don't normally negotiate. Could it be that he's taking you for a ride — that the killing will happen anyway?'

'From what Di Mare told me, Ifran's not your typical terrorist. I have to at least try to listen to him, don't you think?'

Letta sighed. 'All I know is that AISE and their colleagues, both inside and outside Italy, have been playing a dangerous game. They're not going to let some policeman go and ruin it all for them.'

'What game?'

'You must know what I'm talking about.'

Scamarcio just looked at him blankly.

'For God's sake,' hissed Letta under his breath, as if a once-promising student had disappointed him yet again. 'It's shameful. You're a detective — you should try to learn more about the world in which you live.'

'What's that supposed to mean?'

'Which paper do you take?'

'*Gazzetta dello Sport*, mainly.'

'My point exactly — you need to widen your reading.'

Scamarcio shook his head, narked, while Letta took a last desperate suck on the cigarette, smoking it down to the tip, but making no move to throw it away. 'So these jihadists up in the North Caucasus, where you said your Chechen is from — they were getting a fair bit of help — but not from the usual quarters.'

'Where, then?'

'From our own backyard. NATO and the West were propping them up for a while, using them in the fight against Russia for control of pipeline corridors transporting oil and gas out of the Caspian. Not too long ago, some intercepts surfaced which revealed that US officials in Azerbaijan had been backing Chechen rebels during the early 2000s. NATO badly wanted Russia destabilised — they knew if Chechnya could be split off from Russia, western control of the corridor would be enhanced. Of course, this bright idea of befriending the jihadists was nothing new — it was simply an extension of the op launched by Jimmy Carter in Afghanistan in '79 — the same op which propelled the rise of Bin Laden.'

Letta finally gave up on the cigarette and stubbed out what little was left. 'It goes without saying that all this is in total contradiction to the so-called War on Terror. But NATO has been at it for years — and in quite a few places, too: Chechnya, Libya, and Syria to name but a few. They even backed a nasty little Marxist Islamist outfit in Iran called the People's Mujahideen, some of whom they covertly trained in the Nevada desert.' He stopped for a moment and sifted through the chaos on his desk until he located the tobacco pouch again. 'A US journalist dug up the whole sordid tale and got a Pulitzer for his trouble. The yanks were prepping the very people they'd officially designated a terror group. The Obama administration even went so far as to strike the People's Mujahideen from the terror list, much to the fury of Iran.'

Letta rolled up again, smoothing and squeezing until he was satisfied. Scamarcio heard a distant clock somewhere and felt newly on edge. He was desperate for a cigarette, and even though he disliked the smell of Letta's roll-ups, he knew they'd be better than nothing.

'Can I have one?'

Letta looked up, surprised, then handed the cigarette across and lit up for him. The professor reached for the pouch once more and quickly set to work.

'The neat thing is that people are described as terrorists when attacking NATO states and rebels, or freedom fighters when blitzing NATO enemies, for which they are deployed on a much larger scale. In the eyes of a lot of western strategists, it's this imbalance that makes the net effect geopolitically worthwhile, despite occasional blowback. The consensus was always that some stirred-up Muslims were a price worth paying for conducting covert ops against the Ruskies. Unsurprisingly, after 9/11 a few people changed their minds on this.'

Letta took a quick drag on his new cigarette and waved a finger. 'The ultimate targets in these covert wars are always the same: Russia, the world's largest oil and gas producer; and China, the world's largest energy consumer. Neither of these colossi are communist in real terms anymore, which means they're now NATO's main competitors.'

'So, what does all this tell me about the Chechen?' Scamarcio coughed; Letta's tobacco was an acquired taste.

'It tells you two things: one, he may *well* have fought in the Caucasus; but, two, he may have made good friends with the West while doing so.'

'So he could be working for them?'

'Yes.'

'So why is the boy Ifran so worried about him?'

'That, my friend, is why you need to talk to Federico,' said Letta, reaching for the phone again.

17

It is dark beyond the tiny window. Marchetti is snoring in his bunk, farting as he turns. Along the corridor, the squeak of soles on plastic scores out the hours.

I already know I'll see the dawn; the hunchback's words won't let me sleep.

'I was tending my vegetable patch,' said Federico when Letta switched him to speakerphone. 'This year I've planted pumpkins, runner beans, tomatoes, aubergines, cabbages, and courgettes. But I've done too many courgettes. And then I remembered I'm going away and I might not have time to harvest them. They risk growing too large and becoming tasteless.'

Letta rolled his eyes. 'Federico, I have Detective Scamarcio with me.'

There was a brief silence. 'Oh, do you?' Federico had a strange voice. It was low and gentle, but there was no fragility to it. There was something beneath it as hard as steel. 'What's he saying, this detective?'

'You're on speakerphone — ask him yourself.'

'Ah.'

Scamarcio waited for a question, but Federico remained silent.

'He needs answers about a Chechen. I think you two should meet,' tried Letta.

'Can he travel?' asked Federico, after a moment.

'What do *you* think?'

'Hmmm.' Scamarcio heard a hollow tapping — he imagined a pen against a glass.

'Could you come to Rome?' Letta persisted.

'If they see me on the move, they might wonder.'

'You still trying to keep a low profile?'

'Kind of ...'

'So when you said you were going away — that you were worried about your courgettes ...?'

'I'm going to see my sister.'

'Where does she live?'

'... Parioli, as it happens.' Federico sounded put out at having to give up this information.

'Perfect. Couldn't you just leave a bit early?'

'A month early?'

'They killed Di Mare.'

'What?'

'When Scamarcio was in the church talking to him a few hours ago.'

'Christ.'

'Get your shit together and drive to Rome.'

Federico said nothing.

Scamarcio had been about to speak when Federico finally replied: 'OK.'

'Where in Parioli?' asked Letta.

'Via Novelli, number twenty, third floor,' Federico said slowly. 'Ask for Celeste. It will take me nearly an hour.'

'Scamarcio will be there,' said Letta. 'Just look at it this way — at least you'll be home in time to tend your courgettes — you'll have got your sister out the way.'

But the line had gone dead.

Scamarcio put on his sunglasses, pulled his cap down low, and headed towards the address in Parioli, yet again avoiding the main streets and the eyes of CCTV. The roundabout route he'd chosen took him over an hour on foot, and when he arrived he was hot, sweating, and in need of a drink. The apartment was in a nondescript, light-brown block that went up about six floors. He tried the buzzer, and a shaky female voice told him to come up.

An elderly woman with a stoop was waiting in the doorway. Once he was inside, she led him into the lounge and asked him politely if he'd care for coffee.

'We should get him something to eat, as well,' said a man's voice from somewhere within the room. Scamarcio ventured further in and looked around. He found a very thin fellow sat on a sofa facing away from the door. The man was so small that the top of his head hadn't been visible above the cushions. 'Nice to meet you,' he said, rising carefully to his feet. 'I made good time. I've just bought myself an Alfa Romeo Spider — second-hand, but it goes like the wind.'

Scamarcio shook his bony hand. Federico didn't look much shy of seventy.

'Take a seat,' he said, motioning to a flowery armchair. 'We're going to give you some food, and then we're off to the embassy.'

'What?' blinked Scamarcio.

'The British Embassy.'

Scamarcio remained stock-still. 'There is no way I'm going anywhere near the British Embassy.'

'You're jumpy.'

'Half the country's police are out looking for me.'

'You're a policeman; you must know how to evade capture.'

'Yes, by staying as far away as possible from places like the British Embassy.' Scamarcio took a breath. 'Why there?'

'There's someone there who knows about your Chechen.'

'Can't you just pass the information on? Speak to them for me?'

The old woman returned with a large plate of antipasti and a basket of bread. Scamarcio thanked her.

'Eat up,' said Federico. He gave Scamarcio a few moments, then said, 'They tried to turn him, but failed.'

'Who?'

'Your Chechen. If it's the guy I think it is. Describe him.'

'Blond, built like a brick shithouse, weird pale-blue eyes ...'

'Yeah,' said Federico, cutting him off. 'A lot of people wanted him. He was quite the prize catch.'

'But he wasn't working for you guys?'

'My guys? I must stress that I'm no longer with them. But no, he wasn't. Like everyone else, we were after him, but we couldn't get him.'

'So did anyone manage?'

'Not as far as I'm aware.' Federico sniffed and folded his hands in his lap. 'Let's go to Calcata, then,' he said.

Scamarcio looked up from his food. 'Calcata?'

'Did Mr Di Mare show you a picture?'

'Yes.'

'Do you still have it?'

'Sure.'

'The guy who took that picture lives in Calcata — he's your last port of call, given that you won't go to the embassy.' Federico made it sound as if Scamarcio was being difficult.

Calcata was an artists' community some 50 kilometres from the city. Scamarcio couldn't think what that place could possibly have to do with the events unfolding in Rome. Besides, he felt nervous about leaving the city again, about exposing himself to security cameras, motorway police, God knew what.

'You need to speak to him,' said Federico, softly. 'I wasn't properly in the know when it came to Scalisi — I just heard rumours.'

142

'What rumours?'

'You can't work with rumour — you need fact. I need to make a call. Eat up, and then let's go.'

For someone so elderly, Federico displayed remarkable energy, revving the car to the max at every opportunity and waving to pretty girls as they passed. Scamarcio wished he wouldn't draw quite so much attention. He checked his watch and saw that it was past nine. It was as if time was spinning away, eluding him.

When they were heading north out of the city and doing way more than 160, Federico said, 'It's strange he asked for you, that boy.'

Scamarcio told him about his contact with Guerra in Opera. When he was finished, Federico murmured, 'Hmm, I always felt that Guerra was being economical with the truth.'

'In court, you mean?'

Federico nodded. 'He always gave the impression that he had pieced together what the state was up to bit by bit, that it was only towards the end that he had some kind of revelation that they'd been helping him. But if you ask me, he and his band of fascist fuckwits decided early on to throw in their lot with the spooks — they knew exactly what was in play. Guerra was an opportunist, just like the rest of them.'

Maybe, thought Scamarcio. But that revelation didn't get him any further with his current problem.

'So, this guy in Calcata?'

'He worked with Scalisi. They fell out. He wanted leverage, so he took the pictures.' Federico made it all sound so rational.

'Why did he think the pictures would give him leverage?'

'Everyone's looking for leverage. Something might not be of value at the time you find it, but it could become valuable later. That's how we're trained to think in my game.'

'And this Chechen?'

'You didn't want to go to the embassy.'

'Going to the embassy would have been tantamount to capitulation.'

'The British are a law unto themselves. They wouldn't give you up.'

'Maybe not, but from where I'm sitting it's far too risky.'

'So, my friend in Calcata is your last hope. Probably.'

'Probably?'

'You're not very patient, Detective.'

'I don't have time to be.'

'You probably have more time than you think.'

'Probably? You use that word a lot.'

'Who can deal in certainties these days?'

Scamarcio said nothing, then asked, 'You still active?'

'I do a bit of consultancy from time to time, but I prefer to keep it light: too many other commitments.'

'Consultancy for whom?'

'Anyone who comes knocking and has money to spend. I do draw the line at certain r—' He paused and seemed to search for a better word, '*interests*.'

Scamarcio looked out at the ragged crests of the Maremma hills rising above the dark woodland of the Treja Valley. Soon, the fortified walls of old medieval villages began to appear, spires and windows capturing the last of the setting sun. Federico took a right turn, and they joined a steep unmade road that wound high up into the hills. After they'd climbed for a few minutes, Scamarcio spotted a thick curtain of houses. They seemed to be built in higgledy-piggledy layers, each one jumbled precariously on top of the other like a complicated sandcastle ready to topple at any moment. Federico pushed the car upwards until they found themselves at the foot of an immense stone wall. He parked at the beginning of a steep incline, saying, 'The road's too narrow. We'll have to do the rest on foot.'

They made their way up a cobblestone street and past a narrow, locked gate. After they'd climbed for a few minutes, the street began to level out, and they emerged into a wide central square, thick with shadows.

Federico pointed to an old stone church: 'Once the home of Jesus's foreskin.'

Scamarcio frowned.

'Jesus was a Jew, so of course he was circumcised. The famous foreskin was originally kept in Rome, but then a German soldier stole it during the Charles V occupation of 1527. The enterprising soldier brought it to Calcata, where he hid it until his death. Calcata is a good hiding place.'

'Is that what your friend is doing here — hiding out?'

Federico ignored the question. 'He lives up there,' he said, gesturing to the left of the square, beyond the church.

They skirted the edge of the piazza and walked down a meandering street, pressed in on by a hodgepodge of medieval houses in various stages of restoration and decay. Scamarcio took in tearooms, restaurants, antique dealers, and artisan workshops, all thrown together in seeming disarray.

Federico finally came to a stop outside a jewellery shop. The wooden half-door was ajar, and he quickly stepped inside. Scamarcio followed.

Working beneath a circular desk lamp was a man with thick, shoulder-length grey hair and a dense beard. Narrow rimless glasses were perched on the end of his aquiline nose.

'I thought you'd show,' he said, not looking up.

'The detective needs a word.' Federico picked up a necklace of different-coloured glass and fanned it across his palm.

The man at the desk sniffed and pushed the lamp away. He looked at Scamarcio and removed his glasses, rubbing beneath an eye. 'Welcome to Calcata,' he said quietly.

Scamarcio nodded, not quite sure what to say.

'Let's walk,' said the stranger. He shouted to someone out the back, and a young woman emerged through a doorway. Her long, red hair was braided, and she wore a pale-blue tie-dye top and a long, flowing pink skirt. She somehow looked familiar, but Scamarcio couldn't think why.

'I'll be back in an hour,' said the stranger, leading them out.

They walked back to the square, then turned down an alleyway to the right of the church, which led to some steep stone steps. The steps brought them up above the rooftops, and after a few moments, they came out onto a terrace that offered a spectacular sunset view of the Treja Valley and the glinting thread of silver that scored through it.

The jeweller took a seat on a low stone wall that bordered the terrace and motioned Scamarcio to do the same. Federico had already parked himself on a rickety wooden bench and was sitting expectantly, his chin in his hands.

'This is quite a shitstorm,' said the jeweller, narrowing his eyes at Scamarcio.

'Not really of my making,' said Scamarcio.

'I wasn't saying it was.'

'You took those photos — of Scalisi and the boy?'

The stranger nodded.

'Why?'

'Scalisi's lost it.'

'In the sense that he's not behaving normally?'

'In every sense. He's lost control of his man, he's lost control of the situation, and he's possibly lost his mind.'

Scamarcio noticed the man's intense blue eyes; there was a coldness to them, an impenetrability. 'The boy in the picture was working for Scalisi?'

The jeweller glanced at Federico before turning back to Scamarcio. 'How do we know we can trust you?'

'It all depends which side you're on, I guess. I'm clearly not working with the authorities at the moment ...'

This seemed to settle something. The stranger nodded, then said, 'It's very difficult to get someone inside those communities, so when you finally manage it, you go to town and throw everything you have at it.'

Scamarcio wondered why he hadn't answered the question. 'When was Ifran recruited?'

'When he got out of jail, although I believe we started working on him when he was still inside Opera.'

'What was he promised?'

The man frowned. 'Not as much as you might think. A decent salary for sure, but it was more of a PSYOP — the chance to make a difference. The chance to mean something. That can work wonders on guys who have always felt marginalised.'

'What was Ifran's job? What did Scalisi want from him?'

The stranger sighed. 'Forgive me, but we've only just met.'

'I've got the police on my back and a terrorist threatening to blow the city to shreds ...'

The man scratched the back of his head and looked away. Federico coughed.

Eventually, the stranger said, 'We needed Ifran to keep his eyes and ears open, let us know if plans were afoot and who was making them.' Scamarcio noted the 'we' again. He wanted to ask more about this man's past, but the guy was clearly jumpy. Instead he said, 'How was Ifran meant to do that?'

'By making sure he hung around with the right people — the likely contenders.'

'It's all so different from what he told me this morning.'

'What's his version?' the stranger asked quickly.

'He says he was approached by two extremists, and that they tried to persuade him that he needed to do more than a few protest marches.'

'He's probably just inverting roles.'

'So, he was the one persuading *them* to act? Isn't that entrapment?'

The jeweller waved the idea away. 'I doubt it went down exactly like that; they were probably ready to roll before Ifran showed.'

'So you don't have the facts?'

'Of course not.'

'Why "of course not"?'

'It's need-to-know.'

'So, what went wrong?' asked Scamarcio.

Federico coughed again, and they both turned. The old man was leaning forward on the bench, his bird-legs crossed, as if he was enjoying a semi-interesting piece of street theatre. He circled his hand, motioning them to continue.

'Ifran stopped answering his phone, stopped turning up for meets — our boy became a ghost.'

'So what did Scalisi do?'

'He went wild — used anything and anyone he could to track him.'

'Did he find him?'

'He found him today, when Ifran pitched up at the café.'

'Shit.'

'Quite.'

'So who's Ifran really working for?'

'Nobody knows.'

'And where do I fit in?'

'The way I see it, Ifran's using you to blackmail Scalisi.'

'How do you work that out?'

'Federico told me about the DVD. It seems to me that Ifran wanted you to find that disc, wanted to alert you to the Chechen. The question is, Why?'

'Why do *you* think?' asked Scamarcio, but his mind was already turning on a new question: he didn't think he'd mentioned the

DVD to Federico. Was it possible that Letta had told him?

'I don't know much about the Chechen, but I suspect Scalisi does,' said the stranger. 'It's probably quite simple — Ifran wanted to make it clear to Scalisi that he knows about the existence of the Chechen. He wanted to use him as leverage.'

'Leverage for what?'

'Leverage to get himself out of whatever mess he's in.'

'Ifran told me about an American accent on the phone — he took a strange call that was meant for his friend that specified today's date ...'

The jeweller cut him off. '*That* I would write off as a tempting piece of bait to hook you and draw you into the game. Regardless of whether he answered the phone, I doubt it even went down like that.'

Scamarcio got up and walked over to the wall of a crumbling house. He kicked at a few stones and closed his eyes. The fading light was a palish pink beneath his lids. 'I don't know where to take this thing.'

'You need to get back to Ifran. Give him the DVD, and he'll work out the rest. You've done your bit.'

'But was I right to even listen to him?'

'For a while it seemed that Ifran was on the side of good — at least, he did an excellent job of convincing us that's where he stood. He may in fact still be there.'

'How can he be on the side of good if he's holed up in a café threatening to blow the heads off fifteen hostages and then some?'

'It's more complicated than that.'

'Meaning?'

The jeweller just shook his head. He'd said enough.

'And Scalisi?' Scamarcio tried.

'Scalisi is anyone's guess — he could have sold himself to the highest bidder.'

'What does that mean?'

'Exactly what it sounds like. You can't trust him.'

'Then who *can* I trust? Who is going to protect me from Scalisi?'

'There are people: people who've been watching him; people who still wield some power. You're not as alone as you might think.'

Scamarcio frowned and looked down at the darkening valley, at the matchbox cars winding their way along the wisps of road, at the shadowy patchwork of olive groves and farmland. 'Who are you?' he asked.

'Federico and I go back a bit,' said the man, nodding to his friend. 'I waited a little longer to get out, needed a little more convincing.'

Federico rose from the bench and came to stand by Scamarcio. 'Do you still have the photo Di Mare brought you in the church?'

'Yes.'

'Take that to Ifran — it could prove useful. Scalisi won't want it out there. It would destroy him.'

'Why are you trying to help the boy?' Scamarcio asked. 'Like you said, we don't know whose side he's on.'

'For the same reason as you,' said Federico. 'Because your gut's telling you to listen.'

The stranger rose from the wall. 'I need to get back to the shop — keep your cool, and this may all come good. You have the power to turn this around.'

With that, he was gone, and even though the old man was standing beside him, Scamarcio thought he had never felt more alone.

Federico dropped him on the corner of Via Cavour and Via degli Annibaldi, just before the roadblocks started. 'Good luck,' he said, before he sped away. 'Listen to my friend's advice. He knows what he's talking about.'

'Who is he?' Scamarcio tried one more time.

'Better you don't know.' With that, he threw him a cheery wave and hared off into the traffic.

Scamarcio looked around. The pavements were empty, and the sound of the television news was still whispering from the bars and cafés, as if the city itself was heaving one long haunting sigh. He spotted a lone pedestrian at a zebra crossing; he was stepping into the oncoming traffic, his eyes glued to his tablet. It almost ended in disaster.

Scamarcio was about to turn into Via degli Annibaldi and begin making his way towards the Colosseum, burdened with questions and no solutions, when a voice behind him cried, 'Hey, you!'

Clearly the baseball cap and sunglasses hadn't been enough. He glanced around, ready to bolt. Nino Basile was standing there, flanked by two of his goons. 'You're coming with us,' he said, in the same way he might say 'You're going to take a nice swim to the bottom of the ocean.'

'Why the fuck would I want to do that?'

'The Chechen wants to see you.'

'The Chechen?'

'You heard. Come on,' said Basile, striding towards him, the heavies close behind.

Scamarcio tried to make a run for it, but he'd only managed to sprint a few metres before they grabbed him, and then bundled him into a waiting Punto. 'How did you know how to find me?' he panted.

'We've been tailing you and your geriatric buddy. For an old timer, he's fast.'

'Tailing me since when?'

'Since the Chechen legged it — seemed wise.'

'I've been all over the place since then.'

'I have eyes and ears in this city,' said Basile, his tone neutral.

'Besides, I slipped a tracker in your back pocket as you were getting on your bike. It pays to take precautions.'

Scamarcio marvelled at the skill of it. Basile and his mutts were way ahead of AISE.

'Why did the Chechen bolt if now he wants to see me?'

'Fuck knows. We're just the messenger boys,' muttered Basile.

Scamarcio said nothing and surveyed the deserted streets flitting by. His watch told him it was nearing midnight. He still needed to try to make the deadline in case Guerra's message had not got through to Ifran. But how he was going to get to the suburbs and back, escape from the Chechen, and find and convince a news crew to enter a hostage situation by 9.00 a.m. tomorrow he had no idea. He sighed, then glanced over at Basile and his thugs. When he was satisfied their attention was elsewhere, he felt inside his pocket, wound down the window and tossed the tracker into the night.

They reached the pale-grey outskirts of Torpignattara, and Scamarcio immediately noticed the sea of flashing reds and blues. The police presence seemed to have intensified. There were Panthers in all directions now.

'Baby Jesus,' whispered Basile. 'It's a swarm.' His mobile rang, and Scamarcio heard him say, 'Nunzia? What's that tart gone and done?' But then he fell silent for a while, and then said, 'God, it's just one thing after the other with that woman.'

Basile cut the call. They arrived at the warehouse and drove in through the metal gates. Scamarcio noticed that there was a light coming from Basile's office — perhaps the Chechen was inside. The thought of it, and the memory of what he might have done to Basile's sister, made Scamarcio sweat. Yet at the same time, his curiosity was needling him, urging him to find out more.

One of Basile's mutts opened the car door, and as he stepped out, Scamarcio noticed the chemical stink of diesel on the breeze. He looked around the yard, taking in the prefab buildings and rotting vehicles, but couldn't find any immediate explanation for the smell.

He followed Basile and his men into the cabin. There was a new aroma of damp wood and expensive cologne, and as they rounded the door, Scamarcio spotted one huge denim-clad leg dangling from Basile's desk. It soon became apparent that the leg belonged to the Chechen — the giant was resting his massive bulk against the wall as if he owned the place. His eyes were screwed tight, almost shut, as he sucked on a cigarette. With his other hand, he was fingering his fly.

'Detective,' he drawled, his tone giving nothing away.

'I'm confused,' said Scamarcio. 'The first time we meet, you lock me in a room and threaten to kill me, the second time you take one look at me and scarper, and now this time you've sent your monkeys all the way into town to find me. You're either as confused as I am, or something else is going on.'

'It's both,' said the Chechen. Scamarcio thought he detected a hint of New Yorker in his American accent.

'Explain.'

'Take a seat, Detective — this might take a while.'

Scamarcio reached for a shabby swivel chair, and reluctantly sat down. He'd expected Basile and his goons to leave, but they remained stock-still, their stubby arms barring their chests. Basile looked furious. Scamarcio wondered if it was connected to the call he'd just taken about his sister.

'I think you might have this all arse-about-face,' said the Chechen. 'Ifran has muddied the waters — deliberately perhaps.'

'Give me the real story, then. Who is Ifran? And, more to the point, who are you?

'Ifran is exactly who he says he is.'

'No. He isn't. Enough people have told me that.'

'They've probably told you that he's been working for the

153

West — which, in itself, is true. But his identity remains valid — Ifran's family came from Libya fifteen years ago, and he has been living in Torpignattara ever since — doing well at school, acing his exams, but like so many, failing to make great strides. That is the tragedy of children such as Ifran — they will never make great strides. It's this tinderbox of shame and disappointment that lights the fuse.'

'It's actually the tragedy of a whole generation of Italian children now — unless their parents are well connected.'

The Chechen shrugged. 'Ifran was a find — AISE knew they'd struck gold.'

'Why are you telling me this?'

'You're stuck and you need information.'

'That's charitable of you.'

'I think you've been backed into a corner. In a certain sense, so have I.' The Chechen paused. 'Word has reached me of your reputation as a truth chaser. I'm hoping I can trust you.'

'Where do you come into it?'

'That is considerably more complex.'

Scamarcio thought he heard a noise outside, but he was too interested in the Chechen to take much notice.

'I can handle complexity,' he said, holding the giant's gaze, trying to seek out the soul behind the pale, empty eyes. But then Scamarcio's head swung to the window as he heard a clanging of metal and the screeching of tyres. Several car doors slammed.

'*Fuck*,' hissed Basile.

'It's the pigs,' whispered one of his goons, stepping back from the window and reaching for his handgun.

Basile didn't wait for a second opinion. He sprinted for a door to the right of his desk, his men close behind. Scamarcio didn't stop to think, either, and soon they were all spilling out into the night. Basile was already well ahead, running towards a chain-link fence, fast and smooth like a professional athlete. In seconds, he'd clambered onto the metalwork and had scrambled his way to the top.

Scamarcio jumped on, below Basile's goons, their backsides almost in his face, and soon he, too, was at the top, ready to swing his body over the other side. He fell nearly the entire way to the ground and twisted his ankle sharply as he landed. But there was no time for pain — almost before he knew it, he was running across a dark wasteland strewn with ripped garbage bags, worn tyres, and the rotting carcasses of old furniture, toxic foam spilling from the seams. When they had finally made it across and had entered a small street of residential housing, Basile bent his head between his legs and panted, 'We've lost them — for now. Where's the fucking Chechen?'

'They must have got him,' said one of his men, looking back in the direction they'd come.

'No way, I've seen that guy run,' said Scamarcio.

'I'm calling Dino,' said Basile. 'To get us the hell out — this place is teeming.'

He pulled his mobile from his pocket and hurriedly tapped the screen. 'We've got an emergency. Via Bindi — quick as you can, Dino boy.'

He hung up and started pacing, his men looking on nervously.

'We should have stayed well clear,' said one. Basile quickly raised a palm to silence him, and the man said no more.

'Why did the Chechen want to see me?' asked Scamarcio. 'I don't get it.'

Basile turned towards him. 'Do me a favour, pig, and shut the fuck up. You've caused enough trouble.'

A worried silence descended, until, a couple of minutes later, a green Suzuki Jeep tore to a stop in front of them. A fat, exhausted-looking guy was at the wheel. Basile and his men scrambled inside.

'Where are you going?' asked Scamarcio.

'None of your fucking business.'

'Give me a lift. I don't care where — I just don't want the police to find me.'

'You *are* the fucking police,' spat Basile, shaking his head as if he couldn't comprehend the madness of it all.

'I'll make it worth your while. Favours in return. Dante might look on you kindly if you helped me out.'

Basile sighed, then glanced down. His men were growing restless, but one of them was still holding the door open, waiting for a decision.

'What the fuck are we doing?' shouted the fat guy in the front, his voice shaky.

Basile's beady eyes glinted back at Scamarcio in the darkness. 'Greco?'

'Greco.'

'You're in tight?'

Scamarcio shrugged as if it were nothing.

'Hurry up,' hissed Basile, looking the other way, as if he already regretted it.

Scamarcio climbed in beside the two thugs, and they hared away, rubber burning. With some relief, Scamarcio realised that they were heading out of Torpignattara, back towards the centre.

18

THERE WAS A TIGHTER cordon around the café now.
Scamarcio didn't think he'd ever seen so many Panthers and
ambulances out in force; their numbers seemed to have tripled
since the morning, and the dense columns of news cameras and
blinding LED lights were overwhelming. Scamarcio wondered
what his Flying Squad colleagues were doing — whether they
were out at the hostage locations, or whether they were still
toiling in the background, digging up facts AISE probably already
had.

The crowds penned in behind the barricades had grown
thicker, and as he approached, Scamarcio's gut tightened and
his ears started to hum. He removed the cap and glasses, and, as
expected, an old man turned to stare, then a middle-aged woman
two rows ahead did the same. A ripple began to move through
the throng. 'It's him!' he heard a young girl shout. 'The man
from the TV!'

He checked his watch. It was past midnight. He was on
time for a meeting he'd probably never make. As if to confirm
it, Masi chose that moment to emerge from the shadows and
stride briskly towards him. 'Scamarcio,' he said, not sounding
particularly surprised or put out. 'We thought you'd show.'

Scamarcio held his wrists out. 'Go ahead.'

'What are you doing?'

'Cuff me.'

'Don't be ridiculous.'

'Wouldn't look good, I guess.'

Masi took him gently by the elbow. 'Colonel Scalisi wants a word.'

Scamarcio said nothing as Masi led him towards a black Mercedes with darkened windows, idling at the kerb. Scamarcio noticed that the car was different from the one they'd used that morning.

Masi opened the back door, and Scamarcio got in, an unwelcome fluttering in his stomach even though, so far, it was all going according to plan. He really didn't want to be here, but it was the only way to get the missing pieces of the puzzle from Scalisi. Just before the door slammed shut, he thought he caught a camera flash.

Scalisi was sitting in the front passenger seat. He looked back and inclined his head towards Scamarcio, but Scamarcio couldn't read anything in the colonel's hard blue eyes. It was like looking at a blank screen.

The head of AISE scratched at his temple, then said softly, 'You had a crisis of nerves, you freaked. It was all too much for an everyman like yourself, for an average Joe. Everyone will understand.' Scalisi sounded tired, as if he'd already been through every possible outcome, every emotion. Or perhaps he didn't have any emotions; perhaps they'd been trained out of him. Then Scamarcio thought back to Scalisi's behaviour on the American case and understood that the colonel was now exerting considerable self-control. There was something about this that bothered Scamarcio. It bothered him a lot.

'You're too stressed out and panicked to go back in there. We'll explain it to the boy, make sure he understands that his plan has failed. Then, once we've done that, we're going to shoot the shit out of him and his deadbeat friends. The crime scene cleaners will be busy for weeks.'

Scamarcio's jaw tightened. 'You do that and you condemn

those hostages to death, not to mention the innocent victims at the other sites they've got wired.'

'There are no other sites, it's just grandstanding.'

'Bullshit. How can you know?'

'I'm head of AISE — it's my business to know.'

'But this time you failed, as you admitted yourself. However you neglected to mention that you knew about Ifran 'cos he was one of yours. But then he slipped the leash and today came as one nasty surprise.'

Scalisi smiled. It was a complex smile — ambiguous, confusing. It said much, but still held too many secrets.

'It's over, Scamarcio. You'll be charged with aiding and abetting, and with evading the police. As of now, your career is dead in the water. Your life as you know it is finished. Everything will change for you — and very much for the worse.'

'You don't scare me, Scalisi. You're not telling the truth.'

'Scamarcio, you wouldn't know the truth if it bent down on its knees and sucked your tiny dick. I should scare you a lot, Scamarcio. I should petrify you. In fact, right now you should be shitting yourself.'

Scalisi tapped on the passenger window, and a moment later Masi climbed into the driver's seat. With a flick of the wrist, he fired up the ignition, and they pulled away.

'Where are we going?' asked Scamarcio.

But Scalisi just turned his head to the window and said nothing. Scamarcio caught a glimpse of the dark slits of the colonel's eyes in the rear-view mirror. They were the eyes of a man with violence on his mind.

'Give me the picture,' said Scalisi, once he and Scamarcio were seated across a table, alone in a narrow room with no windows.

'Metaphorically speaking?'

159

'Cut the crap.'

'Is this your interrogation suite? I don't see a viewing window.'

'We don't need a viewing window — we're AISE. Give me the photo.'

'What photo?'

'Scamarcio, I'm warning you, it's too late for games. Give me the photo.'

'And I'm telling you, I don't know what you're on about.'

Scamarcio was perplexed by the absence of mikes — the wiring must all be up in the roof, he figured. Scalisi slammed his palms on the desk, commanding his attention.

'I don't understand all this talk of a picture. You think that boy gave me a photo?' said Scamarcio, glancing up. He wondered how the colonel knew he had it. Had his snipers at the basilica told him?

Scalisi looked blank for a moment, then leaned over the desk and brought his face very close. 'Don't play me for a fool!' he yelled. His breath smelt of coffee and something else — something malty, alcoholic.

Scamarcio wiped the spittle from his brow. 'What is in this picture, that you want it so badly?'

'You know.'

'I wish I did.'

'That's it,' said Scalisi, quiet now. 'You had a chance to save yourself, but you've squandered it.' He stepped away and smoothed down his blond hair, which was cropped so short there was nothing to smooth. Then he seemed to change his mind. He approached the desk again, breathing more rapidly now.

'Stand up.'

Scamarcio leaned back in his chair, trying to put more distance between them. 'Why?'

'Stand up, Detective.'

There was something in Scalisi's eyes that made him obey this time.

'Arms out, legs apart.'

'You already searched me when we came in.'

'And now I'm going to search you again.'

Scalisi walked around the desk and began patting him down — his movements clumsy and frenetic, his hands shaky. When he'd finished, he stared at Scamarcio, defiant. 'Where've you hidden it?'

'I haven't hidden it because I don't have it; I've never had it.'

'Have you scanned it onto a drive, a key?'

Scamarcio threw open his palms. 'I repeat: I have absolutely no fucking idea what you're talking about.'

'Perhaps I have something that might help you understand.' There was a look in Scalisi's eye that Scamarcio didn't like.

'Don't go away.' Scalisi was laughing as he left the room. The laughter was strangely shrill and high. *The laugh of a man who's losing it?* Scamarcio wondered.

The colonel sent in two goons, who escorted Scamarcio down some stairs to a basement. He hadn't known there was a prison beneath AISE. Sure, on the inside the small rooms had been designed not to resemble cells, but the horseshoe layout, the guy on guard in the corridor outside, and the small portholes in every door made it clear that this was a holding area for people apparently wishing to do the state some kind of harm.

After a few minutes, which Scamarcio spent worrying in silence, Scalisi strolled in, looking pretty pleased with himself. He was carrying an open laptop.

'You may not have a picture for me, but I have one for you,' he said, laying the computer on a small table in front of Scamarcio. He noticed that fat beads of perspiration clung to the colonel's wide brow, and his chin was wet.

Scalisi nudged the laptop closer to Scamarcio. On the screen in front of him was a blurred frozen video image, but it was too distorted to comprehend.

The colonel swept an arm through the air, like some sick circus ringmaster, and pressed play. As the pixels coalesced, Scamarcio gave a start. Fiammetta was sitting in a high-backed chair. She had been filmed right-side on in a small room, similar to the one he was in now, and there was a small-boned man seated across from her. Between them was a laptop.

As the camera zoomed in, Scamarcio saw with a rush of rage that the right side of Fiammetta's face was badly bruised, and her T-shirt was now ripped open, revealing her bra. Just the sight of it made Scamarcio want to grab Scalisi's head and smash it against the wall until there was nothing left.

'What the fuck have you done to her?' he roared, lunging at him. Scalisi seemed to have been expecting it and deftly stepped back, laughing. 'Just watch the film — all will become clear.'

'Will you confirm that this is Detective Scamarcio's computer?' the man on the screen was asking Fiammetta as he motioned to the laptop. 'And that you were there when we seized it this morning?'

'That could be anybody's — just because the make is the same, it doesn't mean it's his,' she said slowly. She sounded tired, almost drugged. Her hair was a tangled mess, and there were deep grooves beneath her eyes. *Is she here, in the same building?* Scamarcio wondered.

'Check the home screen, please — read through the documents at your leisure,' said the man. 'We have plenty of time.' His tone was soft and unobtrusive — like a dentist or a doctor.

Fiammetta leaned forward and used her right index finger to scroll down the mousepad. Scalisi's film had been shot at such an angle that Scamarcio couldn't tell what she was looking at.

After a minute or so, she said. 'Yes, it *appears* to be his. You could have copied all the files, though.'

'You were there when we confiscated this computer, Miss di Bondi. You were there when we made a note of the serial number. It's the same machine. Check the back, if you wish.'

But she made no move to do so.

'Now, I'd like to draw your attention to a file marked 'Party' in the media folder on the desktop. Open it, please.'

It took quite a while for Fiammetta to find it, and, as she searched, Scamarcio felt his spine grow warm. He had never given any of his files the title 'Party'. He hated parties and always did his best to avoid them. He had no idea what that file contained, but knew that whatever it was would not be good.

Strange muffled noises were starting to come from the laptop in front of Fiammetta. There was something very unsettling about the sound. Fiammetta watched a little longer, her eyes wide, then she placed a hand across her mouth and looked away. 'Switch it off,' she said coldly. 'I feel sick.'

The man in front of her calmly turned the computer around and shut down whatever horror was playing.

When he looked up, he said, 'Detective Scamarcio is addicted to child pornography.' It was all so matter of fact, as if he was telling her that Scamarcio had a nut allergy, or a passion for ornithology.

'He has been for some time. It started with a case he was involved in. It began as a curiosity, and then became an addiction. You need to know the truth about him, Miss di Bondi. You're not defending a hero.'

Scamarcio felt bile push up from his stomach. Sweat was trickling from his chin onto his chest, running down his torso, collecting in his bellybutton. *They're criminals.*

Fiammetta had turned back to the man, but she seemed to be staring straight past him now. She was quite still, blinking slowly, thinking it through, *considering* it. Scamarcio knew that Fiammetta was fiery and impulsive. The fact that she wasn't reacting, screaming at him to go hang, was bad. For a long moment, he wondered if they'd succeeded — if she'd actually been shocked into credulity. Then he prayed she was just playing them, making them *think* they'd won.

'So,' said Scalisi, slamming the laptop shut and jolting Scamarcio back to the present. 'Now that's over with, maybe we can bring this charade to a close. Photo!' He clicked his fingers.

Scamarcio just shook his head, bewildered. 'You're insane. Why the fuck would I give you the picture — after what you've done?'

'That was just for starters, Scamarcio, to give you a taste of what I'm capable of. It will get a hell of a lot worse for Fiammetta before it gets better. And whether it gets better depends entirely on you.'

'Go fuck yourself.'

It was Scalisi's turn to shake his head. 'I thought you'd have the intelligence to work this out, see it in its entirety.'

'That photo is in safe hands,' said Scamarcio slowly, trying to keep control, trying not to end the day with a murder conviction. 'In a matter of minutes, it's going to be shared with the world. The public will know all about the toxic game you've been playing.'

'Ah, so you don't care about your girlfriend ...'

Scamarcio looked down at his old suede Campers and said nothing.

Scalisi smiled tightly. 'You're bluffing. And badly at that ...'

'You were running Ifran, and then he split. When that gets out, you're dust.'

He thought he saw Scalisi's jowl twitch.

'As for the Chechen ...'

Scalisi sniffed. It seemed like an involuntary reaction, almost a reflex.

'As for the Chechen, that's another dismal tale which will need to be told. It's over, Scalisi, it's finished for you.'

'Shut up,' whispered the colonel.

'Give up, go home. Resign before they fire you.'

'I'm not going to let some Calabrian inbred push me around.'

'You are, because you have no choice.' Scamarcio glanced at his watch. 'It's out there now — in the public domain.' Scalisi was right, he was bluffing, but now Scamarcio just kept on going, like a car with no brakes hurtling into the abyss. He wasn't even thinking straight — he was angry, furious. He couldn't see for red mist. Scalisi was dead. If Scamarcio couldn't do it, he'd find someone who would. He didn't care about the price.

'I can tell from your mention of the Chechen that you do *not* understand the situation in which you find yourself. Stop trying to swim with the sharks, Detective. Get me that photo and all the copies you've had made, and then we can end this.'

'Copies? Don't they give you old-timers courses in social media? Try to drag you into the modern age?'

'Have you shared that photo?' Scalisi was breathing faster now. He wiped the sweat from his brow with a starched white cuff and Scamarcio thought he noticed a smudge of hair dye. The spotless façade was starting to crumble.

'If I were to somehow stop its publication, would you release my girlfriend?'

'I doubt she's still your girlfriend.'

Scamarcio said nothing. Scalisi was drawing out a chair and sitting down. He was now staring at the surface of the table as if it held a hidden truth. His fingers started to drum, the rhythm quickening.

'Those are your terms?' he asked eventually, his voice low.

'… And two million euros.'

'What?' Scalisi blinked, then exhaled. After a beat, he inclined his head and assessed Scamarcio with deep contempt. 'I don't buy it.'

'Don't try reading too much into it. Everyone has their price.'

Scamarcio stared at him.

'Hmm,' said Scalisi, holding a bunched fist against his mouth. 'Your loser father left you a lot of money, you're not hard up.'

'If it hadn't been for your petty little stunt, I'd only be asking for one. What is it with you paedophiles that you always try to smear your enemies with your crimes?'

'Shut up.'

'No, you shut up, you sick freak. This is what you're going to do. You're going to escort me out of here. I'm the only one who can find that photo and intercept it before my friend gives it wings.'

'Who's to say he hasn't done so already?'

'Your risk: take it or leave it. But, without me, you're never going to get back some control.'

'I can't raise two million just like that.'

'I'll take 500K as a deposit, but make it quick.'

Scamarcio snapped his fingers.

19

'WHERE'S MASI?' SCAMARCIO ASKED the back of Scalisi's head as they pulled away from wherever it was they'd been holding him. The car they were travelling in had normal windows, and Scamarcio now realised they hadn't been at AISE HQ. He didn't recognise the surrounding area.

'Otherwise engaged.'

'You wanted to keep our little side-trip a secret?'

The colonel remained silent.

'I know someone who has a machine for checking whether euros are counterfeit,' said Scamarcio, pulling out the wad from the top of his jacket and fingering the notes.

'It's legit.'

'It had better be.'

They drove on in silence, Scamarcio wondering whether he'd find Basile in Torpignattara or whether he and his men would still be in town, doing exactly what Scamarcio had convinced them to do. How he had persuaded them was the source of some mental turmoil, but he pushed his doubts aside and tried to focus. It felt altogether wrong to be heading back to Torpignattara, but he didn't want to lead Scalisi into the eye of the storm. He needed to keep him out of the way until he knew Basile had made headway. With luck, he'd find a way to leave Scalisi once they reached the suburbs.

'Take a left here,' Scamarcio instructed the driver. 'Then left again.'

As they made their way up the road to Basile's lot, Scamarcio checked his watch and saw that it was 3.00 a.m. He wondered yet again how much time he really had left until people started dying.

'So, you got your Chechen back?' he tried.

But Scalisi remained motionless, his mountainous shoulders quite still.

'That must be a relief.' It was the mention of the Chechen that had persuaded Scalisi to round up half a million, not Ifran. Scamarcio felt quite sure of it.

They approached the gates, and Scalisi's driver got out to see if there was any kind of entry system. He hung around for a while, but nobody appeared. The place seemed deserted — there were no lights in the outbuildings, and no cars in the forecourt. Scamarcio hoped the clan were all still in the centre, working hard.

'We'll have to sit it out until they get back,' said Scamarcio.

'Where the fuck are they?' asked Scalisi.

'None of your business.'

'I'd say it was, given I've just handed you half a million euros.'

'Half a million doesn't buy much these days. Given the stakes, it's a modest deposit.'

'God, you're one stubborn son of a bitch.'

'When will you get me the rest?'

'By close of play.'

'You make today's events sound like a football match.'

'That, Scamarcio, is the first intelligent analysis you've made.'

'Tell me about your Chechen.'

'He's not *my* Chechen.'

'So whose is he?'

The colonel said nothing.

'Why are you such an incompetent fuck, Scalisi? How did you manage to lose him?'

At that, Scalisi got out of the car, tore open Scamarcio's door, and seized him by the neck. One look at the dark fury in his eyes was enough to tell Scamarcio that he intended to kill him. 'I should have had you finished at the basilica,' hissed Scalisi. 'It wasn't worth the wait — you've given me nothing.'

With one hand still around Scamarcio's neck, he punched him hard in the stomach, and Scamarcio slumped forward. He immediately tried to straighten and mouth 'Stop,' but he couldn't even form the word — the pain was too intense. From a great distance, he heard murmurs and shouts, and then a blast of hot air rushed into the car and two strong hands pulled him away, out of Scalisi's reach.

Scamarcio fell hard onto the pavement, his head slamming against the concrete. The world began to shrink as a black border in his vision grew thicker and thicker. Soon there was nothing left but a tiny pinprick of light followed by a thousand starbursts.

He opened his eyes and tried to raise his head so he could locate Scalisi. But all he could see were tyres and black boots. Somewhere nearby an engine was idling. It made a low hum. It was surprisingly quiet — quieter than he would have expected.

'Motherfuckers,' he whispered, before the world disappeared again.

When he came to, he was in a comfortable bed with clean white sheets and plump pillows. It looked like a hotel bedroom — there were plush burgundy curtains at the tall windows and thick cream carpet. The furniture was antique: some rich, dark wood, polished to perfection. To the right of the bed was a wide desk, but he could see none of the usual accoutrements. There was no complimentary bottle of water with frilly-coaster covered glasses. This was a shame as the back of his throat felt burnt.

He tried to get out of bed, but everything ached: his biceps, his legs, his abdomen. His back felt like it had taken a thousand blows. He wondered if he'd been beaten up while he was unconscious. He lifted the sheet and looked at his stomach. It was covered in bruises, some small, some large. There were a few more on his thighs. He thought for a moment about internal injuries, but he didn't feel unwell — just sore and very thirsty. *How strange*, he thought, *to beat someone when you couldn't witness their suffering — hear them beg, confess what they knew.*

He wondered what had happened to his clothes. All he had left were his boxers.

He eased back against the pillow and closed his eyes. But then he heard the door open. 'Detective.' The Italian word was pronounced with the exaggerated open vowels of a British accent. 'How are you feeling?'

A tall, slender man was approaching the bed. He had a pleasant wide face with square cheekbones, and light-blue eyes behind wide tortoiseshell frames. His strawberry-blond hair was cut in that short-at-the-back, long-at-the-sides style so favoured by the British establishment, and he wore a conservative grey suit with a yellow and blue polka-dot tie. The tie seemed a little ostentatious for the sober suit.

'You beat me up, and then you ask how I'm feeling?'

'We didn't beat you up.'

'Sorry?'

'You should have come to see us, as your friend suggested.'

'What friend?'

'I believe you know him as Federico.'

Scamarcio blinked, then tried to sit up straighter in the bed, but it hurt too much so he remained prone, looking up at the seemingly respectable man before him. 'Are you from the embassy?'

'In a manner of speaking. You've got yourself in quite a jam, Detective.'

Scamarcio chose to say nothing.

170

The stranger pulled out the chair from beneath the desk and angled it towards the bed. He took a seat, draping a relaxed arm over the back and crossing his long legs in front of him. Scamarcio saw navy-blue silk socks and heavy brown brogues — too heavy for the kind of weather they'd been having in Rome lately.

'There are quite a few people who want a word with you, so we thought we'd get ahead of the game. We like to move in early if we can.' He pushed his wide glasses higher up his thin nose.

'You came on a motorbike …?' Scamarcio asked, still trying to piece it all together.

'Yes.' He adjusted the glasses once more. 'We'd been following you and the colonel, keeping tabs, as it were.'

'So who kicked the shit out of me?'

The man opened his palms and shrugged — it was a small, almost fleeting gesture. 'Mr Scalisi lost his cool, I'm afraid, before we could whisk you away. We're not sure whether it was just for show or whether he really hates you. Either way, you should be grateful we eventually got you out of there.'

'"Grateful" is not the word I'd choose.'

'What word would you prefer?'

'What the hell do you want?'

'I think it's more the other way around. We might be in the position to help you. But we require some information from you first.'

'I've heard that line before.'

'I know you come from a tough background and that you've witnessed a lot of violence.'

What the fuck is it with this guy? 'That's got nothing to do with it. I'm just telling you that I'm sick and tired of being played. Don't try to play me, or you'll lose.'

The man looked at him, but said nothing. Scamarcio heard a trapped fly buzzing against the window, its body beating frantically against the glass.

'It's like this, Detective: we know a little, but not a lot. You probably also know a little, but not a lot. But your little might be different from our little, and together that might add up to a lot.'

Scamarcio sighed. 'I haven't got time for this. There's a siege going down; people are about to die. I'd like to get back there and try to help bring this mess to some kind of peaceful resolution.'

'The have-a-go hero. That's all very nice, and the papers would lap it up, but I'm sure you can see that the authorities aren't ever going to let you go back in.'

Scamarcio was no longer listening. 'Fuck, what's the time?' He suddenly realised that he had no idea how long he had been out of it. The curtains looked thick — it could be daylight outside.

'4.30 a.m.'

He took a breath. *Thank God*. 'Where's Scalisi?'

'No idea.'

'I don't believe you.'

'Why would I lie?'

'Because you're a spy and that's what spies do.'

The man flinched as if Scamarcio had called him a murderer or a paedophile. Scamarcio remembered the video of Fiammetta, and his chest felt hollow.

'Ifran has been saying a lot of things. The problem is working out which of them are true.'

'On this, we don't disagree,' said Scamarcio tiredly.

'We believe he was working with Italian intelligence. Is that your assessment?'

Scamarcio felt a strange burning at the corner of his mouth. He touched the spot, trying to come up with a reply. 'Yes,' he said. But that was all.

'Do you think the relationship could have changed? That perhaps, more recently, Ifran decided to strike out on his own?'

'That's possible.'

'Why would he do this?'

'Your guess is as good as mine.'

'Perhaps not ...' The last word trailed off, it was barely audible.

Scamarcio wanted to know about the Chechen. He needed to understand why Ifran was preoccupied with him — why his name had tripped a switch for Scalisi. It felt like time to trade: 'OK, I'll give you my theory. But first, you make a guess for me. Who's the Chechen, and what's he doing in the middle of all this?'

'The Chechen?'

For a moment, the elegant man looked a little unruffled in his perfect suit. 'Describe him.'

Scamarcio went through the same spiel he'd given the guy in Calcata.

'Hmm,' said the Englishman once he'd absorbed it. 'You'll need to give me a moment.'

And with that he left.

20

A FEW MINUTES LATER there was another knock at the door,
— it wasn't the Englishman but a maid in full uniform. She was
carrying a wide tray, on which rested a large bottle of water and
a plate of food. Scamarcio smelt the welcome aroma of fresh
bread, eggs, and bacon. The maid deposited the tray on the desk,
and then left without saying a word.

Scamarcio didn't feel much like moving, but his thirst
compelled him. He hobbled over, the throbbing in his stomach
quite fierce. He drank down the bottle in one, not bothering with
a glass, and then examined the contents of the tray. He took a
seat and ate quickly, immediately feeling better as the sugar
reached his blood.

There was a knock at the door again, and the Englishman
entered, followed by a slightly smaller man with dark hair. He
looked about forty — a few years younger than his colleague.

'I hope the food was OK,' said the blond guy, actually
sounding like he meant it.

'Yes.' As an afterthought Scamarcio added: 'Thank you.'
Perhaps it paid to be polite with the British.

'So, the thing is,' said the man, pulling out a chair from a
small table to the right of the door. 'We know, and *you* know, that
Ifran was involved with Scalisi. Obviously, this will never come
out, but ...'

'Why do you say "obviously"?'

'Well, very few people are aware of the connection, and I doubt you'll be the one to announce it.'

'Why?'

'Because you want to live.'

There was no drama to the words. The delivery couldn't have been flatter, more matter-of-fact.

Scamarcio regarded the two of them. They looked back at him. They had stated a truth that he'd already guessed, but which he now didn't know quite what to do with. He scratched his neck. 'So if I were to reveal to the world that Ifran had been an asset, the intelligence services would kill me.'

'Yes,' said the blond Englishman quickly, as if he was bored of talking about the weather and wanted to move on to something more pertinent.

'They might not leave it at that,' said the dark-haired guy, who was still standing. 'They might decide to go for your family, too. It depends, really — these things can play out in a number of ways. The Italians do business differently. We can't speak for them, but the general picture would probably be the same.'

'The general picture,' repeated Scamarcio, his mind sticking, refusing to move on. 'What am I to do with all this?' he asked after a moment. 'If I'm to do nothing, I mean?'

'Oh, it's not entirely a lost cause,' said the first Englishman, soothingly. 'You could start by talking to us.'

'I thought that's what I was doing.'

It was warm in the room, but Scamarcio suddenly felt cold and exposed in his boxer shorts. 'Any chance of getting some clothes?'

'Oh,' said the dark-haired man, looking slightly vacant. 'Sorry, I was meant to bring them.'

He left the room and was back a few moments later with Scamarcio's things, all clean and pressed — although the jacket and baseball cap still felt damp. The sunglasses had been carefully

175

placed in the top pocket of his jacket, but one of the arms looked bent. 'We'll have your shoes back in a second,' said the guy. Scamarcio wondered about the delay: what were they doing with his shoes? Polishing them?

'Do you know how long Ifran was working for Italian intelligence?' asked the first Englishman.

'No, I haven't got that far,' said Scamarcio as he tried to get into his clothes without cursing in pain.

'Do you think Scalisi had any idea this day was coming?' asked the dark-haired man. It was an important question — a question that had been troubling Scamarcio ever since his last meeting with the colonel. It was the complex smile that had made Scamarcio think that all of this was not as much of a surprise as it should have been. But this was a realisation that had grown gradually, and it hadn't yet properly taken shape. 'I'm not sure. He may have known, but of course he's never said anything to confirm it.'

'What makes you think that?'

Scamarcio sat back down and sighed. 'It's more a hunch: something I read from his body language.' He thought about mentioning the smile, but it would sound lame. 'Why would Scalisi do this? Recruit this guy?' he asked.

'We're always on the lookout for informants inside the suburbs — they're hard to find, but extremely valuable. A kind analysis would say that this is precisely what Scalisi was doing — running an asset inside Torpignattara so Intel knew ahead of the game whether attacks were in the pipeline.'

'Scalisi works for AISE — they're foreign intelligence. Why wasn't this being handled by domestic?'

'AISI probably have their own assets. There's a lot of rivalry between agencies. Scalisi was probably just trying to prove that he was up there with the best of them. If he got a result, that would be a great boost for his agency and a kick in the teeth for his rivals. And there's nothing to lose because if it goes to the wall, as seems to be happening today, his rivals end up with egg on their faces and he escapes the main rap. As you say, everyone expects this to be a matter for domestic Intel, not AISE.'

'You said that was a kind analysis. Is there a harsher one?'

'Of course,' said the blond guy, looking solemn. 'And that's the analysis we're working with.'

'Care to share it?'

'Scalisi leans to the right, as much as that can be said for former military men who become spooks. They start on the right, and then move ever closer to the edges.'

'What happens at the edges?'

'Dark things, darker than you might imagine …'

Scamarcio thought of the video of Fiammetta again and felt sick to his stomach. He had to find her. He wondered if the British might be able to help.

'We believe that Scalisi knew full well that today was coming — maybe he didn't know it as *today*, maybe it was some unspecified date in the future, but he knew it would happen soon enough. We suspect he deliberately ceased contact with Ifran in order to keep his hands clean, but then that picture surfaced, and now he's implicated.'

'But why would Scalisi do this?' asked Scamarcio. 'How could he possibly benefit from a terror attack on Rome? Mass casualties? Sure, domestic would take most of the rap, but he'd still be caught up in the post-mortem. He'd still risk looking incompetent, asleep at the wheel.'

This question had been bothering Scamarcio ever since his meeting with Di Mare in the church, but there hadn't been time to sculpt it, hone it down.

'Scalisi and a few of his colleagues at AISE have a philosophy that they seem to be pursuing, and they're not the only ones in the intelligence community to think this way.'

'What philosophy?'

'Detective, don't take this amiss, but you seem to be the one asking all the questions. We need to turn that around for a moment. We need to know what Ifran told you to draw you into this, and we need to know what you've found out since. When we've covered that, *then* we can give you the finer details. The ones we have, at least.'

Scamarcio didn't really need to weigh it up. Scalisi was the enemy. On the other hand, so far, the Brits had provided a comfortable bed, clean clothes, and a decent meal — and they seemed to know a lot. Some might call him an easy lay, but on this occasion he was prepared to put out.

'OK, but before I tell you about Ifran, I need to ask you one more thing. Scalisi has my girlfriend, he's done her harm. Do you have any ideas where he might be holding her?'

The blond guy shrugged. 'Are you sure he's hurt her?'

Scamarcio nodded, and the guy looked unsettled. 'She's probably at AISE HQ — that would be my guess.' His colleague nodded an assent.

'I'm not convinced she's there. Do they use other places?'

'I'm sure AISE have black sites, but we wouldn't know their location, I'm afraid. That information would never be made available to us. I'm sorry — we can't help.'

Unfortunately, Scamarcio believed him.

'We'll keep our ears to the ground,' said the dark-haired guy quietly.

Scamarcio took a breath and tried to focus on the deal in hand. He talked them through what he knew so far, omitting his more recent discoveries about the Chechen because he wanted to save that card for later. When he'd finished, the blond Englishman said, 'It sounds like Ifran is trying to blackmail Scalisi with the Chechen. The question is, Why?'

'Yep.'

'Do you have any ideas?'

'Probably no better than yours. Is the Chechen Intel? I dunno — you guys tell me. Business in that part of the world seems murky, lines are blurred.'

The Englishman snorted. 'It's not murky, it's impenetrable. You can't see the bottom.'

'Do you have a hunch?'

'We don't like to work on hunches. But as I'm talking to a policeman, and your rules are different, I suppose I might say that the Chechen's strings are definitely being pulled by someone.'

Scamarcio tried to suppress his frustration. 'Someone in intelligence?'

'Possibly.'

'Scalisi?' It was like hammering in nails.

'We deem it unlikely. If the Chechen is who we think he is, he's one of a select few. We don't think he'd do business with Scalisi. He'd have bigger fish to fry.'

'Bigger fish than the head of AISE?'

'There's a huge world out there, full of people with fatter wallets than Scalisi. As the saying goes, follow the money.'

'You guys must have a big budget.'

The blond Englishman laughed. 'Not enough to buy the Chechen.'

'Did you try?'

The Englishman said nothing.

'So, who does that leave?'

'Too many to count.'

'I don't understand,' said Scamarcio. 'I don't get why the Chechen seems so important to Scalisi and Ifran.'

'That is the mystery we're all trying to solve — while the clock ticks down.' He studied his watch, then murmured something to his colleague in English. Scamarcio couldn't catch it.

'This philosophy of Scalisi's — you were going to explain.'

The Englishman turned his gaze from his colleague. 'Yes, we were. But right now, we've got a meeting. We'll be back later.'

'How long is that going to take?'

But they were already through the door. *This is the way with the British*, thought Scamarcio. *They always come across as gentlemen, then rip you off when you least expect it.*

He'd given up looking at his watch. It just brought stress and no solutions. And besides, the Englishman was right — he wasn't ready to be bumped off in some dark alley. He wanted to find Fiammetta. He wanted to return to his former life of semi-challenging cases, interspersed with the occasional head-fuck.

He'd lain back down on the bed and was dozing again, dreams hovering on the edges of nightmares, when the Englishmen strolled back in, newly brisk and invigorated as if they'd just received a pat on the back from a big cheese.

'It's been interesting speaking with you,' said the blond guy. 'What would you like to do now?'

'I want to get out of here.'

'That can be arranged.'

'And I want to know what Scalisi's up to. I need to understand his motives.'

The blond guy nodded sympathetically. 'I'm sure you do. You must appreciate that what we tell you cannot make its way to the media. There'll be severe consequences if it does.'

Scamarcio smiled thinly; he'd expected nothing less.

'You'll need to sign a non-disclosure agreement.'

'I thought that was just for rock stars.'

'Do I look like a rock star?' There was no irony, not even the trace of a smile. The Englishman produced a pen from his top pocket, and his colleague handed over an A4 plastic envelope. The blond guy pulled out a sheet and signed it, then brought

180

it across to Scamarcio. While Scamarcio's English was solid, he couldn't make sense of the legalese in a hurry.

'Do you have one in Italian?'

'No.'

He just went ahead and signed it. The British were no doubt about to get one over on him, but he needed whatever they knew about Scalisi.

Once the document had been returned to its file, the blond Englishman said, 'I'll let my colleague explain. His spoken Italian is better.' He smiled stiffly at the dark-haired guy, who coughed, then said, 'You're a policeman, so I don't need to tell you that surveillance is a troublesome beast. As a detective, if you wish to bug someone or monitor their email, what is the first thing you must do?'

'Usually, I need to get permission from a judge.'

'When you say "usually", how often do you mean?'

'I'd say about ninety per cent of the time,' answered Scamarcio, wondering where this was heading.

'Ninety per cent of the time — that's most of the time.'

'Yes.' What was this, a lesson in percentages?

'So imagine, if you will, a law that gives you the right to eavesdrop on the digital and mobile phone communications of *anyone* linked to a terrorist inquiry, a law that allows you to install secret cameras and recording devices in private homes without requesting prior permission from the judge. Would this new law make your job simpler?'

'Quicker maybe, but perhaps not simpler.'

'Imagine, then, that you have access to a device that records the keystrokes people make on their computers. Imagine that internet and phone companies have black boxes that run complex algorithms that can alert the authorities to suspicious online behaviour. Imagine that these same companies are then forced to hand over all that data when asked. All this information would make it so much easier to solve your cases.'

'And so much easier to make mistakes …'

The dark-haired man just shrugged. 'Scalisi and a few others inside his agency are pushing for the legalisation of mass surveillance. They're not alone and they're definitely following a trend — we've seen it happen in France, and it's starting to happen elsewhere. Scalisi and others are frustrated because, while they have some amazing tech at their fingertips, they don't have the legal clout to use it. Scalisi knew that if an attack came, besides gaining a bigger budget, he'd also be able to secure much wider powers.'

'Isn't that what you *all* want?'

'Our colleagues think the solution needs to be subtler, more measured. There's a danger in taking things too far.'

'The danger of mistakes being made?'

'It's more that they wouldn't want to unnerve their citizens.'

Scamarcio sighed and tried to make sense of it, knocking it around in his head for a while. After a lengthy silence, he said, 'Thanks for bringing me up to speed.'

But on his mind, unspoken, remained the conviction that there was more to this — that the real picture was dirtier and more complicated.

Scamarcio had declined their offer of a car, figuring that some European treaty might oblige them to hand him over. He wondered if they would follow him as he walked back towards the Colosseum. But when he checked behind him, the early morning streets were deserted. He assumed that those people who weren't still asleep were probably glued to their TVs or penned in behind barricades, like rubberneckers at a car-crash.

When he'd left Basile, they'd agreed to meet either back at Torpignattara, if that proved easiest, or at the junction of Via del

Cardello where it met Via Cavour. Basile would post a man there to wait for Scamarcio, in case Basile was busy elsewhere. He'd also station a guy back at his office who could give Scamarcio an update in the event he couldn't reach the centre. Scamarcio had been hoping to give Scalisi the slip when the arrival of the British had put paid to that idea. But as he rounded the corner, Scamarcio was surprised to see the crime boss himself, bathed in the sodium of a street lamp.

'Ah, so you're still alive,' he said by way of hello, sounding slightly disappointed. But although Basile looked tired, his cheeks were flushed, and his eyes were alert. Scamarcio sensed that just the thought of a partnership with Dante Greco was having the same effect as a shot of adrenalin. Sure, Basile had Torpignattara all sewn up but, without a helping hand, he was never going to make it into the premier league. An association with Greco could change that overnight. And if Basile played it well, he could make millions. Scamarcio had grossly exaggerated his connection to Greco and had no idea how he was going to work his way out of the lie, but he decided not to think about that for now. There were more pressing matters to consider.

'Let's walk,' said Scamarcio as they headed down the hill, away from the main road. 'Did you get anywhere?'

'We found a crew. There's a producer who is willing to talk to you. You need to call this number.' Basile fished a piece of paper from his pocket and handed it over.

'I don't have a mobile.'

Basile felt for his phone in his jacket pocket and passed it across. Scamarcio slowed and made towards the entrance of a smart apartment block, where he took a position away from the steps. He dialled, and the number was answered after a few rings.

'Woodman,' snapped an American voice. The man sounded wired on coffee and adrenalin.

Scamarcio introduced himself, his addled mind slow to switch into English.

'Jesus,' said the producer, once he was done. 'Your guy told our fixer that he had an important source, but I didn't expect it to be you. You've got a helluva lot of people after you, Detective.' Woodman paused. 'Obviously, we'd be very keen to get ahead of the curve, but right now I've got no proof that you are who you say you are.'

'I understand,' said Scamarcio. 'Can we meet?'

'Can you get close to the Colosseum?'

'Hold on,' said Scamarcio.

He began walking down Via Cavour, motioning Basile to follow. There was a blue and green awning a few metres down, but Scamarcio couldn't see any chairs or tables outside. Perhaps they hadn't opened up yet. He drew closer and realised that it was a small boutique, not a bar. He kept on going, and soon enough spotted a small, somewhat dingy café. He peered through the glass and noticed that, while chairs were still up on tables and the lights were dimmed, there was a glow coming from a room out back. He guessed they'd be opening for the breakfast rush soon. 'Bar Mirabel, Via Cavour. I'll be waiting for you.'

'Is that far?'

'No more than five minutes, but with the road blocks it might take longer. Come alone — don't bring your fixer.'

Scamarcio didn't want to hammer on the door, but luckily he didn't have to. As they were waiting outside the café, the main lights came on, and a young man started removing chairs and wiping down tables. Scamarcio turned away to face the street. A few minutes later, the guy unlocked the front door, and Basile entered. Scamarcio followed a couple of minutes later. The crime boss had ordered them both cappuccino and brioche, and had found a table by the back wall.

The producer, when he arrived, was sweating, and his face was tight with stress. Woodman was tall and well built, with shoulder-length brown-blond hair and a greying beard. He seemed combat-ready in a tan jacket with a startling array of zips and flaps. On his feet was a pair of sturdy walking boots, and Scamarcio noticed a lurid green K-Way backpack slung over one shoulder. Scamarcio raised his palm in an almost imperceptible gesture, but the American spotted it straight away. He looked hesitant and slowly started to approach. Scamarcio knew that there was no way the producer could recognise him until he removed the sunglasses and cap.

'Er, Detective?'

Scamarcio pushed up the glasses for little more than a second. Woodman's expression morphed into shock, then relief, then back to stress again. 'Good to meet you,' he whispered, extending a quick hand. He sat down opposite and deposited the backpack on the floor by his feet.

'I guess my first question would be, Why us?' he said, reaching into one of the flaps on his jacket and pulling out a small leather-bound notebook and ballpoint pen.

'Can you hold off taking notes?' Scamarcio asked.

'Sure.'

'I didn't choose you. The boy did.'

'The boy in the café? They're saying his name is Ifran Shebani.'

'Yes, Ifran.'

'And what does Ifran want from us? Your associate here,' he motioned to Basile, 'he told my fixer he had a source close to Ifran — he didn't give us further details.'

Basile nodded at the wrong moment, and Scamarcio knew he didn't understand.

'Ifran asked me to bring you back to the bar this morning

with a live link open,' said Scamarcio, knowing the effect this would have.

As expected, the American gave a jolt. He rubbed his chin and said, 'My bosses would never agree to that. It could be carnage — Shebani might be using us to broadcast his sick little snuff movie in real time.'

'I don't believe it's that,' said Scamarcio calmly.

'Why not?'

'What I'm about to tell you is off the record. I might allow it to go *on* the record later, but for now it's between you and me — can you put the notebook away?'

The producer quickly did as instructed.

Scamarcio took a breath, and then began to talk him through his conversation with Ifran. But when it came to the DVD, he held back the finer details. 'That DVD, and a photo that has come into my possession, lead me to believe that Ifran has been working for Italian intelligence. It's also possible that US intelligence is aware.' Again, he resolved to leave the Chechen right out of it — he didn't want Woodman muddying the waters.

'Holy shit,' said the producer. 'Is this for real?'

'I think so.'

'It's one hell of an allegation.'

'I know ...'

'But what would be the point?'

'I'll get to that.'

Woodman took a long breath. 'Let's get this straight: you're telling me there was a DVD — in the exact place the boy said it would be — and that that DVD demonstrates collaboration between him and the intelligence services?'

'That DVD *suggested* it. The confirmation came with the photograph.'

'I'll need to see that photo.'

Scamarcio had been expecting this, and turned to Basile.

'Do you have my wallet and the picture?' he asked in Italian. The crime boss nodded and lifted them from his inside pocket. When he handed over the photo, Scamarcio saw that the corners were now slightly crumpled. He passed it to the producer, who studied it closely. Wordlessly, Basile also handed across the DVD, and Scamarcio pocketed it while the producer's eyes were still on the photo.

'You made the copies?' Scamarcio whispered.

'Sure,' murmured Basile.

'That guy does look like the stills they've released for the boy in the café, but who is the big man with him?' asked Woodman, laying down the photo.

'Colonel Andrea Scalisi, head of AISE. That's our foreign intelligence agency.'

'I know what AISE is, but I don't know this guy. I'll need to verify the image.' Woodman pulled out an iPhone from another of the flaps on his jacket and started tapping and scrolling. Scamarcio presumed he was running a web search for Scalisi. Soon enough, the producer seemed to find confirmation. 'Damn,' was his only reaction.

'Happy?' Scamarcio asked.

'Not exactly …' The producer ran a hand through his hair. 'This is dynamite,' he muttered, looking away.

'In more ways than one. So, do you want the story or not?'

Woodman sighed and ran the tips of his fingers across his forehead, then scratched his neck. 'But why is Ifran insisting on this live link?'

'He wants to tell his story to the world. He thinks this will be his only chance.'

'So what happened with his relationship with AISE? How did it go so wrong?' Woodman stared at Scamarcio hard; he still seemed to be sizing him up.

'I'm not convinced it did go wrong.'

'What do you mean?'

'It could be that the guy running Ifran *wanted* to arrive at this point.'

'You're not serious?'

'I've just had quite an informative chat with some spooks at the British Embassy. The Brits seem to think that Scalisi and a few chums have an agenda — that they're pushing for broader surveillance powers.'

'Why the fuck would the Brits tell you that?'

'That was my question, but it seems that they were looking for information — they showed me theirs, I showed them mine.'

'Information on Ifran?'

'Yes.'

'I can't believe they just let you go with half the world looking for you.'

'They play by their own rules. Ally or enemy doesn't seem to be a solid state.'

'Hmm.' Woodman sighed again and swore softly. After a few seconds spent staring into space, he rubbed beneath his nose and said, 'How did you get the picture — I understand how you got the DVD, but you didn't explain the picture.'

'It was given to me by a guy who recently retired from AISE. He knew there was a shitstorm coming and wanted out before someone switched on the fan.'

Woodman kneaded his chin as if he was trying to sculpt it down, make it less prominent. 'So, he took the photo before he retired?'

'No, someone else took the photo. A guy who'd also left, for similar reasons — I met him last night. I believe him to be credible.'

'Where is he, this photographer?'

'In a village fifty kilometres from Rome.'

'I'll need to see him — I'll need to verify the whole thing.

That photo could be faked. They can do anything these days.'

'You're thinking about your story — all that will come. But we need to focus on the live link — that needs to happen soon. Ifran wants it by 9.00 a.m.'

'Or?'

'Rome burns.'

'What?'

'He says they've got a lot of other sites wired — that we could be looking at thousands of casualties.'

'But how is that even possible?'

'I'm just telling you what he said.'

'How can I make the case for a live link if I haven't corroborated my story? We can't just go blindly in. Not that I believe my bosses would ever let it happen.' Woodman looked at his watch. 'It's 6.45. Christ, I mean, it's not like we even have any time.'

Scamarcio knew there was no way to get the producer to Calcata and back and the crew in place for the deadline. 'He'll come to you,' he said before the thought had properly coalesced. 'I'll get my source to drive here.'

'Well, all right,' said Woodman sounding reluctant. 'I need his name, his former position — I'll need to start checking out his background.'

Scamarcio frowned. He understood where the journalist was coming from, but he was asking the impossible. Scamarcio nudged Basile for his phone and pulled out the card Letta had given him when he'd left to meet Federico. When the professor picked up, he sounded drunk on sleep. 'So, you're still alive?'

It was turning into a theme.

'Federico took me to see this guy in Calcata last night. I need the pair of them to meet me in the centre, Bar Mirabel, as soon as possible — it's an emergency.'

'I thought I told you to back off, Scamarcio.'

'I can't; it's not that simple.'

'I can call Federico, but he might not want to take this further. He's already gone out on a limb, and everyone's jumpy.' Letta said it as if he didn't quite understand why.

'Please, just call him.' Scamarcio paused. 'This friend in Calcata — you ever heard of him?'

'I think Federico may have mentioned him once or twice,' said Letta vaguely.

'I need his name.'

'I can't give you a name.'

'Letta, you've got to trust me when I say this is important.'

Letta whistled down the line. 'At the end of the day, I don't really know you, Scamarcio. I helped you with a case once, but that's it.'

'Trust your gut.'

The line fell quiet for a few moments before Letta said, 'I know him as Alessandro — Alessandro Romanelli.'

'And he worked for AISE?'

'He worked for AISE — high up — with Federico.'

Scamarcio exhaled. 'You've done the right thing.'

'Only time will tell,' said Letta before hanging up.

Scamarcio gave the details to Woodman, who immediately resumed pecking at his iPhone. Then he brought it to his ear.

'What are you doing?' Scamarcio asked.

'What does it look like?'

'No,' said Scamarcio, trying to grab it.

'I need to call my fixer to research Romanelli,' hissed Woodman, trying to move out of the way.

'Don't!' Scamarcio finally managed to prise the phone away.

'What the hell?' seethed Woodman.

'It can't get out that you're looking at Romanelli. I don't know your fixer; I don't know who they might be talking to. Don't you have another way you can find out about him?'

Woodman's expression thawed ever so slightly. 'I could use our Intel guy in the States, ask him to consult his international sources. But that's a roundabout route.'

'I'd rather that than alerting your fixer.'

'People will know sooner or later that I've been asking ...'

'We'll take the risk. Maybe in a few hours it won't matter.'

Scamarcio handed back the iPhone, and Woodman shook his head, still put out. He placed the call and quickly supplied his contact with the details. 'Get it back to me as soon as you can,' he said before hanging up. 'There's an Intelligence Community database that he uses. He'll run the name through that. If it draws a blank he'll call his contacts.' Woodman scrolled down his phone. 'Google has no results,' he said after a few minutes.

'Not exactly surprising,' said Scamarcio under his breath.

Woodman's phone pinged, and when he looked at the message, he laughed. 'That's impressive,' he said. 'He's sent me a file already.'

He scrolled down the screen. 'There is a Romanelli who was with AISE.' He turned the phone to Scamarcio. 'Is this your guy?'

Scamarcio looked at the picture — it was indeed the same man he'd met in Calcata, but he looked very different in this photo. He was clean shaven in a dark suit and tie, and his hair was cropped short. His skin was several shades paler, and he seemed older and more careworn.

'What does it say he did with AISE?' asked Scamarcio.

'It just says counterintelligence. Apparently, he joined two years ago; he'd been at AISI previously — that's domestic, isn't it?'

Scamarcio nodded. There was something bothering him about this information. Hadn't Romanelli said that he and Federico went back a long way? Perhaps they'd known each other privately before AISE? Or perhaps Federico had also come from AISI?

Woodman was patting his jacket for his notebook again. 'I'll need to take some of this down, for background.'

'OK,' said Scamarcio, still preoccupied.

When he had finished, Woodman said, 'I'm just wondering why you didn't do this before — find out about this source?'

'Mr Woodman,' said Scamarcio, trying to keep his tone even, but finding his arm pushing up through the air anyway. 'Until yesterday, I had no idea that there'd be a siege, or that I'd be right in the middle of it. When I got out from seeing Ifran, AISE all but kidnapped me. They seized my mobile, which has meant that I've had no access to digital information. Most of my time has been spent trying to evade capture. Where you come from, you might call that police obstruction or not cooperating with the authorities, but right now I can't be sure that the authorities don't want to do me serious harm.' Scamarcio stopped. He'd been about to tell Woodman about the stunt Scalisi had pulled with Fiammetta, but then thought better of it. It was too private, and besides, he didn't want to scare the man off.

Woodman spent the next forty-five minutes making numerous calls, squinting at his phone and scribbling. Scamarcio had already ordered two espresso and was starting to feel shaky and on edge. He could sense Nino Basile growing increasingly restless beside him.

'My contacts will be here soon,' said Scamarcio, worrying about the amount of time he was spending in one place. He'd thought about sending the crime boss away, but figured that a bit of extra muscle might come in useful. 'Are your boys still at the cordon?'

'Yeah — they're wondering what the plan is. Is there a plan?'

'Sure.'

'What is it, then?'

Scamarcio sniffed. 'I'll share it when the last pieces are in place. No point jumping the gun.'

Basile just shook his head, unimpressed. 'And Greco?'

'He'll be in Rome next week,' Scamarcio lied.

He noticed Woodman glance up from his notes, and when he followed his gaze, he saw Federico and Romanelli entering the café. They seemed irritated and curious by turn.

'What's the big emergency?' asked Romanelli, eyeing the American with suspicion.

'Haven't you seen the news?' said Woodman, looking him up and down, clearly struggling to match this dishevelled hippy with the photo he had just seen.

Romanelli frowned and pulled out a chair. Federico went to the bar and returned with two espressos. As he sat down, Scamarcio noticed that he looked quite nervous, definitely not as relaxed as he'd seemed just hours before. *What or who has got to him?* Scamarcio wondered.

'So,' he said, trying to stay focused, 'this gentleman here,' he gestured to Woodman, 'is with CNN.' He thought he noticed Federico blanch, but he pushed on. 'He's here because Ifran asked me to return with a live TV link open at 0900. He wants to talk to the world. I'm trying to persuade Mr Woodman to grant this request.'

Romanelli pursed his lips, then barred his arms across his chest. 'There's no way that CNN will agree to that. It could be horrific,' he said in English. There was little trace of an accent.

'Quite,' said Woodman, under his breath.

'Mr Woodman is very interested in the tale I've told him so far about Ifran and his relationship with AISE. But he needs to corroborate the story before he calls his bosses.' He turned to Romanelli. 'And that's where you come in. You gave Di Mare the photo; you took that photo. We now know your former position, but we don't know the circumstances surrounding that picture.'

Scamarcio turned to Woodman. 'Is that the essence of it?'

He nodded.

Romanelli sniffed and pushed his glasses higher up his nose. 'Didn't we go through all this?'

'Not really, Mr Romanelli — it's more like we skirted around the edges,' said Scamarcio.

'How did you get my name?' asked Romanelli.

'Does that really matter?'

Romanelli scratched behind an ear and muttered, 'Letta.'

Federico shook his head. 'I doubt it.'

'Who else would it be?'

'Listen,' said Scamarcio, losing patience. 'Can't we just pin down the facts? We have just over an hour before Ifran's deadline.'

Romanelli rubbed his cheek and shook his head slowly. 'I admire your persistence, I really do. But there's no way they're going to let you back in there. You're in cloud-cuckoo-land if you think anything different.'

'Whatever. That's *my* problem. Just tell us how you came to suspect Scalisi. How you came to take that photo.'

Romanelli noticed the espresso in front of him and quickly tipped it back. He glanced up at the ceiling, as if hoping to be spirited out of the bar and back to his workshop.

'Scalisi is part of a group inside the agency who don't like the way things are going. They want to roam free and don't want to have to go running to a judge every two seconds to have their arses covered. They feel that they've been reined in for too long, and, given today's world, it's time for a change. On a certain level, they might be right, but it's the way they're going about things that bothers people like Federico and me.'

'That's what the British said,' said Woodman sounding pleased with himself.

'The British?' asked Federico, now looking even more ill at

ease. 'Have you spoken to them?' he asked Woodman.

'No. But he has,' the producer pointed at Scamarcio.

'When was this?' asked Federico, his brow scored with doubt. 'You were adamant you didn't want to see them.'

Scamarcio sighed. 'It wasn't like that. They found *me* — out in Torpignattara. They brought me back to their place for a friendly chat.'

'Was it friendly?'

'Pretty much — I didn't get the feeling they wanted to kill me, anyway.'

'Why would they want to kill you?' asked Federico, looking at Scamarcio as if he were insane. 'The British go their own way. That's what I was trying to tell you, but you wouldn't listen.'

Scamarcio wondered why Federico was so put out about the British.

'Mr Romanelli, do you think this attitude of Scalisi's, this push for greater powers, could be behind his relationship with Ifran? That it might explain today's attacks?' asked Woodman.

'It's possible,' said Romanelli, drily.

'It's possible, but you don't know for sure?'

'Certainty is a precious commodity. It's rare, and it takes a long time to cultivate.'

'So, you don't know?' said Woodman.

'I have my suspicions, as does Federico,' said Romanelli, gesturing to his colleague. 'But if you're asking us if we're certain, then we'd have to say that we're not.'

'And the photo, how did that come about?' pushed Woodman.

'I took that picture when I was part of a team running Ifran. We had met him in Frascati that day — he could never come to HQ, of course.'

'Of course,' echoed Woodman.

'We were in Frascati to speak to him about some product he'd delivered on two brothers. These brothers were planning a major attack. Ifran had managed to get close. He'd managed to give them the impression that he would help, and be a part of it.'

'These brothers have a name?' asked Woodman.

'Yeah,' sighed Romanelli. 'Barkat and Zabir Alami.' He paused for a beat, he seemed to be weighing something up. After a moment, he added: 'They're the guys with Ifran now. I believe the police have just released the names.'

'Fuck,' said Woodman.

Scamarcio wanted to ask why Romanelli hadn't mentioned this before.

'So, you were running this guy, and he was making progress ...' coaxed Woodman.

'And then he skipped out.'

'You lost contact?'

'We had no idea where he was. When I left the agency, Scalisi was still looking — and looking hard. I heard he spent a fortune — left no stone unturned.'

Woodman whistled softly. 'And then Ifran shows up today.'

'Yes. As for the Chechen, that's anybody's guess ...'

'What?' asked Woodman, looking blank.

'The Chechen,' Romanelli angled his head forward, as if Woodman was being slow.

'Sorry, I don't follow ...'

Both turned to look at Scamarcio. 'I haven't gone into it. I didn't want to confuse things for Mr Woodman.' In reality, because he still wasn't clear on the Chechen's role, Scamarcio knew that any discussion would slow them down.

'I'm sure I can handle it,' said Woodman, sounding peeved.

'Can we just leave the Chechen for a later date?' Scamarcio said. 'You'll get the details, I promise. We just need to prioritise.'

'I don't think you're prioritising correctly,' said Romanelli. 'The Chechen was what got you into this mess.'

'What do you mean?' Woodman's eyes clouded with mistrust.

'The DVD that Detective Scamarcio retrieved showed a Chechen man striking some kind of deal with Ifran, probably to supply arms. Ifran wanted Scamarcio to find the DVD; ergo, he wanted Scamarcio to know about the Chechen. I believe Ifran could have been using the Chechen to try to blackmail Colonel Scalisi.'

Once again, Scamarcio tried to remember when he'd mentioned the DVD to Federico or Romanelli. Regardless of how he'd actually come by the knowledge, Scamarcio didn't understand why Romanelli was now sharing this info so freely. Then Woodman surprised him by saying, 'Hmm, that all sounds interesting, but the detective was right — it's probably too complicated for us. It's more the kind of thing a broadsheet would handle, or our special investigations division.' But then after a moment he asked, 'What do we know about this Chechen?'

'Very little,' said Scamarcio. Thankfully, this time, neither Romanelli nor Federico offered an opinion.

'So, we have no idea how he fits into the picture — who he was working for?' pushed Woodman.

'My guess would be organised crime,' said Scamarcio, grateful that Basile couldn't follow. 'They have been known to supply arms to terrorists.'

'But that doesn't explain why the boy wanted to alert you to his existence,' insisted Woodman.

Scamarcio held his palms open in defeat. 'Like I told you, it's a mystery.'

21

I REMEMBER THE MOMENT *he finally won. We'd been sitting in the gardens of Villa Torlonia as the sun was starting to dip, and the heat was beginning to fade. He'd been telling me about the dead and the wounded: the children he'd helped pull from the rubble; the time he'd cried when they'd found a baby still breathing. There was something in his eyes that told me this was for real, that he wasn't just spinning me a yarn.*

After that, it all made sense — every last part of it.

'I'm going to step outside to make this call,' said Woodman. 'I need to concentrate.'

'You're ringing your bosses?' asked Scamarcio.

'You said it — we're running out of time.'

'Don't mention me, or the police will be all over us.'

'Do I look stupid?'

'OK,' sighed Scamarcio. 'But make it quick. We've been here too long.'

'Five minutes,' snapped Woodman.

Through the glass, they watched him pacing the pavement, one long arm raised, his head nodding from side to side as he spoke. After a while, he started opening his mouth wider and swinging his arm higher, and then he'd turned towards the glass and was kicking the wall below with his big sturdy boot, his red face drawn tight with fury. Scamarcio swore — the last thing they needed was to draw attention. Woodman moved from the window and resumed pacing, his arm pushing up through the air again, his palm flicking at nothing as if he was batting the whole idea away, sending it into the long grass. Scamarcio swallowed.

The producer finally ceased his circuit and lowered his mobile. He tapped the screen, then just stood staring at it, as if he'd forgotten its purpose. But when he finally looked up, he was smiling.

'What the fuck?' whispered Romanelli. Scamarcio felt an unwelcome buzz of anxiety.

Woodman strutted back in like a prize cock, ordered something from the bar, and then threw himself down in his chair.

'So?' asked Scamarcio. Even Basile had gone quite still.

'There's nothing like an ex-wife to give you good advice,' said Woodman.

'What?'

The American smiled again. He had a wide surfer smile — it fitted perfectly into his chiselled chin. Scamarcio guessed that he probably didn't have too much trouble finding women — maybe that's what had killed his marriage.

'My ex-wife used to be a news editor at the network. I just ran the whole thing past her,' said Woodman as if all this were perfectly reasonable.

'You did what?'

The producer just shrugged.

'Weren't you supposed to call your bosses?' asked Scamarcio quietly, his anger a rising tide.

'And risk falling at the first hurdle?'

'What did your ex-wife have to say?' The tide was almost at the shore — it was about to break.

'She says there's no fucking way they'll let this run. I'll need to strike out on my own.'

'On your own?' Scamarcio's hand was twitching; he was about to throttle him.

'I'll tell them I've got an exclusive on something else — something innocuous like "head of police" or "counterespionage" — insider insights into the ongoing operation, et cetera, et cetera. I'll get the live link all set up, and then I'll go in. She thinks they won't kill it immediately — they'll be too freaked out, perhaps even too curious to see how it plays out.'

'And if they shut it down once Ifran starts speaking?'

'They may, they may not — they'll have been caught off guard, they'll be running around like chickens with their heads cut off. It might give us some time to play with.'

'You could lose your job.'

'Or I could become the most lauded producer in the history of TV news. I'll take my chances.'

'Can you trust your ex-wife not to tell anyone?' asked Scamarcio.

Woodman puffed out his cheeks. 'She's one of the few people I *can* trust.'

Romanelli sniffed loudly and shook his head. In Italian, he muttered, 'This is all very nice, but you're forgetting your main problem — how are you going to get back in there?'

Nino Basile surprised them all by saying, 'I have an idea.'

Scamarcio ushered them out of the café. He wanted to find a quieter place to sound out the crime boss.

When they'd filed into an empty car park at the back of a Standa minimarket, Basile took him aside and whispered, 'If I do this, I'll need to see some very solid returns. You really need to get that.'

Scamarcio rolled his eyes. 'I grew up in the life, Nino. I get it.'

'Good.'

Basile grabbed him by the arm and almost pushed him back to the others. Scamarcio did not enjoy the feel of his grip.

The crime boss coughed, then said, 'If there was an explosion, we could distract them long enough to get inside.'

'An explosion?' Scamarcio didn't like the sound of it already.

'They'd be herding everyone back; it wouldn't work,' countered Romanelli.

'Where are the negotiators?' asked Basile.

'In a van to the right of the café — a few metres down,' said Scamarcio impatiently. He wanted to shift the discussion on to something more sensible.

'We rig it there — all eyes will switch to the van. There'll be a few moments of opportunity,' said Basile, as if all this was completely reasonable.

'The area is crawling with cops and special forces,' said Scamarcio, his voice becoming shrill. 'They'll have their eyes locked on that café. They'll have been trained *not* to be distracted by anything. They know all about the danger of diversions — it's textbook.'

Basile held his palms open as if to say, *I was only trying.*

Romanelli said, 'You may be overestimating them, Scamarcio — they'll be tired and they'll be jumpy. The last twenty-four hours have been unprecedented. I wouldn't dismiss Mr Basile's idea out of hand.'

'Are you along for the ride?' asked Scamarcio, sounding colder than he'd intended.

'I'm curious.'

Scamarcio's mind was already turning on something else. 'How the hell are you going to rig the van, Basile? It will be a secure zone — there's no way you'll be able to get close enough.'

'There might be,' said Nino. 'While you lot were wetting your pants about a bunch of stuffed shirts in New York, I was trying to work out how to do the job. Who gives a shit if somebody's boss says yay or nay if you can't even get inside?'

'Quite,' said Romanelli.

'My boys have been watching that van. They get deliveries, take outs — they're human, they've got to eat. The food is coming from a restaurant up the road — Bistro Colosseo. It's brought by delivery boys on Vespas. The Vespas pass a certain junction. My guys can be waiting there to intercept them and make sure the breakfast brioche arrive nice and *hot*.'

'Hot?' Scamarcio felt sick.

'There's a gel we can use. When it reacts with a lighter, it will trigger a blast that blows your balls off,' said Basile with a smirk. Scamarcio imagined him lighting firecrackers as a boy; terrorising the neighbourhood.

'They'll search your guy,' he sighed.

'They won't check the brioche though. And according to my boys, they're getting blasé. They patted down the delivery guys the first couple of times, but now they just wave them in. As your associate says — they're tired. This siege has gone on too long.'

'Are you talking about triacetone — peroxide-based?' asked Romanelli.

'Yep,' said Basile, still looking pleased with himself.

'It's very difficult to create a stable bomb with TATP, and it's even harder to detonate.' Romanelli looked both concerned and intrigued. 'You shouldn't be playing with that stuff.'

'We're not amateurs, we know what we're doing,' said Basile in a tone that didn't invite further question.

Romanelli shook his head. 'No, it's crazy — you can't use it.'

'Why the fuck not?' Basile stepped closer, ready to get right in his face.

Romanelli didn't blink. 'Because it will end in disaster and create more problems than it solves. We need something smaller.' He paused. 'What about smoke grenades? We smoke them out, but nobody dies.'

'How the fuck am I going to get a grenade inside a brioche?'
Basile opened his hands and swung them aloft.

'What if I flash them my ex-Intel credentials — tell them
I have info relating to Scamarcio and that there's imminent
danger,' tried Romanelli.

'Won't they search you before they let you inside?' countered
Basile.

'If I say that there's a bomb threat — that I must speak to the
negotiators, there might be a chance.'

Basile pouted like a child. 'The TATP still gets my vote.'

'It'll turn your guy to mush before he even reaches the van,'
said Romanelli, deadpan.

Scamarcio glanced at his watch and frowned. 'Let's go with
Romanelli.' Then, as an afterthought: 'How do we get hold of
the grenades?'

Basile frowned at him as if he were simple. 'Not a problem,
Scamarcio.'

Scamarcio thought about the last time he'd approached the café.
'I don't think I should try to get back there until the last minute,
when you've got your crew in place, and Romanelli is ready,' he
said to Woodman as they left the car park.

Woodman drew out his top lip with his finger. 'How are you
even going to make it past the crowds? There are a lot of people,
and more will be gathering now it's light.'

'Last time I came close, I was spotted after a minute.'

'I didn't know you'd already made an attempt ...'

'It's a long story.'

'Hmm,' Woodman pinched his nose. He pulled out his
mobile and started dialling. After a moment, he said, 'Can you
leave the location? Come up to Via ...?' He turned to Scamarcio
for the name.

'Leonina.'

Woodman repeated it.

'Tell them to head up Via Cardello if they can, and then swing a right onto Via Madonna dei Monti — Leonina is at the end,' said Scamarcio.

Woodman passed it on. 'I know this sounds weird, but can you bring Jake's cap and sunglasses, a press ID, and a spare D5? I'll explain later.' He paused. 'Well, yeah, put a card in, but we won't be using it until we're back.' He stopped, then added, 'That will all become clear.'

Romanelli, Federico, and Basile were a few metres up ahead, walking briskly. The former spooks seemed to have found common ground with the head of organised crime in Torpignattara.

'My assistant will be here soon,' said Woodman. 'What should we do about those three?' He gestured ahead. 'Will they want to hang out? Do we want them to?'

'No,' said Scamarcio. He began to head over to the group, but stopped and bent down to rub his right heel. The canvas of his shoe was starting to dig uncomfortably into his skin, or maybe it was his heel that was the problem. He wondered if he'd sustained some kind of injury that was only now making itself known. It seemed odd that it would be the shoe, as they'd always been so comfortable. He finished adjusting the heel and walked on, but the pain persisted. He tried to ignore it. He tapped Basile on the shoulder, and he swung round, his street-smart instincts priming him for a fight.

'Do you want to peel off? Woodman and I can go on ahead.'

'Yeah, I need to sort a few things. We'll see you at the press pen.'

'You taking these two?' asked Scamarcio.

'They're strategists,' said Basile, chewing on a piece of gum. 'We're going to put our heads together — there are variables to consider. We'll call the Yank when we're in proximity.'

The language was new, and Scamarcio wondered if it was for Romanelli's benefit. The others all exchanged numbers, and Scamarcio made sure he memorised Basile's. The crime boss started walking away with the others, then turned back to Scamarcio and rubbed his thumb and first finger together, in case Scamarcio had forgotten the terms of their deal. Scamarcio just shook his head.

When the three of them were distant specks, a pretty young woman rounded the corner of Via Madonna dei Monti.

'Ah, great,' said Woodman.

The woman was about thirty, with long dark hair the colour of coal, and huge blue eyes. She was carrying a silver case.

'Now, Clare,' said Woodman, as she drew level. He placed both hands on her shoulders and looked into her eyes. As a gesture, it seemed far too intimate for a working relationship, thought Scamarcio.

'I need you *not* to freak out,' said Woodman.

'Why should I freak out?'

'When I introduce you to this gentleman, I need you to stay calm, stay focused. And then I need you to transmit that calm to the crew. I don't want any of the vipers in the pit cottoning on to what we've got, which, by the way, is a massive exclusive — probably *the* exclusive of your career.'

'Paul, what the fuck?' She had a soft, very controlled New York accent. It could have been the voice of an actress.

'Remember, Clare, no freaking now.'

She frowned. Woodman gestured to the man beside him.

'Clare, this is Detective Scamarcio — the policeman who met the terrorists yesterday morning.'

Clare remained quite still. She didn't blink, she didn't open her mouth, she didn't adjust her hair; her hands stayed by her side, one gripping the silver case. After a couple of moments studying Scamarcio, she turned to Woodman and asked, quite calmly, 'Paul, are you out of your fucking mind?'

Woodman shook his head quickly. 'If you want to make it, you're going to have to learn to take risks, Clare.'

'The police are looking for him, Paul. It's our obligation to hand him in.'

'Clare,' said Woodman, his voice rising. 'Who do you work for? The world's third-largest news network, or the fucking cops?' Woodman sounded like the one who needed to stay calm, thought Scamarcio.

'Fuck you,' hissed Clare, and bit her bottom lip.

'So, are you with me or not? I need you on the same page. This is the biggest opportunity of our careers — don't blow it for all of us.'

After a long time staring at the pavement, she finally looked up. 'OK. I'll indulge you on this one, but I really can't speak for the rest of the team.'

'Indulge me? I'm handing you a freakin' golden ticket here.'

She said nothing.

'Clare — everyone has to be in agreement, or this will end in disaster. Help me make the others see sense. I need to know that you'll try.'

Scamarcio thought Woodman was starting to sound a little crazed.

'I'm guessing the hat and glasses are for him,' said Clare flatly, pulling them from her pocket and handing them over.

Scamarcio thanked her and stepped over to a covered doorway, checking first that there were no street cameras nearby. The cap was a military green with a wide brim and small air holes, and the sunglasses were silver-tinted Aviators. He removed his old pair along with the baseball cap, and stuffed them in his pocket. He looked back at Woodman and his assistant: a terse silence seemed to have descended. Scamarcio didn't like the friction — it felt dangerous. But on the other hand, he was out of options.

They began making their way down Via del Cardello, back towards the Colosseum. Scamarcio carried the silver case, which was lighter than he'd expected. Soon, he saw the backs of the crowds penned in behind the cordon, their T-shirts damp; their hair slick. It had to be at least twenty-five degrees already. There was a strange emptiness about the scene, and it took him a moment to understand: there was no birdsong, he realised. All the birds had fled.

Woodman headed right, where a row of cameramen were standing, their reporters stationed in a line as they recorded pieces to camera. The sky was brightening, but the reporters and their teams were still bathed in the artificial glow of huge lights, their generators whirring and pumping out unwelcome heat.

The press was held back behind its own cordon, and before Woodman could get any closer a policeman asked for ID. The producer showed him his badge, and then gestured to Clare and Scamarcio. Scamarcio had been ready to take out the ID Clare had provided, but the police officer just waved them on behind Woodman. *Sloppy indeed …*

Once inside the pen, they were just fifty metres or so away from the negotiators' van. It was hard to see it through the throng, but Scamarcio reckoned that if he made his way to the end of the line, he'd have a clearer view. Woodman had stopped in front of a strong-boned blonde who was talking into the camera. From one look at her, Scamarcio guessed she'd be called Gretchen or Madchen or one of those Minnesota Dutch names. Woodman tapped him on the shoulder. 'This is us,' he whispered, as if Scamarcio couldn't work that out for himself.

When the woman had finished, and a young man had handed her a plastic cup of something, Scamarcio asked, 'Is there any chance we can all move from here?'

'Not in hell,' said Woodman. 'Why?'

'I can't see the van,' said Scamarcio. 'We need to get closer.'

'These are prized positions,' said Woodman. 'We give this up, we might not get another. We'll have to take it in turns to surveil the van. Didn't Basile say he'd call once they were near?'

'Hmm,' said Scamarcio. 'Do you have a cell phone signal?'

Woodman pulled his phone from his pocket and frowned. 'Yes. Why wouldn't I?'

'Sometimes they're scrambled in emergency situations.'

'Nah, the authorities need to communicate with the outside world just like the rest of us. They'll keep it running.'

Scamarcio said nothing, knowing Woodman was wrong.

'I need to have a word with the team before I introduce you,' said the producer. 'Can you give us five minutes?'

Scamarcio nodded and walked off behind the cameramen towards the end of the press line. He took in six policemen standing guard outside the negotiators' van. He hadn't remembered seeing that many this morning. They were all armed with the standard Heckler & Koch MP5 submachine guns, and their feet were set wide, ready for trouble. Quite how Romanelli was going to get past all that, Scamarcio had no idea. He hoped Romanelli's intelligence credentials would pull some weight, but much depended on who was in charge. He wondered whether Scalisi would be inside the van now.

Scamarcio studied the scene for a few seconds more and was about to turn, when he spotted five snipers on the roof of the building next door to the café. Some had balaclavas and red patches on their jacket sleeves, which told him that they were from the elite SWAT unit of the anti-terror police — the NOCS, or Nucleo Operativo Centrale di Sicurezza. The NOCS were trained in high altitude military parachuting, bomb disposal, and combat shooting, and considered themselves to be the best of the best. They probably were, figured Scamarcio.

He counted two at the front of the building facing the street and one off to the right. They weren't in sniper positions, but it did seem as if they were preparing for something: one was talking into his headset, while the other two scanned the crowds below, guns at the ready. It didn't really make sense for them to be up there — they had no direct view of the café. Then Scamarcio closed his eyes and took a breath. But of course it *did* make sense if they were about to storm the place. He looked for ropes and abseiling gear, but it was impossible to see properly as the lip of the roof was in the way.

He threw one last look at the van and then hurried back to Woodman, his gut churning. The snipers were not good news and just added to his anxiety about the approaching deadline.

When Scamarcio reached the crew, the rugged cameraman took off his cap, which seemed identical to the one Scamarcio was wearing, scratched his grey head, and looked at him hard. The man seemed more perplexed than anything else.

'I've told them not to greet you,' said Woodman. 'The good news is that we're all in agreement: we'll do this thing. For the moment though, you're the camera assistant, so you'll be passing Jake whatever he needs.'

Scamarcio nodded, not really feeling the consensus.

'OK then, back to work,' said Woodman, his eyes dancing.

Scamarcio scanned their faces. The good-looking reporter didn't seem able to take her eyes off him, and this bothered him. He hoped Woodman would say something. Clare seemed to be on the telephone to their office and kept saying 'yes' and 'no', and glancing furtively in his direction. He could hear the crackle of comms coming from the cameraman's headset — someone was counting down from one hundred. The reporter took another quick sip from the plastic cup, then checked her make-up in a small mirror, which she stowed in her handbag.

The cameraman replaced his headset and said, 'OK, Anneliese, thirty.'

They all consulted a small TV monitor on the ground, which showed a head-and-shoulders shot of the reporter on the left of the screen and the studio anchor on the right.

After a few moments, Woodman said: 'Fifteen.'

The presenter readjusted a wire behind her ear, then followed Woodman's hand as he counted down the final seconds. From the small monitor, Scamarcio heard a male voice in the studio say, 'Anneliese van Buren is reporting from the café near the Colosseum. Anneliese, have there been any new developments at this hour?'

'Well, Mason, right now the authorities are not saying much. The terrorists are still in the café behind me, where they're holding fifteen hostages. We have not heard any gunfire and we're certainly hoping this will remain the case. There has, however, been increased activity off to my left, where SWAT teams appear to be mustering. It's possible they're considering storming the building, given so many hours have now passed. From where I'm standing, it certainly does look as if some kind of plan is being put into effect.'

Scamarcio wondered how she could see anything from where she was standing.

'Anneliese, can you tell us exactly what you've witnessed in the last few minutes?' asked the studio anchor.

'I've seen a reinforcement of heavily armed police arriving, along with additional emergency vehicles. This has been in course for fifteen minutes or so.'

'Right, Anneliese — this sounds significant. We'll keep our eyes on developments there,' said the anchor. 'But for now, we'll cross over to our correspondent at the Spanish Steps ...' Woodman killed the sound and said, 'Clare, get back to the muster point and see what's happening.'

She hurried off. Woodman turned the audio on the monitor back up, but Scamarcio was having trouble making out the words above the cacophony of different languages being spoken all around him.

'I'm going to head back towards the van,' he said to Woodman. The producer pulled out his phone and frowned. 'Nothing from Basile.'

'OK.'

When he reached the end of the line, Scamarcio saw that there were now eight police outside the van and ten snipers on the roof. The reporter had been right — something was about to go down. He glanced at his watch. There was now less than ten minutes left till 9.00 a.m. His heart lurched as he prayed that Basile and Romanelli would show soon. If the SWATs were about to go in, it was all over. He'd never reach Ifran.

Scamarcio was about to head back to Woodman when he felt as if he was being observed. He swung around, but couldn't spot anyone looking at him. Then, out of the corner of his vision he saw someone wave, and when he glanced left, there was Basile, looking relaxed. The crime boss quickly pulled down the skin below his eye with his index finger to indicate cunning. Then he inclined his head to the right.

Scamarcio looked and saw Romanelli approach one of the policemen standing furthest from the van.

Why the fuck didn't they call first?

Romanelli had pulled out a card and was showing it to the officer. The policeman turned it over, and then said a few words into his radio. After ten seconds or so, a figure emerged from the back of the van. Scamarcio recognised him as Deputy Chief of Police Leopardi.

Leopardi shook hands with Romanelli, taking him by the elbow in a way that suggested they'd met before. Romanelli spoke, Leopardi listened, a hand at his mouth. But after a few moments he began rubbing beneath his ear, and Scamarcio sensed that Romanelli was losing the argument. Leopardi tilted his head and opened his palms in a 'I'm sorry, but there's nothing I can do' gesture.

Scamarcio bit down on a thumbnail as he watched their one final chance slip away, but then something Romanelli said seemed to change the mood, and Leopardi began to nod, curious now. He stopped, and steepled both hands together at his mouth. Romanelli said a few more words, and then they were both heading towards the van. The deal, it seemed, had been sealed.

Scamarcio was about to hurry back to Woodman when a roar of air lifted him from the pavement and hurled him hard against a car. His arms flailed as he tried to protect his mouth and nose from a searing heat. The heat was followed by a burst of light so bright that it felt as if his eyes were burning inside his skull, and his lungs were melting. There was a ringing in his ears, and a broken hammering in his chest, and all around him he heard people screaming and coughing.

All he could think at that moment was that the explosion was too big and too soon. Basile's smoke grenade was meant to cause a distraction and be let off once Romanelli was *inside* the van, but Romanelli hadn't even made it to the door. He couldn't have.

Then, just seconds later, someone was seizing Scamarcio by the arms and hauling him up off the ground. He was being bumped along the pavement and pulled into a vehicle. But before he could reflect on the efficiency of the ambulance services, he was punched in the teeth, and a black sack was drawn over his head.

22

THE WATERS OF THE Tiber are black and fetid, and I think that if I were to jump in, some monster from the deep might seize me and drag me to the bottom. It's a welcome thought, this chance to drown my doubts, depart unnoticed.

When Scamarcio came to, he found himself in a dim room on a hard, narrow bed. The walls were bare, and there was only one meagre window directly below the ceiling to his right. It felt a long way from British hospitality.

He rubbed his bruised jaw and tried to wet his tongue. His stomach was sore, but not as if it had been punched — it felt more as if he'd eaten something rotten. He tried to straighten, but couldn't — the ache in his gut was too painful. He let out a moan, took a shallow breath, and looked down at his battered shoes. He was exhausted; he wanted this over with. He needed to find Fiammetta and hold her tight. Scalisi had been right: he was just an ordinary guy. This was too big for him to carry.

He heard a door scrape and looked up to see a thin brunette stride into the room. She was accompanied by a shorter muscular man with curly red hair. The woman looked as if she was in her fifties, the man about ten years younger.

The woman scratched at her neck, and then drew out a plastic chair from a table which had been pushed against the wall. She carried it over to the bed. The man remained standing a few feet behind, a lackey waiting for orders.

She took a seat and surveyed Scamarcio, hands folded in her lap, one long red nail tapping her other palm. 'You've caused us quite a lot of trouble, Mr Scamarcio.' She pronounced his name wrong, in the way so many Americans did, with the emphasis on the 'o'.

'That wasn't my intention.'

'Your intentions are irrelevant.' She sniffed. She had an angular, pinched face. Her nose was long and thin, and her chin jutted out. Her eyes, however, were wide and attractive. 'You need to give it up, Detective. You can't help Ifran, and you can't help his victims. It's time to leave it to the people who can.'

'The people who can don't seem to be doing much.'

'About that, you have no idea.'

'Who the fuck are you?'

She scratched at the corner of her lips 'It's not important.'

'I'd say it is, given that I've been dragged into all this against my will.'

'Bullshit. If you'd just shared your information with the authorities from the start you wouldn't be here.'

'I don't understand what it's got to do with the Americans. This is an Italian matter. Why am I being held in this ... cell?'

'It's not a cell.'

Scamarcio said nothing.

'We brought you here to try to make you see sense.'

'"Seeing sense" is giving up and walking away, I take it?'

'It is.'

'I'm not prepared to do that.' That wasn't exactly how he felt, but her arrogance was stoking a new fire in him.

'Why not? You've got a lot to live for.'

'Is that a threat?'

'No. Why did you read it that way?'

'I'm not going to go round in circles. I need to get back to that café by…' The last words vanished. He checked his watch, but it had stopped. He looked at the window, knowing already what he'd see. The glass framed a patch of deep blue; the milky early-morning light was long gone. But he couldn't think about defeat; he couldn't let it distract him. 'Why don't you want me to help Ifran, if it might bring a resolution?'

'We've got our own ways of resolving this. That boy has spun you a bullshit tale, and you've fallen for it hook, line, and sinker.'

'It's *not* bullshit.'

The woman leaned forward, her eyes thin slits in the dim light, the set of her features crueller, harsher now. 'You saw what Scalisi did to your girlfriend. I'd strongly advise you to butt the hell out — before it gets nasty. As far as he and his guys are concerned, your girl's a whore, so it'll be a free for all, believe me.'

She might have been a woman, but Scamarcio wanted to smash her head against the wall, break her jaw, strangle the life from her. But he said nothing and counted to ten: he had to keep ahead, stay sharp. It wouldn't help Fiammetta if he lost it.

'Just what are you so worried about?' he asked when he'd reached eight. 'You've gone to an awful lot of trouble to get me here — you could have just grabbed me off the street instead of letting all hell break loose. Why are you so desperate? Why are you sniffing around in something that has nothing to do with you?'

'That's myopic. Terrorism is a global threat. We cooperate with our allies when we can.'

Scamarcio held up a palm. 'Spare me the crap.'

He let his hand fall as he tried to ignore the burning in his gut. 'You got your precious Chechen back? I heard he'd been arrested. It must be nice to have him where you can see him.'

The woman just kept staring. It was as if a shutter had come down. But Scamarcio noticed the guy behind her scratch at his ear with his index finger, then shift the weight in his legs. It was a small gesture, but it was enough.

'We had an interesting conversation, me and your Chechen. I can't wait to tell my journo friends all about it.'

'You're finished,' the woman snarled. 'Your fuckwit girlfriend, too. And you know what? We'll let you watch. Her suffering will be the last thing you see.'

She sprang up, the chair teetering. Once she and the minion had left, Scamarcio realised that he felt properly sick. Two seconds later, he vomited.

He must have thrown up at least five times. There was nothing left in his stomach, but he was still convulsing and retching, his entire body in spasm.

As he lay prone, his semi-feverish mind kept turning on the same question: could the Chechen have links to both the Americans *and* Scalisi? Was Scalisi running him for them? But where did Ifran fit in? Had he come to understand the real interest groups in play? Had he wondered why the Chechen had been going so far as to supply arms? Maybe Ifran feared an illegal entrapment op, or something more toxic: that perhaps Scalisi and his US 'friends' had set the wheels in motion, and that they were working to ensure an attack?

But behind all this lay a wider question: Why had Ifran cut his ties with Scalisi? Was it possible that he'd reached a point where he no longer trusted his handler? The boy knew he was on his own and the only way to stop the madness was to pull the stunt at the café, draw Scamarcio into the fray, and turn the eyes of the world upon Scalisi. To Scamarcio, this theory had weight. Ifran was trying to blackmail the head of AISE into standing down the operation. He was sending a clear signal that he knew about the involvement of the Chechen, whatever that meant, and that it was time to pull the plug.

Why, then, hadn't the Americans and Scalisi resolved this? led Ifran and his associates out for a debrief, and then released all the hostages? Why instead did they seem intent on spending all their time hunting down Scamarcio, the innocent bystander? It came back around to the same thing: Scalisi and his US backers weren't interested in a resolution; they wanted these attacks at all costs. They wanted the story of the Chechen dead and buried along with the terrorists, and whatever hostages they may have taken along the way. The question was, Why?

Scamarcio retched again, and when he looked up, the woman was back and staring down at him, pitiless. 'You won't be feeling better any time soon.'

'What have you given me?'

She waved the question away and took a seat. She crossed her legs, and then, almost as an aside, said, 'Bendamustine Hydrochloride has a more permanent effect on a foetus, unfortunately.'

Scamarcio frowned, his head swimming. 'What?'

'Oh, didn't you know?' she asked, feigning surprise.

'Know what?'

She smoothed along the outline of her narrow top lip. 'Your girlfriend is expecting. Sorry, *was* expecting.'

Scamarcio bowed his head and retched again. When he'd got his breath back, he said, 'Spare me the amateur mind games. She's not.'

'She was about to tell you — I think she was waiting for the right time.'

Scamarcio tried to swallow, his tongue was bulky, and he couldn't get the saliva down. There was a new ringing in his ears, and his breath felt shallow. He turned hot, and then cold. Was that the big surprise Fiammetta had mentioned? He told himself it might all be coincidence; this woman was just bluffing. But when he looked into her eyes he saw an unmistakeable look of triumph that made him sweat. He retched again, then vomited bile — this time all over her leopard-print shoes.

Scamarcio couldn't be sure if minutes had passed or hours. He was running a high fever, and his thoughts were careering into each other, cancelling each other out, then fighting and coalescing to build frightening new realities. He was so thirsty he would have cut off a limb for water. There was a fire inside his chest — whatever he did, whatever position he took, he just couldn't cool down. His breaths were coming in quick, rapid bursts, and he couldn't even them out — the fever wouldn't let him.

Then — he didn't know how much later — he woke from a nightmare in which a baby had been crying. He hadn't been able to understand what was wrong until he'd realised that there were flames beneath its cot. But when he'd tried to run over to extinguish them, his legs had turned to stone.

Scamarcio looked up at the searing blue beyond the window. He felt cold and spent. He was too exhausted to care anymore, there was no discernible emotion. Had thousands died? Perhaps … But when he thought of Fiammetta, the panic started to build. He *had* to find her.

He shivered. His cotton jacket was stuck to his body — the damp from his shirt had soaked through and the wet fabric was now cooling against his skin. He pulled off the jacket, his arms heavy. As he tried to peel off the sleeve, his fingers passed over something smooth and hard. He felt around in his pockets, but they were empty. After a few moments searching, he realised that the mystery object was inside the lining. There must have been a rip in his pocket, and it had fallen through. He quickly found the tear and felt around inside the lining until his fingers grasped something cool and hard. When he pulled it out, he discovered his blue Bic lighter, glinting in the thin shaft of light from the window.

He sighed. His lighter was a fat lot of good without a fag to smoke. It felt like another cruel twist of fate, but he slipped it into his trouser pocket.

He rose shakily, his head swirling and his ribs aching, and walked towards the wall. When he touched it, the stone was slightly damp. He paced along the edge, tracing the contours, feeling for a break; somewhere a camera might be concealed, or a two-way mirror, but he found nothing. He glanced up at the ceiling, but it was bare. Where was he? It just seemed like a normal room. He walked over to the wooden door. It looked thick, but there was only one large bolt and no spy-hole.

For the lack of anything better to do, he hammered on the wood, then shouted 'Hey!' when no response came. He pushed himself against the door, but it wouldn't budge. 'Hey!' he yelled again, pounding the door with his fists, then immediately feeling weak.

He returned to the bed and flopped down. A few seconds later, a sharp angle of light cut through the room.

'Why the commotion?' said the woman. Her voice was exaggeratedly calm, as if she were making a huge effort to maintain her cool.

Scamarcio remained sprawled. Her heels clicked towards him. When she was standing very near and no more clicks followed, she whispered, 'I'm not in the mood.'

All at once, he jumped up and thrust an arm under her chin, blocking her throat. With his other hand, he pulled out the lighter and lit the flame, bringing it to her skin. 'Get off me! Get off me, you fuck!' she screamed.

He punched her in the stomach, then hit her across the jaw. She was now half-lying on the bed, arms splayed. He knew he should stop while he was still in control of his anger, but he also knew it wouldn't be enough to immobilise her. He tugged back her head and slammed it against the wall so she passed out. His rage was building too quickly. He gripped his own fist and ran for the door.

The makeshift cell gave onto another room, which was lined with shelves containing plastic binders and thick books that looked like manuals. There were maps on the walls and a few fluorescent safety vests hanging from hooks. A couple of desks stood in the corner, laden with computers and telephones.

He came out into a hallway where he saw more fluorescent vests and a row of hard hats tacked to the wall. Below them were sandbags. There was no sign of the ginger-haired guy. Scamarcio felt a current of warm air against his cheek and turned to see a door ajar further down the hallway to his left. As he approached, he caught the unmistakable scent of freshly cut grass and jasmine. But beneath it was a different, chemical smell — like petrol, but not quite. It was headier, more intense.

He opened the door, and his ears were immediately assaulted by a deafening boom. The air all around him was vibrating, humming. About thirty metres from where he was standing, two huge turbines were whirring: a Gulf Stream jet was pushing back from its stand, getting ready to taxi. It was being escorted by a small truck, two guys inside bobbing about like figurines. Scamarcio looked left, then right. There were two stationary planes to his right — small jets, not airliners. To his left, the concrete came to an end and a wide patch of mown grass took over. Terracotta flower pots bursting with geraniums marked the edges. Scamarcio's first thought was, *Private airfield*. His second was, *Run*.

He sprinted off across the grass, his legs already aching, and his lungs burning. Through the heat haze, he could see red brakelights passing behind the metal mesh of a fence some forty metres up ahead. There was shouting behind him, some kind of announcement on a loudspeaker, but he kept on running — he didn't dare look back.

As he neared the fence, he saw an entry gate with a sentry box. A car was at the barrier, getting ready to leave. The barrier was rising, the brakelights were dipping. Scamarcio ran as fast as his battered body would allow until he was through the barrier, the guard yelling at him to stop. He was almost on a road now, a dual carriageway, not a motorway — the traffic was moving fast, and there was very little verge. He kept running, horns blaring, then quickly fading. He noticed a truck in a lay-by some fifty metres ahead — it was heaving off, about to pull away. In an instant, he realised that this was it: his last hope.

His muscles were screaming, and his right shoe was cutting into his flesh as he ran. He cried out from the pain as he hoisted himself up onto the moving ledge of the truck door just in time — it had almost left the lay-by. He hammered on the glass, his palms slipping as he tried to grab the handle. The driver swung towards the window, alarmed. He was a big guy, his hands covered with huge rings. Scamarcio noticed a skull and crossbones.

'Open up,' he yelled. He knew that in his current state he looked less than trustworthy. But he kept pounding on the glass, refusing to give up.

23

THE DRIVER LOOKED PETRIFIED — his hand was still on the gear lever, and he made no sign of being about to release the window. Scamarcio feared that he was about to speed away and throw him to the ground. But if it had been him, he'd probably have done the same.

'Please, I'm Detective Scamarcio from the Flying Squad — open up. I can show you my credentials.'

As soon as he said it, the guy's eyes widened, and he took his hand off the gears. His fingers hovered over the central locking for what seemed like an eternity, then he suddenly seemed to make up his mind and pressed it. Scamarcio ran around the other side and jumped in.

'Where are we?'

'You don't know?'

'I wouldn't be asking otherwise.'

'This is the SS675.'

'That airfield?'

'Viterbo.'

'How far are we from Rome?'

'About an hour.'

'Can you get me to the city? I need to talk to my colleagues. I have no phone, no way to communicate.'

'They're saying those terrorists forced you into doing something bad.'

'Not true,' said Scamarcio. 'Please, can you take me?'

The guy just stared at him, confused now, as well as alarmed. 'I've just been through Calais. What, with the crisis there, and the chaos here ...' The words petered out. He kept staring at Scamarcio. 'My wife won't believe it.'

'Please?'

The driver just looked at him, dumbfounded, then shook his head and pushed the truck into gear. They juddered away. Scamarcio noticed that he seemed to be spending a long time checking his wing mirror. 'Everything OK?'

'No. There's someone in a jeep trying to flag us down.'

'Ignore them.'

The guy's gaze kept returning to the mirror. 'I don't believe this.'

'They still there?'

'Yes.'

Scamarcio waited ten seconds until he asked again.

'Hang on.' The driver lifted a walkie-talkie from the dashboard and said, 'Miki Three, do you read me?'

There was a crackle on the line, and then a big, deep voice said, 'What's up?'

'Can you get between me and that silver jeep in front of you? I'll explain later.'

'Sure,' said the other driver, his tone a question.

A few horns blared, then the guy turned from the mirror, his face pale.

'They've got jammed up in traffic.'

'Thanks,' said Scamarcio. He glanced at a digital display on the dashboard, which read 13:30. 'Is that the right time?' he asked.

'Yep,' said the guy, checking his mirror again.

'You got a phone?'

The guy frowned, but nodded towards a console below the dashboard.

Scamarcio took out the handset and dialled Basile.

'You're alive,' said the crime boss. He sounded more impressed than relieved.

'Were you and Romanelli hit?'

'We lost a few minutes — nothing serious.'

'What the fuck was it?'

'God knows, but it was professional. There were injured. Someone seems to have had the same idea about creating a distraction ...'

'Are you still near the site?'

'I was going to give you another half-hour before calling it a day. Your spook friends were prepared to leave it a little longer.'

'Has anyone been into the café?'

'No-one's been in; no-one's come out.'

'They didn't send in the SWATs?'

'After the bomb, it all went quiet. I reckon they were forced into a rethink.'

'Get Romanelli and Federico and tell them to meet me at Flying Squad HQ in an hour.'

'You wanna meet *there*?'

'I'm out of options.'

'You'll understand if I prefer to keep my distance.'

'Don't sweat it. Just get them there, then head back to the Colosseum. Oh, and bring me a spare cap and sunglasses.'

Basile sniffed. 'Right.'

'And a copy of the DVD.'

'Will that be all?'

The truck driver dropped him ten minutes away from Via San Vitale. He'd wanted to leave Scamarcio at Roma Ostia Station, but Scamarcio feared that the metro would be closed, and even if it was open the police would be a problem. There seemed to be more people on the streets now, and he wondered for a stupid moment if Basile had got it wrong — whether there had in fact been some kind of showdown or resolution.

Scamarcio turned into Via San Vitale and stopped. Parked at the kerb, just a few metres ahead, was a white van with its side door open. Leaning against it, his right arm gripping the roof, was Scalisi. His huge forehead was drawn, and the underarms of his shirt were soaked with sweat. Scamarcio was surprised to see him; somehow he'd expected the Americans would have bundled him off and contained him by now. Yet here he was, keen to welcome him back.

'Get in the van,' snapped the colonel. As he drew closer, Scamarcio noticed that Scalisi was quite pale, and that his eyes were rimmed red with tiredness. His breath stank, and Scamarcio thought he could detect his poison this time: whisky.

Scamarcio wanted to grab him by the neck, wring the truth about Fiammetta from him — but then he noticed an over-tanned and over-ripped musclehead jumping from the vehicle. He sprung onto the pavement, blocking Scamarcio's way. 'Get in the van,' he parroted.

Scamarcio ignored him and turned back to Scalisi. 'I've had it with you and your American pimps. Where's my girlfriend?'

Scalisi just shook his head.

'Spit it out, or I'll take this to my boss, and then his boss. After that, perhaps I'll have a word with the commissioner — send this right to the top.'

The musclehead shoved him, and Scamarcio lunged back. In an instant, the thug had grabbed him by the wrist, spun him around in a violent pirouette, and rammed a rock-hard forearm up against his windpipe. Scamarcio was struggling to breathe, but could do nothing to dislodge him. The guy's other hand quickly pinned back Scamarcio's remaining arm in a vice-like grip.

'You're coming with us,' panted the mutt.

The head of AISE rubbed tiredly at a patch of crepey skin

beneath his right eye. 'We need one final chat, Scamarcio. Then it will all be over.'

Scamarcio didn't like the emphasis he placed on 'over'. He considered his options. He couldn't try to swing back, elbow the meathead in the gut, because both his arms were trapped. Neither could he duck down and wriggle free — the meathead's grip was way too tight. He couldn't even kick back with his foot because the guy was right behind him, like they were dancing some creepy, straight-jacket tango. When it came to options, he didn't really have any. Where the hell were Basile and Romanelli?

'Into the van,' hissed the musclehead. Scamarcio caught a blast of Cool Water and an undercurrent of gum disease.

'What the fuck do you think you're doing?' boomed a voice from down the street. The meathead tightened his grip and turned, dragging Scamarcio around with him. Scamarcio was surprised to see Chief of Police Mancino standing stock-still a few metres away, as if he'd been frozen to the spot. He was flanked by two uniforms — legs apart, Berettas at the ready. The chief looked both shocked and furious.

'Leave it alone, Mancino,' cried Scalisi, his voice rising. 'Leave it *well* alone. This is a matter of state security.' He was almost screaming, and Scamarcio noticed a wave of red making its way up his neck.

'The hell it is. Let go of my detective — right this minute!'

'Let's see what the home secretary has to say about that.'

'Ring him,' shouted Mancino, stabbing a finger towards Scalisi. 'Ring him now!'

As he shakily extracted a mobile phone from his pocket, Scalisi wore the conflicted expression of someone whose bluff had been called. He began to tap a few digits, then seemed to think better of it.

'Call him!' yelled Mancino, now also red in the face.

Scalisi looked back at his phone, thought for a few seconds, and then resumed dialling. Scamarcio could hear the line ringing, and then a click, followed by a muffled greeting. The colonel introduced himself, then said: 'Can you get to Flying Squad HQ? We have Detective Scamarcio. We need your input.' The words were stilted.

Scamarcio caught another garbled sound before Scalisi cut the call. 'He'll be here as soon as he can,' he said, his eyes dead.

'Right, then, I suggest we all head inside and try to finally unravel this mess,' said Mancino. 'Get your monkey to release my detective.'

'Get your officers to lower their weapons.'

'You first!'

Scalisi grunted, then murmured something to the mutt that Scamarcio didn't catch. He heard a sharp intake of breath before he was reluctantly let go. The mutt was glowering and sweating like a disgruntled golem, but Scalisi dismissed him with a quick flick of the wrist. 'Take the van,' he muttered.

The thug ran around the vehicle, jumped behind the wheel, and sped off, leaving Scalisi on the pavement like a rowdy passenger who'd been booted from a taxi.

'Where's Fiammetta?' Scamarcio yelled, stepping closer. They were almost eyeball to eyeball. 'What have you done with her?'

He turned to Mancino. 'He took my girlfriend. They've beaten her up — told her all kinds of shit. I'm going out of my mind. Her health is at risk.' He didn't want to mention the pregnancy. 'Please, Chief, make him tell us where she is. It's unconstitutional. She's being held illegally.'

Mancino just looked at him blankly and said, 'Come inside, and we'll resolve this. This fiasco should never have been allowed to escalate.' It was clear that the dig was intended as much for Scamarcio as it was for Scalisi.

Mancino said nothing more and headed down the street towards HQ, his two officers tightly in step. Scamarcio shuffled behind them, occasionally looking back at Scalisi to check he was following. The spy chief had stopped and seemed to be trying to work out what to do. He was watching Mancino's retreating frame as if he couldn't make up his mind whether to run for it or face the home secretary.

Just as Mancino reached the steps of HQ, Basile drove up in a battered green Fiat and deposited Romanelli and Federico on the pavement. The chief of police scrutinised the driver of the Fiat for a long moment, then shook his head, apparently convinced his eyes were playing tricks. Then Mancino looked at Romanelli as if he seemed familiar, but he couldn't quite place him. The chief ran a tired hand through his hair and continued on inside.

'They're wheeling out the big guns,' said Romanelli, watching Mancino as he disappeared through the doorway. 'You want us there for the debrief?'

'Might be useful,' said Scamarcio.

'Federico's squeamish.'

'Why?' asked Scamarcio, turning to the old man.

'It's a tangled tale. Romanelli will see you right.' He paused. 'Are you still planning to set something in motion?'

'Possibly.'

'If you need me, I'll be near the café with Woodman.' He headed back to the car. He had been about to get in when he patted his pocket. 'I almost forgot — here's one of the copies. Oh yeah, and this ...' He handed Scamarcio the DVD and a leather beret and Ray-Bans.

'It's July ...' moaned Scamarcio.

'I believe that's crime-boss chic year-round.'

Federico got back into the waiting Fiat with Basile, and they sped away.

Scamarcio wanted to ask Romanelli what was eating his friend, but instinct told him to let it lie. He glanced behind him to check on Scalisi, but he'd disappeared.

'Fuck,' hissed Scamarcio. He could guess what Scalisi was thinking: AISE was the law; he shouldn't have to answer to the police. How the hell was Scamarcio going to find Fiammetta now? Would Mancino have any idea?

He took a breath and headed inside with Romanelli.

When they reached the squad room, the few detectives who were in stared at him as if he were a ghost. 'What the fuck?' whispered one as he passed.

Another, who Scamarcio had never liked, started shaking his head. He pushed his trendy glasses higher up his nose and said, 'Scamarcio, as a friend I should warn you that you are now officially in deep, deep shit.'

'Thanks for the searing insight.'

'Fine, but did you know that Mancino's just stormed past?' he pointed to Garramone's office. 'He looked like he just caught his best friend screwing his wife.'

Scamarcio rolled his eyes as if to say 'heard it all before', and headed for the boss's door. He knocked, and Garramone barked, 'Enter.' Just from that one word, Scamarcio knew he was furious.

Scamarcio stepped inside, followed by Romanelli. Garramone gave them a look he usually reserved for career criminals and said, 'This had better be good, Scamarcio. This had better be fucking excellent.'

Uninvited, Scamarcio pulled out a chair opposite the chief's desk, which looked like a hurricane had blown through it. He gestured to Romanelli to take a seat to his right. The place to the left was already occupied by a puce-coloured Mancino.

'This is Alessandro Romanelli,' said Scamarcio. 'Until recently, he worked for AISE. I've brought him with me to help explain what is going on — what I've been doing these past hours.'

He saw a look of recognition cross Chief Mancino's face.

'*These past hours?*' Garramone leaned forward, resting his forearms on a sea of crumpled and coffee-stained papers. 'Scamarcio, you've been gone since nine yesterday morning. The whole country has been looking for you!'

'That's what I'm here to explain.'

'Where's Colonel Scalisi?' asked Chief Mancino.

'He's scarpered.'

'What?' frowned Mancino.

'Surely you didn't expect him to stay?'

'Scamarcio, remember that Chief Mancino is your superior,' muttered Garramone.

Scamarcio closed his eyes, then quickly opened them. He didn't have time for irrelevancies. 'You'll understand when I talk you through it.'

'So get on with it!' shouted Garramone.

'Shouldn't we wait for the home secretary?' asked Scamarcio.

'What the fuck has he got to do with it?!' Garramone was still yelling.

'Sorry, I hadn't got around to explaining,' said Mancino. 'I've called him in. He should be here shortly.'

'Unless Scalisi has rung him to cancel it,' offered Scamarcio.

Mancino grimaced at the thought, then seemed to have a change of heart and pulled out his mobile. 'Yes, sorry, Massimo,' he said after a few moments. 'I just wanted to check you were on your way. Ah, OK, that's great.' Mancino cut the call. 'He's pulling up.'

'I don't get why he's come,' said Garramone, still furious. 'He has enough on his plate.'

'There are big issues here,' said Mancino, seemingly about to say more, then thinking better of it.

A couple of minutes later, there was a knock at the door, and Garramone rose to open it himself.

Scamarcio caught a glimpse of one of the detectives outside, gaping at the famous politician and his entourage. Scamarcio tapped the side of his nose in a 'mind your own business' gesture. Why he was bothering to rile him, he didn't know, but it did give him some small satisfaction when the guy flipped him the bird.

The home secretary was hovering in the doorway, shaking first Garramone's, then Mancino's hand. Scamarcio had never met him before, and was surprised to see that he was much taller than he appeared on TV. Home Secretary Massimo Costantini cut an impressive figure, with his wavy, silver hair, piercing blue eyes, and tanned skin. He was wearing a sharp blue suit that could have been Armani, and a crisp light-blue silk tie against a brilliant white shirt. For a man who was probably experiencing one of his most stressful days in the job, he was impeccably turned out.

Costantini mouthed 'five minutes' to a couple of preppy young flunkeys, and they hung back, the detectives in the bearpit throwing them semi-hostile glances.

Costantini turned from the handshakes to survey Scamarcio. 'So, Detective, here you are finally — and apparently with quite a story to tell. We're all very interested in hearing it, although I'm sure I speak for all of us when I say we *really* wish you'd chosen to share it earlier.' The tone was ice, and Costantini's eyes were hard with a rage he was making no effort to conceal. Scamarcio wondered if there was any hope of reaching him — persuading him that he'd acted, or at least tried to act, for the best.

Chief Mancino vacated the chair to Scamarcio's left, waving the home secretary over, but Garramone said, 'Let's take the table.' He motioned them over to a mahogany conference table at the back of the room. It was surrounded by new high-backed chairs that Scamarcio didn't remember seeing before. His neck and shoulders were killing him, and he thought the new chairs looked highly uncomfortable.

'Where's Scalisi?' asked the home secretary.

'Long story,' said Scamarcio, 'but I think once you've heard what I've got to say, it might become a little clearer.'

When they were all seated, and Costantini had pulled a notepad and pen from his Louis Vuitton briefcase, he said, 'Can we have the news on?'

Garramone nodded and stood up to swing around the small screen on the corner of his desk. He seemed to be having some difficulty operating the remote, and Scamarcio had to help him. He wondered why he hadn't had the TV playing already. Maybe he could no longer watch.

The cameras were still focused on the bar near the Colosseum. The packs of emergency crews had swelled yet again, and the intense sunlight was bouncing off the windows of the café, making it hard to see anything through the small strip of glass not covered by the flags. Scamarcio was relieved that Ifran was still in there, but worried about the state of the hostages. Were they injured? Were they even alive? What was going on in the boy's head? Did Ifran understand that Scamarcio was still trying to meet his demands, or did he think it was all over? Scamarcio didn't really want to ask the question, but he forced himself: 'Has there been any shooting at the café?'

The home secretary frowned as if just the sight of him was somehow distasteful. 'No, not as far as we know. We haven't heard anything, and we have laser microphones trained in all directions. Ifran and his men seem to be biding their time. For what, we do not know ...' He said it like he was expecting Scamarcio to provide the answer.

'And the other locations? Are the hostages still in there?'

'Yes.'

'And the situation with all of them is unchanged?'

'As far as we know, yes.'

Scamarcio suddenly felt a huge wave of gratitude towards Vincenzo Guerra for his role in getting the message through.

Costantini seemed to pick up on his relief and said quickly, 'We have some wounded. Luckily, there's a doctor caught up in the McDonald's siege, and he's doing the best he can. But the injured have been inside a long time. We must bring all of them out alive — they can't become fatalities.'

Costantini pursed his lips and looked down, as if he couldn't face their stares.

'OK,' said Scamarcio like a man who knew his time was up. He wanted to ask them about Fiammetta, get things moving, but he knew they'd need his story first. 'I'll start at the beginning ...'

'That would make sense,' sneered Costantini.

Scamarcio quickly talked them through it, from the meeting at the café, to the drive with Scalisi, to the journey through Ostia and the discovery of the DVD. He realised that the whole thing sounded like some peculiar dream, and he understood that if he were hearing this for the first time, he, too, would have trouble believing it. When he arrived at the part about Ifran's connection to Scalisi, Romanelli helpfully produced the surveillance photograph. The home secretary studied it, and then made a note. Scamarcio wondered what he had written: *1. Fire the Head of AISE*, hopefully. When Scamarcio had finished talking, Mancino said, 'Have you got the DVD?'

Scamarcio handed the disc over, and Garramone slipped it into his laptop.

Garramone pressed play, and the home secretary scratched his chin and frowned, as if he was watching a low-budget drama that failed to convince. After the second clip with the two girls stopped, Scamarcio drew their attention to the hidden audio.

Costantini made a few more notes on his pad and asked, 'So this guy agreeing to get them something — the man they appear to be discussing in the audio — who do we think he is?'

'Don't you know? I thought you were looking for him — that you'd arrested him?' asked Scamarcio, unbelieving.

Costantini just knotted his brows. When he turned to Mancino and Garramone, they looked equally blank.

'But there was a whole appeal on the news for him,' pushed Scamarcio.

Chief Mancino pinched his nose. 'That might have come from

the anti-terror squad, or Intel. Departments aren't coordinating well today. It's a lesson for the future.'

'But surely the home secretary would know!'

Scamarcio looked at Costantini, but he still seemed bemused.

'I'll chase it up,' was all he said. He glanced down at his notepad, and Scamarcio couldn't get any sense of whether he was lying or not.

Scamarcio tried to regain focus. He talked them through the theory he and Rigamonti had formed when they were out in Torpignattara — that the Chechen was in fact Intel's eyes and ears on the ground. Then he brought it all up to date with his encounter with the Americans. The home secretary paled, but said nothing.

'The thing to remember,' said Romanelli, speaking for the first time, 'is that Ifran was being run by Scalisi. It was his pet project, his bid for glory. Then Ifran comes to have doubts about the involvement of this Chechen and his possible links to Scalisi. From experience, I'd suggest that there *is* a US angle — they could well be behind this mystery Chechen.'

'But why does Ifran want us to look into it?' asked the home secretary.

'Because he's worried, and he didn't know who else to ask,' replied Romanelli. 'He signed up to fight terrorism, not to stoke it. And he no longer trusts his handler, Scalisi.'

'But what exactly has this Chechen done? He may have supplied arms, but we have no solid proof. We don't know where he is to ask him, and—'

'I just don't get it,' interrupted Scamarcio. 'The police were after the Chechen; they were all *over* him out in Torpignattara. But now you're telling me that you don't know who he is?'

The home secretary opened his palms. 'Detective, can't you just let it go? The last twenty-four hours have been unprecedented. We've been rounding up a lot of people. Maybe when I consult my paperwork I'll spot a match, but right now I don't have it.'

Mancino was still shaking his head. 'It's not come across my desk,' he said.

'Mine neither,' said Garramone.

Scamarcio wondered for a moment if they were all playing him for a fool.

'So,' said Costantini. 'Let's try to get this straight. We have this boy in the café who for some reason thinks you're the man to help him tell the world about the Chechen. But Ifran *didn't* tell you about his own connection to Colonel Scalisi — that's significant.'

'You think so?' asked Romanelli, clearly unimpressed. 'I think it just shows how isolated Ifran feels. He never expected Scamarcio to believe him, so he decided to let Scamarcio find out for himself.'

The home secretary displayed no discernable reaction. He finished scribbling something on his pad, then stared down at the ink, pen suspended in mid-air as if he were about to add more. 'Mr Romanelli, our paths have crossed, haven't they?'

'I wasn't sure you remembered.'

'It just took me some time to place you, that's all. How are you holding up?'

Scamarcio frowned. It was an odd choice of phrase.

'OK,' said Romanelli. 'I've changed my life somewhat.'

'I can understand that,' said the home secretary, scratching at an elbow and looking up finally. 'Mr Scamarcio, you're telling me the Americans kidnapped you, and that you were held at Viterbo?' He sounded as if his credibility was at breaking point.

Scamarcio wanted to know what the home secretary had meant by 'How are you holding up?' He looked at Romanelli, but the former spook gave nothing away. Scamarcio returned his attention to Costantini; he knew he was losing him, and there wasn't much time to win him back. 'I'm not making this up. They gave me something — I don't know what. It hit my stomach, made me vomit. They were trying to mess with my head. They said they'd harmed my partner, went so far as to suggest she was pregnant … that the foetus would be damaged.'

Garramone's forehead crumpled with concern. 'Is she?'

'I don't know,' said Scamarcio, his desperation clear. 'I've got to find her — I know Scalisi has her — or *had* her. They're trying to use her to get to me. It's their one bargaining chip.'

'Scamarcio,' sighed the home secretary. 'You must understand that all this is a diplomatic and interdepartmental nightmare, and so far, you haven't really given me anything concrete. The whole thing might be nothing more than some nutcase conspiracy theory, spawned by a troubled young lad in the throes of a mental breakdown. It's clear that Ifran has issues.'

'That DVD and the photo aren't concrete enough?'

'That DVD proves nothing until we locate this Chechen and find out who he's working for. The photo could have been doctored — we'll need to run tests.'

'Well, run them, and run them quick — Scalisi is involved in this, I'm sure.'

The home secretary took a long breath. 'That's quite an accusation.'

'I have to say, Sir,' said Romanelli, his tone placatory, 'quite a few people in AISE were worried about the colonel. They suspected that he may no longer have been working for the greater good. His behaviour had become quite odd.'

'Odd in what way?'

'Not sharing intelligence, suddenly losing assets — it deviated from the norm.'

'Don't you spies always keep things close to your chests?' persisted Costantini.

'To a certain extent. But there is a procedure to be followed, and over the last year or so, Scalisi wasn't following it. It raised concerns — and quite high up at that.'

'Why did nobody come to me about this?'

Romanelli scratched at the corner of his nose. 'I think there may have been a plan to approach you. I heard they were waiting to get some final pieces of evidence, nail their case shut. Then yesterday happened ...'

Why didn't he mention this before? Scamarcio wondered.

'This theory of Detective Scamarcio's is illogical,' said Costantini. 'How could Scalisi possibly benefit from an attack on home soil? It would make him look incompetent.'

Romanelli opened his mouth and scratched at his chin, his eyes narrowing as if he was struggling to disguise his surprise at the man's naivety. 'Not quite. It would make his rivals in AISI and the anti-terror police look incompetent. Him — not so much.'

'Perhaps,' sighed the home secretary, non-committal.

'And then there's the whole push for greater surveillance powers,' added Scamarcio. 'The British seem to think Scalisi and a few of his chums are keen on that.'

'Hmm,' murmured Costantini. 'There's been some pressure, but I wasn't aware Scalisi was behind it.'

'Means nothing,' said Romanelli.

The home secretary leaned back against his chair and sighed. He pushed both palms through his hair and said, 'What a clusterfuck. If it comes out Scalisi had links to Ifran ...' He let the sentence hang. Scamarcio knew what he was thinking. Would Costantini sweep all this aside to save his own skin, or was he bigger than that? How many of them were ever bigger than that?

The home secretary sighed again, then said, 'Here's what we'll do. We'll haul in Scalisi — get his side of the story.'

It wasn't exactly a breathtaking solution. 'And?' Scamarcio pushed.

'And then there will have to be a thorough investigation, being sure not to tread on the toes of our US *colleagues*.' Scamarcio took some comfort from the way Costantini said the word: it seemed that he didn't exactly see the Americans as friends.

'But what about Ifran's request for the crew? He's banking on that — he made it clear if he doesn't get the cameras, the killings will start.'

'Detective Scamarcio, you must understand that we can't let him broadcast his theory to the world while it remains untested. There has to be a proper investigation.'

'A proper whitewash, you mean?'

The room fell silent.

'So what happens to Ifran?' Scamarcio's voice was rising, but he didn't care. 'We just let this bloodbath happen?'

'There will be no bloodbath,' snapped the home secretary. 'He was just trying to scare you into action.'

'How can you take that risk?'

'It's a case of lesser evils.'

'A case of saving your own skin?'

'Detective!' shouted Mancino, slamming a fist down hard onto the table.

'How are you going to *end* this, Home Secretary?' asked Scamarcio. 'How are you going to get all those people, all those children, out alive?'

'That's my problem, not yours.'

'OK, so I'll tell you what *is* my problem — my girlfriend. I need to know where she is, and I need to know now.'

'I can assure you that I'll have someone look into that as soon as possible.'

'If I don't have her living and breathing beside me in an hour, I am taking this whole thing to the press.'

He watched Mancino and Garramone trade troubled glances.

'You will not,' whispered the home secretary.

'Just watch me,' said Scamarcio.

'I'll have you arrested,' said Costantini, deadpan.

'No, you won't.' Scamarcio sounded more confident than he

238

felt. He hoped Costantini wouldn't play that game. It would be messy and would raise a lot of questions, but on the other hand Costantini could claim that he'd done it to protect the public — that Scamarcio had been compromised.

The two chiefs were still following the back-and-forth, but neither of them seemed keen to intervene. Scamarcio knew they were wondering the same thing: whether Costantini would have the stomach for anything conspicuous — whether he'd risk a grand gesture.

'*Detective*, I don't need to remind you that you have been obstructing police procedure. You should have come forward with Ifran's demands immediately. Who were you to take it into your own hands?' Costantini looked to the two police chiefs for back up, but they wouldn't meet his gaze.

'What would you have done in my position? Ask yourself that,' said Scamarcio, rising from the table. 'He'd told me *thousands* would die.' He stopped and took a breath, closing his eyes for a second. 'It's been one hell of a day. I'm heading home. I expect to welcome my girlfriend there very soon. And while you're moving heaven and earth, I also need you to locate the journalist Roberto Rigamonti.' He paused. 'Mr Romanelli — a word.'

'Scamarcio,' shouted Garramone, getting to his feet. 'You can't just leave. You and I need to talk — about a whole lot of things.'

'Can't it wait, Chief? I'm exhausted.'

Garramone eyed him sceptically, then said, 'I'll give you a couple of hours, then I want you back here. You'll take an escort.'

'No escort. But I'll show, I promise you.'

'You'd better,' sighed Garramone.

When they were heading down Via San Vitale and approaching the junction with Nazionale, Romanelli said, 'I take it we're not going home.'

Scamarcio adjusted the Ray-Bans. 'Nope.'

'Back to the hacks?'

'You think Basile will come good?'

'I dunno — he's probably still got a few of those WP grenades hidden away somewhere.'

'There's no time left for anything sophisticated.'

'I guess not.'

'Is it worth you calling Federico, finding out how the land lies?'

Romanelli pulled out his mobile and dialled. 'Yeah,' he said after a few moments. 'As well as could be expected. They still there?' He paused, then said, 'See you in ten.'

'They're in the pen?'

Romanelli nodded.

Scamarcio stopped and bent down to rub his foot. His right heel was still killing him. He felt sure that it was bleeding. He grimaced and said, 'Can I borrow your phone?' Romanelli handed it across, and Scamarcio dialled Basile. After today, the number would probably be imprinted on his brain for life. 'Where are you?' Scamarcio asked when he picked up.

'Down near the Colosseum.'

'Do you have any props left?'

'Affirmative.'

'Sit tight, I'm heading your way.'

He handed the phone back to Romanelli. 'There'll be no hanging around. I'll be spotted as soon as we get there, and God knows where Scalisi is lurking.'

Romanelli rubbed at a cheekbone. 'I'll accompany you down there, but I'm going to sit this one out. I've always been a good second man — you wouldn't want me on the inside for this.'

There was something about the way he said it that made Scamarcio wonder.

24

WHEN THEY REACHED THE press pen, Romanelli flashed his old Intel ID, and they were let through. Romanelli shook his head, unimpressed by the lack of rigour.

When he spotted them, Woodman raised his eyebrows before killing the call he was on. 'We thought we'd seen the last of you. Seems like someone set off a small IED — could have been a lot worse.'

Scamarcio just wanted to move on. 'You ready for your exclusive?'

'What? Now?' Woodman looked alarmed.

'No time like the present.'

'Jesus. You don't dick about.'

'On the contrary, there's been *way* too much dicking about.'

'Give me a minute.' Woodman hurried over to his team.

Scamarcio saw hands waving and heads shaking as the crew gathered around. Woodman seemed to be having a hard time of it, but after a few minutes of back-and-forth, things simmered down, and there were a few nods of apparent assent. The cameraman even slapped Woodman on the back in a 'go get 'em' gesture.

He was soon back, the alarm replaced by adrenalin. 'But isn't the deadline long gone? Isn't it too late?'

'It seems like I may have bought us some extra time,' said Scamarcio, praying this was the case.

'OK,' said Woodman quietly. 'I'm going to call to set up the link — it may take a while.'

Behind him the cameraman was paring down his kit, changing lenses, and switching the battery pack. The girl called Clare was following his instructions, opening pockets and extracting equipment from a canvas bag.

Scamarcio motioned to Romanelli for the phone. 'Where are you now?' he asked Basile when he answered.

'Level with the cordon — I can see the press.'

'They probably won't let you in without ID. Someone will come out and meet you, and you'll need to explain that you're a contributor or something. Have you got any kind of ID?'

'This is all getting a little too close for comfort.'

'You could just pass me the grenade, and I'll be the one to throw it.'

'Nah — you might fuck it up.'

'What's to fuck up?'

'I'll try to get close. Any problems and I'll call.'

'Wait a sec — Woodman's trying to get the link. Don't hang up.'

The producer was tapping him on the shoulder, his face flushed. 'An item's fallen through — we can have it in five.'

Scamarcio nodded, his throat tight. 'Basile, count down slowly from three hundred, then toss that grenade if you're near enough.'

'Your man needs to come good.'

'He will, don't worry.'

'Oh, I'm no worrier. Three hundred it is.'

Scamarcio cut the call and turned to Woodman. 'Ready when you are.'

The producer expelled a blast of stale breath and whispered, 'Fuck, I'm nervous.' Then he ran back to the cameraman and started speaking into his ear.

Romanelli coughed and said, 'Time to leave — I'm asthmatic.'

Scamarcio smiled and shook his hand, before Romanelli vanished into the crowd.

'Get a cloth — soak it in water, cover your face,' Scamarcio said to Woodman when he was near. 'Tell your crew to do the same.'

'Shit, of course.'

Scamarcio pulled his jacket over his face, not caring that he was drawing attention to himself. Very soon peoples' focus would be elsewhere. He was still wearing the sunglasses — they were being pushed into his skin by the jacket, but he didn't care. He began counting down, although he had no idea how many seconds still had to pass.

The answer came sooner than expected. There was a hissing to his right, followed by another to his left, like a hundred baskets of vipers being overturned. When he glanced out from beneath his jacket, he saw a column of white smoke rising into the air. All around him people were shouting. Someone nearby was coughing so hard they were almost throwing up — the raspy, dry-retching sound went on and on, and Scamarcio wanted to yell at them to stop. The air was now thick with clouds of phosphorous smog, and when he turned to look for Woodman, he couldn't see anything beyond his own hand. But then he felt a grip on his shoulder.

'Come on,' shouted the American.

As he tried to push forward, Scamarcio was blocked by people kneeling or running in all directions, fearing there was worse to come. The police were shouting at everyone to proceed calmly, but no-one was listening. Scamarcio weaved his way through the chaos, trying to steady his manic pulse. By his calculation, if he turned right a few metres up ahead, he would find the end of the cordon and the start of the pavement running parallel with the coffee bar. He'd identified a landmark earlier to look out for — a wooden tobacconist's kiosk, now abandoned. It lay to the right of the café doorway by a couple of metres.

He pushed forward and nearly stumbled over someone on the ground. He veered round them, narrowly avoiding a slick pool of vomit near their feet. The smog was slowly starting to clear, and he could just about make out people and emergency vehicles parked up at the kerb. He looked to his right, and some twenty metres up ahead, further away than expected, stood the kiosk. He trained his eyes on it and upped his pace. 'Quick,' he said to Woodman, still close behind him, 'Before the smoke clears.'

He made it to the kiosk, and then headed for the café, running the last few metres to the front door. Behind him, he could hear Woodman panting. Scamarcio hammered on the glass, trying to find his breath. 'Ifran! Ifran! Open up. It's Scamarcio. I've got the crew. Let us in.' He closed his eyes for a moment, unable to believe that he'd made it this far.

He turned and saw that, while Woodman and his presenter were now right behind him, Clare and the cameraman had only just reached the kiosk.

Scamarcio kept banging on the door, knowing that they could be spotted at any moment. It felt like the seconds were turning into minutes, but then a shadow appeared on the other side of the glass. The figure was almost level with them, but as the door opened, Scamarcio realised that it wasn't Ifran but the other man, Barkat. The same guy who'd been talking to the Chechen in the video.

'I've brought the crew,' Scamarcio repeated, his nerves jangling.

'Ifran won't be needing any crew.'

'What?'

'Leave now, before I kill you.'

Scamarcio looked around and saw that the cameraman was now filming. And there was a new problem: three snipers, shadows in black, were pounding up the pavement behind them. In an instant, Scamarcio knew that they were about to be caught in a gunfight, chances of survival: zero.

Scamarcio was halfway through the door. 'Let us in, before they kill us all.'

As if he'd just reached the same conclusion, Barkat stepped back so they could rush inside, the cameraman only just making it through before the snipers reached the door.

'Stand down, or I shoot the hostages,' screamed Barkat through the glass. 'Stand down, or we shoot all the children at the preschool. Stand down, or we kill the people at McDonald's. This is a final warning: police, hold your fire!'

Scamarcio heard the crackle of comms outside. Barkat and the other terrorists started throwing tables and chairs against the door, barricading themselves in. 'Help us,' he yelled to Scamarcio and the crew. 'Quick.'

To Scamarcio, it didn't seem that he had much choice. They all started lugging overturned pieces of furniture and whatever else they could find, jamming them up against the glass. When there was nothing left, Scamarcio asked, 'Where's Ifran?'

'You want to see Ifran?' asked Barkat, a strange, whiny tone to his voice.

'That's why I'm here.'

'You give that to me,' screamed Barkat, trying to grab the camera. The cameraman looked horrified and just handed it over. 'What the fuck?' he said, turning on Woodman. 'Is this some kind of set up?'

'Stay calm, Jake,' said Woodman, looking anything but calm himself.

Barkat and two of his men started patting them down, spending slightly too long on the presenter, Anneliese. When they were satisfied, Barkat began herding them towards the back of the café. Scamarcio passed the same line of hostages on the floor — it was as if nobody had moved an inch since yesterday morning. The smell, however, had got worse. He noticed one middle-aged woman with her eyes closed, her head resting against the wall. She was deathly pale, covered in small beads of sweat, and shaking. 'What's wrong with her?' he asked the other people on the floor.

'Diabetes,' whispered a middle-aged man sitting next to her. His short dark hair was pasted to his skull, and his suit was crumpled and stained. Scamarcio realised from his smart shoes and expensive silk tie that he'd normally be considered a snappy dresser; now he was almost in vagrant territory.

'Shut up,' shouted Barkat. 'Don't talk to the hostages.'

Scamarcio fell silent, quickly trying to think of how to help the woman. He remembered something about sugar on the tongue regarding diabetics and their lows, but he wasn't sure of the details — the memory was too vague to be useful. If he'd acted sooner, gone to the authorities immediately, maybe this woman would be in hospital by now. Maybe she wouldn't be in this mess. He willed the thought to disappear, trying to turn his mind blank.

'This way,' shouted Barkat. 'Get a fucking move on!'

Like frightened sheep, they followed him down the stairs, Scamarcio's anxiety mounting. Where the fuck was Ifran? What the hell was he playing at?

When they reached the basement, Scamarcio noticed a new smell: iron, with the hint of something else — something rank and potent, but troublingly familiar. It was a smell he'd encountered at many crime scenes. Barkat strode ahead and snapped on the bare bulb in the storeroom. Like a third-rate magician revealing some mediocre trick, he waved an arm and shouted, 'Tada!'

Slumped against the far wall, a red spray of bullet holes through his chest, was Ifran.

'That's what we do to traitors where I come from,' said Barkat.

25

'WHY?' STAMMERED SCAMARCIO, unable to think of anything better. Behind him, he heard Woodman whisper, 'Fuck, fuck, fuck.' The staccato swearing sounded like bullets from a gun. Someone else was sobbing; Scamarcio didn't know who.

'He didn't have our best interests at heart,' answered Barkat breezily.

'But ...'

Barkat swung the butt of his rifle into Scamarcio's face. It made contact with his jaw. Scamarcio almost passed out from the pain, and when he touched the skin, his fingers came away red.

'But nothing. We got wise to him, and now I need to know exactly what he wanted from you.'

Scamarcio swallowed and tried to quieten his rising panic. His breaths were coming in quick bursts, and he needed to level them out. 'Didn't he say?' he asked lamely. It was obvious now that Ifran wouldn't have told the terrorists the full story, if he was indeed working for AISE.

'He gave me some cock-and-bull, but now I want the truth, and I'll do whatever it takes to get it.'

Barkat motioned to one of his colleagues standing guard over the crew. 'Take them up to the bar — put them with the rest.'

'Scamarcio, what the fuck?' hissed Woodman, as he was marshalled back up the stairs.

'I'm working this out,' said Scamarcio, his voice low.

'Bit late, don't you think?'

When they had gone, Barkat said quietly, 'Stand over there, under the light, where I can see you.'

Scamarcio shuffled over. The bare bulb made him blink.

'So, this is how it goes: you tell me the truth, and it'll be quick. You try to spin me a line, and it will be long and painful.'

Scamarcio shifted his weight from one foot to the other and tried to remember to breathe. He saw that Barkat had a knife pushed into his belt; it had been shoved in there loose, without a case. The blade was wide and sharp, and shone under the light. The ivory handle, Scamarcio noticed, was dented and stained brown.

'Ifran *claimed* you were going to speak to the authorities: help convince them to address our demands. But I've not seen any progress; I've not seen any attempt to meet us halfway.'

Demands, Scamarcio wondered. *What demands? But how do I ask this without confirming the lie?*

'They need more time,' he tried.

'More time? They've had over twenty-four hours.'

'These things take a while.'

'All they need to do is pick up the phone to their faggot friends in Sicily and tell them to stop the drones. It's simple — simple enough for even the Americans to understand.'

'That kind of thing needs to work its way up the command chain. There's a hierarchy to deal with.'

'Yeah, and there are hostages to deal with *here*, and if those strikes don't stop, we're going to kill them.'

Scamarcio thought quickly. *Strikes, drones, Sicily* ... He had to be talking about the US raids on Libya that the Italian prime minister had recently countenanced. 'The government won't allow itself to be blackmailed like that. They won't give in,' Scamarcio said quietly.

'Well, then they're going to have a *shocking* amount of blood on their hands.' Barkat put a heavy emphasis on the word.

Scamarcio fell silent, trying to work out his next move. After a few moments, he said, 'They're defensive strikes from Sigonella. The Americans wanted to use the base for offensive strikes, but we said no to that.'

Barkat just shook his head as if Scamarcio were a fool. 'Offensive, defensive — it's just semantics.'

'So, what do you want?'

'I want you to make them *agree*. We've waited way too long, and I'm starting to think that our demands never reached them — you were here yesterday for some *other* reason.'

'Oh, come on,' said Scamarcio, the fear shifting through his intestines, making him sweat.

Barkat stepped closer and jabbed him in the chest with his rifle butt. 'Ifran was working for your people, it's clear. What were you all planning?'

'Nothing. I'm just a policeman — I didn't understand why he involved me.'

Barkat jabbed him harder, then released his left hand to finger the blade on his belt. 'This will have to get messy.' He almost sounded disappointed.

Scamarcio thought about the real harm in trying to give this man what he wanted. Wouldn't it just show division in the ranks — sow some useful confusion? But confusion, he reminded himself, could be dangerous — and then there was the Chechen. He was an unknown quantity, and his relationship to the terrorists remained unclear.

'Ifran *was* working for the West — you were right,' he tried.

Barkat actually looked shocked for a moment, but then his expression morphed into fury. 'Bastard.'

'But he no longer trusted them. He didn't feel like they had his back — he'd asked me to help fight his case, if it all went to the wall.'

'What do you mean, "went to the wall"?'

'You must realise that there are only two possible outcomes to all this. Either they take you out alive, and you spend the rest of your days in a maximum security prison, or they shoot you dead when they storm the place. Either way, it's not looking good.'

'What makes you think that they'll succeed with a raid?'

'Because you're badly outnumbered — and from the activity outside, it looks like they'll be dropping in sooner rather than later.'

Barkat turned his head and tapped the side of his nose. 'Ah, but that's where you're misinformed. Ifran perhaps neglected to tell you that we have a fallback option — an ejector switch.'

'An ejector switch?'

'A card we can play that will stop them from trying to finish it. As we've seen in the past, the lives of hostages start to matter less towards the end. The security services know they have to be seen to be doing something to end the siege, so the hostage issue fades into the background. You can never rely on hostage collateral to see you through.'

It sounded like he'd attended a lesson on the subject. *Perhaps that's what they're teaching them in the training camps*, thought Scamarcio.

'So, this card?'

Barkat pushed the rifle butt harder into his chest, and Scamarcio remembered his meeting with the boy, when Ifran had done the same thing. Where was good and evil in all this? Was it even where he thought?

'In a few minutes we're going to let it be known that if they raid this place *or* the McDonald's *or* the nursery, we will detonate a bomb under the Colosseum. The blast will be so massive that it will take out a chunk of your city.'

Scamarcio tried to look unmoved. 'I find it hard to believe that you were able to plant a bomb. There is very tight security surrounding the Colosseum.'

'Do you know — it was actually *easier* than we expected. We'd come ready for more of a challenge. The Vatican had been a headfuck.'

'What?'

'You've seen the videos — we couldn't have sent you a clearer message. You were just too busy watching your inane quiz shows or cooking yourselves on the beaches like pigs on a spit to listen.'

That was pretty much what the fascist in Fossignano had said. The same doubts kept coming at him. If he'd gone to the authorities with this threat immediately, there may have been a chance to stop all this. But again, Scamarcio tried to banish the worry. 'But if you scare them into not carrying out a raid, what are you going to do? Sit it out till they send in the disposal robots, and then raid you once the bomb sites are secured?'

'We're not idiots. We want three helicopters.'

'Helicopters to where?'

'Libya.'

'No fifteen minutes of martyr fame?'

Barkat screamed in his face, 'Don't demean me!' Then, after a beat, 'Strategies change.'

Scamarcio frowned. This felt like too much of a deviation. 'So where do I come into it?'

'Ifran thought you might be useful, so I'll use you, too.' Barkat scratched the stubble on his chin. 'I want you to pass on my message to the authorities: shut down the drone strikes and get us our helicopters, otherwise Rome burns.'

'Why can't you just tell them yourself?'

'They'll listen to you.'

Scamarcio rubbed his forehead and closed his eyes. He had a headache and he was thirsty. 'Can I have some water?'

'What do you think this is — a restaurant?' Barkat laughed at his own stupid joke, then walked over to one of the shelves and pulled out a small bottle from a stack encased in plastic. 'I'd ask you if you wanted sparkling or still, but it all seems to be still.'

Scamarcio looked up, but Barkat's expression was surprisingly neutral. He handed over the bottle, and Scamarcio downed it. When he'd got some breath back, he said. 'When I go outside, I want to take that diabetic woman with me.'

'What makes you think you'll be going outside?'

'You just said you wanted me to put your demands to the authorities.'

'Yes, but you'll be doing that from here.'

Scamarcio swallowed and looked down at the chipped concrete beneath his feet. 'OK, but I want that diabetic woman out. It will help your case with the authorities if you show compassion. They will be more willing to negotiate.'

'Have you been listening to *anything* I've said? There is no *room* for negotiation. We have their city wired.'

Scamarcio sighed and slumped down on the hard floor, his shoulders against the wall.

'Get up,' shouted Barkat.

'I don't want to do this anymore. I've been on the run for over twenty-four hours and I'm tired. Just shoot me.'

'What?' screeched Barkat. 'Shut the fuck up, idiot.'

'I've had enough — put me out of my misery.' Scamarcio half meant it.

'Don't try to fuck with me.'

'I'm not fucking with you. I'm tired and I'm burnt out. All the way through, my life has been shit. It's been shit and just seems to get shitter, and I really can't be bothered any more. Let's just call it a day. You'd be doing me a favour.'

Barkat stared down at him, his forehead a mess of confusion.

'What are you waiting for, Barkat?'

'I need you to talk to the authorities.'

'I'm too tired. Why don't you ask those American guys upstairs, or someone else? You have plenty of hostages.'

'They're not connected like you.'

'Does it matter?'

'I'll let the diabetic out.'

'Deal,' said Scamarcio.

26

SCAMARCIO HAD INSISTED ON helping the woman to the door himself. 'I want the media to see.'

'Why?' asked Barkat.

'It will help your case.'

Barkat just looked at him as if he were mad. 'No funny business — we'll be watching every move.'

'I'm not stupid.'

'I'm not so sure.'

They got the diabetic woman to her feet, but she was so weak she was having trouble standing. 'I'm going to have to prop her up,' said Scamarcio. Barkat nodded, then frowned, his AK-47 still trained on Scamarcio's chest.

They began making their way slowly towards the door, the woman moaning with every step. She was small and slight, and because Scamarcio was taking nearly all her weight, her feet were barely touching the ground. For a moment, she looked as if she were about to faint — her skin was now so pale it was almost translucent. She closed her eyes, but then after a few seconds she opened them again, as if she was determined to catch her first glimpse of the outside world. Just before they reached the door, Scamarcio moved his head closer to hers and whispered, 'Tell them to search CCTV on the Colosseum. Go back two weeks. Then check the Vatican.'

He couldn't be sure if she'd heard. She just stared straight ahead, her glassy eyes tightly focused on the door and the world beyond.

'Why the fuck are you talking to her?' screamed Barkat behind him.

'I'm just trying to get her to take some weight — she's getting heavy.'

Scamarcio stopped in front of the door and turned back to the terrorists. 'Tell me when.'

'Wait!' yelled Barkat. They fanned out around Scamarcio so he was covered by a gun at every angle. It wasn't a great feeling.

'Now!' yelled Barkat.

Scamarcio pulled open the door, his every nerve-ending on fire. Immediately, he was blinded by a thousand camera flashes and a sea of electric blues and reds — there were emergency vehicles in all directions, light-bars whirring, radios buzzing. He heard shouts and cries from the press and smelt raw petrol on the wind, and the afternoon musk of baked tarmac and old nicotine. Two terrified paramedics were running towards him with a stretcher. Scamarcio barely had time to push the woman in their direction before an arm yanked him back inside, and the door slammed shut.

'Done,' said Barkat. '*Now* we start the conversation. Do *not* tell them which sites are wired. You just say *important* sites.'

'The phone?'

Barkat pulled an iPhone from his pocket and waved it in the air. 'Out back — I don't want them listening.' He gestured to the hostages, who now seemed fidgety and on edge. Maybe witnessing the woman's exit had made them think that their luck was out.

Barkat strode off towards the stairs. 'That corner,' he said, pointing. 'There's no reception in the basement.' He was motioning Scamarcio towards the back wall of the café where a wooden table was covered in an array of electronic equipment.

He noticed walkie-talkies, AA batteries, and a tangle of black cables of different thicknesses. 'Don't get any ideas,' said Barkat.

Scamarcio didn't know what ideas he was supposed to have, looking at all that.

'Make the call,' barked the terrorist.

'I don't have the number — you want me to speak to the negotiators, I take it?'

'No, you fuck, I want you to call the prime minister.'

Scamarcio looked up, expecting to see another sarcastic smirk, but Barkat's stern expression told him he wasn't joking.

'I don't know his number,' said Scamarcio tiredly.

'Ask the monkeys in the van to put you through.'

Yeah, Scamarcio thought, *I can see how that's going to go down.*

'I don't have the negotiator's number.'

'It's on speed dial under "Infidel bastards".'

'For God's sake ...'

He looked up and again realised Barkat was serious. The day was becoming evermore surreal. Scamarcio found the number and placed the call, his heart pounding. What the hell were the authorities going to say, after he'd led them a dance? But right now, that was the least of his troubles.

'Barkat?' asked the negotiator crisply — it sounded like a different guy. The pair from yesterday had no doubt gone off shift.

'It's not Barkat; it's Detective Scamarcio.'

'Yes, Detective, we just spotted you at the door. We were somewhat surprised to see you.'

'Look,' said Scamarcio, 'there's no time to explain. Did you know Ifran's dead?'

There was silence down the line, and then sudden chatter in the background, like bees swarming. Barkat stirred impatiently beside him.

'We wondered what had changed,' said the negotiator after a few beats, '... why they'd switched. Barkat's listening in, I take it?'

'Yes.'

'What happened?'

'Again, I can't go into that. Barkat wants you to know that they have two major tourist sites in the city wired. If you raid any of the three current hostage locations, these major sites will blow.'

'Which sites?' asked the negotiator, still cool and calm, as he'd been trained. The hum of voices kicked off again in the background.

'He doesn't want me to say. He says they are important sites.'

'What kind of explosives?'

'He says it will be big.'

'We got some of this following your conversation with the home secretary. We'd understood they'd blow the sites if you didn't keep to the terms Ifran set — terms which you chose not to share …'

He broke off, and a new voice came on the line. 'Scamarcio, this is Gianluca Bianchi from AISI. What the fuck are you playing at?'

'It's as I was telling the negotiator: they have the sites wired — they're threating to blow them if you raid the hostage locations.'

'So you didn't give them what they wanted?' Scamarcio sensed that Bianchi had been briefed on Ifran's earlier request, but preferred not to discuss it in public.

'It became irrelevant. These new guys want something different — Ifran's dead, so they're calling the shots now.'

'What are their terms?'

'No more drones out of Sigonella into Libya.'

'They're defensive strikes.'

'Doesn't wash. And they want three helicopters to take them to Libya.'

Barkat snatched the phone. 'And before you think you'll stuff those helicopters with elite forces, think again. If anything happens to us before we reach Libya, our friends will know and they'll blow your city to shreds.'

'How could they possibly know if we kill you when you're 20,000 feet up?'

Scamarcio winced: the guy from AISI didn't seem to be favouring the diplomatic approach. Perhaps after more than thirty hours he could no longer be bothered.

'They'll know — you need to believe me that they'll know, fuckwit.'

Barkat handed the phone back, his neck red. There was a tense silence on the line before the AISI guy said, 'Thanks, but no thanks. We'll take our chances.'

Scamarcio didn't think it was his decision alone to make, then remembered the key question. 'They want to talk to the prime minister. They want you to give me his number.'

'What?'

'You heard me.'

'Or?'

'Or else. They're still holding a shitload of people, remember.'

27

SCAMARCIO WONDERED IF THE message he'd sent with the diabetic woman had got through. That message, coupled with his most recent call to the negotiators, should have set something in motion. But there was no way of knowing.

From his position at the table, Scamarcio watched Woodman and his crew whispering in a huddle. One of the terrorists had also been watching and walked up and kicked Woodman in the small of the back. 'Shut the fuck up, prick!' he screamed in English. Woodman and his colleagues quickly fell silent.

'If they do provide the helicopters, what will happen to all the hostages?' Scamarcio asked Barkat, who was chewing on a dirty nail and scrolling through something on his mobile.

'We'll let them go. We'll tell them to wait five minutes so we have time to leave, and then they're all free.'

'But all this is contingent on being able to talk to the prime minister?'

'Yes.'

'Why?'

'Appearances. Our media arm wants us to demonstrate a position of strength. Speaking with the prime minister would help with that.'

'Ah, so it's just a PR stunt.'

'Kind of,' said Barkat dispassionately. He still hadn't looked up from his phone.

'I need to talk to the negotiators again.'

'Why?'

'I don't think I spelt it out clearly enough. I want another try.'

Barkat frowned, then looked up. 'No funny business.'

'No funny business,' Scamarcio repeated.

The call was patched through, and the same negotiator picked up. 'This thing about the prime minister,' said Scamarcio. 'Don't underestimate it. It all hinges on that: once they get the call, everyone goes free — think of the kids at the preschool.'

'A: we don't believe them. B: it would set a dangerous precedent,' said the negotiator, his tone neutral.

'I understand that, but you guys have got to consider how it's going to look if those kids *are* killed. If the prime minister intervenes and he's seen to be saving lives by doing so, that would have a hell of a lot of positive play in the press. From where I'm sitting, that's worth considering. Italians are pragmatists — sticking to the rules doesn't always score points.' Barkat frowned tightly and nodded.

'We need time,' said the negotiator.

Scamarcio felt a spark of hope. He turned to Barkat. 'They can't get this sorted immediately — you know that. You'll have to give them several hours.'

'Three hours,' snapped Barkat.

'Four,' tried Scamarcio.

'Three hours, fifteen.'

Now he was just being petty. 'He wants it sorted in three hours and fifteen,' relayed Scamarcio.

He heard the negotiator take a breath. 'Tricky.'

'Sure. But what alternatives do we have?'

'Leave it with us.'

The line went dead. Scamarcio knew full well that calling up the prime minister and asking for a decision would take no more than five minutes — given today's events he would be easily contactable.

But now he understood why the negotiators were playing for time: the authorities *were* spooling back through the CCTV, trying to see who had wired the Colosseum and where — and they were doing the same for the Vatican. Once they'd established that, they'd be sending in the bomb squads. It was now up to Scamarcio to keep Barkat sweet and help him pass the time.

'Barkat, what I really don't get is why you want to go to Libya? Why don't you want to die in the fight like the rest of them?' he tried.

Barkat said nothing, just looked the other way, checking his men still had the line of hostages in sight.

'How did you fall into this?'

Barkat looked back from the line. 'If you think it's a case of falling into it, then you understand nothing.'

'Enlighten me, then.'

Barkat sat up straighter. 'We've suffered decades of imperialism and exploitation. It's time to rebuild our empire.'

'But you don't even live over there. You've been in Italy — what? Ten years? Twenty?'

'But I'm not Italian.'

'Why do you say that? You were educated here, you speak the language as well as I; you grew up surrounded by Italians; you lived and breathed our way of life.'

'But that's where you're wrong. We keep to our own world — we don't mix.'

'Whose fault is that?'

'I'd say it's by mutual consent.'

'But I don't get why you want to go to Libya. Don't you want to die a hero?'

'We'll still be heroes.'

Scamarcio fell silent and studied the young man in front of him. He noticed the smart mobile phone, the gold bracelet at his wrist, and the chain at his neck. An idea was beginning to form. It took him by surprise and turned him cold. 'What did he promise you?' he asked after a few moments.

Barkat stopped playing with his phone. 'Who?'

'The Chechen, of course.'

Barkat said nothing. He got up from the table and approached his men. He whispered something, and then they all looked over at Scamarcio. He stared back, his chest tightening. Why had he pushed it? Curiosity? He'd probably die knowing, when it would have been better to survive ignorant.

A mobile rang. Barkat put his phone to his ear, his eyes still fixed on Scamarcio.

'Good,' was all he said, then, 'No.' He ended the call and shoved the mobile back into the pocket of his combat jacket.

'I reckon it was at least a million euros,' shouted Scamarcio across the room.

'Shut the fuck up!' screamed Barkat.

'And you call yourself warriors? Mercenaries, more like.'

'Shut up or I shoot!' hollered Barkat.

'Do I look like I care?'

Barkat moved over to Scamarcio fast and punched him hard across the mouth. 'Silence!'

Scamarcio's jaw was pounding again, and he felt sure it was broken. He tasted blood, but all he could ask himself was, *Why is Barkat so on edge about the Chechen?* Was it because he'd been told never to reveal the true identity of the people funding him?

But Scamarcio knew he'd gone far enough for now. From here on in, it would be a waiting game. He prayed the authorities had an army of analysts going back through the CCTV. It was the only way they'd get the information in time.

He glanced at the five terrorists. Then his gaze switched to Woodman and his cameraman, sitting sullen and cowed, their hands in their laps. As he looked at them, Scamarcio thought to himself, *Just maybe?*

28

SCAMARCIO KEPT STARING AT Woodman and Jake, but Barkat started to notice, so he turned to look at one of the other hostages — the balding man in his mid-fifties with dark sweat patches under the arms of his once pristine shirt. Barkat glanced away again, preoccupied, and Scamarcio immediately returned his gaze to the Americans, willing one of them to look up. But they didn't. He could feel Barkat's eyes on him again, so he bent down and started pulling off his right shoe. He was almost afraid to see what had happened to his heel. It was now giving him as much pain as his jaw, which seemed crazy.

The back of his sock was wet with blood, and he decided not to remove it for fear of infection. He pulled on the shoe again, and could clearly feel something biting into his skin. He removed the shoe a second time, took off the sock, and examined the bruised and bloodied skin. It looked nasty, but it would have to wait.

He glanced up at the Americans, but they were still staring into nothing, looking like they'd given up. *Jesus,* thought Scamarcio, *show some initiative.* He went to put his shoe back on, but as he did so, his finger caught against something in the lining. There was a thick lump the width of a 50-cent coin inside the canvas where it covered his heel — that's what had been causing him all this trouble.

He looked to see what Barkat was doing and, satisfied he wasn't being observed, examined the shoe under the table. There was a small round protrusion sitting just above the stitching at the back. The blue stitches looked as if they had been opened, and then neatly resewn, but the new stitches formed a darker, thicker line when he compared them with those of the left shoe. He checked Barkat again — he was talking to the smallest, youngest-looking of the three terrorists. Scamarcio felt his left shoe — there was no lump under the canvas. *Duh !*

He thought back. What could have happened to his shoes in the last twenty-four hours? He was pretty sure that lump hadn't been there when he'd left his flat yesterday morning, and his shoes had only started to bother him in the past day, really. His mind suddenly flashed on his bare feet on the floor of the room where the British had questioned him. They'd brought back his shirt and jacket, but had claimed to have forgotten the shoes. They'd handed them over just before he left. *You sly fuckers*, he thought. Then, in the next instant he tapped his heel. 'Hey,' he whispered. 'If you're listening, tell NCOS that they'll need to stand by for entry. We're going to try something from the inside.'

'Why are you muttering?' yelled Barkat from across the room.

'Like I told you, I'm losing my mind,' shouted Scamarcio, hoping Woodman would finally glance round. He did. Scamarcio stared at him, unblinking. Woodman just stared back, perplexed.

Scamarcio sank back into a bored silence and noticed a paper napkin dispenser on the table in front of him. He pulled out a few sheets and began making origami birds, trying not to think about Fiammetta, trying not to worry about the baby, trying not to wonder if it had ever existed. How would he feel if she was pregnant? He knew it was too dangerous to allow his mind to go there. He couldn't be railroaded by emotion; he had to stay sharp.

After he'd observed a dense column of ants cross the floor beneath his table and then return fifteen times with tiny crumbs of bread on their backs, after he'd counted over twelve different configurations in the chimes from a nearby church, and watched as the small strips of daylight surrounding the black flag on the window dimmed to almost nothing, Scamarcio finally used up the last serviette, and finished with the birds. Fifty swans now covered his table, miniature and pristine, but destined never to take flight.

'Fifteen minutes left until the deadline,' announced Barkat. He looked back at his phone, nonchalant, as if he was simply counting down the minutes until his favourite show was due on TV.

It was now or never. 'Give me your rifle!' yelled Scamarcio.

Barkat just shook his head, irritated, as if he really did believe Scamarcio was mad.

'Give me your gun!'

'Shut up, cretin!'

Scamarcio suddenly started bashing his head against the table, like a guy possessed. Birds scattered onto the floor in all directions. The four terrorists all turned to look at him. He heard murmurs among the hostages, then shouts. 'Stop it!' Barkat was screaming. 'Stop it, you moron!'

'We need to kill him,' said one of the terrorists. 'Now, Barkat!'

Scamarcio heard triggers being released, breath being held. *Please, someone have some initiative*, he prayed.

'Aaaaaaaaaargh.' There was an almighty roar, like in a rugby haka, and Scamarcio looked up to see the cameraman, Jake, swinging a fist into the side of Barkat's face. The blow sent him crashing into the wall. One of the other terrorists turned and ran at him, but Woodman and his presenter, along with a young male hostage, managed to wrestle him to the ground. Scamarcio caught the glint of something metallic in Woodman's hand.

Jake was still striking Barkat, again and again, until he slid to the floor, where Jake began kicking him while he was prone. But Barkat wasn't their only problem.

A third terrorist was aiming his rifle at Jake, and, with a sick feeling, Scamarcio knew he wouldn't be able to get there in time. The young hostage apparently realised the same thing and threw himself on the terrorist as if he was trying to ride piggyback. The other hostages were now all up off the floor and helping pull at the terrorist's legs and arms, dragging him down. He landed with a crash.

Barkat was writhing on the ground, blood gushing from a wound in the side of his head.

Scamarcio turned and saw that Woodman and the second terrorist were now locked in hand-to-hand combat, the blade in Woodman's hand grinding slowly back and forth between them. Scamarcio suddenly realised that, with his other hand, the terrorist was reaching for a small pistol at his belt. He dove at him, wrenched the gun from his hand, and shot the man in the head, splattering Woodman and his assistant, Clare, with blood and brain matter.

Clare just blinked a few times and wiped her face with her sleeve. She seemed preoccupied with what was happening to her right. Scamarcio followed her gaze, and saw that the third terrorist was on the floor, the hostages all piled on top of him. *We can't kill them all*, thought Scamarcio. *We need answers*. But then a gunshot exploded, and he turned to see Jake sprawled on his back, blood seeping from his chest.

Barkat was attempting to sit up, his rifle shaky. Scamarcio ran over and tried to punch him in the jaw, but missed. His vision was too blurry from blood — whose, he wasn't sure. He swung at Barkat a second time, this time connecting, and Barkat's head fell back and slammed into the floor. His eyes closed, and his mouth drooped open, and Scamarcio knew that he'd be out for more than a few minutes.

Scamarcio tried to breathe, tried to think. The hostages to his right were still wrestling with the third terrorist. Where was the fourth one? Scamarcio hadn't seen him in any of this.

'If you can hear me, send in NCOS. But hold fire,' he shouted, thinking there was no way they'd make him out above the din. But, whether by coincidence or design, just seconds later the glass door shattered, and a troop of snipers crashed in through the barricade of furniture. They resembled a black swarm, their green NiteSites pulsing like fireflies. The commander took a quick look at the scene and yelled, 'Vests?'

But before Scamarcio could reply, there was a bang, and one of the snipers started spinning and twitching. Scamarcio traced the direction of the fire and spotted the fourth terrorist, barricaded behind some tables at the back of the café. He was shooting wildly, panic taking hold. The SWAT team had their weapons trained on him in seconds, and he swirled and jerked like a manic marionette as their bullets took him down.

'No vests,' shouted Scamarcio.

'Contain the suspect,' barked the commander through his mike.

The hostages parted as the snipers took over. The fourth terrorist was rolled onto his chest, and his arms bound with thick black wire. While this was being done, two other snipers were checking for a suicide vest. The procedure was being repeated on each of the other terrorists.

'Any more?' shouted the commander.

'Just them,' said Scamarcio, exhaustion hitting him like a freight train. 'It's just them, now.'

29

As he was led outside behind the hostages, Scamarcio noticed a figure running towards him. It took him a while to realise it was Fiammetta.

'Jesus,' she gasped, touching his face, then examining her bloodied fingers.

'It's not as bad as it looks.'

'This is crazy,' she whispered, pulling him to her. 'I thought I'd never see you again.

He hugged her hard, just grateful for the sight of her, the smell of her.

She wiped her eyes with the back of her hand and looked away. He knew that she had a problem with emotion. She didn't like to reveal her vulnerabilities, and the present situation would be putting that seriously to the test.

Over her shoulder he saw a road full of emergency crews, but no press and public: they must have been moved back. Then he spotted Costantini striding towards him, flanked by a very jumpy security entourage.

'As you can see, we found her,' said the home secretary, his tone noncommittal. Scamarcio noticed Garramone hanging a few paces back. Scamarcio glanced at him, but nothing in his expression helped him understand if he was about to be fired or applauded.

'Thank you,' said Scamarcio. 'What about the bomb sites?'

'In the end, we had just enough time to work with. It took us two hours to identify the locations from the CCTV and forty minutes to secure them. As soon as they were made safe, we prepared to raid the nursery, the McDonald's, and the café. That was just before you started playing the madman.'

Something wasn't adding up. 'It took you only forty minutes to secure the sites?'

'I'll get to that shortly — it's odd.'

'Any civilian fatalities?'

'Two male hostages at the McDonald's, but strangely the other terrorists weren't wearing suicide vests, either. It saved us a heavy death toll.'

'These bomb sites ...'

'Why don't we go back to the van? We can debrief you there.'

For someone whose capital city had just escaped being blown to shreds, the home secretary seemed remarkably composed, thought Scamarcio.

Once they were all inside, and he'd been handed a cup of good espresso along with a tired slice of pizza, Scamarcio looked about him in the rather crowded van and noticed two people lurking behind Costantini who he hadn't spotted on arrival.

'We meet again,' he said quietly.

One of the Brits held up a weary palm. The other just looked strung out.

The home secretary flicked his mane of hair away from his shoulder: 'The British are always cropping up where you least expect them.' He didn't sound pleased about it.

'So — the bomb sites?' Scamarcio pressed.

'We had thirty analysts going back through that CCTV — five days ago, three men turned up in a white van outside the Colosseum. The logo of a local cleaning company was visible on the side, but the van was different from the one that normally comes. The job also took far longer than usual, and the arrival time of 2.00 a.m. was out of the ordinary. Night security tried to call the maintenance manager to check, but their phone was switched off, so the guards just waved the fake cleaners through. This kind of deviation from the rules can never be allowed to happen again.'

'These imposters somehow managed to turn off all the CCTV inside and outside the site. They also interrupted the wi-fi connection to the main control room, which made security think they were looking at an internet problem, rather than a camera issue. Unfortunately for the criminals, though, they forgot one camera. This meant that its feed was eventually backed up to the security hard drive, which allowed us to observe them make their way down to a specific section of the viewing platform above the lower hypogeum, where they descended to the ground below. We searched that area and discovered an explosive device attached to the second pillar. It had been skilfully concealed inside a red housing so it looked like part of the structure.'

'You detonated it?'

'We didn't need to.'

'What?'

'I'll get to that in a minute. It was much harder to locate the Vatican bomb, but we eventually found the same van approaching the Piazza San Pietro on the Borgo Pio at 2.00 a.m. three nights earlier. We'd spotted a similar report of interrupted wi-fi to the control room, which gave us a vital head start.'

'And that device?'

'It's fine.'

'What do you mean, "it's fine"?'

'Again, we didn't need to act.'

'Why the hell not?'

'Because whoever had wired these devices — and we think we know who they are — had wired them incorrectly.'

'But—'

'We believe it was deliberate.'

'Why would it be deliberate?'

'When we find your Chechen, that's the first thing we'll be asking.'

'It was the Chechen?'

'The forgotten CCTV camera at the Colosseum shows him plain as day. And we've matched his gait to a Vatican street cam that night.'

Scamarcio took a moment to absorb this. 'And now you don't know where he is?'

'We're looking hard.'

Scamarcio stepped outside. The evening air was cooler than he would have expected. Beyond the old press cordon, which was now strewn with cigarette butts and discarded food wrappers, he spotted Romanelli. He waved half-heartedly in Scamarcio's direction.

'I just need to speak to this guy,' Scamarcio said to Fiammetta, who was sitting waiting for him by a medical tent. He looked at her for a long moment, anxiety creeping through him, encircling his heart. The fear in her eyes took him back to a past experience, and he felt sick at the thought that he might be about to lose everything that really mattered.

'They didn't do anything bad. I'm OK,' she said, answering his unspoken question.

He pulled her to him.

'They tried to tell me all kinds of bullshit about you, but I never believed them.'

'I knew you wouldn't.'

He kissed her, long and hard, and then reluctantly made his way over to Romanelli.

'Evening,' said the former spy, his tone flat. Scamarcio noticed that his eyes were red, as if he'd been crying or was suffering from some kind of allergy.

'You heard about Ifran?'

'Just found out, as it happens.'

Scamarcio understood then. 'You're cut up?'

Romanelli inclined his head slightly, the gesture noncommittal yet somehow confirmatory.

'I think he tried to stop all this,' said Romanelli. 'He wanted to lead you to the Chechen because he knew that if you brought it all into the open, the Chechen would withdraw. He wouldn't blow those sites.'

'They tell me he hadn't wired them correctly. Deliberately so.'

Romanelli's mouth fell open slightly.

'And you're still telling me you really don't know who he is, this Chechen?' tried Scamarcio.

'Ifran thinks he was working for Scalisi — but who was Scalisi working for? I'm not even sure that the Americans are the answer anymore.' Romanelli ground out a cigarette Scamarcio hadn't noticed, its smoke still dense in the stale city air.

'But they kept me captive.'

'There could be various reasons for that.'

'Anyone seen them? Or Scalisi?'

'Scalisi's gone to ground. No-one in AISE has heard from him in hours.'

'Funny that — both Scalisi and the Chechen disappearing at the same time.'

'Hmm.'

'What did the home secretary mean when he asked you how you were holding up?'

'Ah,' sighed Romanelli, patting down his jacket pocket and

then pulling out a packet of Marlboros.

'This is the first time I've seen you smoke,' observed Scamarcio.

'Desperate times,' muttered Romanelli.

'So?'

'Why can't you just let it lie?' Romanelli extracted a new cigarette, and then seemed to remember his manners and offered Scamarcio one. After he'd lit up for the pair of them, he took a long drag and said, 'He was talking about my wife. She died in an operation last year.'

'Oh, I'm sorry. What was wrong with her?'

'No, not a medical operation, an AISE operation.'

Scamarcio fell silent. 'I hadn't realised she worked with you.'

'Why would you?'

'How did it happen?'

'Our superior led her into an ambush. He should have checked that the situation was safe, but he didn't. He was too eager for results — another ribbon on his shoulder.'

Scamarcio was starting to see it more clearly now. 'Your superior?'

'Do I need to spell it out?'

'Fuck,' he whispered. 'It was you. You had the house in Ostia?'

'Yep.'

'You buried the DVD for Ifran?'

'Guilty as charged.'

'You wanted to see Scalisi go down.'

'Do you blame me?'

In that moment, Scamarcio finally understood one small detail that had been bothering him. The girl with the red hair in Romanelli's shop in Calcata who had seemed so familiar — she was the same young girl playing ball on the film. That was where he'd seen her before — the eyes were the same. The DVD must have been recorded over one of Romanelli's old home movies.

'Why didn't you use a fresh disc?' Scamarcio asked, knowing it was a ridiculous question, but too confused to let it go.

'Scalisi never knew about the DVD, but in the event that he *did* come to learn of its existence, I wanted him to spot a clue. I wanted him to understand that I had his number. Only he could have reached that conclusion. He'd been to the house, you see — met my family in happier times.'

'Did you tip him off about the photo? Tell him I had it?'

'I imagine his gunmen at the basilica would have told him, but, yes, I might have made an anonymous call. I wanted to make him sweat.'

'So, is any of this actually true: his involvement with Ifran; the Chechen?'

'Of course it's true!' Romanelli's pupils flared. 'We just wanted to make sure that Scalisi went out with a bang. A quiet word to Costantini would not have been enough.'

'Hell,' whispered Scamarcio. 'You risked one fucking *big* bang.' He paused. 'Who's "we"?'

'Me and Federico mainly — along with some others still in AISE.'

'Where *is* Federico?'

'Trying to make a swift exit.'

Scamarcio sucked hard on the cigarette, drawing the nicotine down deep. 'What got into him these past hours?'

'He'd been doing a bit of freelancing, then it all got messy and he found himself in the middle of a diplomatic shitstorm. He needed to beat a retreat.'

'Freelancing for the British?'

But Romanelli didn't answer. He just raised his chin and muttered, 'Your gangster wants a word.'

Scamarcio turned and saw Basile locking up a white BMW motorbike. It looked like the same model as Rigamonti's. Scamarcio thought of the reporter and wondered where he was.

Basile did not look happy. But as he drew nearer, Scamarcio changed his assessment: the man was seething. 'Nice wheels,' Scamarcio tried.

Basile just shook his head. 'I won't have you stringing me along.'

'I've only just got out of there alive. I haven't had a chance to call Greco yet.'

Basile looked at his watch. 'Then do it now, while I'm here.'

'I need to go home, have a shower, be with my girlfriend,' said Scamarcio, trying to tamp down his anger.

'I know your reputation. Don't try to pull a fast one — it wouldn't be clever.'

'Yeah, and it wouldn't be great if the police found out you were dealing arms to the Chechen.'

'What?'

'You heard me.'

'You wouldn't fucking dare!'

'I enjoyed meeting you, Nino. I'll be in touch.'

30

GARRAMONE RANG TWO HOURS later, as Scamarcio was getting out of the shower. The basilica near his apartment was striking eleven.

'Chief Mancino just got a call from the home secretary. They've located Scalisi — in an Autogrill on the A1 to Naples.'

'What was he doing there?'

'Not much. He was found slumped in a toilet cubicle.'

'Drunk?'

'Dead.'

Scamarcio ran a tired hand across his mouth. Scalisi had never struck him as a quitter. 'Did he kill himself?'

'Not unless he managed to slash his own throat.'

'Any theories?'

'Your Chechen friend was kind enough to leave a note.'

'Him again?'

'Seems so — they've got him on CCTV filling up at the gas station at around the right time.'

'What's the note say?'

'Actually it was addressed to you — you seem to have made quite an impression.'

'Jesus.'

'If you can finally spare me the time to answer my questions, I might let you take a look.'

The office was a deafening chaos of ringing phones, arguments, and booming TVs. As soon as Scamarcio walked in, one of his colleagues spotted him, and a half-hearted cheer stuttered across the room. Scamarcio would rather have been anywhere else — perhaps his own funeral. He knocked on Garramone's door and went straight in; he didn't want to spend another second out in the pit.

The boss was typing fast. 'You wouldn't believe the number of face-saving reports I'm having to write — as if I don't have anything better to do.'

Scamarcio grunted and pulled out a chair. Garramone looked up. 'What you did was reckless; it was *not* the right way to go.'

'How could I know? Ifran was talking about other sites being wired. It felt reckless *not* to listen.'

'But you risked civilian lives when you took that crew in. A man died for God's sake. If you'd just run it all past us, we could have reached a collective decision. We'd have had earlier intelligence upon which to act.'

'You know as well as I that the top brass wouldn't have allowed me to grant Ifran's request. I couldn't risk giving them the chance to stop me.'

Garramone sighed. 'We could be debating this for weeks.'

'Then let's not.'

'That depends on Chief Mancino.' Garramone scratched the back of his head and pushed some papers away, before retrieving a sheet of A4 that was pinned beneath his keyboard. 'This is a photocopy of the note. AISI is all over it, and the Farnesina are wetting their pants. Nobody thought to let you see it.'

'I appreciate your intervention.'

Garramone pushed the sheet across. 'It's in English,' he said, as if Scamarcio couldn't work that out for himself.

The handwriting sloped elegantly to the right — it looked like something an old lady would write, not some twenty-tonne

Slavic meathead.

'Dear Detective Scamarcio,' it began.

Our paths keep crossing, but we've never really had a chance to talk. From a distance, I've admired your determination, your bravery, and your compelling need to establish the 'truth', whatever that may be. I feel that, given all you've been through, you deserve some kind of explanation.

Ifran pointed you in my direction because he had his doubts — and he was right to have them. Andrea Scalisi got what he deserved — the man is a viper, a cheat, and a double-crossing killer.

Scamarcio thought that was pretty rich from someone who had planned to take out much of Rome, but then he remembered the faulty wiring and wondered if the Chechen's intentions weren't quite so simple.

The letter continued:

But Scalisi was just one cog in a very dirty wheel that keeps turning. He may have thought he was working for the US and faithfully keeping his population quiet, but he wasn't. Sure, the usual suspects were there, calling the shots from Tel Aviv and Washington, hoping that, yet again, the killing would bring Europe to heel, and that the multicultural love fest would spiral into a burning hatred of every Muslim.

But above all that, looking on, was someone with a lot more money and a lot more power. Now here I must hold my hands up: I'm the first to admit that I'm a mercenary whore with no real principles. Where I grew up, they were punched out of you at an early age. So when someone is in on a deal, but knows others who also want the deal to go through but with a bit more colour, a bit more panache, who am I to say no? I've never been averse to a bit of moonlighting, especially when there's serious cash in play.

But this time — I don't know whether it's middle age, or weariness, or boredom — something changed. I made the first steps — found a rabble of semi-enthusiastic 'freedom fighters' with a taste for bling, promised them a few million rather than the usual heavenly harem, and then we all got to work. But the weird thing is that, with time, I came to regret my decision. When push came to shove, I couldn't do it. Don't misunderstand — it wasn't a road-to-Damascus awakening. I just thought, Why make a bunch of rich fuckers even richer?

And so I leave it to you, 'Detective' — for that's what you are in the very best sense of the word. You need to ask 'Cui bono?' And don't pose the question in the comfort of your flat, or while enjoying a stroll by the Tiber. Gather your things NOW and take a trip north. Clear your head, see the sights — maybe enjoy an ice cream at the superb Gelateria Harold. Life is short, embrace the day!

And with that, the letter ended.

'What the fuck?' said Scamarcio.

'Yeah, that's precisely what Intel are asking themselves.'

'Did Scalisi's colleagues at AISE know he was working with the Americans? Maybe it was an official collaboration? a joint op?'

'From what I've heard there was nothing official about it,' said Garramone crisply. 'AISE is in disarray. Costantini has confirmed that both the DVD and photo are genuine — Scalisi is seriously implicated.'

'That reference to bringing Europe "to heel"?'

'Chief Mancino asked Costantini about that. He said that the Chechen was implying that a major terror event might be more likely to keep us in line with the US. The thinking is that it would make us more frightened about going our own way — along with France and the rest.'

'Did the home secretary buy that analysis?'

'If he did, he was hardly going to admit it.'

'Does anyone believe the Chechen's story?'

'Again, no-one's talking to us about that.'

'And the thing about Tel Aviv?'

'Because everyone's so tight lipped, I did a bit of digging myself and discovered that there are a load of conspiracy theorists who say the recent attacks in France were the doing of CIA and Mossad. They claim that Mossad are targeting countries who have said they will recognise the State of Palestine — attacks in Norway, Belgium, and France all followed a short while after those countries said they'd recognise Palestine.'

Scamarcio frowned. 'That sounds like bullshit.'

'The Chechen might just be throwing a load of chaff in our direction — spinning us a few popular conspiracies to distract us.'

Scamarcio scratched his head. 'The thing about me going north though — that's weirdly specific. What did Costantini et al make of that?'

'Guess.'

'No comment?'

'No-one's even mentioned it. Reads to me like the Chechen has a screw loose.'

Scamarcio bit his thumb and thought. 'I'm not sure, perhaps not.'

'We'll talk more in the morning. Go home, get some rest.'

'Yeah,' said Scamarcio, his mind still turning, 'that's exactly what I'll do.'

When he arrived back at his flat it was 1.00 a.m., and Fiammetta was sleeping. There'd been no time to ask her about the pregnancy. When they'd taken a taxi from the Colosseum, she'd nodded off immediately. It had been all he could do to rouse her and get her into bed. He thought about trying to wake her now and asking her outright, but she looked so peaceful.

He padded to the kitchen and poured himself a large glass of Nero d'Avola, then took it to the lounge. The lights of the city were dancing beyond the windows; there was laughter on the streets and music in the bars. It seemed as if Rome was finally breathing again, as if the oxygen had returned to her lungs.

He shut the window, stretched out on the sofa, and closed his eyes, opening them only to sip the wine. It was good — for fifty euros, it ought to have been.

When he'd finished half the glass, he took out the photocopy of the note from the Chechen and read it again. It was true that he spoke in generalities — that his claims could have been fantasy. Whatever the case, it seemed they would remain untested, unless Italian intelligence decided to put it to the CIA that they and their Israeli chums had been interfering. Scamarcio sensed that the etiquette of espionage didn't work this way, though. It seemed more likely that the Italians would perhaps just put it on the slate to be used against the Americans at a later date. *Leverage*, as Federico had called it.

Scamarcio pinched his nose — there was, though, that one very specific reference in the note: The Gelateria Harold. Why was the Chechen telling him to buy an ice cream from this particular place? It was an unusual name, so he pulled out his phone and googled it, in the hope that it might be unique. The first result was the website of an ice cream parlour in Milan. It was the only entry with that name, so he clicked on it and skimmed through the site.

Organic milk used … fair-trade cocoa … so what, so what? … five stars on TripAdvisor … won some gourmet prize last year … opening a new store in Porta Genova soon. Maybe the Chechen just liked his ice cream? Scamarcio was about to leave the site, still baffled, when he noticed the ice cream parlour's address: *Piazza degli*

Affari 4, Milan. 'What?' he whispered. Like most Italians, he knew that Piazza Affari was synonymous with the Milan stock exchange.

He googled the address of the exchange to be sure, and found it was located at number six. The ice cream parlour was right next door. He downed the rest of his wine and tried to focus. 'Fuck,' he murmured. 'He wants me to go there. That's the answer to *Cui bono?*'

Scamarcio rose and started pacing. He thought about waiting until the next morning, but knew that, despite his exhaustion, he wouldn't sleep with all this churning in his head. And besides, the Chechen seemed to be suggesting it was urgent. Why else would he have written 'NOW' in caps? Scamarcio needed to get to Milan, see if there was anything to his hunch. As he was contemplating whether or not to wake Fiammetta, his landline rang.

'Have you seen my piece?'

'Rigamonti! Fuck! Where have you been?'

'Enjoying a nice stay courtesy of your friends at AISE — until the home secretary intervened on my behalf.'

'What did they want from you?'

'The obvious: Where were you? What were Ifran's demands? I kept them occupied for a while, then for some reason they seemed to lose interest. A few hours later, a guy from Costantini's office storms in and starts throwing his weight around. It got quite heated. If you ask me, there's a civil war going down.'

'You've managed to write something already?'

'Go get yourself a copy of *La Repubblica* — they came good this time. They were interested in our Chechen ghost and have been bolder than I would have expected.'

'You want a follow-up?'

'They're after an exclusive with you. That's why I'm calling.'

'I dunno, Rigamonti. This investigation is far from closed, and I've got my police bosses breathing down my neck.'

'You just asked me if I wanted a follow-up!'

'I received a letter from the Chechen a few hours ago — before he disappeared, leaving Scalisi's body behind. The letter was strange, but informative.'

'He killed Scalisi?'

'Yeah, but that's not what you should be interested in.'

'It gets better?'

'The Chechen seems to want to help me understand all this. He's suggested that I should head up to Piazza Affari. It seems like there might be information there which will explain who was really behind these attacks — the people who were pulling Scalisi's strings are not the end of the story, apparently.'

'What do you mean, "pulling his strings"? He *was* involved?'

Scamarcio suddenly realised how much had happened since he and Rigamonti parted.

'His connection to Ifran has been confirmed. He was involved with the Chechen, too.'

Rigamonti whistled. 'So who *does* the Chechen say was behind Scalisi?'

'He calls them the usual suspects — which we think could mean the CIA and Mossad — but he suggests someone else muscled in, and that they wanted these attacks to go off with a bigger bang. I think he's telling me the trail starts at the stock exchange.'

'Money?' Rigamonti paused. 'But why's he helping you?'

'For the same reason he didn't wire the sites like he was supposed to. He says he doesn't want to make a bunch of rich fuckers any richer.'

There was a long silence. He could almost hear Rigamonti's synapses whirring. After a few moments, Scamarcio asked, 'You still there?'

'Yeah,' said the reporter, his voice distant. 'I'm just thinking about how to access that kind of information. I can start with some financial reporters I know — see if they have contacts at the exchange.'

'I went to university with a guy who's now a trader. Last I heard, he was about to retire at the ripe old age of thirty-nine. I was thinking of dropping him a line.'

'Yeah, do that. And I'll try my guys ...'

'I don't want to waste time. I think we should head up there now, before these people get a chance to cover their tracks — there are no trains till six, so we'll have to drive.'

'What's your address? I'll pick you up.'

Scamarcio gave him the details and hung up. When he walked back into the bedroom, Fiammetta was snoring softly. Again, he decided it would be best not to wake her. He'd just write a note.

He was about to leave the room when a small voice said, 'Where are you going?'

'I'm sorry, something has come up.'

'What now — after the day we've just had?'

'I need to check it out — it might help wrap this whole thing up.'

She fell silent. He wanted to know about the pregnancy, but he didn't want to do it in a hurry as he was leaving. It needed to be handled right.

'OK,' she said firmly. 'I understand.'

There was no undertone. He knew that she meant it.

31

PIAZZA DEGLI AFFARI WAS already busy at 7.00 a.m., coming to life in time for the start of trading in an hour. Scamarcio and Rigamonti crossed the square, stopping for a moment to take in 'Il Dito' — the sculpture of a hand with its middle finger raised, by the artist Maurizio Cattelan. To Scamarcio, the huge marble 'up yours' seemed clearly directed at the world of high finance behind it. For the life of him he couldn't understand why two successive mayors had left it in place. He was no great fan of twenty-first-century capitalism, but given that Milan was the economic powerhouse of the country, it seemed a tad disrespectful.

His university friend Dino De Blasi had told them to ring from the foyer of the exchange building. When they entered the office rented by De Blasi's financial services firm, a fat, balding man with rosy cheeks whom Scamarcio didn't recognise waved, then gestured apologetically to the phone against his ear. Scamarcio was about to frown, then managed to freeze his expression at neutral; his old friend might have made a few million, but he had not aged well.

A secretary motioned them to a minimalist leather sofa and assured them that De Blasi wouldn't be long. She stared at Scamarcio with undisguised curiosity, then seemed to remember her manners and returned to her desk.

It was another twenty minutes before De Blasi was able to

extricate himself from his call.

'Leo, so good to see you!' he said, striding over to where they were sitting. Scamarcio stood up to greet De Blasi, who kissed him on both cheeks. 'Sorry — since yesterday it's been a whirlwind. My screen has been a sea of red. But I'm expecting a fair bit of green when we reopen. Given that little damage was done, we have to see an uptick.' De Blasi spoke so fast it was hard to make out the individual words.

'I guess people could remain jumpy for a while,' offered Scamarcio.

'There are a few interesting variables to add to the mix — nervousness about a bond rout, the Europeans moving to phase out QE, not to mention a possible German banking collapse. Sometimes, I wish I'd retired last year.'

'Why didn't you? I hear you're pretty comfortable.' Scamarcio smiled.

'It's the gambler's disease. Just one more spin of the wheel, *then* I'll call it a day.'

De Blasi nodded at Rigamonti, and Scamarcio quickly introduced them.

De Blasi shook Rigamonti's hand, then took a seat on the sofa. 'Sorry about the set-up — I don't have my own office, and it's too noisy on the desks for a decent conversation.' He smoothed down his suit trousers. 'Well, even though I barely came up for air yesterday, I *did* have time to catch *you* on the news, Leo.'

Rigamonti sat back down, but Scamarcio chose to remain standing. 'It was quite a ride.'

'What the hell happened? They said that terrorist put the thumb screws on you.'

'That's about the size of it. The job gets more interesting by the day.'

De Blasi chuckled. 'Who'd have thought it — you, with the Flying Squad!' Then he read something in Scamarcio's expression and changed tack. 'So, what can I do for you? You said it's in connection with what happened. I'll help in any way I can.'

De Blasi had always had a can-do attitude. He'd never been hampered by the semi-depressed lethargy that seemed to have afflicted Scamarcio for so much of his early twenties.

He scratched his head. 'The thing is, Dino, I don't actually know *what* I'm looking for. Someone on the inside has hinted that there were people behind these attacks who stood to benefit if they went ahead. The suggestion is that this would have been a financial benefit, perhaps something playing out on the exchange. What you probably don't know, because it wasn't made public, is that the terrorists told us they had a number of tourist sites wired. We thought they were going to trigger massive explosions and wipe these places off the map.'

The trader's cheeks lost some of their dangerously high colour. 'Which sites?'

'The Colosseum and the Vatican ...'

De Blasi's small eyes widened.

'So I guess my first question is, if these bombs had gone off, who would have benefited on the markets? The second question would be, has there been any unusual trading activity in the last few days — the days leading up to the attack?'

De Blasi stroked his chin. 'Well ... if a number of sites around Rome were to blow — if it was perceived that Italy was in a state of emergency — you'd see free fall. Everything would tumble. Just like 9/11 in the States. The NYSE took a hit of nearly eight per cent — and that was when it reopened a whole week later. They'd kept it closed that long to avoid meltdown.'

'So, nobody benefits?'

'No, somebody *always* benefits. The system will always give you a chance to win.'

'How can you win if all hell is breaking loose?'

De Blasi kept rubbing his chin. 'You ever hear the rumours

about put options on 9/11?'

'What's a put option?' asked Scamarcio, embarrassed by his ignorance.

'It's a device which gives the owner the right, but *not* the obligation, to sell an asset at a specified price by a certain date. After that date, your put option expires and you have to go with the market. Usually, when you buy a put, it's interpreted as a negative sentiment about a stock's future value. The most obvious use is as an insurance: you buy enough puts to cover your holdings, so if there's a dramatic downturn you have the right to sell your stock at the price originally struck. But another use is for speculation — an investor can buy the put option on the stock without trading in it directly. That would be like a pure bet on which way the stock will go, without owning any of the stock yourself. That's what I'd be looking for in this case.'

'Why did you mention 9/11?'

De Blasi scratched an eyebrow. Scamarcio thought he looked slightly ill at ease. 'Just before the attacks, an extraordinary amount of put options were placed on United and American Airlines stock — the trading levels on the Chicago Exchange were abnormally high. The investors in those put options netted a five-million-dollar profit after 9/11, although their names remain undisclosed. Interestingly, the five million still sits unclaimed in the Chicago Exchange account. No other airlines saw these volumes of puts in the days before the attacks.

'Likewise, insurance groups like Citigroup saw about forty-five times the normal trading volume in the three days before 9/11 — but in that case it was on options that *profit* if the stock falls below forty dollars. Morgan Stanley, which had twenty-two floors at the World Trade Centre, also experienced higher-than-normal pre-attack trading of options that profited when stocks fell.' He paused for a moment and looked around to check no-one was listening. 'There were a whole host of abnormal trades on companies who would have been both negatively and positively effected by 9/11.'

Scamarcio pinched his nose and thought. If he'd heard this a few years ago, he would have been shocked. But his experience on the American case had shifted his outlook. 'So, if you were considering yesterday's events, and more importantly, the planned bombings that never came to pass, you'd be looking for these kinds of trades?'

'Yes, I would.'

'But in which industries?' pressed Rigamonti.

'Well, on 9/11 it was pretty obvious that the two airlines and the insurance companies who would be paying out a fortune in claims would be the hardest hit. There was also a defence contractor whose stock surged after the attacks. In this home-grown case, it's slightly more complicated. I'd be thinking about airlines again — Italy's tourist trade would be badly affected by the bombings. Likewise, I'd consider hotel groups. But those industries don't feature on the main FTSE MIB. Also, with the decline of Alitalia, the interests tend to be wrapped up in non-Italian holdings, like easyJet or Ryanair. Same goes for the hotel groups.

'This means it's a subtler thing: the reaction on stock price would be diluted. That said, Italian banks and insurance companies *are* on the MIB. They would take a more direct hit with more drastic moves, so they'd be my first place to look.'

'And how long would it take to get this kind of information?' asked Scamarcio. But De Blasi wasn't listening. He was gazing into the middle distance, his mind turning on where to find the answers.

'Oh,' he said after a few moments. 'There *was* something — a few days back. A colleague was complaining that someone was trying to drive Italian bank stocks down at a time when they were already on their knees. It might not have been puts, but ...'

'Will it take long to find out?'

'I don't trade banking, but no — if I ask the right people it should be quick.' He was already on his feet. 'Don't move.'

Scamarcio took a breath. He thought about the strange tale Dino had told. Would it not be the same here as in the US? That the names of any investors would remain undisclosed?

'What do you make of it?' asked Rigamonti.

'Could be something, could be nothing.'

Rigamonti shrugged in assent. Scamarcio checked his second mobile, which he'd been using since he returned home. Fiammetta hadn't called. He was both relieved and disappointed, but then he reminded himself that she was probably still asleep.

Just fifteen minutes later, De Blasi was back, rubbing his mouth with the back of his hand. 'It's weird.'

Scamarcio got up, keen to stretch.

'We've found the puts — there are a hell of a lot of them — way more than normal. The problem is, they're in the wrong place.'

'What do you mean?' shot Scamarcio. Rigamonti, he noticed, had pulled out a notebook.

'I took a look at banking and insurance, and there *is* abnormally high put activity over the past four days. Italian banks are not seen positively right now, so you've got to factor that in, but the trading is still *way* above the norm.'

Rigamonti laid down his pen. 'So it's in the *right* place, then? You said before that banks would take the most direct hit.'

'Yeah, but they *haven't*. Meanwhile, the biggest activity has come in the past forty-eight hours. There's a major aerospace firm outside Rome — you'll have heard of it: Ferromeccanica. Someone's bought over 3,000 puts on their stock. A colleague of mine was told about it just this morning.'

Rigamonti and Scamarcio fell silent, not knowing what to make of it.

'And then there's Salucci motors, who trade on the MIB — they've seen nearly 4,000 puts since Monday. It's mad. I mean, if you have a big terror event in the capital, those stocks will slide along with the rest, but I wouldn't target them specifically. It makes no sense.'

When Rigamonti and Scamarcio said nothing, De Blasi sighed. 'Sorry guys, I'm at a loss,' he opened his palms and sat down. 'I dunno, maybe someone has info on those companies we don't — maybe there's some big surprise in the accounting coming.' He stopped and shook his head. 'Jesus, we really don't need another Parmalat.'

Scamarcio had been about to concur, when a thought struck him. 'You said a put option gives you the right, but not the *obligation* to sell?'

'Yes.'

'So what if you decide your asset isn't going to slide; that you don't want to sell it anymore?'

Dino shrugged. 'You simply don't exercise the option.'

'That's it,' said Scamarcio, his voice rising. 'They knew their plans were going to the wall, so they made new ones.' He looked at Rigamonti. 'They've put a bomb under them, that's what they've done. They knew the Chechen wasn't going to deliver, so they found new sites, and a new bomber. They needed to act quickly, so they could use events in Rome as cover.' He paused. 'Do you know when these two options expire?'

De Blasi paled again. 'I checked, 'cos I was curious. Both run till close of trade today.'

Scamarcio pulled out his mobile and dialled Garramone. There was no time for hello. 'There are bombs under the factories of Ferromeccanica in Rome and Salucci cars in Turin. All staff need to be evacuated, and the robots sent in.'

'Scamarcio, is that you? What the fuck?'

'The Chechen's note made sense — whoever was backing him was planning to profit from the attacks. Then he let them down, and they switched to a new plan. Get squads to these sites and get the workers out. If I'm wrong, then fire me.'

Scamarcio killed the call, not wanting Garramone to waste a second. He didn't care if he was wrong; he just didn't want to be *right*.

32

THAT EVENING'S NEWS WAS wall-to-wall with the two explosions. They had killed over three hundred and torn a huge hole through Italy's already wounded manufacturing heart.

Scamarcio's interrogation seemed to have gone on for days. Why had the bombs been set up to fail at some sites and wired correctly at others? Why had the terrorists not worn suicide vests? What was the Chechen's real role, and why was he communicating with Scamarcio and no-one else?

At a certain point, the questions had stopped and were replaced with a series of complicated non-disclosure forms, which Scamarcio had been asked to sign. No precise threat had been articulated, but one wasn't needed: he knew that if he wanted to keep his job he must comply — Rigamonti's earlier piece in *La Repubblica* had already ruffled too many feathers.

It was, of course, a one-way street: Scamarcio's enquiries to AISE about Colonel Scalisi were shot down. Likewise, his questions about why the Americans had held him captive, and whether anyone was actually holding them to account.

There was, however, one issue that the home secretary and his remaining intelligence chiefs had deigned to address. The trades against the two leading FTSE MIB companies had been handled by two respected brokerage firms. Under police caution, their employees claimed the options had been purchased by the same trader: a twenty-nine-year-old Anglo-Italian New Yorker by the name of David Morrati. It came as quite a coincidence when Morrati was found some hours later, hanging from a light fitting in his apartment near Central Park. The trail seemed to grow cold as quickly as Morrati's decomposing corpse.

When Scamarcio had finally shaken off the spooks, he sat down with Garramone for a beer in the café at the end of Via San Vitale, which was usually avoided by his colleagues due to its greasy brioche.

'Christ,' was the boss's opener. 'I'm going to move you to Vice for a quiet life.'

Scamarcio still felt he owed him an explanation — that he hadn't made his point well enough. 'I know it looks off, but I was just trying to do what I thought best. I had to believe Ifran would blow those sites, because if he did, and I hadn't tried to find that DVD, I'd have those deaths on my conscience forever.'

'Sure, I get that now ... After what happened today,' Garramone added quietly.

'As for Milan, I had no idea whether I was on a fool's errand. It didn't become clear until too late.' He fished in his pocket and pulled out half the wad of hush money Scalisi had given him for the photo. 'That's for the victims' families.'

Garramone riffled through the pristine notes, then said, 'Fuck!'

'Scalisi parted with it willingly.'

'Again, what the fuck, Scamarcio?'

He just waved the question away and sank back into silence. He could think of nothing but the carnage he'd seen on TV.

'No point beating yourself up,' tried Garramone. 'I don't think you were really meant to find out in time — you just stumbled upon it at the last minute.' He paused. 'The picture's becoming a little clearer now. AISI discovered a diary belonging to Ifran. It seems like he no longer knew which side he was on. He was a very confused young lad.'

'I'm not convinced. I still think he was trying to do the right thing.'

Garramone studied his beer. He seemed to be debating whether to share something. 'There's a war being waged,' he said eventually.

'Isn't there always?' muttered Scamarcio.

'The prime minister is locked in combat with AISE.'

Scamarcio looked up. 'Really?'

'The Brits weren't far wrong when they said Scalisi and his cronies were pushing for wider powers. The PM had been keeping an eye out, apparently, knowing there was trouble brewing. Now this Scalisi business has thrust it all into the open. There are major firings in the offing — they don't like to call it a purge, but in essence that's what it will be.'

Scamarcio raised an eyebrow.

'Could be you end up with a well-placed contact inside AISE.'

'Who?'

'Alessandro Romanelli is set for the top job, if I've heard correctly. They're trying to persuade him to come back.'

'Oh ...'

'I've got another piece of good news. Well, some might interpret it as good, but in your case I'm not so sure.'

Scamarcio felt his shoulders tense; he didn't know whether it was excitement or fear. 'Spit it out,' he said, taking a long drink.

'The president wants to award you the medal of honour.'

He almost choked.

'Steady on,' said Garramone. 'What doesn't kill you makes you stronger.'

33

Fiammetta looked tired. Actually, if he thought about it, he'd never seen her look quite so drained. There were deep, grey grooves beneath her eyes, and her skin was pale and drawn.

'Let's go for a drink,' he tried.

'I don't feel like it.'

'You *always* feel like a drink.'

'Well, today I don't.'

The question was still there, hovering between them, but he couldn't bring himself to voice it. He needed to know, but he was scared of knowing. He was unsure of his own reaction; he didn't trust himself not to run screaming for the hills. After all this time, he was still working hard to get a grip on himself, salvage the inner wreck.

'Why don't we go for dinner, then? There's that Thai place round the corner.'

She smiled unconvincingly. 'If you like ...'

They left the flat and headed out into the dusty chaos of a Rome summer evening. The heat was still throbbing off the pavement in long, suffocating blasts, and the air was heavy with a confusing blend of warmed citrus, fried garlic, and overworked drains. Colour had returned, the people keen to taste their freedom. With so much energy all around, Scamarcio's plans to wait until later vanished. There was so much life, so much hope on the streets, that he suddenly wanted to be a part of it. 'Are you pregnant?' he asked, still walking, not even looking at her.

Fiammetta came to an abrupt stop, causing someone behind her to curse. 'What?'

'Are you pregnant?' His tone was unintentionally cold. He didn't know why — perhaps he was angry that she hadn't told him. Perhaps he was angry that she'd let it happen. Perhaps he was just trying to protect himself.

She turned. There was a hardness in her eyes that he hadn't seen before. 'Why do you ask that?'

'Those Americans said you were.'

She frowned. 'Why would they think that?'

'Maybe they got it from Scalisi …'

She said nothing.

'Are you?'

'No,' she said softly. There was a lost look in her eyes that suggested this wasn't the end of it. But he was too blindsided by his emotions to focus. It felt as if someone had kicked him in the stomach; the disappointment was so intense, so biting that he almost couldn't take the weight of it. He wanted to sit down, but he couldn't see a wall.

'Leo, are you all right?'

He had been about to lie, fob her off, but he could no longer be bothered. 'No. I'm gutted.'

'You're … *disappointed*?'

'Of course I'm fucking disappointed.'

She looked at him, her eyes wide with concern, but then the sound of a car screeching to a stop made them turn. A silver Bentley had pulled up at the kerb. A tall grey-haired chauffeur emerged and opened the back door. In an instant, Dante Greco materialised. *Like an evil spirit escaping from a bottle*, thought Scamarcio. Greco wore a light-blue shirt and pale chinos, but without his cashmere coat he seemed naked.

'Leone,' he said, turning up his nose as he caught a whiff of the summer drains. He studied Fiammetta from head to toe, then gave her a long approving stare.

Scamarcio's mouth turned dry. 'Give us five minutes,' he said, nudging her towards the window of a nearby shop.

'I'm not happy,' snapped Greco.

Scamarcio clenched his jaw. *Why couldn't that little shit Basile have waited?* He'd given him the rest of Scalisi's hush money — a quarter of a million euros, for Christ's sake — that was supposed to buy him some time. 'Is this about Torpignattara?'

Greco pressed the heels of his hands and fingertips together and shook them up and down. 'How dare you promise favours on my behalf to the little league? What gives you the right?'

'I was in a bind — I needed Basile's help. I didn't know who else to ask.'

Greco stabbed a finger into his chest. It hurt. 'Just remember this: every time you use my name, I will use yours, Scamarcio.'

'What does that mean?'

'You know *exactly* what it means.'

With that, Greco turned and disappeared back inside the Bentley.

Scamarcio watched as the car evaporated into the dusk. 'When will it be over?' he sighed.

'You're about to receive the medal of honour,' said Fiammetta, reappearing beside him. 'Buck up.'

34

THE MEAL HAD BEEN good, but there was still something unsaid occupying the space between them — some secret doubt that neither of them was able to acknowledge. Its presence felt dark, and Scamarcio worried that it might signify the start of a bigger problem — perhaps even the beginning of the end. Fiammetta hadn't said so, but he wondered whether the fact she'd gone so long without hearing from him had been a turning point — whether this was something she couldn't forgive, regardless of whether he was at fault or not.

He poured himself a large glass of Amarone and sat at his living-room window, trying to work it all out. *Are things going wrong? Was she even telling the truth about the pregnancy? Did she lose a baby?*

His mobile buzzed. There were half a dozen new emails, some disturbingly headed 'Congratulations'. Then he spotted a sender he didn't recognise — an Ivan Lovov. He opened the email. There was no 'Dear Mr Scamarcio', no introduction.

Don't give up, my friend! Take a trip to the States — start with a little outfit on Wall Street called Mason, Simons and Brown. Then pay a visit to Julius Nevitt (212 645 3618).

These men had everything that money can buy, but now they've lost their most vital asset: immunity. I am stripping it from them piece by piece, favour by favour, bribe by bribe. And you are helping!

Sleep tight, my friend.

'The Chechen'

Scamarcio emptied the glass. Whoever these men were, they'd worked hard to stay hidden. Could he really be the one to smoke them out?

He turned. Fiammetta was standing in the doorway, a hand on the wall. 'I owe you an apology.'

'Why?'

'I haven't been honest with you.'

She's been having an affair, was his first thought. His second was, *Who? Someone from TV? Some sleazy producer, or that fake-tanned arse of a host on her show?* He took a breath. *No, Fiammetta is better than that.*

'What?' was all he could come up with.

'I *am* pregnant. I just needed time to understand how I felt. Your question took me by surprise — I realised that, with everything that had happened, I hadn't had a proper chance to think things through.'

'Think things through?' he echoed, his mind suddenly vacant.

'I'll be the mother. I'll be the one giving birth — the one looking after the baby. It's a huge change; my life will never be the same.'

Scamarcio was silent.

'I ...' She hesitated, gave up. After a long moment, she said, 'I do want this baby. I'm sure of that now.'

She looked scared, standing there in the doorway — as if she knew she was throwing her cards into the wind with no idea where they might scatter.

Scamarcio said nothing, didn't move. 'But they told me they'd harmed you ... harmed the fetus ...'

She shook her head. 'One of them punched my face. That was it.'

She was standing quite still, as if she feared the slightest movement might change the course of her life. He knew he should walk over and embrace her, but he didn't feel like it. He wasn't in the mood.

'Aren't you going to give me a hug?' she said quietly.

He rose slowly. He felt like he was carrying some dead weight. He walked towards her and pulled her to him, but he didn't look at her. He couldn't. He felt her hot tears against his neck and knew he should say something. But the words wouldn't come.

His mind hurtled forward. Everything would change now: their life together, his work. There'd be someone else to think of — someone who'd need protecting. He thought about his father and how he'd died. Would he make that same mistake? Would he let his child suffer because of his own flawed choices?

He remembered the new email from the Chechen. One day, Scamarcio would try to find the answers, but it couldn't be now. But then a new, more troubling thought hit him: was it already too late? A child would be his weak spot, his Achilles's heel. For the first time, he'd be truly vulnerable. Sure, he might *want* a baby with this challenging and beautiful woman more than anything, but that wasn't the issue. The issue was, *could* he? Was it fair to allow a child into his world? Wouldn't it mean a life of paranoia, a life of constant worry for both he and Fiammetta? He wasn't sure of the answer, and it frightened him. It frightened him more than anything had ever frightened him before.

Acknowledgements

I'D LIKE TO THANK my lovely agent Norah Perkins at Curtis Brown, and the superb team at Scribe for their continued encouragement and razor-sharp feedback. I'd also like to thank my husband Marco for putting up with my mood swings. He and our two little monsters constantly remind me of what's truly important in life.

Letter to my readers

IT HAS MEANT A lot to read all the comments from readers who have taken the trouble to contact me. Thank you.

If you enjoyed *The Extremist*, I'd be very grateful if you could write a review. It need only be a few words or so, but it makes a big difference and helps new readers discover the Scamarcio series.

I'd also welcome hearing your thoughts. What did you make of Scamarcio? And what would you like to see happen next in his life?

You can reach me through Twitter, Goodreads, or my website (nadiadalbuono.com). I read every message and will always reply.